STICKY
FINGERS

STICKY FINGERS

Nancy Martin

Minotaur Books
New York

This is a work of fiction.
All of the characters, organizations, and events portrayed in this novel
are either products of the author's imagination
or are used fictitiously.

www.minotaurbooks.com

THE LIBRARY OF CONGRESS HAS CATALOGED THE HARDCOVER EDITION AS FOLLOWS:

Martin, Nancy, 1953–
  Sticky fingers / Nancy Martin.—1st ed.
     p. cm.
  ISBN 978-0-312-57373-7
  1. Single mothers—Fiction. 2. Pittsburgh (Pa.)—Fiction. I. Title.
  PS3563.A7267S75 2011
  813'.54—dc22

                                                                    2010041089

ISBN 978-1-250-00165-8 (trade paperback)

First Minotaur Books Paperback Edition: February 2012

10 9 8 7 6 5 4 3 2 1

❈ Acknowledgments ❈

Many thanks to Deborah Harding from the Carnegie Museum. I love my lunch buddies Lila Shaara, Kathleen George, Rebecca Drake, Heather Benedict Terrell, and Kathryn Miller-Haines. (Welcome, Little G!) Thank you, Nancie Hays, Ramona Long, Terri Sokoloff, Mary Alice Gorman, and Richard Goldman at Mystery Lovers Bookshop. Kisses to Kathy Sweeney and my wonderful blog sisters at TLC—Sarah Strohmeyer, Hank Phillippi Ryan, Elaine Viets, Harley Jane Kozak, Margaret Maron, Nancy Pickard, Brunonia Barry, Cornelia Read, and Diane Chamberlain. I'm waving to the backbloggers at the Lipstick Chronicles and my Sisters in Crime. And I owe Deb and Bill Foster for Shelby. As for Meg Ruley and Kelley Ragland—I'll see you at the Love Shack, ladies!

STICKY FINGERS

1

The first thing I noticed as I was sitting in a squad car was that police cruisers don't have seatbelts in the back. Me, I'm used to traveling through life without a seatbelt. I'm a no-retraints kinda girl. But today my wrists were in handcuffs so tight I felt like a Christmas turkey, and I planned on bringing up the issue with my arresting officer.

Trouble was, Detective Duffy was already plenty ticked off at me. Behind the wheel, he snapped his cell phone shut, turned around, and said through the screen, "Roxy, behave yourself. I gotta take a detour."

"What? You gonna show me all the romantic sights of Pittsburgh before you book me?"

"Shut up," he said. "Or I'll drop you in the river."

I'd met Bug Duffy years after he earned his nickname eating crickets on the playground of St. Raphael Elementary. He'd been a year ahead of me in high school, when we'd both done time wearing our respective Catholic school uniforms. Back then, he was vice president of his class, and I was a member of an unofficial club called Future Delinquents of America. Things hadn't changed much.

He made a U-turn in front of a convenience store and cut down through the North Side—a maze of cobblestoned streets lined with boarded-up storefronts and magnificent old houses either crumbling to bits or under rehab by hopeful do-it-yourselfers. A pair of stone-faced teenagers melted back from the curb at the sight of the cop car. On the next block a young woman in a ponytail and expensive sneakers briskly jogged behind a high-tech baby carriage. Funny thing was, I knew the teenagers, not the mom.

In a few minutes, we were bumping along a deserted stretch of road that ran parallel to the Ohio River. It wasn't exactly scenic there, and like most old Pittsburgh industrial sites, the ground probably hadn't passed an EPA inspection even back in the day when bribes made a difference.

A river patrol boat bobbed offshore with its crew leaning on the rail to watch. A tug cruised past, engine low, pushing six empty barges, going downriver fast. On the shoreline, a couple of crime-scene guys stood hunched against the November wind, hands in their pockets, looking down at a sodden, rolled-up carpet that had clearly just floated up on the river.

A police photographer snapped pictures of it.

Bug shut off the patrol car's engine, got out, and came around to the rear door. He pulled me out and unlocked the cuffs. He was just about my height, and I could have kicked him in the nuts and made a break for it, but he gave me a look and said, "What do you bet this is her?"

I saw what he meant and said, "Oh, shit."

We walked across a stubbly field that had once been a steel mill, and he said hello to the crime-scene guys. I looked at the foot sticking out of one end of the carpet—a woman's bare foot with a pink pedicure. I felt the wind bite through the layers of my sweatshirts, but the cold wasn't the reason I suddenly had to clench my teeth to keep them from chattering.

Bug hunkered down over the carpet and used a pocketknife to cut the twine. Somebody had tied it with Boy Scout precision—little loops and knots every twelve inches or so. Like a rolled steak braciole, I thought. Bug handed the twine to one of the techs, who put it into a plastic bag. Then Bug unrolled the rug—a lot more gently than he'd handled me.

"This her?" Bug looked up at me when the gray, flattened face came into view.

"That's Clarice," I said, although I hardly recognized my own voice.

Clarice Crabtree had been shot a couple of times in the head—not the way you'd expect a distinguished museum curator to die. She probably never broke a sweat doing her work—but it was work that a lot of people seemed to think was valuable. In the last second of her life, I bet she'd been surprised to feel the barrel of a gun against her skull.

As I looked at Clarice, my own mother's death swam up in my head. I tried to shove it down into the blackness where all bad memories belong. But it was the sight of Clarice's ear—the one that was now missing a sedate gold earring, the mate of the one that remained clipped to her other lobe—that took me fast into a shadowy kitchen with blood on the floor next to a dead or dying woman whose earring—not gold, but a cheap one—had been torn from her by a glancing fist. I had hidden in another room while my parents shouted. While he beat her. As he killed her. A day later, while packing up some clothes and books for foster care, I'd found the missing earring embedded in a loaf of moldy bread on the kitchen counter.

I doubted Clarice Crabtree's kids ate moldy bread.

Still kneeling, Bug said, "I don't like that look on your face, Roxy."

Too late, I wiped away all expression and turned away, shaking and sick.

Bug said something to the techs, then came over and put one hand on my shoulder. "Don't even think about it."

I pushed his hand away. "About what?"

"Doing something about this on your own."

I said, "She has two kids."

3

He sighed. "Oh, hell. Look, I know how you get about mothers and kids, but this is my case now, Rox. I don't want to be tripping over you for weeks while I figure out who killed this lady."

"I won't get in your way."

"Better not," he said.

❧ 2 ❧

A few days earlier on a sunny November day, I had strolled into a noisy Strip District deli to meet Marvin Weiss, my uncle Carmine's lawyer. The deli specialized in sandwiches with hot fries and drippy coleslaw smashed between the meat and thick slices of Italian bread. The lawyer specialized in doing Carmine's dirty work.

I put my sidekick Nooch onto a stool at the counter and handed him enough cash to buy a sandwich and a Coke. "Chew your food," I told him. "Make it last longer than two minutes."

Then I threaded my way through small tables still crowded with guys who worked in the neighborhood.

Marvin sat in a back booth, already halfway through a corned beef big enough to choke a bull. He had his lunch in both hands, but the sandwich was dripping all over the waxed paper in his plastic basket. Those sandwiches had once made for a quick workingman's lunch for guys who labored in the nearby warehouses, but eventually the after-midnight club crowd in search of munchies found the restaurant to satisfy late-night cravings. Now tourists flocked to the place, and it was busy day and night.

I slid into the booth across from Marvin, unzipping my sweatshirt and peeling the scarf from around my neck. "This is your idea of a secure meeting place, 007? Half the guys in here are on lunch break from the newspaper."

Marvin had a long, bony nose and a receding chin, which made him look like a bunny rabbit in a striped tie. He dropped his sandwich and mopped his hands with a fistful of napkins. "How do you know? Have they all slept with you?"

"I bet they slept with your mama," I shot back. "Shut up and get down to business, okay? I've got work to do."

Some kind of child brain prodigy, Marvin had graduated from law school before he got through puberty, and he still looked like he played video games. He also still lived with his mother, who cooked his meals, washed and ironed his shirts, and maybe tucked him in at night, for all I knew. She hadn't given him many social skills. I figured he was destined to be president of the *Star Trek* club until he qualified for AARP.

He wiped his mouth and said, "You're late. What happened? You break your vow of celibacy already?"

Time stood still when I heard that. Like, all sound evaporated except for the rush of blood pressure in my ears. I grabbed the edge of the table to keep myself from falling over. "What did you say?"

Marvin smirked. "I heard about your pledge of abstinence. Everybody has. What happened, Roxy? Did you finally get scared straight?"

"Who the hell told you—"

"It's all over the neighborhood. You decided to give up sex, right?"

"Keep your voice down!"

"What's the matter? Afraid somebody hasn't heard yet? Believe me, the whole city knows you've had a change of heart."

I reached across the table, grabbed a fistful of Marvin's tie, and jammed it against his protruding Adam's apple. "Listen up, Marv. You say one more word about my sex life, and I'll put your head on a sandwich and slather it with mustard. You hear me?"

"Take it easy!" he yelped. "This is my favorite tie!"

"Your mom can get another one next time she visits Kmart." I released him.

"Okay, okay! Jeez." He patted his tie back into place. "I'm the last to know, anyway. If the story trickled down to me, even the mayor has probably heard by now."

A couple of factors had pushed me to make the decision to straighten out my bent life a little. First, my teenage daughter had a pregnancy scare that made me think maybe I wasn't the best role model going. I'd managed to enjoy a lot of guys over the years on my own terms, but maybe that wasn't the right message for a kid to learn about her mom. And second, I'd recently gotten naked with a man who turned out to be a murderer.

An awful thought hit me, and I said, "Has my uncle Carmine heard?"

Marvin mustered some dignity. "Usually, I'd deny any association with Carmine Abruzzo."

"Yeah, I'm kinda surprised you actually said his name in public."

"I'm not a mob lawyer," he said firmly. "How should I know what's on his mind? We barely speak."

Marvin had come home from law school and hung his shingle on the second floor above his parents' dry cleaning shop. He didn't attract many clients until my uncle Carmine plucked him from obscurity to do some transactions for a couple of sham businesses that shielded Carmine's real line of work. Only in the last year or so had naive Marvin finally figured out he was working for one of the last old-time crime bosses in the city of Pittsburgh.

I said, "How's the old crook doing these days?"

"Watching too many game shows, if you ask me. He's hooked on *Let's Make a Deal*. He likes the costumes, I think. He's happy with the way your last job turned out, though."

"Huh," I said. "Does he know the details? I got a little carried away."

Marvin raised his eyebrows. "You? Carried away?"

A day earlier on a mission to collect a gambling debt for Carmine, I'd busted into an apartment in the Oakland neighborhood and rousted scrawny Gino Martinelli out of bed—a bed he was rocking with the help of a fifteen-year-old girl who was late for her after-school babysitting job. For his day job, Gino ran a corrupt city tow truck business, which gave him plenty of free time to prey on teenagers who didn't have sense enough to stick with the sex maniacs in their own age group.

I had grabbed Gino by his hair—a mistake, because turns out he must be one of the last men on earth who wears a toupee—then by the scruff of the neck. I pulled him off Kiley Seranelli and threw him on the floor. Bare-assed and furious, he'd come up fast and tried to punch me, but I'd brought along a baseball bat and managed to chase him out onto the porch. Despite my finely honed powers of persuasion, Gino scrambled into my truck, where we tussled a while longer and I maybe broke his nose.

I kicked him out onto the main boulevard, which ran through at least three universities.

To Marvin, I said, "I delivered Carmine's message, but I kind of left Gino in the middle of Forbes Avenue. Without his pants."

Marvin shrugged. "Gino paid off his debt. Carmine's happy about that. He wouldn't care about the no-pants thing."

"Don't be so sure. Gino's daughter's getting married this weekend."

"So?"

"So Carmine's invited to the wedding. Gino's liable to want some payback."

"Maybe he should learn not to gamble."

Marvin clearly didn't understand the implications of liquored-up Italian relatives crammed into a restaurant ballroom with booze, bridesmaids, and brass knuckles in the pockets of their rented tuxes.

Marvin leaned forward across the table. "Forget about that. Carmine needs another favor."

In the last few months, my business in architectural salvage had hit a dry patch, and I'd finally done a couple of little jobs for my uncle. Nothing too strenuous. In fact, it was a kind of work that appealed to me. I discovered I didn't mind threatening the occasional gambler with a tire iron. And it turned out I was good at recovering cash Carmine figured was long gone. He shared a percentage with me, and we were both happy.

Sort of.

I was a little worried my daughter might learn about my new career path.

But a family's gotta eat.

"What is it this time?" I asked. "Am I supposed to shake down another retiree who owes bingo money?"

"No. Something bigger." Marvin glanced around the deli. "Somebody contacted Carmine for a service."

I grinned. "Tell me the truth, Marv. When you were a kid, did you dress up like James Bond on Halloween? Carry a martini glass around the neighborhood, asking for Snickers bars?"

"Why?"

"Because if anybody's watching you right now, they're going to think you're soliciting a hit."

"You can make jokes," he said. "But I hear your kid is going to college next year. You have the tuition saved up?"

Okay, so far I had managed to buy everything my daughter required, including the latest silly-looking shoes and a lot of electronic equipment that every teenager needed to survive. But somebody had finally showed me what it costs to send a child to college these days, and I'd nearly fallen off my chair.

I said, "What's the job?"

"A kidnapping," Marvin said.

I laughed. "Your mom finally wants rid of you?"

Marvin's face remained stiff. "Keep your voice down. Somebody wants a woman snatched and held for ransom."

"A woman?"

"Yeah, kidnapped."

I blinked. "Marv, are you wearing a wire?"

He shook his head firmly. "Not me."

I sat back against the vinyl seat. "Either you've decided to save your skin by turning state's evidence against Carmine, or you're pulling my leg."

"I'm not kidding around, Roxy."

I put my elbows on the table and leaned forward. "Marvin, you're talking felony here, with big time attached. It's a lot different from hassling people about their gambling debts."

"I know that."

"And you'd be an accessory, sweet pea. Did you skip that day in law school?"

"I didn't skip any days of law school."

"Besides, what idiot thinks Carmine can mastermind a kidnapping? He's eighty years old now, and he wasn't too swift to begin with. He was the one who left his craps-game winnings on the bar on St. Patrick's Day, remember?"

Without answering, Marvin pulled a sheet of paper from the inside pocket of his suit. He slid it across the table to me like he was handing off a mission impossible.

I unfolded the paper and looked down at a page made up entirely of letters cut from magazines and newspapers.

Marvin said, "That's a photocopy of a photocopy. The sender must have kept the original. There were no fingerprints either."

"You checked?" I said. "Tell me you still have a chemistry set your parents got you for your bar mitzvah."

"It was a birthday present. It has a perfectly good fingerprint kit," he said. "And I know how to use it."

"Yeah, you probably practiced on all your friends on the debate team."

I read the letter.

Mr. Abruzzo,

I need you to kidnap someone on Tuesday. I will pay you ten thousand dollars. For the details, call my telephone number at five o'clock today.

At the bottom of the page was a local phone number.

I looked up to find Marvin gnawing on one fingernail. I said, "Did Carmine call the number?"

"No, I did. It was a recorded message, with all the information we needed to complete the request. The voice was distorted by a computer, very high-tech. Two hours later, I called back, but the number had been disconnected. I received a small down payment via PayPal online."

"Gee, a computer-savvy crook. That's unusual. What's supposed to happen to the woman once she's kidnapped?"

"What do you mean?"

"Well, you kidnap somebody, you don't exactly sit around playing Parcheesi and eating Doritos together."

"I don't know. Does it matter?"

"Of course it matters." I refolded the letter and skimmed it back across the table. "There's a cop behind this, Marvin. It's a sting. Somebody's trying to put Carmine in jail once and for all."

He shook his head. "I don't think so. The details were very specific—where and when the snatch could happen, everything. Except for the Parcheesi and Doritos part. Are you interested?"

"Hell, no," I said. "I stay away from felonies. And besides, I don't pick on women."

He took the letter and tucked it back into his pocket. "The guy who normally does this stuff for Carmine turned me down because—well, he's had two knee replacements."

"Carmine's whole crew have pacemakers and live on Metamucil."

He smiled unpleasantly. "So that leaves you, Roxy."

Sure, I liked the idea of causing a little trouble. But I had a daughter to think about, and Nooch, too. So I shook my head. "Forget it."

"You sure?"

I fixed him with a look. "Read my lips, Marvin. I don't hurt women. Not for anybody."

He stopped smiling.

Curiosity got the best of me, though. I said, "Tell me one thing."

"What?"

"Who's the woman? The mark? The one who's supposed to be kidnapped?"

"Name of Clarice Crabtree." Marvin picked up his corned beef. "She works at the museum."

I stopped worrying and burst out laughing. "Marvin, you've been scammed! I went to high school with Clarice! She got straight A's and never said a word to anyone unless it was to brag about how great she was. Hell, if somebody wants her kidnapped, it's probably just to shut her up."

❊ 3 ❊

Back in the truck, my dog Rooney woke up with a slobbery snort and gobbled the remaining half of Nooch's sandwich, wrapping and all.

"I wasn't finished with that!" Nooch cried as his snack disappeared.

"Take it easy," I said as Rooney licked his chops. "You ate lunch an hour ago. You didn't need another whole sandwich, for God's sake."

"I can't help it if I get hungry," Nooch said. "And you said you'd quit cussing. It's bad for business."

Most of the guys in my business cussed a hell of a lot more than I did. But Nooch had almost the same brain as a barnacle, so disagreeing with him could turn into a long afternoon. It would be easier to clean up my language.

Nooch Santonucci had been my wingman since back in our high school days, when kids taunted him for being a retard, and I busted their heads for it. The partnership lasted because he was the size of a triceratops and could do my heavy lifting without protest. And in daylight, I preferred his kind of company—a man who did what he was told. To tell the truth, I liked that kind of man at night, too.

"What did Marvin want?" Nooch asked when we were buckled up with Rooney panting between us on the front seat.

"He wanted to buy me lunch." The less Nooch knew about Marvin's proposal, the better.

"I been reading this book," Nooch said, "that says being evasive is an early warning sign."

"Who says I'm being evasive? And since when do you know what that means? Wait a minute. You're reading a book?" I shoved Rooney out of the way and stared at Nooch. "A real book? What's it called?"

"*Wonderful You*. Father Mike gave it to me. He said it would help me realize my potential as a human being. The book says the power of positive thoughts will dissolve all the world's problems. A golden stream of positive energy, that's all we need to become magnets for wealth and health."

"Magnets for—?"

"Wealth and health. It's a great book. Here, Father Mike gave me a notebook to write down the important stuff." Nooch fished a battered ring-bound notepad out of his pocket and thumbed it open. A few pages bore carefully penciled block letters. "See? Positive thoughts, that's important. I'm supposed to close my eyes and visualize what I want. Trouble is, when I close my eyes, I keep falling asleep."

"You're actually writing stuff down?"

"Yeah, Father Mike says it'll help me remember."

I started the truck. "So what's being evasive an early warning sign of?"

"I forget, but it's bad. So is cussing, which degrades your respect for— for something, but I forget that part, too." He tried paging through his notes to find the right answer. "Anyway, you're supposed to surround yourself with stuff that reflects positive energy, which I figure is sandwiches and pizza, because everybody loves sandwiches and pizza. But cussing isn't positive."

"Suddenly I'm having a close encounter with my own personal Doctor Phil," I said. "Put your notebook away before Rooney eats it."

Nooch placidly obeyed. "You should read the book, Rox. You're always reading books. But this one is all about having a positive outlook on life."

"I'm plenty positive."

My cell phone rang before he could argue the point, and I pulled it from the pocket of my jeans. Without checking the ID, which is always a mistake, I answered.

"You bitch," Gino Martinelli said in my ear. "I'm coming after you."

Last I'd seen, little Gino had been hopping up and down barefoot and buck naked like some kind of furious Italian leprechaun.

"You're a pest, Gino," I said. "And not a very positive person, if I might say so."

"You're not as tough as you think you are," he snarled, and added some curses.

I switched ears so Nooch wouldn't hear Gino's nonpositive language. Gino once boxed flyweight—at least, that's what he bragged down at the Sons of Italy–but mostly he was just another old guy blowing a lot of hot air. I said, "Don't threaten me, Gino. You know I hate being terrified."

He said, "Just watch your rearview mirror, bitch, because I'm coming."

"Put extra glue on your toupee," I advised. "Your wife will be mad if you lose it. Does she know about your latest girlfriend yet? The one you pulled out of kindergarten class?"

He cussed some more and hung up.

Nooch said, "Gino doesn't like talk about his toupee."

"Then he should get a new one. It looks like he's wearing a weasel up there."

"You're just making him madder. You should be positive. Be a magnet for wonderfulness."

"There's nothing wonderful about Gino." I pulled into traffic. "I thought his wife would be keeping him busy with wedding stuff this week."

"My nonna says I need a suit for the wedding."

"Okay, we'll go shopping. I can probably afford something from the thrift store." There was no use spending real money on a suit that Nooch would wear once. "But right now, we've got work to do. It's okay to work, right? Is it positive enough for you?"

"Yeah, sure," Nooch said. "I like working. Work is positive."

An old bank was being torn down in the Garfield neighborhood. Nooch and I put on our hard hats and went inside.

"Roxy!" Speeder Reed spun his wheelchair in the middle of the bank's dusty floor and rolled over to me. "Glad you could make it."

"Hey, Speeder. What do you have for me?"

"The marble counters and the iron bars. Can you believe a bank in this neighborhood wasn't using bulletproof glass?"

"Maybe that explains why they closed this branch."

Speeder's dad had been in the salvage business for years, and his son accidentally got caught in the collapse of an old church. Since losing the use of his legs at the age of thirteen, Speeder had showed a lot of determination to stay in the family trade. His arms and shoulders were huge from spinning the wheelchair around, and he fearlessly drove a specially equipped van into the most dangerous parts of the city. He could always be found scooting through demo sites, covered in dust and giving orders.

"Take whatever else you can carry out of here," Speeder said. "We're gonna drop this building in the morning."

"Thanks."

Half the success in the salvage business is the dumb luck of finding stuff of value after everybody else has given up. It takes the sensitive nose of a beagle and the instincts of a treasure hunter with a little Gypsy fortune-teller thrown in. I sifted through the bank's cash drawers but didn't see any old bills stuck in any cracks. But I did find treasure under a broken desk.

"What're those?" Nooch leaned over my shoulder.

I gathered up a handful of narrow plastic tubes. "Dye packs," I said, handling them carefully. "Banks used to put these in the bags they handed over to robbers. Once the thief touched the money, the dye pack blew up and made him obvious to the police."

"Cool!" Nooch grabbed one out of my hand, and it immediately burst.

"Watch out!" I waved my hand in front of my face to dispel the orange cloud.

When I opened my eyes, a huge orange blotch had stained the front of Nooch's brown sweatshirt. With his yellow hard hat, he looked like the Great Pumpkin.

"Oh, man." He stared down at himself. "Orange is the color of the Cincinnati Bengals. How am I going to explain this?"

Wearing the colors of an archenemy team was treason to a Pittsburgh Steelers fan.

"I don't think there's any need to explain," I said. "One look pretty much tells the story."

"Is it a positive story?" Nooch asked. "If I'm supposed to be on a path of fulfillment, I think it should be a positive story."

I figured Nooch should read the next chapter in his book because at the moment, he looked like he'd robbed a bank. But he and I spent a couple of hours hauling the marble counter and the iron bars out of the bank. The whole time, Nooch moaned about his orange shirt.

I tuned out his complaints. While we worked, my thoughts kept circling back to kidnapping Clarice Crabtree. The whole idea sounded like a joke to me.

In high school, there are cool smart girls who share their civics homework when you forget to do it, and there are mean smart girls who laugh when you can't explain the themes of *Ethan Frome* when Sister calls on you in English class. Clarice was the laughing kind.

She also had a neat blond ponytail and a little button nose in a school full of girls whose grandparents came from the hill country of Italy. She had her high school uniform tailored, while the rest of us rolled up the skirts and tied our shirttails tight around our waists. For a while, she pretended a fascination with the tattoos of the girls I ran around with in those days, but eventually she took to curling her lip when she walked past the gang of us who smoked cigarettes at the bus stop every morning.

Worst of all, she ratted out people who sneaked cherry bombs into the Spanish class Cinco de Mayo piñata.

I spent two weeks in detention for the cherry bomb incident, and had to work off the damages, too, washing blackboards for the rest of the school year. Clarice gave me smug smiles in the school hallway until classes let out in June.

Yeah, I hated her, but why anybody'd want her kidnapped, I couldn't figure. And I knew that whatever the ransom was, it wasn't enough to put up with being alone with Clarice for ten minutes.

Eventually I figured the whole kidnapping plot was definitely some kind of plot to entrap Carmine, and I decided to forget about it. I had better things to do than worry about my high school's top mean girl.

Nooch and I finished loading stuff I wanted from the bank and went inside to say good-bye to Speeder. When we came outside, we discovered somebody had spray-painted the tail of the Monster Truck:

BITCH

Nooch stood beside me, staring at the word. "I don't think that paint's going to wash off easy."

"No it's not. And I smell Gino Martinelli."

"Huh?"

"Gino did this. I'm starting to think maybe I shoulda handled things differently with him."

Nooch looked astonished. "You never say that! Rox, this could be some kind of breakthrough for you. You should definitely borrow my book."

"I'll wait for the Cliff's Notes." I tapped my foot on the pavement. Gino was really starting to annoy me.

Nooch and I unloaded the truck at the salvage yard and drank some Red Bull in my office. Then I dropped Nooch off at the house he shared with his grandmothers. Done for the day, I went up to Bloomfield, the Little Italy neighborhood of Pittsburgh, in hopes of grabbing dinner with my daughter.

I'd given birth to Sage when I was just a kid myself, and even now I knew she was better off living with my aunt Loretta, whose house was filled with cozy fragrances and slip-covered furniture. My lifestyle wasn't right for Sage. I had a tendency to move around a lot—not always staying one step ahead of trouble. I also needed to keep my eye on the various houses I bought, renovated fast, and flipped. Usually I camped out in the half-empty buildings rather than let local druggies destroy my property.

Loretta was a better influence. Homework got done. Healthy meals were consumed. Dinner table conversation was civilized. Nobody spray-painted insults on Loretta's car either.

The house usually smelled deliciously of marinara sauce and garlic, but tonight I found Loretta in her kitchen surrounded by cookies. Mountains of cookies. The scent of anise and cinnamon was almost thick enough to chew, and the dining room table was stacked with Tupperware containers brimming with ladylike treats with pastel frosting and confetti sprinkles.

"Wipe your boots!" Loretta cried when I popped the door back on its hinges.

When she wasn't practicing law, Loretta did a damn good imitation of a sitcom housewife—cooking, cleaning, and dispensing motherly advice even though she wasn't technically anybody's mother. Her husband had died years ago, and she'd distracted herself from the grief by trying to raise me after my own parents left the picture. Now she was shepherding Sage through the tumultuous teenage years.

The second time around, Loretta was having more success.

She stood at the stove with a frilly apron tied over a pin-striped business suit, stirring a pot. The apron had pink ruffles and said, Eat Dessert First, a mantra she would never embrace herself. Loretta was big on eating your vegetables first, which was one of the reasons I bugged out of her house as soon as I could.

She scuffed around the kitchen in her slippers. Most of the time, she tried to dress herself to be taken seriously, but it was a lost cause. Loretta was naturally soft bosomed, with big hair, lots of eye makeup, and the kind of cleavage that Hugh Hefner probably dreamed about as a pipe-smoking teenager. She had tried making the transition to the modern age by buying her suits at Brooks Brothers and getting them altered to fit her prodigious bust size. The result was a voluptuous middle-aged lady lawyer who occasionally caused elderly judges to snap their gavels.

I kicked off my boots and unzipped my sweatshirt. "Wow, did the Pillsbury Doughboy explode in here?"

Still stirring, Loretta said over her shoulder, "Before I took this new case, I promised I'd help with the cookie table for Shelby Martinelli's wedding."

"Gino Martinelli's daughter?"

"You know perfectly well she's Gino's daughter. Did you fall on your head today? They've got four hundred people coming to the wedding on Saturday. Fortunately, the judge on my case got the stomach flu and sent us home early. Otherwise, I'd be in big cookie trouble."

Loretta was an attorney, specializing in championing the elderly. Lately, she'd been suing some slacker for telephoning old people and claiming he was their grandson, stuck in Amsterdam because his pocket had been picked. You'd be surprised how many grandparents are willing to give their life savings to get their idiot grandsons out of a jam. Even grandparents who don't have grandsons old enough to ride their tricycles in Amsterdam.

The mere mention of the Martinelli family wedding, though, put me on red alert. That, and the way Loretta didn't meet my eye and kept her voice brisk.

Just as I had when I was a teenager and knew I was in trouble, but wasn't sure for which infraction exactly, I tried to sound casual. "How many cookies do the Martinellis expect four hundred people to eat? After dinner and wedding cake?"

"There will be take-home containers. You know the Martinellis. Shelby's cousin had a cookie table that ran the whole way around the Sheraton's ballroom."

"So they have to beat the cousin." I took another look at the Tupperware containers. There might have been a hundred, stacked everywhere. "You baked all these cookies?"

"Heavens, no. I promised I'd do the collecting. I've got plenty of room in the freezers. Everybody's dropping off tonight. By the way, I said you'd help deliver to the reception hall on Saturday morning."

"Sure thing."

Loretta's basement freezers were usually stuffed with homemade pasta casseroles that could be thawed, baked, and delivered to sick neighbors, the homeless shelter, or the social hall at St. Dominic's Church at a moment's notice. Now and then, she helped out friends who were collecting offerings for wedding cookie tables. Sometimes, ten thousand cookies were required to make an appropriately festive cookie table. Only Loretta had enough freezer space.

A knock sounded at the back door, and Loretta handed me the wooden spoon. "Here, stir."

"But–"

Loretta bustled to the back door and opened it. The upper half of the person standing there was obscured by the stack of more Tupperware containers.

"Hi, Loretta." The voice came from behind the cookies. "It's me, Irene Stossel. I've got buttercream horns from my mother."

"Oh, Irene, your mother's cream horns are the best! Everybody says so. Step inside."

Irene did as she was told, and Loretta closed the door before pulling the top four containers out of Irene's arms. She gave Irene the customary two kisses, then hotfooted it into the dining room to stash the new arrivals with the cookies that had already been delivered.

Obediently, Irene stood on the rug, holding the rest of the cookies. She spotted me at the stove. "Hey, Roxy. Long time, no see."

Irene had been famous for eating glue back in kindergarten—big globs of it off her finger, the way most of us eat chocolate frosting from a can. But later, she didn't have a regular bunch of friends to sit with in the cafeteria, and she was always one of the last girls to get picked for teams in gym class. In other words, since the glue-eating incident, she had become a pariah. It's kind of sad when your big moment in the spotlight happened when you were six, right?

After our days in Catholic school, Irene became one of those dutiful daughters who stayed behind to take care of her parents after her siblings fled the neighborhood. As far as I knew she spent her days driving her mother around in a beige Buick to the grocery store and the salon. Irene also tended to dress like she was part of her mother's generation. And talking with her—she could go into excruciating detail about how to choose a standing rib roast—could be like trying to make conversation with drywall.

But I took a closer look and decided Irene had changed lately. She was wearing jeans, a manly sort of orange parka, and combat boots instead of the standard beige London Fog with beige Naturalizers and beige pants with an elastic waist. I wasn't sure what the transformation meant. Her hair—usually neatly permed into a helmet like her mother's—was now long and frizzy.

It looked to me like Irene had untied the apron strings at last. I stayed at the stove, stirring. "Hey, Irene. Your mom okay?"

"She's fine. I just dropped her off at the bingo game."

"So what's new?"

"Not much. Except I got a job managing the Greentree gun range."

"Gun range? You mean, like, shooting?"

"Yeah, ducking bullets, that's me." Irene gave me a cheerful grin. "Today I had a guy who complained to me about his new gun. Said the weapon kept dropping parts every time he fired it. Turns out, it was the shell casings."

"Wow," I said. "What an idiot."

"Scary who's allowed to carry a firearm."

"I'll say."

I stayed at the stove, but took a look at Irene's parka. I wondered if she was packing while she delivered cookies.

Brightly, Irene said, "How's your uncle Carmine?"

"Carmine? Fine, I guess."

"I heard he's been sick lately."

I shrugged. "Could be. I don't talk to him much."

"No? Too busy? I could look in on him once in a while, if you want."

Lots of folks in the old neighborhood still looked up to Carmine for the crime boss he used to be. Even people who never asked him for a favor or to bet on a baseball game thought he was Robin Hood or something. Sure, he used to give a few bucks to old ladies who couldn't pay their rent, but mostly Carmine preyed on the weak and the stupid. If people knew how he'd cheated their fathers or taken advantage of their neighbors? Believe me, they wouldn't act like he was such a great guy.

But if he kissed the bride at a wedding and tucked a hundred-dollar bill into her hand, people talked about it for years.

And here was Irene Stossel looking eager to take him chicken soup.

"Sure," I said. "Knock yourself out."

Loretta came back and took the remaining containers from Irene. "There you go, dear. Tell your mother I'm so relieved she could contribute. I don't know what I'd have done without her."

"You know Mom," Irene said, still standing on the rug. "She'll make cookies for anybody, anytime."

"That's a blessing. See you at the wedding?"

"Maybe, maybe not. I might have to work. I have a job at the gun range now."

"Goodness," Loretta said. "Does your mother know?"

"Yeah, she thinks it's great. She wants a Glock for Christmas."

"Happy holidays," I said.

Loretta shot me a dirty look. But she said to Irene, "Just be careful, dear. And thanks for the cookies!"

I noticed Loretta didn't invite Irene to sit down at the table for a cup of coffee and a biscotti. She practically shoved Irene out the door. "Bye, now!"

"Jeez," I said. "What happened to Irene? She finally get laid, do you think?"

"Don't talk like that." Loretta went straight to the sink and washed her hands. "She's a nice girl. Devoted to her mother. But . . . all right, she's a little strange. Why would she take a job shooting guns when she could have worked at her grandfather's bakery? He always has those pizzelles in the window—they're so popular. Come to think of it, why hasn't he sent any pizzelles for the wedding? I should give him a call. Here, let me stir."

I handed over the wooden spoon and peeked into the goop in the saucepan, wrinkling my nose. "What kind of cookies are these? It doesn't smell like anything I recognize."

"It's not cookie, it's depilatory wax."

I backed up fast and clamped one hand over my upper lip. "I don't have a mustache!"

"Wait until menopause. It's not for you. Your aunt Roberta is here." Loretta pointed at the powder room door, closed, but with a bead of light shining under the door.

I relaxed, glad not to be tonight's victim. "Has she moved in? I thought I saw her Dodge Neon parked outside."

"She's staying here for a little while. Tonight we decided to try getting rid of a few dark hairs."

"A few? Loretta, in dim light, she'd pass for Uncle Salvatore."

Aunt Roberta wasn't really my aunt, but a cousin of Loretta's. She was a former nun, known in the family as Sister Bob. Which explained the Dodge Neon—the car all nuns drive, for some reason. For years, she'd worked as some kind of bigwig hospital administrator, but the hospital was sold to a conglomerate and Sister Bob was asked to retire.

Instead, Sister Bob suddenly turned in her rosary and quit the nun gig. Since then, she moved from family household to family household, and everybody was working on Sister Bob's appearance. The crazy hope that at sixty-two she might still find happiness as a married housewife burned as brightly as a candle in church.

I said, "Is she praying for courage in there?"

"I think so."

At that moment, Rooney nosed the back door open and rushed past me. He'd probably been pooping in the neighbor's yard. Or maybe killing their Chihuahua. In a flurry of slippery paws, the dog skidded to a stop and parked his butt at Loretta's feet. He fixed her with an adoring stare and dropped a splat of drool on her clean floor.

"What does the baby boy want?" Loretta cooed, blind to the drool. "He's such a good puppy! He loves his aunt Loretta, doesn't he, sweet puppy?"

A hundred-plus pounds of pit bull, rottweiler, and mastiff mix quivered and whined. The mutual admiration society.

Loretta stopped stirring the wax long enough to drop Rooney a piece of cookie, which he snatched out of the air the way a frog zaps a fly over a lily pond.

I reached for a cookie, too, but Loretta slapped my hand away.

"Not that one! Have an oatmeal raisin." She pointed down the counter at a collection of misshapen lumps. "Mary Pat Caravello brought those over. Poor thing doesn't even know oatmeal raisin cookies don't belong on a cookie table."

"Why does Rooney get a cookie and I don't?"

"Because you don't deserve it."

"Why the hell not? What have I done?"

Loretta's mouth tightened, and for a second I thought she was going to hold back. But with a tart snap in her voice, she said, "I hear you tricked Gino into leaving his girlfriend's apartment in his underwear."

Aha. I'd sensed a certain chilly air in Loretta's manner from the moment I stepped into the house. She'd given Irene Stossel a welcome kiss, but not me.

I said, "How'd you hear about that?"

"Gino's sister told Mary Pat at the Shop 'n' Save, who told me last night at the ladies auxiliary meeting." Loretta fixed me with a stern stare. "Roxy, Gino's an important man in the neighborhood. What were you thinking?"

I said, "First of all, he's married. And second, she wasn't his girlfriend, Loretta. Gino was banging a fifteen-year-old."

"Don't say things like— Wait. A fifteen-year-old?"

"Yeah, one of Sage's friends, in fact. Gino Martinelli is a slimeball, and the rest of the Martinellis ought to throw his ass in the river before he gives away the bride on Saturday."

Loretta crossed herself as if she'd just had a whiff of the devil. "Where did you hear such a rumor?"

"It's no rumor. I saw the girl myself. Talked to her. Dropped her off at her babysitting job." I munched the cookie. "She's fifteen, and Gino is scum."

Okay, maybe Kiley Seranelli was one of those oversexed fifteen-year-olds who took the impact of Britney Spears on American culture very seriously. When I'd gone back and dragged her out of Gino Martinelli's love nest, Kiley had been smoking a postcoital cigarette with the aplomb of Marlene Dietrich. But you can't blame a fifteen-year-old for fornicating with a middle-aged man. He's the one who's supposed to know the difference between right and wrong.

Loretta took her hand from her mouth. "So it's true? What you did?"

I wouldn't have gone after Gino Martinelli purely to regain Uncle Carmine's investment. But when Sage told me her friend was sneaking away from basketball practice to hook up with an older guy, I'd done some snooping. I learned Gino kept an off-campus apartment where he and his jagoff sons regularly took very young girls for afternoons of marijuana-fueled corruption of minors. So I took it upon myself to bust the party.

After I'd tossed Gino out of my truck, I'd gone back to rescue Kiley— only to find she really didn't want rescuing. She was smoking and weeping because Gino had removed her belly button ring. With his tongue. She couldn't figure out how to put it back in place.

"Yeah, Gino and I had a meeting of the minds," I said. "I think he'll stay away from little girls for a while."

"Good heavens."

"There's nothing heavenly about Gino."

Frowning, Loretta went back to tending the saucepan. "So are you going to the wedding?"

"Hell, no!"

"If you don't go, everyone will assume you were the one in the wrong."

"It'll just make Gino mad if I show up. Plus, all those Martinelli aunts will make comments about my hair."

"I can take care of that." Loretta lifted her spoon and with a critical eye watched a long ribbon of wax dribble back into the saucepan. "I could use my influence and make you an appointment at Valentino's for Friday."

"They hate me at Valentino's!"

"They hate your hair," she corrected, sounding gentler. "Not you. Big difference."

I wasn't so sure. The neighborhood beauty salon was the kind of place where I was talked about, not talked to. But complaining to Loretta was only going to result in me going to bed hungry. So I said, "I'll check my schedule."

"If I make an appointment, you'll rearrange your schedule. An hour at Valentino's is hard to get on a Friday. I don't want to waste my influence."

"I'll think about it." I opened the refrigerator. "Is there any real food for people to eat?"

Loretta went back to the stove. "There's egg salad on the middle shelf. I've been too busy to make anything else for dinner."

It took a big event for Loretta to skip making dinner.

After my mother died, it was Loretta—my father's cousin—who came to rescue me in Jersey. Loretta found me in foster care, packed my clothes into her car, buckled my seatbelt, and drove me three hundred miles across the Pennsylvania Turnpike to her home. I didn't said a word on the trip, she told me later, but I remember that at the first meal she cooked for me—pasta shells stuffed with a savory mixture of ricotta, cream, and gently steamed spinach, unlike anything my own mother threw on the table—I cried like a baby. Since then, she'd raised me pretty much as her own daughter—or as close to it as I'd allow.

The idea of egg salad wasn't very satisfying, though, so I closed the refrigerator door.

As I did so, the powder room door burst open, and Sister Bob bustled into the kitchen. She stood five feet tall and was shaped like a beer barrel. Since I'd seen her last, her gray hair had been poufed, her wardrobe primped. She was wearing a purple velour track suit with racing stripes down the outside of her chubby legs—an outfit I'm pretty sure even the most progressive convent would veto.

"Roxana Marie! Where have you been keeping yourself?"

"Hi, Sister Bob."

Sister Bob gave me an exuberant hug, squeezed my face, and planted noisy kisses on my cheeks. Her mustache prickled, but she gave me a sparkly-eyed smile. "I heard what you did to Gino Martinelli. Bless you, dear! That man is a weasel."

"How on earth do you know about Gino?" Loretta demanded.

"What? You think the nuns can resist listening in on confession sometimes?" She had a raucous laugh. "Just kidding. That's convent humor. I volunteer at the public library now. Kids talk there, and they say the most awful things. Gino deserves worse than what Roxy gave him. He should escort his daughter down the aisle with a black eye."

I couldn't help grinning. "That's pretty Old Testament, Sister Bob."

"Darn tootin'," she replied. "If you need backup next time you decide to administer some street justice, you can count on me."

"Thanks." Dirty Harry had nothing on Sister Bob.

"I'm not listening," Loretta said. "I'm an officer of the court. I'm not hearing a thing. Vigilantes simply get in the way of the judicial system."

Sister Bob winked at me. "Don't listen to Loretta. If that man went after Sage, she'd be first in line with an ax and garbage bags."

"Yeow." I dusted cookie crumbs from my hands into the sink. "Where is Sage, by the way?"

"In the living room." Loretta lifted her spoon again to judge whether the wax was ready, and she sent me a glance that said I'd better hightail it out of the kitchen before I got stuck helping with Sister Bob's mustache. "Go make sure she isn't doing something she shouldn't be doing with That Boy."

"Zack Cleary is here?"

"Yes," Loretta said darkly.

Sister Bob said, "He looks very sweet to me."

I snorted.

A year ago, Loretta and I wouldn't have worried about what Sage was doing, because she was either studying or playing basketball. But in the last several months, Sage had found love—or something like it—with Zack Cleary, a kid a few years older who was going to cop school.

We'd already had one pregnancy scare, and none of us wanted to go through that again.

So when I exited the kitchen and caught sight of Zack Cleary with his tongue in my daughter's ear, I blew a fuse.

❧ 4 ❧

I could have grabbed a table lamp and clonked my daughter's boyfriend over his crewcut head. Or used the extension cord to strangle him.

But at the last second I caught sight of the untouched Italian sub sitting on its waxed paper on the coffee table, and my heart did a happy dance.

"Is that sandwich from Bruno's?" I asked.

Sage and Zack sprang apart, and Sage flushed the color of a pomegranate. Zack, the horndog, sat back, stretched his arms out on the back of the sofa, and smiled at me.

"Yep," he said. "Capicola and mozzarella. With hot peppers. You hungry, Mrs. A?"

Zack Cleary had been a skinny, long-haired sneak a couple of years ago—the youngest of seven, who rebelled against his father, the city's chief of police, by shoplifting cigarettes at convenience stores. But after two years of college, Zack must have drunk the family Kool-Aid, because he suddenly quit school, cut his hair short, put on some muscle, and got himself into the police academy, where he was working hard—to hear the neighborhood tell it—at getting into the Cleary family trade.

The fact that my daughter was dating the chief of police's kid had given me more than a few sleepless hours.

Sage, on the other hand, seemed as happy as any teenage girl coming into her own. Instead of a T-shirt, basketball shorts, and sneakers, she was lounging around the house in black tights and a long shirt with a bunch of bracelets on one wrist. She wore hoop earrings, too, tangled in the curls of her glossy dark hair.

I said, "You forgot your pants, Sage."

She rolled her eyes. "This is a dress, Mom."

"It's too short for a dress."

"It's *fashion*. As if you'd know anything about that."

"I know you need to go put on your jeans before your butt falls out of that outfit."

"At least I won't be humiliated by my mother."

"Say, what?"

Sage had a hard look in her eye. "Kiley Seranelli, that's what. Mom, did you have to make a spectacle of her boyfriend?"

"Boyfriend? Do you know who her so-called boyfriend is?"

"No, but she said—"

"He's Gino Martinelli. Shelby's dad."

"What?" The information shook the disdain out of Sage's attitude.

"Yes, and he's old enough to be Kiley's— Hell, he's a statutory rapist, that's what he is. And you were the one who told me about it!"

Sage clamped her mouth into a severe line. "I didn't tell you so you'd go off like a crazy woman on him."

"Oh, no? I was supposed to wait for Gino to grow a conscience? Or your friend to reach legal age?"

"Mom, everybody in school heard about what you did. Somebody's cousin even took pictures with her cell phone."

"Good," I said. "Let's hope the photos are admissible in court."

"Kiley can't go to court!" Sage cried. "Her mom would kill her! Her whole life is practically ruined now."

"All I care about is Gino getting punished. For Kiley, things will blow over."

"No, they won't. She's already talking about transferring to a whole different school. We need her for basketball season! Mom, you really screwed up this time."

Being the mother of a teenager, I had learned, means screwing up all the time. There is no winning with teenagers—only staying one step ahead of them if you're really vigilant. One day you're up, maybe, but the next day you're the lowest form of life known to man.

"Look," I said, "Kiley needed help, whether she realized it or not. I did what needed to be done."

"As usual, you bullied your way into a situation with a bazooka instead of a sensible argument."

"If I'd had a bazooka, I'd have used it."

"You're a bully," Sage snapped. "You can't be a sensible human being in a crisis. You always explode."

"I do not, damn it!"

"Kiley's life sucks, and it's your fault!"

Before I could make a snappy comeback, Sage's phone, sitting on the coffee table, began to buzz.

Zack, who had been observing us argue like he was watching a tennis match, suddenly rolled his eyes and grunted his disgust.

I pointed at the phone. "You going to answer that?"

"She doesn't have to," Zack said. "She knows who it is."

"Who is it?" I asked my daughter.

Sage, who had never been a pouter, suddenly had a lower lip big enough for a bird to land on. "Brian."

"Who's Brian?"

"Brian Stinkler," Zack said.

"Sinkland!" Sage corrected.

"He calls every five minutes," Zack told me.

I said to Sage, "Why don't you just answer? He'll stop calling."

"She doesn't want him to stop," Zack said. "She's got a crush on him."

"I do not!"

"Then why are you going out with him Friday night?"

"I haven't decided if I'm going," Sage said.

"You're stringing along the mystery man?" I asked. "Meanwhile, you're going to first base with Zack?"

"I'm not going anywhere with Zack." She grabbed the phone and leaped off the sofa. "I don't know why I try to make conversation with either one of you. I'm going upstairs."

Sage took her phone and ran up the stairs. When she was almost out of sight, she answered her phone with a sweetened voice. "Hello?"

We didn't hear the rest of the conversation because she slammed her bedroom door.

Usually, I cut Sage a lot of slack. She was a better kid than I had been at her age. The thing I didn't like was her growing up at all. I'd been happier when she was ten and showing me how to use a computer than I was now, when she had one sly boyfriend in the house and another one on the phone. And a skirt so short I could practically read the tag on her panties.

Zack laughed, and I swung on him. He had seen my expression. "She's hot, isn't she?"

"Shut the hell up."

"Hey, she comes by it naturally."

"What's that supposed to mean?"

Zack stayed relaxed on the sofa, looking up at me. "You're not exactly the PTA type, Mrs. A. So don't get all bent out of shape about Sage. Just be glad she's with me most of the time."

"I should be glad about that?"

"She could do worse."

"Like this Brian kid?"

"Maybe."

I cocked both fists on my hips. "Who is he?"

"He's a senior at one of those snotty prep schools. His dad is Mr. Squishy, the frozen-custard guy."

"Who?"

"You know—the ice-cream stands that are all over town. Mr. Squishy. He's a self-made bazillionaire, so his kid's got money to burn, not to mention a fancy Escalade to impress girls with."

"How'd Sage meet a guy like that?"

"Who am I, your spy?"

He was still smiling when he said it. I wanted to drop-kick his ass out the front door, but I'd had a long day, and my head was fuzzy where Sage was concerned. I knew she had to grow up. Of course I did. I just didn't want her plunging headlong into adulthood the way I had. Hanging out with rich kids and horny neighborhood guys like Zack seemed like she was going down exactly the wrong path.

As for Zack, it felt like he was trying hard to become my second kid. I wasn't sure how to handle him exactly. I wanted to kick him out.

But he had that sandwich.

Zack noted the direction of my gaze. He gave me a crafty smile. "You look hungry, Mrs. A."

"Quit calling me that. I'm nobody's Mrs."

"Okay, okay." He paused before saying temptingly, "Want half my sandwich? Consider it a peace offering."

In my own defense, I hadn't eaten anything since a Slim Jim at breakfast. A few oatmeal cookies had only started my belly growling. And the delicious fumes of the sub were soon going to make me drool on the floor just like Rooney.

With dignity, I decided to accept his peace offering. "If you insist."

I sat down in an armchair. Zack hunkered forward and handed over a paper napkin. He plunked half the sandwich down next, which I grabbed and bit into right away. I almost moaned with pleasure. Bruno's made a sub like no other—orgasm on a fresh-baked roll.

I ate, and Zack watched as if pleased with the situation. We could hear

Loretta and Sister Bob banging around in the kitchen, but the two of us were alone.

Small talk wasn't my specialty. But Zack looked like he was expecting a discussion of football scores or something. Probably, he wanted to talk more about Sage, but that seemed like a bad idea.

My mouth full, I said, "What's with the shirt?"

Zack's grin widened. He was wearing jeans and a blue shirt proudly printed with the words Event Security in bold white letters across the chest. "I got another part-time job until I can take the police exam. I'm working a security detail at a big concert later this week. They even gave me a free shirt. Cool, huh? I get free admission to the concert, too."

"I hope you don't get assigned to the parking lot."

He frowned. That possibility hadn't occurred to him.

I said, "I thought you got hired full-time somewhere else. What happened? You lose that job already?"

"It's only part-time. I got hired at the gun range. But they don't pay me enough, so I took a security gig, too."

"Which gun range? The same place Irene Stossel works?"

"Yeah. In fact, old Irene hired me."

Since I was the same age as Irene, I tried not to be offended. "How'd that happen?"

"Irene lives next to my uncle and heard I needed some income. I know she's weird, but she was nice to hire me. But, man, you take your life in your hands at that place. You know how many idiots want to shoot at targets? Half the time they're waving loaded weapons at each other. Irene's always in the line of fire, but she doesn't lose her cool. I'm telling you, it's dangerous work."

The thought of Zack getting himself blown to bits was kind of appealing, actually.

But further make-nice conversation was in order.

I swallowed and said, "Your mom's a volunteer at the big museum, right? Has she ever heard of somebody named Crabtree?"

Zack's expression turned to surprise. "You mean Professor Crabtree? The dinosaur guy? He's way famous."

I used the paper napkin to wipe some of the sandwich juices off my chin. "That's not who I'm talking about. This Crabtree is a woman."

Zack tore open a bag of chips and didn't appear to hear me. "My oldest brother studied with Professor Crabtree for a while. They went on a class trip to Alaska, looking for extinct animals in glaciers."

"Extinct animals, huh? Now there's a useful knowledge base for getting a job."

Zack popped a chip and grinned a little. "Paleontology. It's actually very cool. My brother took me to a lecture once, let me sit in the back. It was great. I wanted to take Crabtree's intro course when I got to college, but I didn't have the grades to get into that school."

Zack slouched back into the sofa, his legs spread comfortably, eating chips with confidence in spite of his bad grades. "Crabtree's lecture was unbelievable—slide shows and wild stories. That's why I wanted to take his class. The trips were big adventures, you know? Indiana Jones stuff."

"Does he work at the museum?"

"He was a professor at the university. Maybe he did work for the museum, too. I mean, they'd be crazy to ignore him. I think there's even some kind of national park named after him—one of those places were dinosaur bones are, like, spread all over the place. The museum has some of the stuff he dug up."

I didn't want to need Zack for anything. The kid had seduced my daughter at least once—hell, they might be doing it regularly now even with another boyfriend in the wings—and I really wanted to shove his sandwich down his throat and stomp on his chest while he choked on it. But somebody was looking to kidnap Clarice Crabtree, and it only seemed right to ask around a little.

So I said, "You know anything about Clarice Crabtree?"

"Clarice? That's really her name?"

"No kidding."

Zack frowned in concentration. "He mentioned something about a daughter, in the class I visited. She used to go on digs with him. She the one you mean?"

"I don't know, maybe."

I thought about things for a minute. Even though I'd gone to high school with Clarice, I didn't know anything about her family or where she came from. Marvin had said she worked for the museum now, but that was news to me.

I said, "Is there anybody in the neighborhood who works for the museum?"

Zack frowned at the ceiling and finally said, "My cousin's brother-in-law used to work security at an art museum. Night shift, before he joined the force."

That wouldn't do me any good. "Anybody else?"

"I'll have to think about it."

Me, too.

"What are you trying to find out, Mrs. A?"

Zack was no brain surgeon, but he could probably put two and two together if I let slip too many details. I shrugged. "Nothing special."

"You have something going on?"

"More than you do, Zack. You're necking with my daughter, but she's got Mr. Squashy on the phone. You lost your charm?"

He smiled winningly. "How about you put in a good word for me?"

I laughed. "Dream on, tiger."

My cell phone rang in my pocket. I pulled it out and checked the ID. It was Gino Martinelli.

"Damn," I said.

Zack said, "Trouble?"

I put the phone back in my pocket without answering. "Nothing unusual. Just a man trying to prove his dick is bigger than it really is. Thanks for the sandwich, tiger."

"Anytime, Mrs. A."

After talking with Zack, I went back to my place that night. But I had trouble getting to sleep. It wasn't the hot peppers that kept me awake. I was thinking about Marvin's job offer. I didn't want any part of it, but knowing that somebody wanted to kidnap Clarice Crabtree—well, maybe I was going a little soft, but I wondered if I ought to look her up and warn her.

❊ 5 ❊

In the morning, I got a call from my longtime friend Adasha Washington, another high school pal who'd had nothing to do with hiding cherry bombs in piñatas. Unlike me, Adasha had studied hard and loved school so much that she was now an ER doc at the hospital around the corner from my house.

After a big yawn in my ear, she said, "I had a lousy shift last night. I can't go running this morning."

"Damn," I said into my cell phone. "I'm all warmed up and ready to go."

She laughed. "Yeah, right. Your lazy butt is still in bed, isn't it?"

"Hey, I've been up for—well, half an hour, at least."

"Did you have a late date last night?"

It was a loaded question, and the word "date" didn't quite cover how I used to spend a lot of my evenings. I popped open a Red Bull and took a slug while rummaging in a drawer for a Slim Jim. Breakfast of champions.

Hearing my silence, she said, "Oh, Rox, I thought you quit sleeping with strangers."

"I did," I said. "Cold turkey."

After I'd fooled with the guy who turned out to have killed two people, I started thinking about the patterns of my life. I ended up talking to Adasha about it over a couple glasses of wine. I had bad impulse control to begin with, but when things got hairy, I tended to go looking for men to take out my frustration. Maybe it was unresolved anger related to my mother abandoning me when she got killed, like Adasha said, but I don't know. I was reckless, yes, but maybe I just liked sex. It was fun. Exhilarating. Therapeutic in a weird way. Satisfying, too, if only for a couple of hours. I liked having a few laughs with a man, then forgetting about him. No need to remember any phone numbers. No awkward conversations. Just good times.

"I'm glad to hear you're sticking to the plan," Adasha said. "Because you had a hell of a wake-up call, my dear."

"I know, I know."

"Look, I don't want to beat you up about this, but I heard about a therapy group that might be good for you. It's for sex addicts."

"Sex addicts! Is that what you think I am?"

"This group could be just what you need."

I couldn't help laughing. "Wait, somebody actually puts a bunch of sex addicts in the same room together? What do you think they're going to do? Have a prayer meeting?"

"It's *therapy*," Adasha insisted. "With an experienced therapist who leads the group. Everybody participates and—"

"That's some great group participation, I bet."

"Very funny. I'm just saying, it could be good for you."

"Is this like the time in seventh grade you conned me into joining the Kitchen Klub? Those girls who spent all their time weaving potholders and discussing good nutrition?"

"That was a mistake, I'll admit. I thought it meant we'd get free cupcakes."

"Mostly, we cleaned out cupboards in the home economics room."

Adasha and I had been through a lot together. She knew me well enough to make a suggestion and not get all upset if I didn't take it. I said, "Look, I'm not going to do any group therapy. I do things my own way."

"But—"

"I can handle my situation."

"Okay," she said mildly. "Think about it, Roxy. It couldn't hurt, right? Meanwhile, it's me who's got a problem."

"What's going on? More ER patients throwing up on your shoes?"

"Nothing that easy. Can you meet me on the porch?"

Barefoot, I went out to the porch and found Adasha there, still wearing her hospital scrubs, standing with a slim, pretty young woman and two scared little kids. On the street in front of the house sat the Monster Truck, and both kids blinked at the paint sprayed on the tailgate. I figured they couldn't read the word, but just the same, I wished it didn't look so scary.

Adasha said, "What's that orange stuff in your hair? Paint?"

"Dye pack from a bank. Long story."

She gave me a sideways glance. "Did you make a good getaway?"

"No gunfire. Who's this?"

"Roxy, this is Jane Doe."

Jane smiled and held out her trembling hand for me to shake. "It's not really Jane Doe. But I'm supposed to keep my identity secret. Social worker at the hospital suggested it."

Her identity was plain to me. I recognized her face from the news channel where she gave the weather every morning. Except today her face was a mess—black eye, bruised cheek, swollen lip with stitches. I couldn't remember her name—Ashley or Nicole or something trendy like that. She had a chirpy voice with a tinge of southern flirtation that got stronger when she bantered on-camera with the guy with the hair plugs who read the news.

From behind Jane Doe, her two young kids peeped at me with big eyes. The little girl clutched a pink blanket to her face and sucked her thumb. The little boy—he was maybe three—looked like he might burst into sobs any minute.

Feigning a brightness she obviously wasn't feeling, Jane said, "These are my children, Michael and Emily. Say hi, kids."

The kids didn't say a word, so Jane turned back to me. She was jumpier than a frightened rabbit. "I share custody with my first husband, and I don't want him to get the idea that anything's wrong with my—my current relationship, but I—um—I mean . . ."

Adasha got down to business. "Jane's a patient who came in last night. She needs a safe place to keep the kids for a few days. Somewhere her boyfriend can't find her."

I kept my voice low so the children couldn't hear. "Why can't she go to Social Services? They're in the business of helping women like Jane."

"She needs a place to hide," Adasha corrected. "This boyfriend is a city fireman, and he probably knows all the shelters where Social Services could put her."

"That's what restraining orders are for."

Adasha shook her head. "She can't do that, either. Takes too long, and the cop community might pass the word to the firefighters. And she's likely to be recognized at a hotel. Believe me, she shouldn't be found. Not until her face heals up."

A well-known television personality with a beat-up face wasn't going to keep any secrets for long.

On TV, Jane was perky. I could see she was trying hard to keep up the perk factor, but she looked like a battered hooker with a crazy pimp. Her smile was too bright. Her eyes gleamed with suppressed hysteria. It looked to me as if her fireman boyfriend could have finished her off without too much trouble. I wondered if the kids had watched him beat her.

I scooped up her little boy. For a second, he arched away from me, sucking in a big breath to scream, but then he caught sight of my necklace—the gold cross I usually wore around my neck—and he grabbed it with a sticky hand.

Adasha said, "I told Jane that you have an extra house next door. It's nothing fancy, Jane, but it's safe and clean."

"Not so clean at the moment," I said, hefting Michael on my hip. "Unless you're handy with a broom. The last tenant moved out fast."

In fact, my last tenant had gone to jail for stabbing her man with a broken beer bottle. I'd emptied the house myself—to make sure all her needles were gone—but I hadn't swept out the last layer of dust yet.

Little Emily had attached herself to her mother's leg. Putting her hand on the top of her daughter's head, Jane mustered more spunk. "I'm a good housekeeper. And we won't make any trouble for you, I promise. We'll be gone in a couple of days."

"Then what? You going back to the guy who messed up your face?"

"He was upset," Jane said, defensive at once. "He was tired, and I pushed the wrong buttons."

"Honey," Adasha said, "don't make excuses for that dirtbag. He beat the crap out of you, and—"

The kids didn't need to hear anymore, so I cut across my friend's harsh lecture before she really got going. "You don't have to leave him if you don't want to. But maybe it's a good idea to get some space for a while. You know—a cooling-off period. I can let you have a place for a couple of weeks while I look for a long-term tenant. After that, you can decide for yourself."

I had learned to say what needed to be said to get the job done. I could change my tune later. Is it a form of lying? You got a problem with that?

Adasha frowned, but Jane had started nodding at the first mention of a cooling-off period. "Okay, I guess that makes sense. It wasn't really his fault, see."

"It wasn't?"

"Not really. I didn't—I should have seen he was under a lot of stress."

The pressure behind my eyes began to pound at this familiar refrain. It seemed impossible that a girl who looked this bad could make excuses for the asshole who had sent her to the emergency room, but I had heard the same old story a hundred times.

"Okay," I said, rubbing my nose against Michael's until he smiled shyly. "Here's what we'll do. Adasha can take you over to the house here. See? I live in this one, and Adasha's next door." I pointed for Michael's benefit. "There's some furniture—nothing great, but it'll do. I see Adasha thought ahead and brought you some sheets and blankets."

"Thank you."

Balancing Michael on my hip, I dug into my pocket for my keys and flipped through them to find the right one. Peeling it off, I handed it to Jane. "Adasha can show you around the neighborhood, too."

"Great! Thanks! C'mon, kids, let's get your suitcases out of the car, okay?"

I carefully pried my necklace out of his fingers and gave Michael to his mother. While Jane led the two children back to the street, Adasha stood beside me and we watched them go. Adasha said, "Thank you, Rox."

"No problem. You getting her some of that group therapy you like so much?"

"I'll do what I can. She needs to calm down first, get the kids settled. The little girl didn't say a word all night while we worked on her mom. You okay?"

"Sure. Why wouldn't I be?"

She gave me a punch on the arm. "No reason. I'll check on them before I go to my shift tonight."

"Listen, Dasha, before you go to sleep for the day, I gotta ask you something."

"Shoot."

My feet were cold, and I wanted to go back inside, but I'd spent the night tossing and turning, so I asked, "Do you remember Clarice Crabtree from high school?"

If the change of subject surprised her, Adasha didn't show it. "Snotty white chick? Always bragging about herself?"

"That's the one. Know anything about her now? Isn't her dad somebody famous?"

"He's Leeford Crabtree, the dinosaur guy." Guessing the gap in my education, Adasha said, "He's a big deal. Dug up dinosaur bones? Wrote books? Did those TV documentaries we watched growing up? He was like Jacques Cousteau, only dustier."

"Right, right. How come I never knew they were related? Clarice bragged about everything else under the sun. Why not her father?"

"Who knows? Teenagers are always ashamed of their parents. Why are you asking?"

"Something came up at work." I decided to skim over my motivation. I hadn't quite figured out why I was interested except I had an inkling Marvin might screw up and accidentally mention my name to the cops someday. Adasha didn't need to hear about that. "Any idea how I could learn more about her?"

"Why don't you just look her up in the phone book and call?"

"Uh, I'm thinking it might be better to sneak up on her a little. Do you know anybody who works at the museum, for instance?"

"No." Adasha looked suspicious. "Wait. When you adopted Rooney, wasn't there somebody who got a dog at the same time? Didn't he work somewhere in the museum?"

I snapped my fingers. "You're right! Thanks, Dasha."

I even remembered where I'd scribbled down his phone number. Slugging down the last ounces of my morning Red Bull, I called him. He seemed pleased to hear from me.

"Sure, darling, come over this morning," he said on the phone, and he gave me directions.

Showered, dressed, and feeling jazzed on caffeine, I climbed into the Monster Truck and pulled out of my parking space on the street. Singing along with Aretha Franklin on WDVE, I swung by the salvage yard to pick up Rooney after a night of patrolling. We snagged Nooch about ten minutes later. He was waiting on the corner reading from his little notebook. Now and then, he glanced around, looking like a serial killer. When he saw the truck, he lost the menacing glare that kept the neighborhood thugs at a distance and got on his happy face. He tucked his notebook into his pocket and came over to the truck.

Wet but cheerful, he climbed into the passenger seat with a paper bag in one hand. His sweatshirt still had a big orange blob on the front. "Lookit! I brought breakfast."

"Wow." I peeked into the bag, elbowing Rooney's curious nose out of the way. "What's the occasion?"

"My bubbe baked muffins for Father Eugene. I swiped a couple when she wasn't looking."

"You stole a priest's breakfast?"

"It's okay. He should be on a diet. He says he's watching what he eats, but he can't turn down Bubbe, can he?"

I couldn't remember which of Nooch's grandmothers was Bubbe and which was Nonna, but one of them was enormous and the other not much bigger than a bird. The two were crabby old ladies that neighborhood kids feared. Nooch was adept at avoiding both of them, except when they were cooking. Then, he couldn't resist.

I pulled out a muffin and took a tentative bite. The texture was that of a soggy softball. Bubbe cooked a lot, but she hadn't learned much. I slipped the rest of my muffin to Rooney.

Nooch didn't notice and gobbled his before we reached the end of the block. With his mouth full, he said, "I read another chapter in my book last night."

"Oh, yeah? More thoughts on positive energy as a path to fulfillment?"

"This chapter was more about visualizing ways to be magnetic."

"You're plenty magnetic already."

"No, no, I have to make myself a magnet for good stuff."

"Like what?"

"The book talks about making a million dollars. Trouble is, I don't know how to be a magnet for a million dollars."

"You write a book about magnets, I guess."

"Huh?"

"Never mind."

Nooch looked around and realized we were traveling beyond our usual territory. "Hey, where are we going?"

I hung a left onto Penn Avenue, passing a few hipster night spots and a lot of boarded-up storefronts. "Do you remember Tito Garibaldi? The guy who adopted a dog the same time I got Rooney?"

Nooch scrunched up his face.

I said, "His dog was a white pit bull? Almost as big as he was?"

Nooch continued to frown.

"The guy who gave you a pepperoni pizza after we helped him jump his car battery," I said finally.

"Oh, him! Yeah, he was nice."

"We're going to see him this morning."

"Why?"

"To see if he knows Clarice Crabtree." I took a chance and said, "Do you remember Clarice? She was a year ahead of us in school. Tall? Blond hair? Kinda stuck-up? Picked on you?"

"Everybody picked on me in high school," Nooch said, suddenly weary. "I don't remember no Clarice."

I gave him a knock on the arm. "That's a good thing, right? You're only visualizing the positive stuff."

"Hey, I guess you're right."

Rain started to spatter the windshield. I flicked on the wipers.

Turns out, my friend Tito didn't actually work in the museum. His unglamorous workplace was officially and somewhat unimaginatively called the Remote Storage Warehouse, located in a bad part of town. Because the museum honchos didn't want their neighbors to figure out they were keeping priceless stuff in the building, they made the warehouse look completely nondescript. It was a big, square block hulk painted gray with a couple of large garage bay doors in back. There were no windows. No signage. Only the street number hung over a small front door.

I parked the Monster Truck, and we crossed the street in the rain. At the door, I pressed a button, according to Tito's instructions, and a moment later Nooch and I were inside, standing in front of a security desk.

The security guard looked like he hadn't visualized anything positive in years. "Sign in, please."

Nooch accidentally knocked a clipboard off his desk.

"Hey, be careful," the security guard said. "You can't go around like it's the demolition derby in here."

Nooch hastily put his hands into his pockets while I signed us in. I noticed the last visitor had been in the building two months ago.

Tito appeared and gave me a hearty hug. It was like getting the Heimlich maneuver from an elf. The top of his head barely came to my collarbone. "Roxy, darling! I'm so glad to see you! How's Rooney?"

"He's great. Hasn't bitten anybody in ages. How's Lucy?"

Tito had a small, animated face with bright blue eyes. A mop of soft flyaway hair curled around his head. Built like a jockey, he wore fashionable jeans, wool clogs, and a thick purple sweater that looked as if it had been knitted by Norwegian drunks. A knot of keys and plastic security and ID cards jingled around his neck.

At the mention of his dog's name, though, his sprightly expression faltered. He stiffened his lower lip manfully. "I had to let Lucy go. It's a long story, but the postal service was involved."

"Gee, I'm sorry."

While I had gone to the pound looking for a dog to guard my place of business, Tito had hoped for a house pet and ended up picking the worst case in the shelter—the neediest, most vicious dog, the one that had been rescued from a fighting pit and probably had no chance at rehabilitation.

Tito smile sadly. "It's all for the best. I can't really leave a dog at home if I'm here all day, right? So I got a rabbit from the shelter. Do you know how many rabbits are dropped off at shelters every year? Thousands. So I got one, and then another and another. Now I've got a whole rabbit community! I'm thinking of writing a screenplay for a children's movie."

"Actually, a children's movie about you and a bunch of rabbits sounds terrific."

"Thanks. I'll find the time eventually. Hello, Nooch!" Tito grabbed Nooch's paw and pumped it vigorously. He smiled up into his face. "Great to see you again! Did you ever find out if your family comes from eastern

Europe, by any chance? Poland? Maybe Gdansk? Perhaps the Wrzeszcz district?"

Nooch looked charmed, but confused. "Huh?"

"Genetic markers! It's your ears. And the way your forehead is shaped. Very much from Wrzeszcz. C'mon, let's go upstairs."

Nooch reached for his ears. "Huh?"

"Tito is an anthropologist," I said as we started up a set of industrial steps. "He knows all about people and where they come from."

"And their music, their arts and crafts, their work. Nooch, the people of your hometown mostly worked in breweries. Cistercian monks ran waterwheels and mills on the creek, but that was back in the thirteenth century. I don't suppose you know if you had any monks in your family tree?"

"Huh?"

I said, "Nooch is focusing on being positive these days. Sometimes that takes all of his mental energy."

"*Wonderful You!* Extraordinary how such flimflammery resurfaces every few decades. How's it going for you, Nooch?" Tito asked.

"So far, it turned me orange." Nooch indicated his sweatshirt.

"That's not so bad, is it? Orange is the color of sweet potatoes and mangoes, two of my favorite foods."

Nooch said, "I like marshmallows and brown sugar on sweet potatoes."

"Who doesn't? See? Already, you're radiating positive vibrations."

Nooch said, "I'm on a path to fulfillment."

"A very admirable endeavor." Tito swiped a security card to get us through a steel door on the landing, and another card to get us through a second door. "I love Poland," he went on. "I once spent two weeks hiking around the Carpathian Mountains. The birds are incredible there. I met a man from Ukraine, big fella like you, Nooch. We didn't speak any languages in common, except the language of love. But that's another story. Watch your step. Those are Japanese *naginata*. A traditional weapon for women now, but with samurai origins."

The door opened into a storage space about the size of a football field.

The temperature hovered somewhere between meat locker and the garage where I rotated my tires. Some kind of crazy music floated on the air— maybe a klezmer band with a clarinet playing on the edge of hysteria. Hundreds of bright yellow steel lockers stood in rows before us.

A stack of machetelike weapons leaned against the nearest locker, and Nooch bumped into them. The machetes fell over with a clatter.

"Sorry!" Nooch stepped back.

He backed into a mannequin dressed in rustic-looking armor and holding a club. I grabbed the mannequin to keep it from crashing over, but one of the breastplates fell off and hit the floor with a clang.

"Sorry," I said.

"No worries!" Tito cried, picking up the weapons and restacking them. He put the breastplate on top of one of the lockers. "These things haven't had a scratch in three hundred years, so why would they break now? Come this way."

"Be careful," I muttered to Nooch.

"I am," he whispered back. "There's just too much stuff in here!"

Tito talked over the music as he led us through a maze of lockers. He pointed to some junk sitting on top of one of them. "Those are Peruvian death masks. And up there you'll see a fine example of Aboriginal carving, see? And some feathered arrows over there, from Africa. It's all cataloged, so don't think anything's lost. Exquisite, right?"

Nooch tried to be polite. "Real nice."

To me, all the stuff looked like a big garage sale.

Eventually, Tito quit giving us the grand tour and marched to his office, which was maybe eight feet by eight feet, all of it packed with computers, racks of CDs, boxes of old-fashioned photographic slides, and a line of coffee cups standing on a shelf, each with a different Latin phrase printed on the side. A space heater hummed on the floor.

It took Nooch four seconds to kick over the space heater.

Tito leaped to upright it. "Oh, dear, oh, dear. Maybe this is the wrong place to be if we're worried about maintaining positive energy. I do keep a few important pieces here for—"

Nooch shouldered a pot off a shelf, and I caught it in midair.

Tito let out an unsteady breath. "That's third century BC."

I handed the pot to him carefully. "I guess I should have left Nooch in the truck."

"It's okay," Tito said, clearly lying. He placed the pot firmly on a different shelf, then opened a shallow desk drawer and began to rummage in the clutter there. "Where's that leash you gave me? It was definitely the right idea for Lucy. I just couldn't bring myself to use something that dug into her neck."

"I know what you mean. I couldn't use it on Rooney, either."

"Here we go. One spiked collar. Sorry for not returning it sooner."

"No problem." Before he could launch into another lecture, I said, "Tito, I wonder if you know somebody I went to school with."

Tito smiled and fixed me with his intent blue gaze. "I figured there was something else on your mind. Picking up a dog collar you wouldn't use seemed like a flimsy excuse."

I grinned, too. "I should have known you'd see through me."

"Who do you want to know about?"

"A lady by the name of Clarice Crabtree."

Surprise showed on his face. "Why do you want to know about her? Is it personal?"

"No."

"Business?"

"I—"

"Or something to do with your uncle?"

I was almost too distracted to grab Nooch just as he was about to bump a priceless sculpture off Tito's desk. But I managed. "My uncle?"

Tito's smile broadened. "I'm a researcher, Roxy. When I met you, I did a little reading, and of course Carmine Abruzzo's name popped up. Before we have an accident, why don't we talk elsewhere? Nooch, would you like a cup of green tea? I guarantee positive results."

"Uh—"

"You've got him buffaloed," I said. "Yes, he'd like some tea."

Tito led us back downstairs to an employee lounge. Concrete floor, folding table cluttered with magazines and coffee cups. Tito put Nooch safely into a folding chair and proceeded to pour hot water from a coffeemaker over a fragrant tea bag. "To answer your question, yes, Clarice Crabtree works for the museum. Not at this facility. She's at the main branch, in the natural history collection. She works in megafauna, but I hear she's on the road quite a bit. She lectures and still visits digs, I believe. She's in great demand, probably because of her name."

"Her dad is Professor Crabtree."

"Yes, of course, darling. That's enough of a credential to get her dozens of lecture offers every year. Her husband works for the museum, too, by the way. His expertise is mollusks."

"He must be a thrill a minute."

"Actually, they both do fascinating work. But that's not why you're here. What do you want to know about Clarice?"

"Just—I don't know exactly. What's megafauna?"

"Shall I show you?"

"Sure."

"Let's leave Nooch here. Our insurance is paid up, but I'm thinking we should do everything possible to protect world culture."

With Nooch content to sniff the contents of his teacup, Tito took me back into another part of the huge warehouse, a section cordoned off with a chain-link fence and padlocks.

As we walked, I asked, "Do you know Clarice personally?"

"Not well. I met her a few times—at large functions. At those things, all academic types brag about their prestigious awards and their important speeches. She was right in the scrum of battling egos. Otherwise, though, she was very cool."

"She was cool?"

"In the standoffish sense. I've observed that characteristic in many wealthy people. They keep their distance. They're afraid, perhaps, that everybody's after their money."

"Clarice is wealthy?"

"I believe her husband came from an important family. And, of course, there must be money in Professor Crabtree's account, right?"

Money was enough to explain why somebody might want to kidnap Clarice.

"Unfortunately," Tito continued, "her father has lost his marbles, I hear. Clarice packed him off to an Alzheimer's facility a few weeks ago. We heard all about it, through the grapevine. Are you going to the house sale? That's your line of work, right? Buying and selling junk from houses?"

"Not junk. Architectural salvage," I corrected.

"Sorry. I heard Clarice was selling off things from her father's estate. Furniture and whatnot. Probably things from his collection. Could be worth a fortune."

Anything worth a fortune interested me.

Tito stopped in front of some large items heaped untidily behind the chain-link fence. I peered at the dim shapes and finally realized I was looking at bones. Very large bones.

Tito said, "Andrew Carnegie started this museum with dinosaur bones, did you know that? Dinosaur bones were very exciting back then—a surefire way to draw the public into a museum. Later, this was the first dinosaur Leeford Crabtree ever dug up. He named all his finds, by the way. This one is Trixie. We usually cast the bones in plaster and display the casts in the museum, not the originals. The real things are too heavy, so we keep them here."

"Wow. Those bones are huge."

"Early paleontologists often couldn't find the smaller parts of skeletons. The right technology didn't exist back then, which is why there isn't enough of Trixie to make a good display. Her skull was missing—probably washed away or carried off by scavenging carnivores, and skulls are what give dinosaur displays their personality."

"But you keep Trixie anyway?"

"We could have sold her parts, I suppose. But selling to collectors is very bad form in our world." Tito blew some dust off a label. "Professor Crabtree eventually left dinosaurs for later species, of course. Some of us have the opinion that he surrendered the field because other, younger scientists were more successful. In the middle part of his career, he found a full saber-toothed tiger in Siberia. You've probably seen that one at the museum. He called that specimen Fred. Fred makes a very good display."

If I had seen Crabtree's tiger, it hadn't made much of an impression on me.

I said, "You mentioned Clarice is into something called megafauna. What's that?"

"Technically, it's an animal weighing more than a hundred pounds, anything from deer and kangaroos to humans or elephants. But Clarice specializes in Pleistocene megafauna—those giant animals from the last ice age. You know—aurochs and the *Elasmotherium* and so forth."

"The *Elas*—what?"

"A kind of giant rhinoceros." Tito strolled further along the chain-link enclosure, gesturing at the dusty lumps on the other side. "And, of course, the granddaddy of the Pleistocene era—the woolly mammoth. Here are some mastodon bones." He consulted a plain index card stuck on the chain link, lettered by hand in blue ink. "Shirley, I believe. Yes, it's Shirley."

"Can you make a lot of money stuyding megafauna?"

"Perhaps. Why don't you ask Clarice? I'm sure she'd be forthcoming."

"Hm."

Tito had been observing me while he spoke. "You seem reluctant to communicate directly with Clarice."

"A little. We have some history."

Tito's brows rose.

"Just a high school thing."

"Ah," said Tito. "High school. The great leveler. I hated high school."

"Who didn't?"

"Cheerleaders, probably."

I laughed. "You're right."

"I think we should be getting back to Nooch, in case he's destroyed something priceless. Is there anything else you'd like to know, Roxy?"

"Just this," I said. "Do you know anybody who might have a beef with Clarice Crabtree?"

"That's quite a loaded question, isn't it? Is she in some kind of trouble?"

Yes, I thought. Clarice is in big trouble. I decided I better warn her.

❦ 6 ❦

But after visiting Tito, I took a phone call from a demolition guy who wanted me to take a look at a staircase in an old house he was tearing down in Millvale. Since business was so bad, I figured I'd better check it out. In my line of work, you never know when you might hit the jackpot. The staircase turned out to be junk, but at the home next door was a punk who wanted rid of his dead grandmother's household stuff. In the heap of rubble he'd piled in the backyard I found what looked like a Russian icon.

It was a painting on a big splintered board, depicting a hollow-cheeked Christ figure with spaniel eyes and a starburst crown. I hauled the heavy painting out of the pile and sat down on the back steps to admire it. Things don't often take my breath away, but this was a masterpiece. And, judging by its size, it might once have adorned one of the local Russian Orthodox churches.

A lot of immigrants had come to Pittsburgh a century ago to work in the mills, and some of them brought priceless heirlooms from their countries of origin. Especially religious stuff. The old folks were still the keepers of their ethnic traditions, but their offspring were often impatient with the old ways.

"Ugly, isn't it?" The punk blew a lungful of cigarette smoke at the painting. "Gram collected all kinds of crap. Is this worth anything?"

"It's not in great condition." I balanced it awkwardly to point out the faded gold paint and the big scrawl of Crayola crayon across Jesus's face.

"Give me fifty bucks and it's yours," the kid said, dropping his cigarette and grinding it out on the porch floor. "If I don't have to do any work, that is. Your moron can carry it out of here."

Most of the time, I try to do the right thing by people who are scraping by. But I talked Prince Charming down to thirty bucks.

I drove the icon over to a gallery owner, who fell to his knees when he saw it. Later, he brewed us some espresso, and we talked over the wisdom of getting someone to restore it or just send the icon to an art auction house and hope for the best. He warned that it would take months—maybe a year or more—to get any definitive answers. I trusted the gallery owner. With luck, it might help start Sage's college fund. Or not. I was out just thirty bucks. Not a bad bet.

After that pleasant interlude, I had to go back to my office to return some calls from people looking for architectural stuff for their houses. While I did that, Nooch moved stuff in the warehouse. I did my best to drum up some good business, but nothing panned out. I decided to take the advice from Nooch's book, though, and think positively. Tomorrow was another day.

So it was a few hours later when we piled into the truck. The cold rain had finally let up, and evening was just starting to gather. I'd looked the Crabtree name up in the property tax rolls and found Professor Crabtree's address, but not Clarice's. I drove up to the neighborhood and parked in front of the Crabtree house.

Why? I wasn't sure. I didn't owe Clarice a damn thing. But I figured it wouldn't hurt to warn her that something was up.

Nooch and Rooney and I sat in front of a dark, sagging house in a once-respected part of town. Old age was getting its claws into the side-walks and the homes. The location—near enough to the universities—had caused their value as single-family residences to drop like a block of yellow ice from an airplane.

I'd expected Professor Leeford Crabtree to live in grandeur. I mean, if he was such a big deal in the dinosaur game, he ought to have a few bucks, right? But instead, the house was practically a pile of sticks. Most of the Victorian houses in his neighborhood had been broken up into apartments for students. A few mildewed sofas sat on porches with beer cans scattered around—sure signs of student living. The brick street was nothing but bumps and potholes, and piles of wet leaves hugged the curbs. Half the trees were dead, just waiting to fall on a car and make some in-surance agent miserable.

"Pretty house." Nooch looked at the tilted porch and the broken stairs, but even he saw the obvious signs of past glory—the Victorian trim, the elegant proportions and scale the architect had put to use. "At least, it used to be. Who lives here?"

"Professor Crabtree."

"Who's that?"

"An old guy. He's gone to a hospital."

Nooch's eyes bugged out. "He get hurt or something?"

Nooch might have been the size of a sumo wrestler, and he could scare the shit out of most petty criminals, but he had the personality of a lamb. Okay, maybe a lamb with a learning disability.

"His brain got hurt gradually." I shut off the truck's engine. "He couldn't take care of himself anymore, so his family found a safe place for him."

"You mean the old-folks home. Man, that stinks."

In our final moments together, Tito had mentioned that Clarice de-cided it was time to do something about her father when Professor Crab-tree took to spending most of his days and nights sitting on his front porch with a sawed-off Holland & Holland elephant gun. Neighbors became alarmed for their children. So his daughter, Tito said, finally clapped him into a nursing home.

Tonight, a gray Volvo station wagon sat parked in the driveway. The vehicle of university professors, arty types, and liberal ministers. A university parking sticker glowed on the back bumper. A dry-cleaning bag hung on a hook inside the back window. Good chance this was Clarice's car.

The house looked as if it was being emptied out, all right. On the porch, somebody had left some sad-looking furniture—a rump-sprung armchair and an end table missing a leg. The front door was propped open with a brick. A dim light shone from inside the house, and I could see a ladder standing in the front hallway. Boxes were stacked by the door.

"Look," I said to Nooch, "how about we play it this way? I go inside for a minute while you stay here and keep an eye on things."

"What are you going to do inside?"

"Talk to somebody. Crabtree's daughter, if I'm lucky."

"How come you want to talk to her?"

"Because maybe she needs some help."

Nooch said, "Looks like the house needs help."

"Yeah. So you stay here and watch out for things."

"What things? You mean cops?"

Nooch hadn't been in trouble with the law for ten years, but he was still spooked about the police. I said, "Anybody. And don't start visualizing. I don't want you falling asleep."

"Right." Nooch nodded firmly, as if accepting a very difficult task.

I bailed out of the Monster Truck. Before I could stop him, Rooney jumped out too. The dog had been cooped up for most of the day, so he made a beeline for the picket fence, where he lifted his leg and peed for about a minute. When he finished, he nosed open the gate, ran across the small, overgrown yard, and disappeared around the bushes into the darkness at the side of the old house. I called him, but he didn't return. But he'd come back eventually, so I wasn't worried.

I knocked on the jamb. When I didn't get an answer, I leaned into the foyer and called, "Anybody home?"

It was a big, gloomy house. Some doctor or college professor had probably built it back in the heydey of steel mills. But not a lick of maintenance had been done since then. When I stepped inside, the wooden floor creaked, and it slanted downhill at a fun-house angle. An oak staircase marched up crookedly to the second floor. The oak paneling's veneer was peeling.

I poked my head into the parlor, where the remaining furniture had once been kinda froufrou. But now the upholstery was stained and patched with duct tape. Tall bookshelves were so stuffed with books and archive boxes that they seemed to lean into the room.

I checked out the clutter on the big desk. More books and lots of papers. The drawers hung open and overflowed. A lot more papers were scattered on the floor. Some were filled with numbers, but most of them were printed with long paragraphs. I picked up one page and scanned it. Lots of big words.

Glancing around, I decided somebody had ransacked the desk looking for something.

From deep in the house, a voice called, "Back here!"

I followed it, my boots grinding grit into the floorboards, and found Clarice Crabtree standing with a clipboard in the middle of kitchen.

"You're not the electrician," she said at once.

I put my hands into the front pockets of my jeans to look as unthreatening as possible. "Sorry, no. I do architectural salvage. I'm Roxy Abruzzo."

Clarice hadn't changed much since high school. Thin as an icicle, she still had blond hair that stayed perfectly combed no matter what, and a certain curl to her upper lip—like Elvis, only not sexy.

"Roxy," she said slowly, trying to remember. "Roxy Abruzzo."

"Yeah," I said. "I heard you might be breaking up the house."

I don't know why I didn't come clean immediately and just warn her that somebody was looking to kidnap her. I guess it's just not my nature to be honest right away.

She skewered me with a look, still not sure why she recognized my name. I was a little insulted. But she said, "Who did you hear that from?"

"In my business, word gets around. Plumbers, carpenters, you know.

This is a beautiful place. I mean, it was beautiful once. Shame about the current condition. You the homeowner?"

She said, "I'm in charge of the estate. It's my father's house, but he won't be coming back. I'm Dr. Crabtree. Clarice Crabtree."

I put on my good manners and shook her hand firmly.

"Architectural salvage," she said, wiping her hand on her pants. "What's that, exactly?"

"I strip stuff out of fancy houses and resell it. Woodwork. Fireplaces. Staircases. That kind of thing. Here's my card. I only deal in quality goods, though. Has anyone else been here yet?"

Clarice accepted my somewhat grubby card, read it carefully, and then gave me a more complete once-over, an inspection I let happen even though I felt the old sensation of dislike and resentment rising up inside. My uncombed hair and the layers of jeans and sweatshirts that passed for my fashion statement didn't seem to impress her. My sartorial choices hadn't changed in . . . well, not ever.

"You're the first," she replied.

By contrast, Clarice wore a trim silver pantsuit with gold cuff links on her sleeves. The cuff links might have been old coins. I thought, What kind of woman wears cuff links? Her earrings matched, only the coins were smaller. Her face had always been kind of snooty, but it was patrician now—short nose, pointed jaw. Her shoes had straps and very high heels, as if she were one of those desert birds that try to make themselves as big as possible. She still looked like the kind of person who'd laugh if you couldn't fake reading stupid *Ethan Frome.*

She had two cell phones clipped to her belt, both of them blinking with messages. What kind of person carries two cell phones?

In a different tone, Clarice suddenly said, "Roxy Abruzzo."

"Yeah." I smiled. "Remember me now, Clarice?"

"Vaguely." But her face said she recalled every unfortunate second we'd ever spent in each other's company.

Like Tito had said, high school was the great leveler—the last time in life that everybody's almost on equal footing. We were all subject to the same pressures and humiliations. Some of us emerged smarter and stronger for all the tortures, though, while others simply walked out of the hallowed halls the same jerks they had been from the beginning.

Clarice said, "I never liked you."

"Sorry to say, I didn't care much for you, either."

"It's odd," she said. "Because you were the only person with whom I had anything in common."

"Let's not get insulting here, Clarice."

She ignored that, but fixed me with a stare, tapping her pencil on her clipboard. Finally, she said, "Our mothers were both murdered."

For once, I couldn't make a comeback.

"You'd think that might draw us together," she said, "but actually it made me want to avoid you even more."

As teenagers, you really don't care much about why people act the way they do. You're too busy trying to survive yourself, I guess. It never occurred to me that Clarice might have some baggage, too.

When I could breathe again, I said, "I didn't know your mom was killed."

"Yes. She was mugged outside a bank when I was fourteen. Yours?"

"I was thirteen," I said stiffly.

"How did she die?"

Normally, I wouldn't have answered. But I said, "Beaten. Strangled."

"At random? By a stranger?"

"No," I said.

"I see." Her smile returned. "Well, at least I have that to hang on to. Nobody in my family is a murderer."

A delicious white heat of rage promptly seethed in my veins, and I felt almost happy again. "Still the same humanitarian, huh, Clarice?"

"We all find ways to cope, Roxy. At least I'm a productive member of society."

I could have knocked her down and shoved all her stupid gold coins down her throat just then, but I held back. That's me—the new master of my impulses.

If I'd had any urge to protect her—to warn her that somebody wanted to do her harm—it evaporated. Suddenly I didn't care if Muslim terrorists snatched Clarice off a street, tied her up in a cave, and left her to rot. They could have her, for all I cared.

And the whole sisterhood of the murdered mothers? Screw that. I'd lived through it and done just fine on my own.

With a cold smile on her face, she watched my storm of emotions. She enjoyed it, I could see. When I finally got control of myself, she said, "Are you interested in wine racks?"

"Wine racks?" I knew I sounded stupid and hated myself for it. "Like—you mean wooden racks for bottles?"

"Is there any other kind?" Her tone was withering. "The realtor tells me I should get rid of all the junk in the basement. Your arrival is timely. There are some big wine racks I'd like to dispose of. Would you like them? Could they be removed soon?"

"Sure. We do our own demo."

She lifted her eyebrows. "We?"

"My assistant and me. He's outside." I hooked my thumb at the door. "You want to meet him? Maybe check his résumé?"

She gave me the smug stinkeye for another second. Then she put the pencil in her mouth and champed down on it. I could see she'd already chewed it so there was barely anything left of the yellow part. She removed the pencil and said, "That won't be necessary. Shall we take a look at the racks?"

"Lead the way."

With military precision, Clarice led me across the gritty-floored kitchen.

As she walked away from me, I couldn't help noticing her butt. It's not like I'm in the habit of looking at women's bodies, honest. But there it was. Unmistakable evidence that under her expensive, professorly pantsuit, Clarice wore a thong.

Kind of surprising, since she'd been a cold fish back in high school.

I shrugged and followed her down a set of wobbly steps, past the fuse box to the cellar, where only a single bulb with a dangling pull string cast a gray light across the eerie shapes of junk the old professor had collected over the years. Not just boxes and barrels of crap, but a whole crazy zoo was spread out across the vast floor.

Maybe I was already off kilter. But suddenly I had to clamp down every iota of self-control not to break out in the screaming meemies.

Because it was a horror show down there. Stuffed animals frozen in weird poses, glass eyes gleaming. An antelope, a leopard. A stuffed grizzly bear stood beside a rusted deep freeze, alongside a pair of barrels that contained something that smelled disgusting. A dozen stuffed birds hung upside down from the ceiling, laced with cobwebs. An arctic fox stared out from a corner, teeth bared in a snarl.

I could hardly keep from running back up the stairs and into the night.

Clarice enjoyed watching my reaction.

But suddenly one of the beasts growled. It lunged out from behind a wooden crate. Ferocious growl, huge body, threatening teeth. I almost shrieked.

Except the monster turned out to be Rooney.

I sagged against a pillar, relief sweeping over me so fast I felt weak.

But Clarice screamed, dropped her clipboard, and jumped up on the freezer, fancy shoes and everything.

I grabbed Rooney's collar and held him back. "Easy, big fella."

He twisted in my grasp and gave me a whine of complaint. He liked scaring people.

"Good boy," I said, patting his huge head.

Instead of looking smug, Clarice was spazzed out, on her hands and knees on the freezer. It was good to see her looking unhinged.

She snapped, "How did that get in here?"

"I feel a breeze. There's a door open somewhere."

"That's impossible! I checked all the doors myself."

"Then the wind must have come up. Say hello, Rooney."

My dog was as big as the wild boar in the corner and twice as ugly, blind in one eye, and with a head that was a mass of scars. He looked right at home in the professor's menagerie.

When she realized Rooney wasn't on the attack, Clarice climbed down off the freezer and pulled herself together. She dusted the dirt from the knees of her trousers and accepted the clipboard as I handed it back to her. "You should keep that animal on a leash."

"He can't do his job on a leash." I patted him and set him loose again. He went straight to Clarice and put his nose in her crotch. "Hey," I said to him, and he obediently shied away.

Clarice brushed invisible hairs from her pants. "Just keep him away from me, will you? Or I'll send you the dry-cleaning bill."

Rooney knocked into one of the dead animals, and I reached down to prevent it from falling over. As I set it upright again, I said, "What the hell is this? Some kind of badger?".

"It's a *Castoroides*. A relative of the modern beaver." Clarice smoothed her hairdo. "It's been extinct for a hundred years."

"Shouldn't it be in a museum?"

"Most of my father's mounts are infested with moths. No curator would want them contaminating an important collection."

I looked around a little more. Of course, I had never been one of those Girl Scout types that hiked around in the wood, breathing fresh air and learning how to treat snakebites with leaves and berries, but to me the grizzly bear had teeth that didn't look like they belonged in the real world, and the rhino head hanging on the wall had plates on his neck that might have been designed for a sci-fi movie.

I said, "What did your old man study, exactly? Mutants?"

"He researched many things. None of them thoroughly." Coldly, Clarice added, "He was more of a dilettante than people thought."

"That means you aren't?"

"You're asking my academic specialty? I don't think you'd understand, Roxy. Let's just say I didn't fly on my father's coattails. I've made my own success," she went on, starting to sound like her high school self. "I'm sought after in my own right. I do some seminars, but my research keeps me very busy. Plenty of international travel. I'm the foremost expert in my field."

"Impressive," I said. "Now, about those wine racks? I don't want to waste any more of your valuable time."

She glowered. "Very well. This way."

We brushed past more junk. I took care to stay away from the creepy animals. Eventually we came to the back of the basement, and I took a look at some dusty shelves that had been built into the original frame of the house. They were crude wine racks, nothing special, built of hickory, I guessed. But Clarice got all rapturous.

"My parents once kept a vast wine collection." She ran one finger down the edge of the racks, then looked at the dust with distaste. "But it was my mother's interest, really. After she died, Dad just drank it all. He wasn't an alcoholic, but he had a bottle with dinner every night for twenty years—so the collection dwindled to nothing."

The family tragedy didn't interest me. "Well, the racks look in good shape. I know a restaurant that's looking to make some upgrades. These might appeal to the owner. I can offer you a couple hundred bucks."

"That's all?"

"If they were carved or imported or something, I could offer you more. But these are nothing fancy. See? Even the joints don't match. You could ask around, try to find somebody else who will offer you more. No skin off my nose."

"Oh, never mind. I'm just glad to be rid of them. I'd like all of this mess out of here as soon as possible. And a check, of course."

"You want me to pay you now?"

Clarice checked her watch. "I have an important meeting this evening, and I don't want to be late. Can you send it to me? To this address?"

"Yeah, sure. I could write you a check now, if you want. I just have to go out to the truck and dig out the checkbook."

"No, I'm in a rush."

"Okay, I'll send the check. Where are you headed?"

"That's none of your business."

"Whatever you say." I shrugged. "You don't have to stick around to supervise. If you've got big places to go, go. I'll get the racks out of here tonight, put a payment into the mail tomorrow."

She hesitated. Either she needed the dough or she didn't trust me. I was willing to bet on the trust issue.

I said, "I'm bonded. Go to your meeting. Just—when you leave, send my guy down here. He's waiting in my truck. Can you do that?"

She turned briskly. "Yes. There's nothing worth stealing in the house, by the way. And I have your business card, if there's anything out of order when I return. Turn off the lights and lock the front door when you leave."

She left and went up the steps. I considered making a spitball and hitting her in the butt with it, but she was already gone.

It was only after I heard her footsteps cross the floor upstairs that I realized I hadn't gotten around to warning her.

That's when Rooney reappeared from the darkness. He jumped up and put his front paws on the freezer. He clawed at the lid and gave me a hopeful woof.

"Now what?" I asked him.

He barked again and smiled at me, his big tongue hanging out the side of his mouth.

"You want something inside?"

I looked at the freezer. Maybe all those weird animals had made me jumpy, but all I could think about was stupid heroines in horror movies who were always stumbling around in dark basements, opening doors that should have stayed closed. But the freezer beckoned. Rooney clawed at it some more.

Gently, I lifted the lid on the freezer.

Preparing to find a dead zombie, I peered inside.

But all I saw was a heap of colorful frozen vegetable bags sitting alongside various sizes of packages wrapped in white butcher paper—probably meat. A soup bone sat on top. A really big one.

Rooney jumped up and leaned his head into the freezer. The interior light glowed up on the wrinkled features of his face. Snuffling eagerly, he tried to climb into the freezer to get at the bone. But his hind legs couldn't quite get enough traction to make it over the edge.

I figured the old man had moved out of his house, and what were the chances of his bitch of a daughter wanting to eat his frozen food? Plus she'd said she was going to empty out the house in time to show it to a realtor. So I grabbed one of the white packages and hefted it. Maybe five pounds, I guessed. I ripped open the edge, and inside it looked like beef to me. With considerable freezer burn.

But Rooney stretched his nose closer to the huge bone sitting across the top of all the white packages.

I dropped the meat and reached in to push the bone closer to Rooney's jaws. It weighed a ton, but he wrestled it out of the freezer and dragged it onto the floor. There, he crouched down and immediately fell to gnawing on one knobby end.

"Enjoy it," I said. "With Clarice's compliments." I closed the freezer. "Where the hell is Nooch?"

Either he'd been sidetracked—which happened a lot—or Clarice had forgotten to deliver my message.

I went upstairs to find him myself. Rooney grabbed up his big bone and followed. The bone clunked against the walls, and he had trouble getting it through the doorways, but he managed.

On the front sidewalk in the dark, Rooney pushed ahead of me, then stopped dead and growled.

I couldn't see much, but I trusted the dog's instincts and froze. The wind hissed in the trees overhead. A distant siren wailed. Rooney dropped his bone on the sidewalk, and I grabbed his collar. I could feel the hair on his neck bristling.

I glanced up the street, my heart skipping. The streetlights weren't much help. No traffic.

Then a car door opened somewhere in the darkness and slammed a second later. I steeled myself, thinking fast about a weapon. Should I turn the dog loose? Or prepare to use my fists?

But it was Nooch who pushed through the Crabtree gate.

I expelled a breath I hadn't realized I'd been holding. "Where have you been?"

Nooch halted in his tracks in the act of muffling a yawn with one hand. "In the truck, like you said."

"Didn't Clarice Crabtree tell you I wanted you downstairs?"

"Who?"

"The lady who came out of the house a few minutes ago."

"Nobody told me nothing."

I glanced over at the driveway. Clarice's car was still parked where she'd left it. The interior lights were on. Nobody was sitting inside. I could hear the bing-bing-bing of a key in the ignition, though. I headed over to the car.

"What's going on?" Nooch ambled after me.

I reached the station wagon and peered inside. No Clarice. But the keys dangled from the ignition, and the car kept binging. I leaned in the open door to get a better look and saw her purse half hidden under the seat. Careful not to touch anything else, I snagged it off the floor.

"What are you doing?" Nooch asked. "Jeez, you're not purse snatching, are you?"

"I'm checking her stuff. You fell asleep, didn't you?"

"Aw, Rox, don't yell at me. I started visualizing a nice plate of gnocchi, but I must have dozed off for a couple of minutes, that's all, and—what are you doing?"

I had already pulled my cell phone from the hip pocket of my jeans. "I'm calling the cops."

Nooch's eyes bulged. "All I did was fall asleep!"

The first squad car arrived in less than three minutes. In half an hour, the street was crowded with cops and their vehicles. I guess it was a slow night for crime fighting. After the initial rush, Bug Duffy finally showed up.

✳ 7 ✳

Bug flashed his detective's shield at the cop who'd been assigned the job of keeping sightseers away. He spotted me perched on the porch railing with Nooch. Shaking his head, Bug limped across the small yard toward us. He'd done something to his knee a few weeks back, and it looked as if he'd thrown away his crutches a little too early. He wore his rumpled jacket and corduroys with hiking boots, and he carried a big flashlight in one hand, turned off.

He said, "We didn't believe it was you who called in a car with keys in the ignition. Are you the new neighborhood watch?"

"You mean I should have stolen the car?"

"That would have been easier to handle than the homicide we're working in Homewood. Drug bust turned into a shoot-out, thirteen-year-old kid killed. Depressing as hell. I had to get away for a while." He looked down at Rooney. "That's some bone."

The dog lay on the ground at my feet. He must have sensed Bug was referring to his prize, because he kept his teeth clamped on his bone, rolled his eyes up, and growled.

"Easy, Rooney," I said without moving from my spot on the railing. "Nooch, how about putting him in the truck before he starts thinking somebody's going to steal his new toy?"

The last thing I needed was my dog attacking a cop.

"Sure," Nooch said amiably.

When Nooch was out of earshot, Bug said, "What's this I hear about you giving up your religion?"

"What's that supposed to mean?"

Bug leaned against the porch railing. He tried holding back a smile. "I hear you've taken a vow of chastity." He turned on the flashlight, and the glare hit me in the eyes. I put up my hand to cut the pain, but he kept it on me. I heard barely suppressed laughter in his voice. "Is it true? You're on the straight and narrow?"

"Mostly straight, rarely narrow," I said, avoiding the light. "It's a little less exciting than I'm used to, that's all."

I hadn't expected my life-changing decision to make the headline news at police headquarters, especially during a big homicide investigation. The fact that even Duffy knew my business was a little embarrassing, I guess. For some reason, I didn't mind everybody knowing I liked a quickie now and then. But now that I was trying to control my impulses, I felt kinda foolish.

Maybe Bug noticed, because the flashlight went dark. "Less exciting can be a good thing."

"Is that the attitude in your marriage, Detective Duffy?" I asked. "How are Marie and the kids?"

Full of affection, he said, "Driving me crazy. Your daughter?"

"Pretty much the same."

Bug was the kind of name that stuck, especially to a skinny kid who'd worn huge eyeglasses right through high school. But somewhere on his life's trajectory, Bug Duffy had filled out in the shoulders, gotten some Lasik done on his eyes, and grown into a not-bad-looking guy with a steady job, a nice family, and a couple of citations for bravery. We'd been acquaintances in high school. I wouldn't call Bug a friend, exactly, but he tended to look me in the eyes, not any other part of my body, which elevated him in my esteem.

How Bug felt about me, I wasn't sure. Mostly, he seemed amused.

"This neighborhood doesn't usually have much crime." He thumbed the switch again and pointed the flashlight's glare on the station wagon. "Whose car is it, do you know?"

"Isn't this where the city's finest technology comes into play?"

"The city can barely afford telephone service, let alone fancy technology. To me, this looks like somebody walked away from their car, that's all. What's the big deal?"

Nooch had come back, and was standing at the edge of the sidewalk. "I don't feel so good."

Bug trained the flashlight on Nooch's orange belly. "What's the matter, big guy? Queasy?"

"Hungry," Nooch said. "I didn't have no dinner yet."

I got to my feet and pulled the truck's keys from my pocket. "Mind if I take him home? He's on a quest for fulfillment, and he needs food."

"Send for a fulfilling pizza instead." Bug lost his sense of humor. "So what's the story, Rox? You wouldn't call 911 without a good reason."

"A lady named Clarice Crabtree was here a while ago, but she seems to have disappeared. That's her car. She said she had some important meeting and took off in a hurry, but when I came upstairs, here's her car, lights on, keys in the ignition, purse on the floor."

"Who's Clarice Crabtree?"

"The homeowner's daughter."

"Where's the homeowner?"

"She mentioned a nursing home."

Bug flicked his flashlight up to get a better look at the dilapidated house. The nursing-home story made sense to him. People in Pittsburgh took good care of their homes, unless they were poor or too old to climb ladders.

He swung the flashlight around and spotlighted the station wagon. "Anybody have a look inside the car yet?"

"I might have taken a peek while your buddies first searched the house." I decided it wasn't worth mentioning that I'd taken a quick look through Clarice's handbag and found the usual junk women seem to collect. Lipstick, a scrip for Prozac, wallet with credit cards, eighty-two bucks in cash. The only interesting tidbit was that she had two valid driver's licenses— each with a different home address. Maybe she had recently moved. Bug would find those on his own.

Bug flashed the light into my face again. "Why are you so worried about this lady? Your level of concern seems out of character."

Explaining that I knew somebody had plans for Clarice didn't seem like a good idea. So I said, "I owe her two hundred bucks."

"That's it?"

"And . . . Clarice went to high school with us. Don't you remember? I think she graduated the same year you did."

He dropped the light. "I think I'd have remembered somebody named Clarice. But I don't."

Bug had been in love with Marie back in high school. Even then, he hadn't looked at other women.

A shout from behind some bushes drew everyone's attention, and Bug pointed his light in the direction of the commotion. A moment later, one of the uniformed cops pulled a man out from behind a hedge.

He was a rangy old guy in pajamas and a blue corduroy bathrobe. I pegged him at once. Professor Crabtree. Had to be.

Maybe he'd had a dignified bearing in the past, but tonight he shuffled out of the bushes looking like a scarecrow in a pair of too-large rubber boots. A couple of days' worth of grizzled beard bristled on his chin. Mud spattered the hem of his bathrobe.

"Hey!" Nooch called to him. "Be careful. You should have some better shoes."

Bug kept his flashlight trained on the man's confused face. "What's your name, sir?"

"Professor Crabtree," I guessed, already on my way down the porch steps. "The aforementioned homeowner."

It took two uniformed cops to drag the old man out onto the grass, and he resisted every step.

"I'm not going back," he was saying. "Let me go! Get away from me."

"Take it easy," I snapped at the cops. "He's just a harmless old guy."

Behind me, Bug said, "Don't agitate him, fellas."

The professor stopped short and glowered at me. Peevishly, he said, "I want to go home."

"Right," I said. "This is your home. You're Professor Crabtree, aren't you?"

At the mention of his title, he pulled himself together. "Yes, indeed. I belong here. I have to check on Rhonda."

"Who's Rhonda?" Bug asked. "Your daughter?"

"No," he said. Then hesitated.

Bug could see he was confused. "How'd you get here, sir? Take a cab? A bus?"

"This is my home. I belong here," the old man repeated. "Ask anyone. I'd like to go inside now. I have things to check on."

"Your daughter was here a few minutes ago. Rhonda, right?"

"Clarice," I said.

The old man looked pathetic to me. Not a famous scientist or whatever. Just a confused old guy who needed help.

Bug touched Crabtree's arm. "Did you see your daughter, sir?"

Crabtree's eyes lost their focus, and he started to get upset again. He rubbed his arms with his hands, half hugging himself. "I don't know who you're talking about. You're trying to trick me. I'd like my dinner, please."

"Me, too," said Nooch.

The old man stopped rubbing his arms and peered at Nooch. "Do I know you?"

"I don't know," Nooch replied. "Do you?"

"I'd like a sandwich. A bologna sandwich."

"Yeah, that sounds good. With pickles?"

The old man mustered some dignity. "I'm not fond of pickles."

Once started on the subject of food, Nooch was hard to suppress. As the two of them talked about sandwiches, Bug grabbed my elbow and pulled me over to stand under the big tree in the middle of the Crabtree yard.

Bug let me go and shoved his hands into his pockets to stay warm. "What do you think? The old man busted out of the nursing home? And found his way back here?"

"He's supposed to be in an Alzheimer's unit somewhere. Don't they lock patients in those places?"

"He must have given them the slip."

"He used to be a smart guy. But now . . ."

"Yeah. Who's Rhonda?"

"No clue."

Bug was frowning at the Volvo. "Think this has anything to do with your missing station wagon owner?"

"Oh, hell," I said. "I hope not."

My cell phone rang in my pocket. It was probably Sage calling me to ask for help with her trig homework or something. I made a move to answer the phone, then paused, raising my brows at Bug.

Then his cell phone rang too, and he checked the screen. "The Homicide guys," he said with a sigh. "I gotta take this."

As he walked away to talk to his colleagues, I answered my phone.

Instead of Sage, I heard the voice of Stony Zuzak, the bass player of Rusted Roses. I sometimes sang backup for Stony and his rotating band of musician friends. His voice was unmistakable on the phone. He had ruined it screaming into microphones and smoking two packs a day since he was twelve. Now he sounded like a poor man's Meat Loaf.

"Rox?" Stony rasped. "You busy Friday night? We might have a gig to play."

I watched Bug limp away, his ear to his cell phone. I could have told him more about the Crabtrees, I suppose. Part of me wondered why I kept secrets, but at the moment it felt like self-preservation.

"Rox?" Stony said in my ear. "You there?"

Rusted Roses was never going to make it big, but Stony always hoped. He worked hard at getting the band into the South Side clubs where college kids paid to drink and dance. I joined the band when I felt like it. Stony's gigs often meant being paid in beer, which wasn't all bad.

I liked Stony, but then, I'd always had a soft spot for lost causes.

I said, "Yeah, I might be free. What's up?"

Stony said, "An old friend of mine is playing a concert here and invited me to play with him. He could use backup. If I send you some tapes, will you listen? We could rehearse Friday, before the gig. Kate's coming, and so is Deondra. We could use you, too."

My mind wasn't totally engaged by Stony's details. I was watching Bug question Professor Crabtree again. I said, "Yeah, sure, send me a tape."

"Wear something sexy," he advised.

His standard order, which I ignored. I sounded the same wearing jeans as I did in a miniskirt, but I felt less stupid.

I hung up. Watching Professor Crabtree's worried face, I doubted he was the one who had contracted to get his daughter kidnapped. But somebody had. And I wondered if the deed had been done.

✳ 8 ✳

Duffy got called back to his homicide scene, so I took Nooch home. After dropping him off and when I was alone in the truck again, I called Marvin Weiss to find out what he knew about the Crabtree job. When I turned down the kidnapping, who had he offered it to?

But it was after midnight, and he didn't answer his phone. I left a message.

I parked the truck in front of my house and took a minute to check the house next door where Jane Doe and her kids had moved in. I noticed a light in the kitchen, but I peeped in the windows and saw nobody. I guessed Jane had left the light on for comfort. Upstairs, they were all probably asleep. I checked the back door and found it locked, so I went home. I ate two apples, drank a Yuengling, and hit the sack.

The next morning, my cell phone woke me at six. I expected to hear Marvin on the line. Or Adasha. Or maybe Gino Martinelli, making more empty threats.

Instead it was Patrick Flynn, of all people. I grabbed the headboard to keep from falling out of bed. In the year or so since he'd come back to Pittsburgh, I could count on one hand how many times he'd actually dialed my number.

He said, "Rox, I need to talk to you."

I sat up in the bed, rubbing my face to wake up fast. Maybe it was his tone, but I felt immediately guilty. Like I had done something and the school principal wanted me in his office. "This minute?"

Flynn didn't sound like a school principal. His voice had a low, sexy timbre that still had the annoying ability to curl my toes. He said, "This morning, if possible. Come by the restaurant?"

I made a point of uncurling my toes. "You making breakfast?"

He laughed. "Still a mooch. Yeah, sure, why not? C'mon over."

Hanging up, I leaned back against the headboard and looked at the ceiling. Last night had been hard. First Clarice had found a way to get under my skin. Then her old man had showed up looking helpless. All the tension had put me in the mood to grab a nameless guy and get my rocks off. But I'd listened to the little voice in my head instead—the one that sounded a lot like Adasha. I had come home and climbed into bed alone. Did I feel better this morning?

To be honest? No.

I rolled out of the bed, took a fast shower, and pulled on a clean pair of jeans and a couple of sweatshirts. My hair was a lost cause.

Fifteen minutes later, I went outside and discovered somebody had soaped the windows of the Monster Truck.

"You're getting real annoying, Gino," I muttered.

I used an ice scraper to rub most of the soap off the windows, then ran the wipers and a lot of washer fluid onto the glass. It made a streaky mess, but I figured I'd run the truck through a car wash later. Too bad the car wash couldn't remove the paint on my tailgate.

I started the truck just as the sunlight peeked through the trees, and I flipped on the radio. Punching through the buttons, I searched for some local news that might include a report on Clarice Crabtree's disappearance.

No luck. The local news was about the teenager who'd been shot in Homewood. The drivetime DJs were yakking about an upcoming concert.

Driving across the river, I tried dialing Marvin's cell phone again, thinking I'd catch him as he got out of bed. Still no answer. I left another message.

Ahead of me, Pittsburgh was in one of its pretty silvery phases—looking a little like Camelot with the tops of the handsome buildings poking through the fog. The fog hung low enough to hide the city's less attractive issues. I'd lost track of what construction jobs were under way downtown.

I drove under the convention center and popped up on Smallman Street, heading upriver along with the usual morning throng of tractor-trailers making warehouse deliveries. I wasn't sure what bee Flynn had buzzing up his butt this morning, so I decided to swing by the salvage yard and pick up Rooney in case I needed backup. Plus, after a night of patrolling my place of business, the dog would be hungry. Flynn might feed him.

Rooney jumped into the truck, dragging the gigantic bone he'd taken out of Clarice Crabtree's basement. He made happy-to-see-me noises and tried to slurp my face.

"Hey, big guy." I avoided his tongue and roughed up his head. "You eat any trespassers last night?"

I tried to shove the bone out of the way before it broke my windshield. Usually, Rooney could crush up a bone in a few hours, but this one must have been particularly resilient. In daylight, it seemed bigger than ever.

Rizza's restaurant was a macho meat place that served steaks and pork belly and pig's ears mostly to executives who thought they were Rust Belt tough guys. To keep that illusion alive, the place was located on the lower side of the Strip District—Pittsburgh's still-thriving warehouse neighborhood. The restaurant's owner had made his fortune in software and now liked to hang out at his own bar drinking scotch and making customers feel special. He had chosen the location because it sat near downtown, straddling the line between upscale and low rent. In the evenings, there was valet parking, and women came in wearing sparkly jewelry. In the early morning, though, you might find a homeless person sleeping on the restaurant's pretty patio.

I parked in the alley behind the restaurant and let myself in through the back door to the kitchen. Rooney trotted after me with his bone in his teeth.

The restaurant kitchen looked bigger when it wasn't jammed with cooks and waiters and busboys servicing the dinner crowd. This morning, the stainless-steel surfaces gleamed under dazzling overhead lights. All the dishes were stacked and ready, the pots and pans lined up in perfect order for the evening shift. Some cases of fresh produce sat on the counter near the door—evidence that someone had done his grocery shopping before dawn.

Patrick Flynn, the restaurant's exec chef, stood before a gigantic stove. Wearing snug jeans and a black T-shirt that clung to his shoulders like powdered sugar on a doughnut, he'd wrapped a kitchen towel around his slim hips and wore a motorcyclist's skullcap on his shaved head. He'd been a hellraiser back in our high school days, but a couple of tours in Afghanistan had given him some hard edges and wiped the merry gleam out of his blue eyes.

Part of me wanted to see that gleam again, but our history was messy enough already.

He shot one glance at Rooney and said, "Leave that animal outside. The Department of Health will give me hell."

"If I put him outside, he'll attack somebody. Besides, even the health department isn't awake at this ungodly hour."

"Where'd he get a bone that big? The zoo?"

"Good morning to you, too, sunshine," I said. "Where's my breakfast?"

Usually? I had a lot of self-control where Flynn was concerned. But I grabbed the front of his shirt, pulled him close enough to snuggle my breasts against his chest, and kissed him on the mouth.

He made a noise in his throat—half surprise, half protest, and a dash of *gimme more*.

He dropped his spatula, and it clattered on the floor.

Just as he started to slip his hands into my hair, my hands hit the hand-gun tucked into the small of his back. I broke the kiss, stepped back, and gave him a push.

He rocked back on his heels. "What the hell was that for?"

"You looked grouchy. Feel better now?" Already, I was regretting my impulse, but I decided to bluff it out and grinned. "I want a good break-fast now. Food, that is, not sex."

He put the back of his hand to his mouth and blew out a soft, smiling curse. "You're always trouble."

"You must be expecting more trouble than me if you're packing that weapon at this hour. And I'm not talking about a hard-on."

"The gun? Aw, sometimes characters come in here early, looking to score enough money for their daily drugs."

"Why don't you just lock the door?"

"I was unloading the truck. No big deal."

Except to me. I hated guns. To an ex-marine like Flynn, though, carry-ing a weapon was like wearing a wristwatch—nothing out of the ordinary.

My feelings toward Flynn were definitely mixed. Our history was long and complicated—with good chapters and bad ones, too. Sure, he was still the sexiest thing on two legs. But the fact that he was insinuating himself into Sage's life, experimenting at being her father, was a slow process I had decided to watch from afar. If their relationship went sour, I planned on being on Sage's side.

Besides, there was the small complication of Flynn living with Marla Krantz now, a part-time hostess for the restaurant and probably one of the most beautiful women in the city.

He was still touching his mouth—maybe savoring my kiss just a little. His eyes were flickering with amusement. "I heard a rumor about you."

"What kind of rumor?"

"That you quit seducing every man who tickles your fancy. It must be true if you're kissing me all of a sudden."

"Very funny."

"What's funny is you giving up sex, hot stuff."

"Where'd you hear that?"

"Around. How's the abstinence going?"

"Terrible. I'm ready to strip you naked right here."

He laughed easily—an old friend who knew me well. "How about breakfast instead?"

"I hope you made a hell of a lot of food." I kept my voice light. I boosted myself up onto the counter and sat back, bracing my hands behind me like I was sunning myself on a beach. "I need to satisfy my cravings. Eggs and bacon? Waffles? What's on the menu?"

He shook his head, amused, and turned back to the stove. Grabbing a pepper grinder, he ground fresh pepper into the sauté pan where a perfect omelet was just crisping up at the edges. "Ready in a minute. Just don't let Rooney get into my soup bones, okay? And keep your boots out of my clean napkins."

I crossed one leg over the other. "I wonder if Rachael Ray gives orders like that?"

"I'm ten times the cook Rachael Ray is."

"Prove it, big guy."

Flynn grabbed a plate in one hand, the handle of the sauté pan in the other. He flipped the omelet effortlessly, then reached for parsley. I liked watching him work his magic. A minute later, he skimmed my breakfast onto the counter in front of me. He walked away and came back with a fork and a napkin.

I leaned over the plate and inhaled the heavenly fragrance. The omelet had hunks of asparagus and red peppers, a hint of cheese, and bits of prosciutto, too.

While Flynn was busy pouring coffee into two white mugs, I tossed a corner of the omelet to Rooney. He dropped his bone and gulped it whole.

When Flynn came back, sipping coffee, I said, "What are you doing in here so early? Don't you have minions who can do your shopping?"

He slid the other mug to me. "I like doing it myself. Especially this week."

I took my first bite. The eggs were creamy and rich—just enough salt, just enough pepper. Flynn did a lot of things very well. But cooking was his art. Around a second mouthful, I said, "Something special going on this week?"

He pulled the second stool closer and leaned on it—tall and easy with his own body. "You could say that. We've got a big foodie coming in for dinner tonight. He came last night, too, in fact, but this time he wants the chef's table. That's eighteen courses, plus wine pairings. If it goes well, he could put us on the map."

"Not the local restaurant critic, huh?"

"Nope." He grinned a little. "You'll never guess who he is."

"Okay, tell me. Who's your important guest?"

"Dooce."

"Dooce? Wait—you mean, Dooce, the rock star?"

"The very one." Flynn borrowed my fork to sample the omelet.

"He's in town for a concert?" I remembered Zack Cleary saying something about working a concert. I hadn't realized Dooce was the headliner.

"Yep."

Suddenly Stony's phone call took on a whole new meaning.

Flynn said, "Dooce came to town early for the concert because he's got relatives here. And he collects stuff. Those big stars are always looking for stuff on tour—antiques and crap. But while he's on tour, he's taking a whole entourage around with him. Including a food writer."

"And they're eating here? Wow, pretty cool."

Flynn took a look at me and saw that I was being sincere for once. "It takes a lot to impress you, Roxy. I guess you must be a big fan."

Okay, yeah, I liked Dooce's music. Classic rock with a workingman's sensibility. He wrote songs about steelworkers and waitresses, and they were good songs, too. I could see why Stony hadn't mentioned Dooce's name, though. Dooce was too pop for Stony's taste. Not hairy enough.

"What's he like?" I asked.

"I have no idea. I cooked, he ate. We didn't meet. He has an assistant, Jeremy, who does his bidding. Jeremy jumps through hoops if Dooce tells him to. Tonight, though, I'll have to do the whole routine for the man himself."

Flynn had learned to cook in a French restaurant after his military service. Then he'd bumped around the world, refining his skills and his palate. Also doing incredible amounts of smack, which he claimed he'd kicked. I liked the animation in his face when he talked about cooking. And he seemed to devote every muscle when he worked at the stove, which was nice to watch. Most of all, though, I was glad he'd found a passion that didn't require needles.

"Eighteen courses? What will you make?"

"A little of everything. We're known for meat—pork belly and steaks. But I've got some sushi-grade calamari to play with. Jeremy says his boss is very big on sushi. Plus lamb—I've experimented with a way of braising a leg of lamb that's pretty incredible. It'll all be good."

"Dooce likes that fancy stuff?"

"You think otherwise?"

"Hey, his songs are not exactly the work of a gourmet, you know?"

Flynn leaned against the counter and smiled down at me. "You really go for Dooce, huh?"

"He's a little old for me," I said lightly.

"Oh, yeah? You have limits?"

"What, you're jealous?"

"I've been over you for a long time now."

I grinned with him. "You'll never be over me, mister. What does Marla say about Dooce? She excited for you?"

Flynn got busy cleaning his knife with a towel. "I haven't told her about tonight."

"Huh? Why not?"

He shrugged. "I dunno. It didn't come up. I don't know why I'm telling you. I guess I knew you'd get it."

"I get a lot of things."

"Yeah, maybe." He looked at me again, then shook his head, blue eyes alight in a way that made something in my chest feel funny. But then he mastered his face and said, "Look, the real reason I called you this morning is Sage."

Seventeen years ago, when Flynn and I were a couple of wild teenagers and doing it like bunnies when we weren't raising hell in the neighborhood, we conceived our daughter, Sage. But as soon as the bun started growing in my oven, Flynn got himself arrested and took off for the marines to avoid a jail sentence. When I knocked on his door the day he enlisted, his mother answered. He was already gone, she said. Even now, I wonder if he was running away from jail or from the responsibility of having a family at seventeen. Or maybe he ran away from me.

I still wasn't sure how I felt about Sage's father butting into our lives after all these years. Was he going to stick around this time? Or hightail it out of town when it suited him?

I never wanted to feel the same way I had the day he took off the first time. And I didn't want my daughter feeling it either.

So I kept my voice neutral when I said, "What about Sage?"

Flynn drank more coffee. "She's supposed to be doing her college applications, right?"

"Yeah, most of 'em are due in December."

"Just a couple of weeks away."

"What's your point?"

"I had lunch with her on Saturday. She mentioned a boyfriend."

"You mean Zack?"

"Not Zack. Some other kid. New. Ryan or something."

"Brian. What about him?"

"While we were at lunch, he called her, like, a dozen times. Wanted to know where she was, who she was with, when she would be finished. The guy's either a total wiener or he's . . ."

I had always been able to read Flynn. I said, "You think he's abusive?"

"Controlling," he said.

"Sage would never fall for a guy like that."

Flynn toyed with his coffee mug and let me think a little longer.

I said, "You think she's falling for it?"

"I think she found his attention flattering. He's some rich kid with a big car and money to blow. He's taking her to the Dooce concert, you know. And some big ski weekend after that."

"A ski weekend?" That was the first I'd heard of making the Friday-night date into a weekend event.

"His family has a chalet at Seven Springs."

"She's not going away for the weekend with anybody, let alone a kid I've never met."

"Yeah, well, the ski weekend is the least of our problems. Here's the big deal: Brian thinks college is a waste of time."

I put down my fork. "He's trying to convince her not to go to college? That's ridiculous."

"Turns out, his father is some kind of self-made millionaire who barely passed eighth grade. Have you talked to her about school?"

"All the time. Look, Brian is new on the scene, and she's not serious about him. It was Zack sitting in the living room with her the other night. And she's got all kinds of other boyfriends. This one's nothing."

"I know I'm new at this," Flynn said stubbornly. "I know my opinion doesn't count for much, but—"

"It might if you had changed a few diapers instead of running around the world learning how to make fancy eggs."

"Shut up for a minute. I'm just saying that she's talking to me. Is she talking to you? Because shit's happening, Rox. There's a new boy whispering in her ear, and she's listening to him."

The idea that Sage might skip college and marry some ice-cream scooper was the worst-case scenario in my opinion. I'd made a few mistakes when I was her age, but I'd learned from my experiences and hoped she'd noticed. I was getting along fine now, but life was a tough hand-to-mouth struggle sometimes. I hated the thought of Sage doing the same stupid things I had—thinking with her hormones when there were far better options.

But I didn't like Flynn sticking his nose in our business either. Hinting that I wasn't doing a good job made me fume. And maybe I hadn't forgiven him for opting out at seventeen, either.

I said, "I think you should buzz off. I know a lot more about teenage girls and their various problems than you could fit into your frying pan. So let me handle my daughter."

Flynn shrugged. "Be my guest. Handle her. I just don't want you ignoring the situation."

"Is that all?" I tossed down my fork. "Because I'm finished with breakfast."

"And finished listening." Flynn refused to get mad. "Okay, have it your way. Going to Shelby Martinelli's wedding on Saturday?"

"No," I said.

"Good thing." Flynn reached for my empty plate. "Because I hear Gino's planning on having you thrown out if you show up."

"He wouldn't dare. Not if Uncle Carmine makes an appearance. Gino's happy to piss me off, but he knows better than to cross Carmine."

"So you're going to the wedding?"

"I haven't decided yet."

"Well, I'm supposed to tell you to wear a short skirt. Everybody wants a good show."

Normally, I didn't lose my temper so fast. But a lot had been happening, and he was pushing my buttons. I grabbed his shirt again and tried to pull him close.

Flynn blocked me, though, and turned his head to avoid another kiss. He said, "Stop it."

"Really? You don't want me?"

"Hell, yes." He looked me in the eyes again. His were burning. "I'd like to unzip you right here and see if we still have the old steam. But maybe you ought to think about why you're so anxious to fuck me now."

I released him as if my hands were seared. "I must be more desperate than I thought."

I whistled for Rooney, and he reappeared with his bone. We left. That's me. Miss Congeniality.

❧ 9 ❧

I knew I'd let Flynn get a rise out of me for no good reason. We had both moved on with our lives, even though something elemental kept pulling us together again—like gravity. Being around him always got my blood pressure zinging.

With the radio blasting another old Dooce tune, I drove up into Lawrenceville to pick up Nooch for the day. But he wasn't on his usual corner, so I checked my watch and realized I was an hour early.

On an impulse, I cut down through the neighborhood and ended up in the parking lot of the Carnegie library branch. I'll admit I was uneasy about what might have happened to Clarice Crabtree. It wouldn't hurt to do a little reading about her.

Sister Bob's Dodge Neon sat in the spot designated for Our Angel Volunteers alongside the dilapidated vehicles the librarians drove. I backed into a parking space so the word painted on the tailgate wouldn't offend any library patron who might peek out through an upstairs window. I left Rooney in the truck with a window cracked. He was happy to be left alone with his bone.

I cut around the back of the building to the employee entrance.

Inside the dark stairwell, a plump gray-haired figure screamed when she saw me come through the door. A coffee cup flew out of her hand and smashed on the steps.

I barely dodged flying shards of the cup. "Sister Bob, it's just me—Roxy."

Sister Bob clutched her bosom and sat down heavily on the top step. "Roxana Marie, you gave me a terrible scare!"

I leaped up the steps and sat down beside her. "You okay? I'm so sorry. Need a drink of water?"

She laughed shortly and showed me her trembling hand. "What I need is a shot of whiskey, but that would blow my image once and for all, wouldn't it?"

"Got a bottle hiding in a desk drawer somewhere close?" I grinned encouragingly and nudged her with my elbow. "I'll go get it for you."

Sister Bob shook her head, good humor returning. "I was only joking, dear. What would they think of me at St. Dom's, if anyone heard I was drinking at my volunteer job?"

"Yeah, you should be at the front desk adding up my late fines instead."

She smiled ruefully. "The library's not open yet. I went downstairs to get a cup of coffee for Mary Lou. And I wanted to make sure the door was locked now that all the employees are here for the day. They've been having— well, not break-ins, but a young man has come in a couple of times before we open. He steals the petty cash. It's not much, I know, but he's frightening. He gave Cora Blawski such a terrible scare that she may never come back. She's our periodicals expert. We can't afford to lose her."

"Does he have a gun?"

"He said so, but kept his hand in his pocket the first two times. Last week he pulled his hand out and had a tube of Banana Boat sun-screen."

"He held you up with suntan lotion?"

"Well, how were we to know?" She clenched her fists. "Oh, I wish I

89

had my old BB gun! I'd like to give him a good scare. I used to be a pretty good shot, you know."

I didn't like hearing about a robber menacing the librarians, even one brandishing a ridiculous weapon. What a lowlife. But I tried to sound soothing. "The guy's probably just a junkie desperate for money to buy his next hit. Did you call the police?"

"Of course. And they parked in our lot a few mornings to make sure he didn't come back. But they can't wait around every day. So when you opened the door and—"

"Sorry. I didn't mean to scare you. Your thief is probably watching for the police car."

"I know," she said sadly. "He'll be back for more money when he thinks the coast is clear."

"And he'll keep coming back until he's caught."

"Yes, I'm sure you're right."

"I have an idea. I got my hands on some old bank dye packs—you know, those tubes of exploding dye? They're the old-fashioned kind, very fragile, not the ones that need a special detonator at the door. All you do is slip one into your guy's hand or the bag of cash, and it blows up. If the police can't catch him in the act, at least they'll see him in the neighborhood and pick him up."

Sister Bob looked anxious. "Would the exploding things hurt anybody?"

"Hell—I mean, heck no. They just make a mess. You want me to bring you some?"

"It might work," Bob said slowly. Then she managed a smile. "It's a comfort to have you here, Roxana. You're so capable. What are you doing here this morning? Are you returning a few of the books you've been hoarding?"

"Uh, not exactly. I came to look up some old newspaper clippings."

"We don't have the clippings, of course, but you can look up newspaper archives on the computer."

I figured Sister Bob might need a distraction. "You mind showing me?"

"Let me clear away this mess first."

It seemed only right to help her clean up her broken coffee cup and wipe up the spill on the steps. I went out to the truck and carefully brought in a couple of the dye packs we'd gotten out of the bank. We locked the employee door together. Then she showed me into the library's computer room and booted up a machine. Within a few minutes, I was reading about the murder of Clarice Crabtree's mother.

"There's not much information, is there?" Sister Bob sat beside me and tried scrolling down the screen for more to the story. "Just that the poor lady was shot outside a bank. The killer was never caught."

"It was probably some random thing," I said, staring at the computer screen and wishing there was more information. "Like your petty-cash thief."

Bob tapped the screen with her forefinger. "This woman's daughter is a friend of yours, Roxana?"

"I knew her in high school, that's all. We were talking about our dead mothers last night. When she said her mother had been murdered, I thought I'd try to find out more."

"You have a strange sort of bond with her, then. I suppose you both miss your mothers."

I said, "Mine wasn't much to miss."

Sister Bob nodded in sympathy. "And, of course, you had Loretta."

"Not exactly the same thing, though."

"But she loves you unconditionally. And took good care of you."

"Yeah, I know." I grinned and said, "Thanks for your help, Sister Bob. You going to be okay if I leave now?"

"You're welcome, Roxana. And of course we'll be fine. But come back anytime." Her eyes twinkled. "Especially if you bring some of those books you borrowed."

I let myself out the back door and got into the Monster Truck.

"Aw, yuck! Rooney!"

He had managed to smear the passenger seat with gunk from his bone. Happily, he panted at me.

I used an old crumpled shirt of Nooch's to wipe up the worst of the mess. But it was a lost cause. I'd have to get the truck steam-cleaned, and soon.

As I pulled out of the parking lot, I glanced around for anybody who looked like the kind of slimeball who'd steal cash from a library. But I didn't see anyone.

Nooch was waiting on the corner by his house.

When he opened the passenger door, he said, "What happened to the windows?"

"I think Gino Martinelli soaped them while the truck was parked out in front of my house last night."

"Wow, he really needs to do some positive visualizing. I bet if he could think about something nice he'd forget about making such a mess."

"Gino's idea of something nice is jailbait."

"Ew." Nooch climbed into the truck. "What's this all over the seat?"

"Rooney's bone. He must have chewed it open."

Nooch sat in the mess and forgot about it.

That morning, we had some business to take care of in a tony neighborhood with the ridiculous name of Squirrel Hill. I had a few linear yards of quality porch railing that a very nice rabbi and his wife might like for the home they were renovating on a shady side street. All we had to do was show them the stuff and close the deal.

When we got to the salvage yard to pick up the samples, though, we discovered somebody had spray-painted my gate while I was eating breakfast at Flynn's.

BITCH EAT SHIT

"That's rude." Nooch stared at the gate.

"Gino Martinelli sure gets around," I growled. "When I find the time, I'm gonna run over him with this truck until his guts squirt out. If you'll pardon the negative visual."

"You seem a little mad, Rox," Nooch said.

"Not as mad as I'm gonna make him."

Nooch loaded porch rails into the truck while I went into the office. Stuck through the mail slot was a CD from Stony. Probably the songs he wanted me to practice before the Friday-night gig.

I checked my office voice mail. Nothing from Marvin. Insults from Gino. I slammed down the phone, and Nooch and I headed for Squirrel Hill.

I popped Stony's CD into the truck's player and hummed along with the first song—one of Dooce's standard anthems to the working class, which immediately got Nooch tapping his foot. For me, the harmony was easy—but my mind wandered away from the music.

Rooney sat between us on the front seat, clenching his bone and looking out the windshield for other dogs being walked on the sidewalks. When he saw one, he lunged onto Nooch's lap and growled possessively around his bone. The thing had begun to smell, though, and it was oozing plenty of goo, too.

The morning had turned cool and gray, with a little drizzle spattering the windshield and making a mess of the residual soap. Not good weather for unloading anything, so I found myself turning down the street where Professor Crabtree lived. I had a bad feeling about the way Clarice had dropped out of sight. The fact that Marvin hadn't returned my calls just added to my anxiety.

To Nooch, I said, "Hey, how about thinking back to last night for a minute, will you? While you were sitting in the truck, before the police came, did you see anything at all before you went to sleep?"

"I didn't sleep. I was—"

"Visualizing, yeah. What about this time?"

Nooch looked embarrassed. "I was making myself a magnet for good bowling scores."

"Okay, okay, before you closed your eyes to go bowling, what happened? Was anybody hanging around? Looking suspicious?"

"No. Except for the limo."

"What limo?"

"A black limo came down the street and sat in front of the house for a couple of minutes."

"Who uses a limo on that street?" I asked. "Unless it's prom night?"

"Nobody uses black limos for proms. Only white."

I forced myself not to scream. "Okay, okay, so who was in the limo?"

"I couldn't see inside. And it didn't stick around. Just sat in front of the house, then moved on."

"You're sure about that?"

"Sure, I'm sure. How come you want to know all this stuff?"

Giving Nooch too much information meant that eventually some of it would come leaking out of him—probably at the wrong time. But I said, "The lady I saw in the house? Clarice Crabtree? I think somebody grabbed her."

"What do you mean?"

"I mean somebody kidnapped her."

The idea seemed impossible to Nooch. "Why would somebody do that?"

I wasn't going to tell Nooch about Marvin's effort to hire me for the kidnapping. Nooch would misinterpret. "I don't know, I just— Look, think about it again. Did you see anybody besides the black limo or not?"

"Not," said Nooch.

I pulled down the street where we'd parked the previous night. In daylight, the Crabtree house looked even more drab than its neighbors.

Except for the emergency van and the police cars parked in front of it. Blue and red lights flashed, and various police personnel bustled around. Clarice's station wagon was gone. Maybe towed by the cops.

"Hey!" Nooch sat forward in his seat at the sight of the emerging vehicle. "What's going on?"

Rooney jumped forward and planted his paws on the dashboard to get a better look, too. He growled in case one of the cops decided to steal his bone.

"It's the bomb squad." I stamped on the brake on the truck to avoid hitting the pudgy uniformed cop who was stopping all traffic on the street. I rolled down the window and leaned out. "What's happening?"

The pudgy cop strolled over. "Hey, Roxy."

It was Gary Sedlak, a guy I knew from high school. Back in those days, he'd been a big man on the football team and me a lowly freshman when he showed me his eagle tattoo in his mother's basement laundry room. After graduation, he'd fulfilled his dream and gone into the army. He'd had the cocky stuff kicked out of him in the desert, then come home and become a city cop. Now that he was married to Janine, who ran the shop that sold religious trinkets in a storefront around the corner from St. Dom's, he pretended we'd never given each other hickeys on his mom's Maytag.

Gary leaned his forearm on the truck's window and looked past me. "Hello, there, Nooch. What happened to your shirt?"

Nooch said, "A dye thing exploded in a bank."

Gary looked at me, and I said, "It's not what you think."

He shook his head like he'd seen it all and couldn't be surprised anymore. "I wasn't thinking anything." Looking at Rooney, Gary said, "Wow, that's some bone."

"Don't try to take it away from him," I said, holding Rooney back. "What's going on?"

"A neighbor called in a suspicious package. After last night's excitement at this house, nobody wants to take any chances. So the cowboys are here. They're mad because they're supposed to be hanging out at the concert venue, looking for bombs but hoping for an autograph from Dooce. So they're going to work off their frustrations by blowing up whatever this is."

Together, the four of us watched a couple of guys in SWAT-style uniforms help one of their buddies into a big padded bomb suit. When he was all zipped up, they fitted the helmet over his head.

Nooch said, "He looks like the marshmallow man."

The marshmallow man gave a thumbs-up to his buddies and grabbed the end of a length of wire that unspooled from a wheel inside the panel van marked Bomb Squad. Then he waddled across the front yard toward the bomb.

"That's no bomb," I said. "It's a messenger bag. Like a briefcase for hippies."

"It might look like a messenger bag," Gary said. "But it could be a bomb rigged inside of a messenger bag."

"Some kid dropped his school bag on his way to the university," I said. "That's all. There's probably homework and a peanut butter and jelly sandwich inside."

Nooch said, "You mean there's a kid who might not get a lunch today?"

"A teacher will help," I said. "Teachers are always lending kids lunch money. That's why they need a union—so their paychecks can afford all the kids they have to subsidize."

By that time, the marshmallow man had reached the lunchbox. He tried to hunch down in front of it, but his suit made him too clumsy. Eventually, he kneeled down in the grass.

We couldn't see what he was doing, but Gary got all ex-GI and said, "He's planting the det line. They're gonna blow it up, whatever it is."

"Right there in the open?" I asked. "What if there's a big explosion? It could blow all the windows in the houses around here. Or else I'm going to get peanut butter and jelly all over my truck."

Gary shrugged. "If they didn't tell us to evacuate the area, they already figured out it's nothing. They're just showing off now."

So we hung out while the detonator got installed. But then the marshmallow man's suit was so bulky that he couldn't get up by himself, so his assistants had to jog into the blast zone and help him to his feet. Then they went back and hid behind the panel truck.

Gary said to me, "I hear you're singing backup for Rusted Roses."

"Now and then."

"Somebody at the station said he saw you wearing, like, a lace tank top at a club over on the South Side a couple of weeks ago. Said you looked like Joan Jett."

"Better than looking like Janis Joplin," I said.

"What's taking so long?" Nooch asked.

About that time, one of the bomb squad guys leaned on a lever, just like in the movies, and the messenger bag blew off the grass, turning end over end as it arced into the air in a spray of what looked like shreds of paper and maybe some of those little peeled carrots. A couple seconds later, my theory was confirmed when orange carrot bits splattered my windshield like confetti at a parade.

"Cool!" Nooch said.

Rooney turned around on the seat and growled again. I looked out the back window. A car had pulled up behind the Monster Truck. It was a silver Mercedes—a big one, very expensive once, but old now.

Gary signaled the driver to back up the street to turn around and leave, but the driver's-side door of the Mercedes popped open and a middle-aged Albert Einstein got out onto the street. He had a lot of curly gray hair and bags under his eyes. He left the engine running.

Hanging on to the door like he needed the support, Einstein said to Gary, "May I inquire? What's going on?"

Gary read the anxiety on the man's face and said easily, "Nothing to be concerned about, sir. If you'll just back up—"

"I'm looking for my wife."

"Your wife," Gary said.

"I'm extremely worried about her."

I bailed out of the truck. I could tell this was going to be interesting.

Einstein looked to be somewhere between forty and fifty. He wore rumpled but expensive-looking gray trousers and a preppy-looking blue blazer that was spotted with coffee dribbles. His white shirt's collar was frayed, and his red-striped bow tie was faded but perky. A museum tag like Tito's hung from a clip on his shirt pocket.

He had to be the mollusk guy. Clarice Crabtree's rich husband. The bow tie was the biggest nerd alert I'd ever seen. I figured if Clarice Crabtree ever arm-wrestled her husband, she probably made him cry.

Einstein pulled out his wallet and opened it up with shaky hands. "I'm Richard Eckelstine. My wife didn't come home last night. Her name is Clarice Crabtree. I thought she might be here. This is her father's house."

"No kidding," said Gary, looking at me instead of Eckelstine's wallet ID. Which made Eckelstine look at me, too.

I said, "I saw Clarice here last night about seven."

"Oh, that's such a relief." He put the wallet away and took out a wadded-up handkerchief to touch his forehead. "When I drove up and saw all the police vehicles, I was afraid that—well. I haven't seen my wife in two days. She doesn't answer her cell phone either."

He wore rimless eyeglasses, but behind the thick lenses, his eyes looked full of worry.

I said, "When your wife left here last night, she said she had a meeting."

Eckelstine nodded. "Probably one of her committee meetings. She's on dozens of committees. Association committees, department committees, research committees. She's in great demand on national committees, too, which is why she travels so much. But . . ."

"But she didn't come home after last night's meeting."

Eckelstine pushed his eyeglasses more firmly up on his nose. "Correct."

Gary said to me, "I'm going to call Duffy."

"Good idea."

"Who's Duffy?"

Neither one of us wanted to tell Eckelstine that Duffy was a homicide cop.

The passenger door of the old Mercedes opened with a creak, and a teenager said, "Dad?"

"It's okay, Richie."

The kid took that to mean he could get out of the car. He was about sixteen, I guessed. He had the same curly hair as his father, but a silver stud shone in his nose and another poked through his eyebrow. He wore an expensive-looking black leather jacket, and underneath it, his faded T-shirt had a skateboard company's graffitilike logo printed on it. I wasn't sure, but I thought he was wearing eye makeup.

He slouched against the hood of the Mercedes, looking bored. "Where's Mom?"

"We're trying to establish that, Richie," Eckelstine said.

Richie rolled his eyes. "Was she here, or not?"

The kid wasn't necessarily addressing his father, so I said, "She was here last night."

"I don't know why she keeps coming back." The kid sent a glare up at the house. "She already took everything she wanted."

"What did she want?" I asked.

"Richie."

The kid ignored his father. "Grandpa's research papers, probably. Who cares? It's all bullshit anyway."

"Richie—"

"Oh, who gives a flying fig? Can I go to class now? I'm late already."

If he'd been my kid, I'd have told him to start walking. But his father said, "Just a minute. Let's get some information."

Richie turned around and kicked the bumper of his old man's sixty-thousand-dollar car.

Gary ambled back. "Duffy's on his way."

"Who's Duffy?" Eckelstine asked again.

I was standing there thinking about Clarice, the woman who had married an absentminded professor, which seemed in character. What didn't make sense was that her son was sixteen. I'd been pregnant with Sage at my high school graduation, which meant Clarice must have had her baby within the same year or so. She hadn't struck me as the kind of teenager who got pregnant by accident. Rather, she had seemed like a girl who wouldn't discover sex for another decade. So . . . how did she end up with a snotty teenager who wore eye makeup?

There was obviously more to Clarice's story than I had first figured.

About that time, another vehicle pulled up—a snazzy Volvo station wagon.

Just like the one Clarice Crabtree drove, I noted, except this one was black, not silver.

A tall, athletic man got out of the station wagon. Late thirties, I guessed, and handsome as hell. He knew it, too. Fluffy brown hair, a golden tan. When he stepped out of the car, he straightened his broad shoulders as if a camera crew might catch him in action. He wore a blue warm-up suit with clean white sneakers, perfect for acting in a commercial for men's deodorant or maybe jock-itch cream. He approached us in long, brisk strides. "Excuse me, Officer."

Gary looked him up and down like he was dressed for a costume party. "Yes, sir?"

"I'm Mitch Mitchell."

"Congratulations," Gary said.

"I'm looking for my wife." Mitchell glanced around, but appeared unconcerned about the emergency vehicles and the bomb squad cleaning up their gear. "She was supposed to be here last night, checking on her father's house. Clarice Crabtree. Have you seen her?"

Gary said, "Your wife is Clarice Crabtree? Or she's your ex-wife?"

"Wife," Mitchell said crisply.

Eckelstine said, "What?"

As the two men sized each other up, I thought about Clarice's thong underwear and wondered which one she wore the sexy stuff for.

Mitchell squinted at Eckelstine. "Who are you?"

Gary said, "This is Mr. Eckelstine. He says the lady is *his* wife."

"No, no, she's *my* wife. We've been married almost ten years."

Gary looked hard at Eckelstine, who squeaked out, "We've been married for eleven years."

The two men stared at each other. Angry, at first. Then with seeds of doubt clearly sprouting in their minds.

"You're married to Clarice Crabtree?" Mitchell said finally. "Curator at the museum?"

"Yes, exactly." Eckelstine fumbled with his ID tag and held it up like Exhibit A. "We both work for the museum."

Mitchell said, "I don't get it." He glared accusingly at Gary. "What's going on here?"

Gary looked at me. "I think I better call Duffy again."

"Tell him to hurry," I said.

Gary left, and the next person to join the extended family group was a girl who climbed out of Mitch Mitchell's Volvo. Another teenager. She had a long black ponytail and wore tight black pants and a fleece jacket unzipped to reveal a tight pink T-shirt that said, When the Going Gets Tough . . . in sequins. The main thing? She was Asian. If she was the daughter of Clarice and the jock-itch commercial, she had been adopted.

"What's going on, Daddy? Where's Mommy?"

In my lifetime I've been known to whap a tire iron upside a few heads, and I don't take guff from anybody, but I have a big, gooshy soft spot for kids. I'd kick the ass of anybody who'd say so, of course.

But one glance at that girl, and I wondered if I was staring at a kid who'd soon be losing her college tuition money to a kidnapper demanding ransom.

Her dad said, "Just a minute, sweetheart. There's a mix-up about Mommy."

"What kind of mix-up?"

Eckelstine had been staring at the kid like she was a snake that might bite him. "Who's this?"

Mitch Mitchell put his hands protectively on the girl's shoulders, and with gentler pressure he spun her around. With a fatherly push, he sent her back to the station wagon. "That is my daughter. Our daughter. Clarice's daughter and my daughter. Sherelle. Her name is Sherelle. We call her Sugar."

Eckelstine suddenly lost his balance. He staggered over to the curb and sat down hard, hyperventilating. He put his head between his knees and gasped for breath.

Mitchell jutted his jaw at me, belligerence in his eyes. "What's he so upset about?"

"Because you're both married to the same woman, dipshit."

Which I guess was the wrong thing to say, because Mitchell punched me in the mouth.

❋ 10 ❋

Bug Duffy pulled up about the time the bomb squad slammed their doors and started their engines. He got out of his cruiser with a cup of coffee in one hand and went over to talk to the driver of the panel van. Whatever they talked about made Bug laugh, so I assumed the bomb squad admitted they'd just blown up somebody's lunch. They pulled away, and Bug strolled over to us.

The Eckelstines still sat on the curb. The father looked sick. The son looked annoyed. Mitch Mitchell had joined his daughter in their Volvo. Through the windshield, he glared at me. Like the situation was all my fault.

Me, I was holding a wad of fast-food napkins against my bleeding mouth and wondering if I might lose a tooth.

"Hey, Gary." Bug put out his hand to the uniformed cop. "How come you're not at the concert venue, learning how to protect the life of a rock singer?"

Gary shook his hand. "I don't need the overtime. You?"

"I don't need the aggravation." Bug took a slug of coffee and eyed me over the rim of the cup. "What's with the blood, Roxy? You getting too slow to duck a punch these days?"

I said, "You're just worried about the paperwork. Well, cool your jets, Detective. I'm not pressing charges."

He nodded once. "Okay, that makes my morning simpler. What's the story here?"

Gary gave Bug the lowdown, and during the telling, Bug glanced from the Eckelstines to the Mitchells and finally back to me. I held his gaze while Gary finished up the story.

"A woman bigamist," Bug said finally. "There's a switch."

"Must not have been getting enough attention from the first team," I said. "She needed a second string."

"And what are you doing here, exactly?" he asked. "Again?"

"You mean before I was assaulted? Just watching the bomb squad have their fun."

"Did they let you push the detonator?"

"Darnit, no. Did you find Clarice Crabtree yet?"

"I haven't been looking. We've got the Homewood homicide on the front burner at the moment. And she's not even officially a missing person."

"But . . . ?" I prompted.

Grimly, he said, "I'm thinking maybe it wouldn't hurt to get a jump start on things. I'll go talk to the husbands. Which one looks the guiltiest?"

"They both seem pretty shaken up," Gary observed.

Bug sighed. "My money's always on the husband in these disappearance cases. But this time it's a crowded field."

Gary said, "I'd go after Mitchell first. The pretty boy with the bleeding knuckles. What do you bet he has a girlfriend on the side?"

"Libido's not a motive for making your wife disappear," I said, surprising myself.

Bug raised one eyebrow. "I think I'll talk to Eckelstine first, give

Mitchell time to get nervous. Maybe you ought to go use your feminine wiles on him, Rox. Get him to confess."

"Or maybe he'll just hit me again."

Bug smiled and strolled over to talk with the Eckelstines.

Mitchell worked up the courage to get out of his car and come over to me.

"I'm sorry about hitting you." He almost managed to look contrite. "I was upset."

"No kidding," I said.

"Considering the circumstances, I hope you won't press charges."

I glanced past him at his daughter. She had pulled a cell phone from her jacket pocket and was listening to a call. And sobbing softly.

My heart twisted at the sight of tears streaking down her cheeks. "Yeah, okay," I said to Mitchell. "No harm done."

"I'm sure there's an explanation for all this." Mitchell wagged his head in disbelief. "Clarice will be able to straighten everything out as soon as we locate her. I've been trying to reach her since yesterday, but she'll call soon. Clarice always keeps in touch."

I remembered the two cell phones Clarice clipped to her belt. "She's a good communicator, huh?"

"Yes. Usually, I know where she is at any time—even making a speech in California, maybe, or working at the site in Siberia."

"Siberia?"

"Yes, she travels to important digs." Mitchell looked surprised at my ignorance. "That's where we met, working together."

I remembered my discussion with Tito. "Digging up dinosaur bones?"

"Not dinosaurs. Later mammals."

"Megafauna."

"Exactly. We worked on the site where her father discovered all those woolly mammoths. We had some great success there. It's where we married. And adopted Sugar, too."

I couldn't help glancing at their daughter one more time. "You got married and started a family all at once, huh?"

"Yeah. Clarice ran across Sugar in the village where we had a base camp. She'd been orphaned, and Clarice wanted to help. It's impossible not to fall in love with Sugar." Mitchell glanced back at his daughter and glowed with pride. "Even back then she was obviously something special."

"So you married Clarice and adopted the kid before you left Siberia?"

"Yes. And since then, she's made my life complete."

"Daddy?"

Sugar had gotten out of the car and come over. She tugged at her father's sleeve. "Daddy, I need to get to practice. My coach says we only have the rink reserved until eleven."

Mitchell checked his watch. "We'll leave as soon as we get some answers, sweetheart."

"But, Daddy—"

From the curb, Eckelstine's teenage son mocked her in a falsetto sing-song. "But, Daddy!"

"Shut up, kid," I said to him.

"Make me," he shot back.

"I could make you eat that face jewelry you've got on."

"You try, you'll eat something else, too, bitch."

"Give it a rest, jagoff," I said.

Which was enough to get his father on his feet and swinging a punch at my face. He missed and hit Mitchell instead. Sugar screamed. The Eckelestine kid burst out laughing. Mitchell made a fist and swung for Eckelstine. He missed, too.

And hit me again.

This time, I hit him back.

❈ 11 ❈

When the brawl ended, Bug loaded me into the back of his cruiser, and we headed downtown for me to be booked for disturbing the peace, which was totally bogus. I sulked in the backseat.

I also thought about Mitch Mitchell and his angelic daughter, and Eckelstine and his snotty son. How did Clarice fit into those family portraits? And why did she feel the need to have two whole families? Wasn't one set of problems enough?

Boy, there was a lot more to Clarice than I first thought.

That's when Bug took a cell phone call. Then he drove down to the bank of the Ohio, where I saw a river patrol boat bobbing offshore, and the forensic cops standing over a rolled-up carpet. Bug got me out of the car, and we went over to check out the scene.

"Hell," Bug sighed after we established that the body in the carpet was that of Clarice Crabtree. He looked up at the sky for a while and finally said, "You going to stay out of my way while I work this case?"

I didn't feel so good.

Clarice was definitely dead. Not kidnapped. Dead.

To Bug, I said, "Why would I get in your way?"

Maybe I sounded too flip. Or sarcastic. But suddenly he was angry, and I was the nearest target.

"How about this for a reason?" He got right in my face, his voice going up a notch. "I talked to my wife this morning. She has a better memory of high school than I do. She says you and Clarice not only knew each other back in the good old days, but you hated each other's guts."

I tried to rouse my temper to match his. "What does that make me? Your prime suspect now?"

"All I know for sure is you're probably lying about something."

"I did know Clarice," I snapped, "and okay, we didn't get along. But until last night, I hadn't seen her since Mrs. Strohman's sixth-period science class. So back off, Detective."

Bug's face was dark. "You notice me using a nightstick on you?"

"I was handcuffed in your car a few minutes ago!"

He threw up his hands. "How else am I supposed to calm you down? Besides, I'd have cuffed your hands behind you if I'd been serious. You're a heck of a lot easier to handle when you're tied."

"Is that supposed to be suggestive, Mr. Clean?"

"Shut up." He blew a sigh of frustration. "You're just— You could trust a person once in a while, Roxy, that's all I'm saying. I'm trying to be your friend here."

"I don't need any more friends," I shot back.

"You just don't know how to handle a man who doesn't care about getting into your pants."

"Maybe we ought to climb into the backseat and get off a quick one," I said. "It might establish who's in charge."

"Shut your dirty mouth." He flushed, and for the first time I thought he might lose his temper in a big way. "Why do you make it so hard to get along with you? I can see why Mitchell and Eckelstine popped you in the mouth."

"You want to try it yourself?" I stuck my jaw out to be socked.

"Cut it out."

I saw, finally, that Detective Duffy wasn't cool with dead bodies the way TV cops seemed to be. He was a little green, in fact. Unhappy. Maybe feeling just as sick as I was.

I turned away from the carpet and its awful contents. "Okay, sorry. It's been a bad day."

"You got that right," he muttered, turning to glare at the river.

"For those kids, especially," I said. "Who's going to tell them their mother's gone?"

"Not me, that's for sure."

"That daughter of Mitchell's—the girl—she— Did you see her? Talk to her? This could really screw with her head, you know."

The words stuck in my throat after that. I felt a tsunami of sympathy for Sugar Mitchell. She seemed like a sweet kid. She didn't deserve what was coming.

Bug's face softened. "Sorry. I should have seen this from your point of view. I know how your mom died, Rox. With you there, a witness to everything. That probably messed you up for life."

I don't know what I hated more—the sympathy people were always trying to give me, or the painful hole that seemed to widen inside when the subject of my mother's murder came up. I liked things better when I didn't feel anything.

Voice harsh, I said, "Yeah, well, buy me an ice-cream cone and I'll be fine."

Bug sighed.

We stood for a moment, staring at the river, trying to forget what was behind us. Out of the blue, I said, "You know anything about Mr. Squeegee?"

"Who?"

"It's an ice-cream chain or something."

"Mr. Squishy." Bug sounded tired. "It's frozen custard. My kids love that stuff. The Oreo swirl is pretty good." He dug into his pocket and came up with a pack of gum. He peeled off a stick and offered it to me.

I took it and unwrapped the stick. "My daughter's dating the heir apparent."

"Did she meet him scooping butter pecan for his father?"

"She's not working at any damn ice-cream parlor. She's going to get an education, dammit."

Bug popped his stick of gum into his mouth. "Trouble at home, huh?"

"It's not trouble yet. I'm going to try to visualize Sage in college. Learning to make something of herself. Do you believe in that visualization stuff?"

"Not so much."

"Me neither. Look, can't I say something about Clarice's kids without triggering a sapfest? What happened to me is long buried."

"Whatever you say, Rox." He sighed again. "Hang around, okay? You're still in my custody."

He turned away and walked over to the crime-scene team.

I hung around for a while, freezing my ass off. Getting mad, calming down, feeling sick, then pulling myself together. Wondering about Clarice. Thinking about her daughter, then out of nowhere wondering if Sage was somewhere safe. I shoved the mental images of my own mother's dead body as far down into the darkness of my soul as I could manage.

Seemed like I'd spent the whole day watching cops work at a glacial pace.

Finally, I'd had enough. I waited until Bug was on his phone, and then I walked away, stopping by the cruiser only long enough to grab my cell phone from the front seat where Bug had put it after taking it away from me. While I was there, I took Bug's police parking medallion from the dashboard, too. Might come in handy someday. You never know.

I walked up to the casino, cut cross the parking lot, and went past the weird statue of Mr. Rogers putting on his sneakers. As usual, there were some tourists taking pictures of their kids sitting in the statue's lap. The kids didn't think the statue was weird. For a few minutes, I lost myself in the crowd to be sure the cops hadn't decided to follow me.

Nobody came looking, so I kept walking.

I dialed Nooch on my cell phone. I'd left him in charge of Rooney and the truck.

When he picked up, I said, "Come pick me up in front of the baseball stadium, by Willie Stargell."

"What are you doing there?" he asked. "It's not baseball season."

"Just come get me."

I tried Marvin's phone again. I wanted to know everything about the kidnapping job he'd offered to me. Because obviously somebody else took the job, and it had gone very, very wrong. But he didn't answer.

I reached the baseball stadium within a few minutes and hung around the statues of long-gone players, waiting for Nooch and thinking about Clarice and how she must have died. My teeth chattered in the cold, and I kept my arms folded across my chest.

I considered all the guys who did favors for Uncle Carmine over the years. But my memories were dim. Most of the colorful old hit men were gone now—half out of commission in nursing homes, the other half buried in Catholic cemeteries all over the city.

The Monster Truck pulled up, and I almost screamed.

Somebody had pelted the windshield with eggs. And smashed in one of my headlights. Nooch had turned on the wipers, and the yellow egg mess was now streaked all over the glass and leaking down across the hood. Even Rooney hunkered down in the seat to avoid my wrath.

I grabbed the passenger door and yanked it open. Nooch sat behind the wheel, holding a Pepsi can against his swollen face. Seeing him hurt made my heart jerk.

"What happened?" I demanded.

"It was Gino Martinelli," he said. "I'm sorry, Rox, I really am. I wasn't going to hit him, but—"

"You hit him?" I tried not to panic. "What happened to positive energy and all that jazz?"

"I dunno," he moaned. "I went a little nuts."

"It's understandable." I pulled myself together and climbed into the truck, pushing Rooney out of my way. "Next time we see him, you can beat him into hamburger."

"No kidding? Usually, you—"

"Just kidding," I said. I gave up trying to be calm for Nooch's sake. All of a sudden, I was really tired. Exhausted, almost. "Don't go hitting Gino, or you'll get arrested for busting your parole. What happened?"

Nooch took a deep breath. "I was getting myself a hoagie in Bruno's. Ham and capicola with provolone. My favorite. I was gonna share with you, Rox, honest. But when I came out of Bruno's, there was Gino kicking in your headlight."

"He kicked it in?" My voice cracked.

"Well, he tried," Nooch said. "I picked him up—you know, to stop him from doing any damage, and he started swinging at me. He hit me in the face with his elbow, see?" He stuck out his cheek for me to see the blotchy welt there.

I clenched my teeth. "Yeah, I see."

"Anyway, I kinda tossed him onto the sidewalk. Then I lost my balance."

"You fell?"

He blushed. "It was me who broke the headlight, Rox." He pushed up his knit cap to show me the bruise swelling on his forehead. "I'm really sorry."

What bugged me more than anything was seeing Nooch with all his positive energy drained like somebody had pulled a plug. That son of a bitch Gino had picked on Nooch because he was too chicken to come at me instead.

I rubbed my face, trying to hold on to my temper. "That Gino is a scamp, isn't he?"

"What are you going to do, Rox?"

"I'll figure out something. When I get a minute to think straight. A lot has happened. I need to cogitate a little. How about driving me over to the Wainwright Hotel?"

"On Sixth?"

I turned up the heater, buckled my seatbelt, and flopped back against the headrest. Gino was like a boil on my butt, but the real problem was Clarice. Now that she was dead, things had really changed. While Nooch drove, I said, "Tell me more about the limo you saw the night Clarice disappeared."

"What limo?"

"You said you saw a black limousine outside the Crabtree house while you waited in the truck. You said it sat there, but went away after a couple of minutes. Did you get the license plate?"

"No."

What was I thinking? Of course Nooch hadn't memorized the plate number. "Was it a Premier Limo? Premier has the little star decal on the back bumper. Visualize. Do you remember any little star?"

Nooch squinched up his face. "I don't think so."

"Maybe it was from that company that has the little flags on the antenna? Was there any little flag?"

Nooch shook his head. "I'da remembered a flag."

"What about Anderson Transportation? Their cars always have the A-1 magnetic sign attached to the—"

"Yes!" Nooch bounced in his seat, causing Rooney to growl. "Yes, there was an A on the trunk!"

"See? Now we're getting somewhere. All of your positive crap is paying off."

I directed Nooch to pull under the canopy in front of the Wainwright Hotel—one of Pittsburgh's refurbished landmarks. A couple of taxis were letting off passengers with suitcases. I bailed out of the truck and told Nooch to sit tight.

Alongside the hedge sat an Anderson limo, engine running, driver sitting behind the wheel reading a magazine, waiting for a passenger. I hustled over and knocked on the window. The window hummed down, and the face that looked up at me was none other than that of Pam Anderson herself, daughter of the company's owner. She was wearing a black suit with a white shirt underneath, very professional. Pearl necklace, pink nail polish, matching lipstick. Nothing like the way she looked when she enjoyed her favorite pastime—her roller derby team. Pam was famous around town as the Bumper—a ruthless member of the Burgh Bombers.

She recognized me and said. "Well, if it isn't Heidi Klum. How's life at the top of the best-dressed list, Rox?"

Okay, so I'm not a fashion model. But I didn't spend my weekends knocking other women on their cans in front of bellowing fans.

I pointed. "You've got a spider on your shoulder, Pam."

She shrieked and jumped out of the limo, then tore off her tailored jacket and threw it on the pavement. She danced around, screaming for a while, then saw my face and finally stopped the hysterics.

"You bitch," she said.

"I'm getting a lot of that lately. Got a minute?"

"I should shoot you right now."

She reached behind the waistband of her pencil skirt, but stopped before yanking out whatever firearm she had concealed there. Already, she'd drawn the attention of everybody within shouting distance. The Bumper shooting me in the driveway of the hotel was going to make headlines her company didn't need. Plus mess up her outfit.

Pam's dad, Roger Anderson, had made his fortune running numbers before he finally opened a used-car dealership that specialized in not asking questions. He went to jail a few times and finally tried a legit business, driving limos and special-event buses for senior citizens who wanted to visit Gatlinburg and Niagara Falls. He made a pretty good living at it, and now all of his kids were vying to run the operation. Pam, the youngest, was obviously trying to learn the business from behind a steering wheel for the time when her roller derby career finally dwindled.

"Take it easy, Pam. Let's remember who testified in your brother's favor last year."

Pam narrowed her already slitty eyes at me. "He went to jail anyway."

"But only for three months. He was out in time for your mom's birthday, right?"

She stopped reaching for her gun. "What do you want?"

"There was an Anderson limo out last night, up on Cherry Street, about seven. Were you the driver?"

"No," she said sullenly. "I had a date last night."

"Congratulations. Anybody I know?"

"I hope not!" She bristled as if insulted. "Are we done?"

"I need to know who was driving last night. Who the passenger was."

"Why should I tell you?"

"If you tell me, I won't tell the police one of your cars was up there."

"Why should it matter where the car was?"

"When you read the paper tomorrow morning, you'll know why it matters. Your dad will be happy you cooperated. Just tell me, okay?"

Pam was savvy enough to understand that something had happened that didn't need the addition of an Anderson vehicle to the mix. She picked up her jacket and dusted it off. "It was Dooce."

"What?"

"The rock singer." She hooked her thumb at the hotel. "He's staying here. We're on call for him, night and day. Last night, he went out for dinner. Him and his assistant—Jeremy somebody. My brother Donnie says they took a drive up into the city first. Some neighborhood. Could have been Cherry Street, for all I know."

"What were they doing up there?"

"How should I know? They wanted to drive around, so Donnie did what he was told."

I stood in the driveway and tried to figure out what it meant. Dooce was in town for his concert. Dragging around a food writer, too. What the hell connection did he have with the Crabtrees? Or was it some coincidence he'd been near their house?

Pam said, "Be careful, Roxy. The steam coming out of your ears might ruin that hairdo of yours."

"Relax, Pammy. Bad hair's not contagious. You know anything else about this evening drive Dooce took?"

"Only that his assistant lost a briefcase somewhere. Donnie had to retrace their route today, but he didn't find it."

"Briefcase?" I said. "Or a messenger bag?"

Pam shrugged. "What's the difference?"

What the heck had Dooce's assistant been doing up at the Crabtree house? I wondered. Had they been mixed up in Clarice's kidnapping? Seemed impossible.

I left Pam and walked back to the Monster Truck.

I told Nooch to move over, and as I climbed into the driver's seat, my cell phone vibrated in my pocket. I checked the screen. There was nobody I wanted to talk to, except Marvin Weiss.

"Who is it?" Nooch asked, wrestling with Rooney for possession of the passenger seat.

"Bug."

I let the call go to voice mail, then dialed Marvin's number.

"Marvin," I said when his recorded voice invited me to leave a message. "Call me when you get this, or I'm coming to cut your tiny balls off."

I snapped the phone shut.

"That wasn't nice," Nooch said.

"Shut up." Then, "Sorry."

"It's okay. You're mad about the truck. Let's visualize it clean and fixed, okay?"

"Okay, okay."

Instead of worrying about the truck, I thought about what I knew so far. Clarice Crabtree, a bigamist, had one egghead husband and one idiot spouse quick with a rabbit punch. Somebody wanted her kidnapped—for ransom, or maybe just to get her out of the way for a while. But now she was dead—probably shot by a pro.

If I hadn't seen the mystified expressions on their faces, I'd have guessed that one of her husbands had already figured out the marriage was crowded and had killed Clarice for it. But they both looked genuinely astonished to learn about the other guy. Besides, neither one of them looked like he had the stones for killing. The police surely assumed one of the husbands was guilty of killing his two-timing spouse. I could leave the job of interviewing the husbands to the cops.

Clarice's father was in the loony bin, but he obviously had an escape route. Still, I didn't see him as a murderer.

And now I had a wild card. What the hell was Dooce doing, cruising around the Crabtree house in a limousine? Had his assistant dropped his messenger bag in the Crabtree's front yard?

I should probably call Bug and tell him about that development.

But the fact that earlier in the week somebody had tried to hire a kidnapper worried me considerably. If Bug found out I'd been high on the hiring list, I could be in some seriously hot water.

The picture of Sugar Mitchell weeping in her dad's car, though—that really stuck in my head.

The way I figured it, one of Carmine's minions had screwed up and killed Clarice. Had to be. I needed to find out who so I could save my own skin. And maybe make things easier for Clarice's kid.

There was one person who could give me right answers.

"I'm going to take a cruise past Marvin's office," I said to Nooch. "I definitely need to see him."

I drove out of downtown along with rush-hour traffic. The other drivers were mostly well-dressed professionals leaving their offices in BMWs and Mercedes sedans, heading for the upscale neighborhoods of the East End. Everybody steered clear of the Monster Truck. City buses tried to crowd me, but I was hard to bully. Still, it was slow going. Then I heard an ambulance behind me and pulled over. When it went past me, though, I cut in behind it and followed. All the other traffic got out of our way. Drafting behind an ambulance was still the speediest way to get through rush hour.

When we got to Shadyside Hospital, the ambulance went into the emergency-room entrance, and I continued down Aiken. At a more sedate pace, I continued a few more blocks and turned left through a bunch of grad students walking away from the universities. Within four blocks, I hit a neighborhood where lots of schoolkids crowded the sidewalks, strolling home from after-school activities as the streetlights started flickering on. The houses we passed were lit up from inside. Through the windows, I could see kids doing homework. Moms making dinner. Then I crossed into a small commercial district. There was a Mr. Squishy store-front on one corner, but I passed it by.

Slowly, I drove past Marvin's office. Closed. Lights off, blinds down. His parents' dry-cleaning shop was open, though. Customers were dashing in and out, picking up their laundry.

I craned to see who was running the shop and saw it was the Weiss family's efficient employee, Mrs. Wong. I parked the truck at a fire hydrant, left it running, and went inside to talk to her. The bell over the door jingled when I entered.

All business, Mrs. Wong rang up the customer ahead of me and handed over a plastic bag stuffed with dress shirts. Whatever chemicals were used to dry-clean clothing, they had the added benefit of preserving certain human beings. Mrs. Wong looked to be about thirty, but she was probably nearer eighty. Not a wrinkle in sight.

When I stepped up to the counter, her expression of polite attention faded. Her oversized eyeglasses were decorated with rhinestones, but the sparkle did not extend to her eyes.

I pasted on a cheery grin. "Hi, Mrs. Wong. How you doing this evening?"

She didn't crack a smile. "Marvin not here. Mr. and Mrs. Weiss not here either."

Mrs. Wong and I weren't exactly best buddies. In my own defense, she got all her information about me from Marvin's mother, who didn't trust me for reasons that probably had to do with me not treating her son like God's gift to the human race.

I said, "I can see they're not here. Where can I find them?"

"Gone away. Gone on vacation."

"No kidding?" I leaned comfortably on the counter. "Where'd they go?"

"Mrs. Weiss not say anything about where they go."

"Oh, come on, Mrs. Wong. You can trust me."

She gave me a look that said she wasn't crazy.

"I want to send them a postcard," I said. "Did they go to Atlantic City?"

She shook her head.

"New York to take Mr. Weiss's sister to see *Jersey Boys* again?"

Mrs. Wong continued to sternly wag her head.

"D.C.?" I asked. "What about Cleveland? Doesn't Marvin have a cousin in Cleveland?"

"Not Cleveland. No cousin. No phone call. You go now. I have work to do."

"But—"

"Weiss family not want to talk to you," Mrs. Wong said.

"Just tell me where they went."

Nothing.

"Well, okay, Mrs. Wong. Nice to see you." I turned in the doorway. "By the way, I saw your grandson yesterday. James is in my daughter's study group. He says he's applying to Harvard."

Mrs. Wong started to smile, then squelched it.

I said, "Too bad Harvard only takes one kid from every high school. Did you hear that? I read it in the paper. Only one kid who applies from the same high school. I think James and Sage have grades that are the same, but how about her SAT score? She beat James by twenty points. Maybe I should encourage her to apply to Harvard, too."

"She not want Harvard."

Yes, threatening nice old ladies was a sign of poor character. What else is new? I said, "Sage hasn't had time to look at it carefully yet. I think she should apply—you know, as a safety school or something."

Mrs. Wong's mouth flattened as she thought over the situation. Finally, she said, "Weiss family gone to Bermuda."

The destination surprised me. "Really? When did they leave? When are they coming back?"

Mrs. Wong frowned. "Don't know. Don't want to know. They leave in a hurry. Marvin say it a surprise vacation."

As long as I had her gushing like an oil well in the Gulf of Mexico, I wanted to ask more questions, but the bell on the door tinkled again, and another customer came into the shop. No use making a scene.

"Thanks, Mrs. Wong."

She said, "No apply to Harvard."

I shrugged. "Sage doesn't listen to me much. Who knows where she'll end up?"

While Mrs. Wong fumed, I went out to the truck.

"Well?" Nooch said when I got back into the truck. "You find Marvin?"

"He's gone on a vacation. Took his parents, too."

"You don't look happy for him. Rox? You okay?"

"Yeah, fine," I said.

"You look worried."

Maybe it was the wrong thing to do, but I couldn't help myself. I said, "That woman I talked to last night? Clarice Crabtree? She was murdered. The cops found her in the river today."

A storm of shock, sympathy, and compassion blew across Nooch's big features. "Wow. That's bad."

"Those kids at the house this morning? Those were her kids."

Nooch's face puckered again. "They don't have a mom anymore."

"Right."

"That's really sad."

I looked at my sidekick. When brains were handed out, he'd been standing in the line for muscles. But he had a big heart, which was the main reason I kept him around. Again, I started feeling guilty that he'd gotten his face messed up by Gino. Gino was my problem. Not Nooch's.

I gave him a gentle sock on the arm. "Yeah, I know. Tomorrow? I'll pick you up at the regular time."

"Okay, Rox. Whatever you say."

I threaded the Monster Truck through traffic back to the Lawrenceville neighborhood. Parked out in front of Nooch's house was a big Chrysler, the vehicle owned by the only stable male figure in Nooch's life—his uncle Stosh, who ran the steamfitters' union. Stosh checked up on Nooch now and then, and he was standing beside the Chrysler when we drove up.

Stosh raised one enormous hand and gave me a wave. We had an unspoken understanding. Whoever was with Nooch at the time was responsible for his safety. Today, I hadn't done my job. Nooch's battered face wasn't going to make his uncle happy.

"Hey, look! It's Uncle Stosh!" Nooch's good humor was back. "Maybe he brought some of his homemade pierogies. He makes the best." When he climbed out of the truck, he looked back long enough to give me a loopy smile. "You want to come for dinner?"

"Thanks, Nooch, but not tonight."

"Stay out of trouble, okay, Rox?"

"Yeah, sure."

"Don't worry too much about those kids. Not tonight. Tomorrow we can visualize some good stuff for them."

I managed a smile. "Good plan. Thanks, Nooch."

He jumped out and lumbered over to his uncle. I watched Stosh throw his arm around Nooch's shoulder—no easy task—and they disappeared into the house together.

Rooney jostled my arm with his nose, which made me realize I'd been staring into space long after Nooch went inside.

I put the truck in gear and drove down the hill, heading for the salvage yard.

❈ 12 ❈

I'd left the gate open earlier in the day. Gino Martinelli's graffiti was still there, bringing down my property values.

I parked. Rooney grabbed his greasy bone, jumped out of the truck, and made a quick tour of the property. He was the ideal junkyard dog. He liked to patrol his territory, and he was big enough to terrify trespassers, even with his mouth full. I let him go.

I unlocked the overhead door and rolled it up. Flipping the light switch, I went inside the old garage, where my uncles had once run a scrap business. Now I had the place full of architectural stuff that I'd salvaged around the city. Trouble was, lately the bottom had fallen out of the salvage business. Nobody wanted to buy old things for their houses anymore. In fact, construction was at a new low, as far as I was concerned. So I was hurting a little.

Next to the garage, connected by a steel door, was the old barbershop that I'd converted into an office for myself. I went inside, turned on the lights. I could see my breath in the office, so I clicked on the space heater.

Next door, I could hear the sounds of the new tenant who'd taken over the former chop shop. I'd heard he was some kind of artist or metalworker or whatever. He ran a blowtorch or pounded like a blacksmith day and night, that's all I knew.

I closed the door, sat on my squeaking office chair, and scooted it closer to the heater. I noticed the light blinking on my answering machine, so I hit the button. A crazy part of me hoped to hear Flynn's voice.

First came a couple of messages from Bug, both the same.

"Call me."

Another call was the voice of a guy I knew who often tossed work my way. "Hey, Roxy, how about coming over to the old high school in McKeesport tomorrow? I got a bunch of desks and chairs that need a good home. I thought maybe you'd want to bid on 'em."

I had no use for desks and chairs, so I deleted the message. My business was starting to look seriously awful.

Next came Stony Zuzak's voice. "Rox, did you get a chance to listen to the CD I dropped off? What do you think? Can you make it Friday night? Sound check's at five."

He sounded excited, and I could understand. If somebody as famous as Dooce was his old pal and asking for Stony to play in his concert—well, that was pretty cool.

The last message was from Marvin Weiss. He'd been too chicken to call me on my cell. I sat up straight when I heard his voice.

"Roxy, hi. Sorry about this, but I'm getting out of town for a couple of weeks. Maybe you should, too."

I slammed my hand on the desk.

"Thanks for the warning, Marvie," I snapped at the machine. "One little problem comes up, and you take a powder. You candy ass."

I had been left to twist in the wind, all by myself.

A few months ago, I'd have taken out my frustration with Marvin on the first guy I could pick up in a bar or a club. The fastest way I knew to calm myself down was a quickie with someone I'd never see again. Most men were ready and willing to oblige me.

The guy next door with the blowtorch. Maybe I should go check him out.

But I was trying to get a handle on that behavior. I knew it wasn't safe. Sure, I was careful to keep plenty of condoms in my hip pocket, and I knew how to wield a blunt weapon if I needed it. So far, I'd been okay. But taking risks like that was probably going to get me in trouble eventually. And I really hated the thought of Sage finding out. It was high time I grew up.

Quietly, I opened the drawer in my desk—the drawer where I kept a lot of things I stole from the guys I hooked up with. A key chain, an earring, a rabbit's foot. Just junk, but I remembered each encounter. I'd heard about wacko killers who kept trinkets from their victims, but, hey, that wasn't what my collection was about. I just liked the sex.

And I missed it.

I closed the drawer and found myself thinking about Flynn. For some reason, being with him didn't feel the same as the sex I should be avoiding.

I tried to shake off that thought by pouring some water into a bowl for Rooney. I left his kibble around the yard to keep him moving on his nightly patrol. Then I drove up to Aunt Loretta's house.

More Dooce songs on the CD. I sang along, but my heart wasn't in it. Sometimes I liked to roll down all the windows and scream the song lyrics while blasting along the highways. But tonight, I didn't feel like it. Instead, I hit all the lights right, so it was only a few minutes before I parked the truck in the alley behind Loretta's house.

Loretta's car was gone, I noticed. She had probably taken Sister Bob over to the Meals on Wheels planning meeting at St. Dominic's.

I found Sage just where I needed her: alone, in her room, on her bed with her laptop humming on her knees. She was listening to music through earbuds, bobbing to the beat. She'd pulled her hair into goofy pigtails. I liked seeing her this way—happy, occupied, no boyfriend in sight. She was wearing flannels and a tank top with the name of her basketball team emblazoned on the front. She smelled of bubblegum.

When she looked up and saw me in the doorway, her face hardened. Then instantly changed.

"Mom! OhmyGod, what happened to your lip?" She pulled out her earbuds and scrambled off the bed. "What's wrong?"

"Nothing's wrong. I bumped it at work. Nothing serious."

"You need ice!"

"I got some in the kitchen." I held up a paper towel wrapped around a couple of ice cubes from Loretta's freezer.

"Here, let me help."

Carefully, she took the ice from me and used the wet paper to daub at my lower lip. I held still. With my tongue, I checked to see if the tooth Mitchell had loosened still felt wobbly. But it was fine now—probably held in place by swelling, but that was a good thing. Sage frowned in concentration.

I felt a softening in my chest. It was amazing that I could have a screaming fight with Sage one night, and she could welcome me home without so much as a cross word the next. She was a good kid that way. Didn't hold a grudge for long.

I said, "You should become a doctor."

She smiled reluctantly. "I hate the way hospitals smell. Remember the time I broke my finger playing in the city tournament? I threw up in the emergency room."

"Not because of the smell. You were in pain. And upset."

"I was not." She argued without heat, still concentrating on the examination of my wound. "I don't think you need any stitches, but this looks very sore."

"I'll live. Did you get any supper yet?"

"We had pasta fagioli and salad. There are leftovers in the fridge for you." Sage smiled. Her face was a thing of beauty—perfect cheeks, expressive dark eyes that reflected everything that's young and full of promise.

But she flicked a teasing glance up at me. "Loretta said to tell you to stay out of the cookies in the freezer."

"Too late." In my other hand, I already had a handful of frozen treats cradled in a square of paper towel.

She grinned and accepted a cream-filled horn made by Irene Stossel's mother. Sage popped it into her mouth. "I love them frozen. They last longer this way."

I handed over the rest of the cookies, sprawled onto her bed, and held the sopping ice cube to my lip. "Loretta will never miss them."

"Are you kidding? She keeps a tally on a Post-it note."

"Good thing I threw away her Post-it note."

Sage climbed onto the bed and sat cross-legged beside me, just the way we had when she was little. Around us, her collection of well-loved stuffed animals sat crowded against her textbooks, her computer, and a tangle of electronic charger cords. She took an inventory of the cookies in her hand. "I better not get blamed."

"Blame Zack. He's always around."

Sage sucked on her cream horn, eyeing me warily. "Are you going to go ballistic again? About Zack?"

"You could do worse than Zack." I threw the ice cube into her trash can and picked out a frozen pecan sandy from her lap.

Here was my opening—a chance to talk to Sage about all the stuff Flynn was so worried about, including Mr. Squishy.

But her cell phone began chirping on the bed. Sage didn't move to answer it. But her gaze landed on the phone, then cut to me.

"You ignoring somebody?" I asked.

She shrugged. "It's just Brian again, making sure I'm okay."

"Hmm," I said. "How are the college applications coming? Is that what you're working on here?" I waved my cookie at the nest of papers on the bed.

"Not at the moment." She avoided my eye. "They're coming along, though."

"You sent any yet?"

"Applications take time. There are lots of questions to fill in. Essays to write. I have to collect recommendations from teachers too, and that takes forever."

"You need any help?"

Her cell phone stopped chirping, and she shook her head. "It's all stuff I have to do myself, really. I've been busy. You know—with homework and stuff. Don't worry. I'll get 'em done."

Most of the time, I let Sage pretty much do whatever she liked. If something looked like it might get out of hand, I trusted Aunt Loretta to play the heavy. Loretta was much more attuned to the subtle signs of looming disaster. Me, I tended to notice the bad stuff only when it blew up in my face.

I knew I should be asking Sage about why she was avoiding her college applications. Why she wasn't talking to me about Mr. Squashy. Why she hadn't thrown Zack out of her life completely.

But I couldn't do it. The moment felt too good just then—too sweet to be ruined by a lot of squabbling about stuff that seemed very far removed from that warmly cluttered room.

As if enjoying the same lull of peace between us, Sage said, "I'm sorry I got so manic last time you were here. About Kiley, I mean."

"I probably deserved it." I popped the cookie into my mouth. "Sorry about the yelling."

She nodded her acceptance of my apology. Simple as that. "Kiley told her mom everything, by the way. This afternoon."

"Wow, I thought I heard a nuclear explosion today."

"It wasn't that bad. I mean, it was pretty awful, don't get me wrong. Her mom went insane."

"Did they call the police? About Gino Martinelli?"

"I don't know the details. Kiley only had time to text me, real fast, in between shrieking sessions." With a sidelong glance at me, she said, "I guess it was pretty icky that she was sleeping with a guy old enough to be her father."

"Super icky."

Shaking her head, my beautiful daughter said, "Kiley can be impulsive. She has no judgment."

"It wasn't her fault, Sage. Gino was the adult. He was a predator, simple as that. She has to take a little responsibility for being susceptible, maybe, but he's the criminal, the one who deserves to be punished."

"But for him to get punished, Kiley has to go through a lot of hell. Police, doctors, lawyers, the whole bit. Her mother wants to sweep it under the rug so nobody else finds out."

"Everybody's going to find out anyway. If they go to the police, they get to control whose side of the story gets told. And Gino gets what's coming to him."

Sage sighed. "I dunno. It's all pretty awful."

"Have another cookie."

She took one. I did, too. Sage smiled at me, and my heart did a loop-deeloop. Having a kid has its moments.

Her cell phone went off again, and she sighed with impatience.

"Go ahead and answer," I said. "I'll step outside, if you want."

"No need for that." She snatched up her phone and flipped it open. "Yes?" she snapped. "Brian, I'm still here in my room, so chill, okay? I'm with my mom. . . . Yes, my mom. You want to talk to her? . . . I didn't think so. Stop calling and go to bed, will you?"

She clicked the phone shut.

"Problem?" I asked.

"He just wants to know where I am," she said, instantly serene again. "It's no big deal. But it gets a little annoying sometimes."

I could have asked her more, but instead I reached out and tugged on one of her pigtails. "I need some information. You mind doing a little Googling for me?"

She sat up straighter and pulled her computer into her lap. "Sure. What do you want to know?"

"A woman got killed last night. A person I knew from high school, in fact. Turns out, she was married to two men at the same time. And had two kids, one with each husband."

Sage's eyes opened with surprise. "How'd she pull that off?"

"It must have been tricky. I mean, she had a lot of secrets to keep straight. And how do you keep track of what goes on with two kids? I've got half my brain designated to knowing when your next basketball game is."

"Do you?" Sage seemed surprised.

"Have I missed a game yet?"

"No, but—I guess you're right. How'd she keep everything straight?"

"She was a smart lady. Smarter than I am, that's for sure."

"What do you mean?" A suspicious frown. "Why do you want to know about her, Mom?"

I'd prepared my answer for this question during the drive over. Smoothly, I said, "I was doing some business with her just before she was killed."

"You mean you were there when it happened? Were you in danger?"

"No, nothing like that. She died after I met with her. I wonder if there's something I could have done that might have kept her from getting killed."

Sage smiled gently. "That's a nice thought, Mom, but you can't be everywhere at once. Just be thankful you weren't hurt."

"Yeah, I suppose so."

Sage was back on her computer. "What's her name?"

"Clarice Crabtree. One husband is Mitch Mitchell. The other is Eckelstine—Richard, I think."

Sage went to work, happily rattling her computer keys and munching the last of the cookies at the same time.

"Here's a little info about Mitch Mitchell," she reported after a couple of minutes of muttering at her computer screen. "Looks like he owned a company called Cultural Excavations. Cool! See this? He dug up stuff at archaeological sites. Here's his picture on one of those little bulldozers at that place in New Mexico where they find Native American artifacts."

I looked at the photo, now several years old, judging by Mitchell's current hairline. "He might get a bad sunburn with his shirt off like that."

Sage laughed. "You think he's selling more than his bulldozer, much?"

Mr. Beefcake had posed himself in a dramatic setting with his abs highlighted by the sunset. I began to understand what Clarice Crabtree might find so appealing about Mitchell. I felt pretty sure she wasn't wearing thong underwear for the mollusk man. "What else do you see?"

"Some pictures in Siberia where they found all those woolly mammoths in the permafrost. Pretty cool, right? They pulled whole animals right out of the ice—hardly any damage after thousands of years."

"Yeah, cool, but what about the people?"

Sage continued to type on her keyboard. She frowned some more. "Funny thing. The stuff about Mitchell kinda dies out, like maybe he's not in business anymore. The last picture of him actually digging stuff was years ago. But there's a lot of information here about his daughter. Sugar Mitchell. See? She's an ice-skater."

Sage spun the screen so I could see photos of Mitchell's daughter Sugar in her spangled skating outfits at various ages. Sugar twirling on the ice as a toddler. Sugar skating with one leg up in the air like a Rockette. Sugar accepting a trophy as a teenager, triumphantly smiling into the camera. And another trophy. And another and another.

"She's cute," I said.

Sage gave me a horrified look. "You've got to be kidding! Mom, in some of these old pictures she looks like one of those five-year-old sexpot beauty queens. Lipstick at that age? It's just creepy."

"Her outfit is cute."

"She looks like a hooker! Who puts a push-up bra on a kid?"

"How old do you think she is?"

"In this picture? Maybe ten. Now she's—what? Fifteen? But she's really successful." Sage pointed at the screen. "Look, here's a newspaper article about her."

We both bent over the laptop and read a piece about Sugar being a big ice-skating champion, maybe heading to the Olympics someday. In the background of Sugar's photo, we could see Mitch Mitchell, smiling proudly. No sign of Clarice, though.

"Huh," I said, skimming the gushy article. "Looks like Sugar's been on the road more than she's been at home. Her dad travels with her. That's one way not to notice your wife's married to somebody else."

"Let's look up the other husband." Sage tapped her keys again. "What's his name?"

"Eckelstine. Richard."

The information about Richard Eckelstine started with a family tree.

"His family was real important a long time ago," Sage said. "His great-grandfather invented some kind of iron-processing thingie. I bet they had buckets of money. See this mansion? It belonged to them, like, a hundred years ago. Now it's an apartment building. And here? Looks like they gave a lot of money to a museum once."

We found some incomprehensible articles Richard himself had written about snails. Lots and lots of articles about snails. Apparently, he hadn't shared his wife's interest in digging up dead animals.

"Mostly, he does research," Sage said. "Oh, wait, here's a picture of him at a charity ball. With Clarice, I guess?"

"Yeah, that's her."

I peered at the screen. Richard Eckelstine wore a stiff tuxedo, and Clarice was gussied up in a long gown with earrings the size of hotel chandeliers. The photo had been a candid shot, I could see, from a couple of years ago. The photographer caught them entering a ballroom with tall flower arrangements on either side of the doorway. Clarice looked like she was going to a funeral, not a party. Her husband gave the camera a feeble smile.

On a hunch, I said, "Try looking up their son. He goes by Richie. Maybe he's an ice-skater, too?"

I waited while Sage glared intently at her screen. She had always been a cute kid, but lately Sage was growing into her nose and her long limbs. No wonder all the boys were taking notice of her. By the time she graduated from high school in the spring, she was going to be a knockout.

I just hoped she planned on being a knockout in college, not working at some ice-cream stand and taking cell phone calls from slacker boyfriends.

Sage chewed her lower lip. "Nope, no ice-skating for Richie. I see his name in a kids skateboarding competition a couple of years ago, but that's it. Whoa!" Sage sat back from the computer. "Get this. Looks like Richie Eckelstine has been arrested."

"For what?"

"Can't tell. Juvenile records are sealed."

If Richie Eckelstine had lived in my neighborhood, at least two hundred people would know what he'd been charged with, the result of his court appearance, the name of his probation officer, and what color socks he wore on Wednesdays.

"Let me check Facebook," Sage said. "Maybe I can learn something."

Facebook checking involved going through the steps of being "friended," which sometimes took a while, so I finished off the cookies and put my head on Sage's pillow. She typed and clicked, and I closed my eyes.

Sage's room had been mine up until she was born. I hadn't spent much time in it when I was a teenager. Mostly, it was a place to crash when I wasn't out running around. I'd painted the room pink before Sage was born, though, and the two of us had shared it until she started first grade. I kept her in a crib in the corner at first; then we shared the double bed.

Gradually, though, I'd moved my life out of the house. As Sage grew into a person who needed a parent, Loretta took over more and more of the daily routine of child rearing. I checked in most nights and helped her with her algebra, her geometry, and finally trigonometry. But Loretta was the grown-up in Sage's daily life. Maybe that had been a bad thing for me to do.

The more Sage had watched me, though, the more I'd felt like I was doing everything wrong.

Tonight it felt nice to be back in the room we'd shared. Cozy. Uncomplicated.

Fleetingly, I wondered if Clarice had been a good mother. Did she tuck her kids into bed every night? Check their report cards? Make special sandwiches? Set a good example? How had she pulled it all off?

I woke up in the morning when Sage hit her alarm and rolled out of bed for school.

While she bustled around the room, she told me what she learned about Richie Eckelstine.

"He got arrested for graffiti." Sage wriggled into a pair of black leggings and pulled a short dress over her head. "He did a couple thousand dollars of damage at his school and got caught when his friends turned him in."

I yawned. "Nice friends."

"Graffiti might look cool, Mom, but it's the first sign of neighborhoods going to pot, not to mention expensive to clean up. After the school incident, the police figured out he was responsible for spraying paint all over a bunch of businesses. Even some university buildings. He was in big trouble. His parents agreed to pay damages, though."

I sat up and pushed away a throw blanket that somebody had tucked around me during the night. "How did you learn of all this? Facebook?"

Sage grabbed a couple of shirts out of her closet and held them up against herself, looking in the mirror to check her reflection. She gave me a grin in her mirror. "I have my methods."

"You're a genius." I stretched in the bed. "Can I give you a lift to school?"

"No, thanks. I like walking. It clears my head. Gets me ready for the academic challenges of the day."

I peered up at her, my juvenile-delinquent antenna on alert.

"What?" she said. "I'm serious."

Just then, her cell phone buzzed on the nightstand. I made a swipe for it, but Sage scooped up the phone.

"Study buddy. Big chemistry test today," she said, and took the phone into the bathroom. She shut the door firmly.

I leaped out of bed and listened at the door, hoping to learn a little more about Mr. Squeegee. But Sage turned on the tap water, and I couldn't hear anything.

Because Loretta had an early day in court suing the Amsterdam grandson, I used her bathroom across the hall to take a shower. I came back to steal a pair of clean panties and a pair of socks from Sage's top drawer. I could still hear the water running in Sage's bathroom, so I took a quick tour of her other drawers, too. And her shelves and under her mattress.

Under the mattress, I found four blank college applications.

Worse yet? Under the bed, I found a gigantic pile of college catalogs and brochures. There must have been a hundred different colleges represented in all that paper.

A dull pain throbbed behind my eyeball. Clearly, Sage hadn't even looked at half the stuff she had hidden under the bed. She hadn't done a damn thing about applying for college.

Did Loretta know about this? What kind of talk had she conducted with Sage on this subject?

Because I sure as hell didn't know what to say.

How did other parents handle this kind of passive-aggressive crap? Especially those who had screwed up their own lives and certainly didn't have a college diploma to wave around?

Annoyed, I shoved the catalogs and brochures back under the bed and hurried downstairs.

Sister Bob had Loretta's television on, and she listened to the morning news from the floor where she was grunting, doing sit-ups.

"Good morning, Roxana! Do you exercise every morning? Isn't it a pain?"

"Give it up to God, Sister Bob." I crouched down to hold her ankles.

As she finished counting off her sit-ups, we listened to the tail end of the Clarice Crabtree story, complete with footage of the rolled-up carpet.

When Clarice's name was finally mentioned, Sister Bob paused in the act of sitting up. "That's the woman you were looking up in the library yesterday, isn't it?"

"Yeah."

She gave me a frown. "Did you know about this yesterday?"

"I knew something was up," I said.

The reporter started talking about bigamy, and how none of Clarice's neighbors could imagine she'd had two husbands.

"Doesn't that beat all?" Sister Bob remained paused, her hands linked behind her head. "What woman wants two husbands? Surely it's hard enough to train one properly."

"I wouldn't know."

Sister Bob gave up on exercise. She rubbed her stomach muscles and eyed me. "Why didn't you marry that nice Patrick Flynn, Roxana? I heard he liked getting into trouble, but I always thought he was a good boy."

"Who told you he liked trouble?"

"Oh, everybody at St. Dom's. His father used to say he'd rather get a switching than a medal for good behavior. Why didn't you marry him?"

"Maybe because he ran out on us?"

"Oh, what do you expect from a boy that age? Most of them, their brains don't develop until they're in their twenties, right?"

"He didn't deserve to be Sage's dad."

Sister Bob reached for the remote control on the floor beside her and snapped off the TV. She peered at my face. "What's wrong with your lip? Did somebody punch you?" She clapped one hand over her mouth to stifle a cry of dismay. "Oh my heaven, you didn't go after that man at the library, did you?"

"Nope, sorry. He's still on the loose. No, this was something else. At work. Nothing big."

I poured myself a cup of coffee from Loretta's De'Longhi and sat down at the table, where the newspaper was spread out. I saw a photo of Clarice Crabtree on top of the fold. The headline read, Double Life?

I wanted to know who ended Clarice's double life.

Sister Bob struggled to her knees and used a chair to leverage herself to her feet. She went to the stove and turned up the heat under a frying pan. A fragrant sizzle rose up, and she used a wooden spoon to stir.

Today Bob wore a pair of white sneakers with sparkles on the laces and a lavender track suit that drooped around her butt. Beneath her nose, her upper lip was still red, as if burned by hot wax. Somebody had pulled out most of her eyebrows, too. She had two skinny half-moons drawn in brow pencil on her forehead.

"Sister Bob, you grew up with Carmine, right?"

"Yes, I did."

"And the guys who ended up working for him. You knew them, too?"

"Some of them." Sister Bob cracked eggs into the frying pan over some onions and peppers and bacon that had been mingling their own deliciousness. As the eggs cooked, she sliced a loaf of Italian bread for the toaster. For a nun who'd lived for several decades in the strict life of a convent, she certainly had reverted smoothly to her upbringing.

Within a few minutes, she slid a plate in front of me and set the frying pan in the middle of the table on a kitchen towel.

I caught her wrist. "I need to know about the guys who did the really dirty jobs for Carmine. I only remember cigar smoke and a lot of slips of paper and dollar bills on the kitchen table. But who did the wet work?"

If my question horrified her, she managed not to show it. Instead, she gave me the Look—a hot laser beam that nuns probably learned in weekly seminars. The Look was a weapon deployed to remind naughty children of the brevity of life—or at least the power of a nun to stand a kid in a corner for a few hours of humiliation.

Radiating disapproval, she said, "Why do you want to know all that awful stuff?"

"It's complicated."

"I understand complicated." She poured two glasses of orange juice and sat down at the table, the power of the Look only mildly reduced. "I hear your uncle Carmine has been paying you to do his errands."

"Just a few."

"Are you hard up for money? Is that why you're on his payroll all of a sudden? Or is it the excitement that appeals to you?"

"I wouldn't call it excitement, exactly."

"For the adrenaline rush, then. Sure, I know all about adrenaline," she said when she saw my skeptical smile. "I know that's half of the appeal of working for Carmine." She met my eye. "You're on a slippery slope, Roxana."

"I'm not sliding anywhere," I said. "I just want to know who Carmine might call if he had a really big job he wanted done. A kidnapping, maybe."

"Kidnapping! That sounds sordid." Sister Bob put a modest amount of breakfast on a plate for herself. "I knew all those slick fellows who worked for Carmine. They were his muscle. It was the thing to do in the neighborhood once—be a big man, be dangerous. Get special treatment in restaurants. Maybe get a discount on a car. But that's all gone. That glamorous life of crime—it doesn't exist anymore, not the way it looks in the movies. And eventually, each of those big men developed a guilty conscience." Bob tapped the back of my hand with her fork. "You will, too, Roxana. Mark my words."

"I'm not Carmine's muscle."

"No?" She speared a pepper. "Maybe Patrick Flynn isn't the only one around here who likes getting into trouble."

"Me? I've got a daughter to think about."

"Good," said Sister Bob. "Keep your priorities straight. You lie down with dogs, you get up with fleas."

"Do you see me scratching?"

"No. I know you don't want to be anything like your own mother, God rest her." Bob ate some eggs, obviously thinking about me. "She didn't pay enough attention to you, Roxana, but you turned out just fine in spite of everything, didn't you?"

I toyed with my breakfast and said nothing.

Sister Bob said, "You turned into a terrific mother yourself."

Hardly terrific, I thought. My face must have said as much.

"You're good with Sage," Bob insisted. "Whether you recognize it or not. You're a good influence on that girl, and when you can't be, you have the sense to step aside and let others take over."

"I give Loretta all the credit for how Sage is turning out."

Bob nodded in agreement. "Loretta's wonderful. It's a good thing you see that. It wouldn't hurt to say so once in a while."

Yeah, I'd been avoiding Loretta lately. I wasn't sure why, but I didn't want to talk to her right now.

Watching Bob eat her breakfast one dainty bite at a time, I went back to my original question. "You gotta trust me when I say I'm staying out of trouble, Sister Bob. I need to know who would Carmine call to do a kidnapping, back in his heyday? You know any names?"

"Sure, I knew all of them. Larry Spezzante, Tommy the Tank, Dutch Campisano. But they're all dead now."

"All of them?"

"Well, Dutch is in assisted living. Some people say that's worse than a cemetery."

If I got lucky, Dutch might know somebody in Carmine's organization who might still be called upon to do a kidnapping. "Hey, wait, doesn't Dutch have a son? That guy with the road rage? Always getting arrested for rear-ending senior citizens in traffic?"

"I don't know. He sounds awful. I suppose I should start praying for him."

Half to myself, I murmured, "Maybe I should go talk to Dutch."

"He won't have much to say. Alzheimer's, I think."

"I'll go see Dutch anyway."

"We both should go." Sister Bob slapped the table. "Visitors might cheer him up. And I like the idea of being your sidekick on this mission. I can keep an eye on you. I'll see what I can set up for us. Maybe this afternoon?"

"Sure." Sister Bob worked fast, which I liked. "Aunt Roberta, can I ask you one more thing?"

She sipped her juice and waited.

"You really moved in the neighborhood when you were a girl. I mean, you had dates every weekend, Loretta says. You shocked everybody when you decided to be a nun. And you stuck with it for how long? Thirty years? That's a really long time to do something and then give it up. How come you left the convent?"

She set her glass back on the table. "A hot flash."

"Huh?"

She grinned at me. "I had my first hot flash just after I was told to resign from the hospital. I flashed right on the steps of the convent and decided it was a sign from God. Time to leave. Time to do something with my hormones before they dried up completely. Why should you young people have all the fun?"

I laughed and thanked her for the breakfast and went outside.

While I was still standing on the porch, my cell phone rang. I checked the ID.

Uncle Carmine.

Now, that was one guy I really didn't want to talk to right now.

I closed the phone without answering, and that's when I noticed that parked behind my truck in the alley was a police cruiser with its engine running. A thin blue cloud of exhaust hung in the cool morning air behind the vehicle. Bug Duffy rolled down the driver's-side window.

❊ 13 ❊

"You look well rested," Bug said when I strolled over to his car. "For a fugitive."

I leaned my hip against his rearview mirror. "If I'd known you were hanging around out here to arrest me, I'd have invited you in for breakfast. Sister Bob made bacon and eggs."

"No, thanks. I've been up all night and snacking on doughnuts to stay awake. If you've got a Tums, I'll spare the handcuffs."

He wore a pair of reflective sunglasses. I couldn't see his eyes, and apparently he wanted to keep it that way.

I said, "Sorry, I don't have any Tums. I guess I'll just have to outrun you."

"Forget it, then. I don't feel up to chasing you."

"Find Clarice's killer yet?"

"Nope."

"I— Look, I'm sorry about yesterday. Losing my temper, I mean." I didn't want to get into a big deal about my mother and all, but I said, "You were right. I was kinda torn up about things. I didn't mean to take it out on you. This whole friend thing—well, it's new territory for me."

"Forget about it," Bug said easily, to my great relief. "I talked to both husbands again last night. I guess we'd have figured this out sooner if I'd checked those two IDs in Clarice's handbag, but that's the way police work goes sometimes. ME said she was probably killed right after she was snatched, so I don't think we could have stopped that. Both of the husbands claim they had no idea Clarice was married to somebody else."

"Do you believe them?"

"Not exactly. We also started looking at Clarice's financial records."

"And?"

"She drew a small salary from the museum. So did Husband Number One—Eckelstine. But they had big expenses—nice cars, big mortgage, legal fees to keep their kid out of jail. They used credit cards erratically—ran up big debt, then paid them off in big chunks."

"Where'd they get the chunks of money?"

"Eckelstine says she was paid to give speeches, but he wasn't sure about the details. Either that, or he's lying. Clarice took care of all their finances, he said."

"What's the story with the Mitchells?"

"Same deal. She handled the financial stuff. He mostly takes care of their kid. She's a figure skater. Here's where it gets interesting. You won't believe what it costs to train a teenage ice-skater. Tens of thousands of dollars on coaching, travel, tournaments. Plus she goes to a private school—some online education with assignments the kids do on their own time. Huge tuition, plus extra fees for tutoring when she travels. I've got a guy working on figuring out where Clarice got the money to pay for everything. Mitchell, incidentally, has no job at all except driving the daughter back and forth between skating rinks. He devotes all his time to the kid."

"Maybe Clarice's father gave her dough?"

Bug shrugged. "Maybe. She had recently taken over his financials, too, but at first glance his assets were modest."

"By the looks of his house, Professor Crabtree didn't have much extra cash. What are you doing next?"

"Talking to banks to follow the money. Then back to the husbands. One of them probably offed her."

"Did you figure out who Rhonda is? Crabtree kept asking about her. I wonder if she was maybe a secretary or something. Or a sister?"

"I forgot about Rhonda."

"You've had a lot on your mind. Look, there's something I haven't told you."

Bug squinted up at me through his sunglasses. "Just one thing?"

I tried to smile, but couldn't. "When I was in the house talking to Clarice that night, Nooch saw a black limousine pull up on the street."

Bug waited for more, saying nothing.

"It took Nooch a while to remember to tell me. He's forgetful. It's not his fault. Anyway, yesterday I asked around, and it sounds to me like Dooce was in the neighborhood that night."

"Dooce? You mean the singer, Dooce?"

"Yeah, him. And his assistant, some guy named Jeremy."

"Dooce was at the Crabtree house? When were you going to mention that?"

"I'm mentioning it now. Look, they didn't get out of the car or anything."

Bug's expression didn't waver, and I wanted to pull off his sunglasses to see what he was thinking. Finally, he said, "A rock singer driving by the Crabtree house doesn't sound like a promising lead right now, Roxy."

It sounded pretty stupid to me, too, suddenly. So I said, "I'm just putting my cards on the table, that's all. You know—sharing information with a friend."

His phone jingled, and he answered it. He checked his watch while listening to the voice on the other end. "Yeah, I'll be there in ten."

"Hot lead?" I asked when he snapped the phone shut.

He shook his head. "I'm taking my boys to their dentist appointment."

Bug's wife, I knew, had MS. He'd shouldered a lot of parental respon-
sibilities in the last year. I felt a twinge of guilt for giving him a hard time.
He had his hands full already.

Bug tossed his phone on the passenger seat. "Look, I still need to talk
to you about what happened yesterday with Clarice's husbands. What they
said to each other before I got there—that kind of thing. You available
later?"

"For you to arrest me?"

"Not unless you provoke somebody into another street brawl. Lunch?
At Roland's? One o'clock?"

I wondered if he'd still be awake at one o'clock, but I liked the fish
sandwiches at Roland's, so I said, "Yeah, okay."

Bug rolled up his window, put the cruiser in gear, and left the alley.

I climbed into the truck and started the engine. While hunting for
a radio station that would tell me more about Clarice Crabtree's life and
death, I saw a black Escalade pull into the alley.

An Escalade. In Loretta's alley. My urban-dweller radar switched on.

The vehicle of city drug dealers and bad guys in general was a sleek
truck with tinted windows and the full package of chrome wheels and
door trim. From the angle of the sunlight, I couldn't see who was behind
the wheel of this one.

The driver beeped his horn, and a second later Sage pushed out the
door and came skipping down the sidewalk, munching on toast and smiling at the driver. She climbed in the passenger seat, and I could see her
silhouette as she leaned across and kissed the driver, long and sweetly.

I laid a hand on my horn and blasted it.

Sage sat up quickly and buckled her seatbelt. The driver pulled away
fast, throwing up a spray of gravel.

That's when I saw the license plate: SQUISHY.

It was no drug dealer. It was my daughter's new boyfriend. I considered
ramming the Squishy Escalade with the Monster Truck, but I couldn't get
the beast turned around fast enough. I grabbed my cell phone and dialed
Sage's number.

No surprise, she didn't answer.

At the traffic light, I saw a flash of chrome as the Escalade turned left. Away from the direction of Sage's school. When I reached the light, I got caught behind a bus and missed which way they went after that. Cursing, I trolled a couple of side streets, hoping to catch sight of them, but no luck. Sage had disappeared, and I knew she wasn't going to study for a chemistry test.

I tried her cell phone a couple more times. She didn't answer.

Fuming, I picked up Nooch. He got into the truck and sniffed. "You smell good. Like bacon."

"We should invent a perfume that smells like bacon. Men would love it. Of course, men love everything as long as there's food or sex involved, preferably both."

Nooch blinked fearfully at me. "What are you so mad about this morning?"

"Sage has a new boyfriend, and I think they're skipping school together."

Nooch looked grave. "That's not positive."

"It's about as negative as it gets."

"But Sage is a nice girl. She wouldn't get into any trouble."

"Don't bet the farm on that."

But Nooch was right. Sage was a good kid, and I had to trust that—especially on a day when I had other stuff to worry about.

I tried to think through what I could accomplish in the hours before I had to meet Bug for lunch. First, I drove down to the salvage yard. Rooney was waiting for us at the gate, holding his bone in his teeth.

Nooch yelped. "Oh, no. Look!"

We jumped out of the truck. Rooney bounded over and shoved his face into mine, and I realized somebody had spray-painted him, too. His face was splotched with green paint, and his body had a fine green tint all over.

"What happened to you?" I asked the dog.

"Somebody painted him!" Nooch cried.

"Probably through the fence." I examined Rooney more carefully. He was green, all right, but it didn't look as if it hurt him any. He waggled his whole body—happy to see us. I pried open his mouth to check if maybe he'd inhaled anything poisonous, but his teeth and tongue were clean.

"It was that idiot Gino." I hugged Rooney. "Damn it, it's time to saddle up and go after him."

"Oh, jeez," Nooch groaned. "It makes me nervous when you go all cowboy."

I gave Rooney more pats and pulled out my keys again. "Nooch, I need you to pull out all the pocket doors in the inventory. The beveled glass ones. Tomorrow there's a guy coming from Fox Chapel who's interested. You do that. I'll go after Gino."

"What about lunch? Will you be back for lunch?"

"If I'm not, you can order a pizza. There's money in the petty-cash box."

I went into the office and looked up some addresses in the phone book. Then I loaded Rooney and his bone into the truck. I phoned Flynn from behind the steering wheel.

"What?" he said, sounding hostile.

Better to skip any pleasantries. "Do you still play hockey at night with your friends?"

If the topic of conversation surprised him, he didn't sound that way. He said, "Yeah, couple nights a week when I can. Why?"

"Do you know any ice-skaters?"

He paused. "You're going to have to be more specific."

"Not hockey skaters, but the girls in the sparkly outfits."

"You mean figure skaters?"

"Yeah, any of those?"

"A couple. What's this all about?"

"Do any of them teach little kids?"

"Yes. Rox, I'm busy here—"

"How about a name? Somebody I can talk to?"

"Is this about Sage? She wants to learn to skate?"

"No, I just need to learn in general about skating."

"Sometimes you're more nuts than others," he said. "Try Jenny Osterman. She works at the Harmar Rink, teaches lessons after school. She's a nice girl, Rox. Don't go trying to intimidate her, okay?"

"What kind of jerk do you think I am? Wait—don't answer that. How was dinner last night?"

"Crazy," he said. "I'll talk to you later."

He hung up.

I had other things to do before I could intimidate the skating teacher after school, but first I headed over to Petrone's gas station to wash the truck. On the way, I tried to think up an appropriate punishment for Gino. I envisioned everything from pelting him with water balloons to eviscerating him with a sharpened pencil.

Outside the car wash, I did a double take.

"Holy shit," I said. "Maybe this envisioning thing works!"

Pulling through the big-rig bay was one of Gino Martinelli's tow trucks. I pulled in front and blocked it.

Gino himself leaned out of the cab. "Bitch!"

It was all I needed. I was out from behind the steering wheel in a heartbeat, and I yanked open Gino's door. He gave a squeak as I grabbed a handful of his jacket and dragged him out of the truck.

He fought me, kicking and scratching. I kneed him once and he went limp, but only for a second. In another instant, he reared up and tried to bite me on the neck. He got a mouthful of hair instead.

I snapped. Okay, I'd had a bad couple of days. On the front seat of his tow truck I saw a clipboard, some jumper cables, and a bunch of other stuff. I leaned in and seized the jumper cables. In another second, I wrapped them around Gino's scrawny neck.

He wound his fingers through the cables and turned purple, chanting, "Bitch, slut, dirty whore—"

"Call me all the names you like, hamster man. I saw you without your pants, remember? You go after little girls 'cause you can't make a real woman happy?"

He choked and gagged and struggled.

I hauled him up by the neck. "Listen up, Gino, you miserable shit. You painted my gate. You messed up my truck. But when you try to hurt my dog, you son of a bitch, you get what's coming to you."

He made gargling noises and started to slide to the ground. Panting and cursing, I tightened the cables until the muscles in my forearms screamed. I heard Rooney barking like crazy, but he sounded very far away. If Nooch had been there to pull me off Gino, it might have turned out okay. But I could feel the wildfire in my veins. My brain stopped functioning on anything but the most primitive level.

Then suddenly a police cruiser passed the entrance to the car wash.

The cop stopped the car. As he backed up to get a better look at what was happening, Gino and I both caught sight of him.

I dropped the jumper cables and put my arm around Gino's shoulders, hoping it looked convincing.

Likewise, Gino straightened up and smiled at the cop. He even waved.

The cop rolled down the window of his cruiser to take a longer look at the two of us. He stared hard.

We smiled back.

After an eternity, the cop put up his window and drove away.

The interlude gave me enough time to regain my wits. With a little less fury than before, I slammed Gino into the side of his truck and pinned him there with one hand against his throat. "Listen to me, you baby-screwing asshole. You come near one of my daughter's friends again, I'll get out my hedge clippers and do some serious damage, you know what I mean? And picking on Nooch? That'll get you something just as bad. But if you touch my dog, I'll core you like an apple."

"Whore," he snarled.

I reached inside the cab of his truck and came out with a stapler—the one he used to attach his overpriced receipts to the credit card slips of the car owners he cheated. Then I pulled a five-dollar bill out of my hip pocket and slapped it into the palm of his hand.

"Here," I said. "This should cover the damages."

I stapled the five into his hand.

Gino howled, but I threw the staple gun and walked way. I got into the Monster Truck and drove out of the car wash.

A little while later I drove into a pretty residential neighborhood. By then, I was no longer blind with rage. I could almost think again. I was wishing I could summon a little of Nooch's positive energy, because I was still shaking with diffused anger.

But I'd managed to find myself in the Eckelstine neighborhood.

The Eckelstine house was a century-old brick two-story with Tudor beams on the front, like Henry the Eighth might drop by to behead somebody. Similar homes lined the street—mansions built back during the first steel boom and still well maintained. They had rolling front lawns and sculpted flower beds, and brick driveways led to garages out back—garages once big enough to hold carriages and a couple of horses, too.

Today, a bunch of satellite trucks were parked in the street in front of the house. Now that the story of the bigamist lady was out, news reporters milled around on the sidewalk, drinking coffee out of Starbucks cups and waiting for the next update. As I cruised past, I recognized a guy who wrote up crime stories for the newspaper. I'd slept with him last summer, except we hadn't exactly slept.

He caught sight of me going by, and his head nearly swiveled off his neck as he tried to make sure it was really me.

To avoid talking to the reporter, I decided not to park and stroll through the crowd to Eckelstine's front door.

Instead, I drove around the block, past a bus stop and a lady walking a sheepdog.

The next block over was another row of nice old houses that shared backyards with the houses on Eckelstine's. I parked the truck and looked through somebody's driveway at the back of the Eckelstine house. What I hadn't seen from the front was a plumber's truck parked beside the Eckelstine garage.

The side of the truck said, Busted Flush Plumbing.

"Aha," I said.

Before I formed a complete plan, who should come popping out from behind a hedge but Richard Eckelstine himself. He must have gone out his back door and crossed the neighbor's yard and come out on this side.

It was him, all right. There was no mistaking his gray corona of hair. But instead of his bow tie and khaki pants, today he was dressed in a shapeless army surplus jacket and jeans. A throwback to grad students back in the hippie days. He hit the sidewalk, walking fast and adjusting his backpack straps on his shoulders.

To me, he didn't look like a grieving husband. He looked a lot like my daughter when she was happily bebopping down the porch steps to skip school with her new boyfriend.

Which raised my blood pressure all over again.

What the hell did I have to lose? I drove up beside Eckelstine and pushed the button to roll down the passenger window. "Hey," I said. "Can I give you a lift somewhere?"

Next thing that happened didn't seem like the act of a grieving husband either. Eckelstine's face got all surprised, and he bolted. He ran pell-mell down the sidewalk, holding on to his backpack straps for dear life.

"Something I said?" I asked Rooney.

I pulled to the curb, shut off the truck, and told Rooney to stay. Then I bailed out and started chasing Eckelstine. It was purely instinct—like when a lion sees a juicy gazelle come running out of the tall grass. Hard to suppress the urge to run it down and kill it.

I was lighter and faster than Eckelstine, but I held back, letting the pace tire him out. When he turned the corner and began to run for his life, I ducked into somebody's driveway. It was another big house—this one with lace curtains in all the windows and a decorative wreath on the double doors. I headed for the backyard, dodging trash cans, skirting a vegetable garden covered in straw, and jumping a koi pond with a little bridge over it. I hurdled a picket fence into the next yard and nearly landed on a dachshund taking a crap on the lawn. Two more dachshunds jumped out from under a deck and streaked in my direction, yapping murderously. I guess they didn't notice I could have crushed them with my boots. But I like dogs, so I jumped another fence and ran across several more backyards.

The lawns were soft underfoot, and I ran until I reached the corner. Then I popped out and there was Eckelstine, running toward me and glancing over his shoulder.

When he turned back and saw me in front instead of behind, he missed a step, tripped over a hump in the sidewalk, and fell, *splat*, on his face. His backpack went flying.

I went over to the grass and picked up the backpack. Surprisingly heavy, like maybe he had a bowling ball inside.

"Jeez." I stood over him, listening to his labored breathing. "You okay?"

He panted and groaned at the same time. "No, I'm not okay!"

"Want some help up?"

He rolled over, clutching his nose. "No!"

I crouched down on one knee. "Wow, you sure took a header."

"You were chasing me!"

"Following," I corrected. "I was following, not chasing. Why did you run, anyway? Got something to hide in here?"

I dangled the backpack over him, and he forgot about his nose and made a grab for it. I pulled the backpack up again, playing keepaway.

He summoned some anger, which was quite a trick being that he was still on his back on the sidewalk. "Give me that. It's private property."

"This? Whatcha got in it, Mr. Eckelstine?"

"Doctor. I'm Dr. Eckelstine."

"Oh, yeah? Got a minute to look at the rash on my ass?"

"Not that kind of doctor."

"Then how about you give up trying to impress me? What's in the bag? Should I take a peek?" I tugged at the zipper.

"You open it, I'll have you arrested." He sat up stiffly and touched his nose with tentative fingers. "It's just some of my wife's papers. Confidential papers. And a key to her safety-deposit box. She's dead, you know. There are matters to take care of."

"My condolences. That still doesn't explain how come you took one look at me and ran like a rabbit. Or why this bag weighs a hell of a lot more than papers."

"I ran because I—I thought you were the press. From a newspaper or something." He gave me a disgruntled glare. "They're all knocking on my door, trying to get a statement. Trying to get me to say something incriminating."

"Incriminating?"

"They think I killed my wife." Eckelstine looked insulted.

"Did you?"

"Of course not! I loved Clarice! We made a good team."

"That's what keeps a marriage fresh, I hear. Teamwork." I was starting to think Clarice married the other guy because Eckelstine's view of married life was Dullsville.

His glare turned suspicious. "What do you want?"

"How about a little information?"

"Will you give my bag back?"

"Sure, why not? Just tell me this. Did you know your wife was married to somebody else?"

Eckelstine opened his mouth, but nothing came out.

I said, "I had a feeling you weren't totally blown away by Mitchell when he showed up. Did you know Clarice had married him?"

"No." Carefully, Eckelstine said, "I knew a little about him, but not that they had married."

"You knew they worked together? In Siberia?"

"Yes." Eckelstine gingerly felt his left arm, maybe searching for broken bones. "Years ago, Clarice called me from a dig in Siberia, wanting to adopt an orphaned child. I refused, of course, and—"

"You refused to adopt an orphan? Why?"

"Because Clarice wasn't fit to be a mother."

I had expected him to say he didn't want a kid who might have fetal alcohol syndrome or whatever problems he imagined came with foreign adoptions, but he surprised me. "She wasn't fit? Why not?"

Coldly, Eckelstine said, "May I stand up now?"

I put my hand down and pulled him to his feet.

He dusted himself off. "If you must know, Richie isn't Clarice's child.

He is my son with my first wife, who died. Clarice became his stepmother when we married. Richie was seven. She—well, she never really took to motherhood where Richie was concerned, and I didn't want her trying a second time with another child—let alone a girl."

"What's wrong with a girl?"

Eckelstine didn't want to answer, but I began to swing the backpack, so he said reluctantly, "Clarice had too many unresolved issues concerning her own mother. I knew she'd make a terrible mess of a daughter, so I refused. But she was very stubborn, and I should have guessed she'd find a way around me."

"So she married Mitchell in Siberia to get custody of Sugar?"

Eckelstine rolled his eyes. "That's her name? Sugar? See what I mean? Clarice had no common sense where children are concerned. I knew it would turn out badly, and I was right, wasn't I?"

"Sugar seems okay to me."

"But isn't it obvious? Mitchell must have killed Clarice. Probably over some issue with the girl."

"What issue?"

"Who knows? Clarice ran hot and cold with Richie, either ignored him or went overboard with discipline. It all stems from her own childhood and abandonment issues, I'm sure. Somehow, Clarice blamed her mother for dying, and her displaced resentment boiled over."

I was trying to process all the psychobabble and didn't say anything.

As if I were a dense student, Eckelstine sighed and said, "Don't you get it? Clarice and Mitchell must have clashed over their adopted daughter. And Mitchell killed her."

"Or maybe you found out about Mitchell," I said. "And you got mad at Clarice and killed her for stepping out on you."

"That's ridiculous. I'd never let my emotions run away with me like that."

I could see Eckelstine was more annoyed with Clarice for getting herself killed than grieving for his loss. I said, "You wouldn't lose control? Not even if you learned Clarice was having great sex with another man?"

"Don't be insulting," Eckelstine said with disdain.

"What about Clarice's father?"

"What about him?"

"Could he have killed Clarice?"

"Why would he do that? He was a giant in his field, and Clarice followed in his footsteps. He should have been proud of her."

"Should have been?"

"I'm sure he was," Eckelstine amended. "What parent wouldn't be proud of a woman like her? Besides, he's hospitalized now. For his own safety."

"Could he be violent?"

"Leeford Crabtree is an intellectual, not violent. Mark my words, it was certainly Mitchell who killed Clarice. Isn't it usually the husband in these cases?"

"Usually, yes," I said, looking him straight in the eye.

Icy again, he said, "May I have my property now, please?"

I handed over the backpack. "Can I ask you one more thing?"

"If you must."

"How did Clarice's mother die?"

"She was killed during a robbery."

"Could she have been deliberately murdered? Targeted, I mean, and the killer made it look like a robbery gone wrong?"

"I very much doubt that," Eckelstine said. "It was a mistake, that's all. She was in the wrong place at the wrong time."

"And Clarice?"

"What about her?"

"She never got over her mother's murder?"

"She never wanted to," Eckelstine said. "That's my educated guess. She liked blaming all her problems on a thing that happened long ago. It was a kind of crutch for her."

When I didn't respond, Eckelstine shouldered his bag and walked away.

I let him go. I walked back to my truck, and Rooney gave me a wet greeting.

I sat in the truck for a while. Thinking. Trying not to feel anything, but thinking about Clarice and her kids. About her dead mother. And her screwed-up life.

Then I thought about her kids a little more and decided they deserved to understand how their mother died.

As for me, I needed some sex before I killed somebody.

❊ 14 ❊

Before any of the reporters caught sight of me, I trotted up the back porch steps of Eckelstine's house and looked through the glass in the door. I had pulled my hair into a ponytail and jammed a ball cap over it.

Inside, the kitchen was a mess. I saw dirty dishes and glassware everywhere. A carton of milk forgotten on the counter. Bowl of bananas turning black. A stack of pizza boxes four feet tall. Sure signs of men living alone. I guessed Clarice hadn't been here in days.

The door was unlocked. Which is practically an engraved invitation, right? So I opened the door and went inside.

From under the sink, the lower half of Reggie Ricco, owner of Busted Flush Plumbing, stretched out onto the kitchen floor. I recognized his belly, because his sweatshirt was all hiked up. He had a tattoo of a mermaid on his stomach, riding the wave of his considerable body hair. His head, shoulders, and arms were inside the cabinet, at work on the water pipes.

"Reggie?"

"Huh?" He banged his head as he came out from under the sink. When he saw it was me standing there, he dropped his wrench.

Reggie had graduated from high school with me, and his wife was Stripper Betty. She wasn't really an exotic dancer, but back in tenth grade she'd accidentally lost her shirt when it got caught on the school bus door, and she'd been known as Stripper Betty ever since. High school humor is timeless.

The color drained out of Reggie's face. "Roxy! What are you doing here?"

"I'm your assistant."

"I don't have an assistant."

"Shut up and listen, Reggie. For the purposes of the newspeople outside and anybody else who might wander in, today I'm your assistant, and if you say otherwise, I'm going to tell Betty about you and me."

Okay, I'm not proud of it. One afternoon a bunch of years ago, I'd bumped into Reggie, bought him a couple of beers, and ridden him like a circus pony. It was before he'd married Betty, but the interlude had so frightened Reggie that he still lived in fear that anyone—particularly his wife—might find out what he'd allowed to happen.

On the floor, Reggie stared up at me and gulped.

I said, "I'm not here to jump you, Reggie. I'm just going to have a look around the house."

"You c-can't do that. I'm bonded. If you steal something—"

"I'm not going to steal anything. I'm just looking."

"But—"

"Dammit, is there anybody else in the house?"

"A kid. Teenager. He's upstairs in his room, I think."

"Okay, when does the father get back?"

"He said he'd be gone a couple of hours. He called me because the sink backed up, and he says they're having some kind of funeral thing here soon, so I came right over to— Look, Roxy, I—"

"It'll be okay. Forget I'm here."

While Reggie stared in horror, I prowled out of the kitchen.

I peeked into the dining room. The table was covered with books, newspapers, and coffee cups. And more pizza boxes. In the living room, I decided the furniture had been chosen by a decorator who liked hotel lobbies. A big sofa and chairs in contrasting prints, tables with no scratches, color-coordinated lamps.

The only weird thing about the living room was a giant, ugly painting over the fireplace. It depicted an elephant with long hair, chasing what looked like cavemen with spears.

Art is something I don't understand. Weird stuff is what people like now, not pretty things. Me, I like a nice painting of Italian beaches or maybe flowers.

I went over and looked more closely at the hairy elephant. There was a little brass plate at the bottom of the picture frame. I blinked and looked closer.

RHONDA

It was printed right there on the frame. The hairy elephant's name was Rhonda.

"I'll be damned." My voice echoed in the living room. "The professor was looking for his elephant. Rhonda is an animal."

Was an animal. Some kind of animal. Megafauna. A mastodon or a woolly mammoth or something. What was the difference?

I shook my head at the strangeness of people and took a cautious look through the window curtains at the street. The press hadn't moved from their stakeout. I twitched the curtains closed and started nosing around again. I wasn't sure what else I was looking for. But I figured I'd recognize something useful like an elephant with a name.

A stack of bills lay in a basket by the front door. I flipped through them. Recent postmarks. Utility companies, a Nordstrom bill, and a bunch of junk mail. Nothing Sherlock Holmes might interpret as a clue.

About that time, I heard music somewhere and followed the sound to a den in the basement. There I found Richie Eckelstine, the snotty son, sitting at a big table under the glare of fluorescent lights, hacking up some cloth with a huge pair of scissors.

My first thought was that he had good taste in music. The Clash finished up one of their hits, and then the tortured voice of Joey Ramone started wailing.

Richie caught sight of me and used his thumb to turn off the CD player. Instant silence.

He sat on a tall stool in jeans, a T-shirt, and a webbed belt with fringe. His bare arms were skinny and pale. His face was punctured with less jewelry than before, but he still had a ring through one eyebrow. He paused in the act of cutting with the scissors.

He stared at me. "What are you doing here? Looking for somebody else to beat up?"

The room was clearly his lair—Big-screen TV, video games, several pairs of sneakers left on the floor. He had painted graffiti all over the walls. Neon colors swirled around in big, puffy letters that made no sense. Ugly as hell.

And the big table in the center of the room—I decided it was an old Ping-Pong table—was littered with shredded cloth. And of all things, a sewing machine.

I said, "I was just talking to your dad. Apologizing. You know, for yesterday's—uh—incident."

He gave me a suspicious stare, then used the scissors to point at my face. "You have a fat lip. Did my old man do that to you?"

"Either him or the other guy. I forget which one has the million-dollar arm."

"The other guy," the kid said. "My father couldn't hurt a flea."

"He did a pretty good imitation yesterday." I don't know why I wanted to make Eckelstine sound like a hero, but here I was, doing just that. Something in the kid's manner, I guess. He didn't have yesterday's bravado anymore. I said, "Yesterday must have been a bad day for you."

The kid went back to concentrating on the scrap of cloth in his hands. He focused closely on trimming an edge. "You mean me finding out my mother is a slut."

"Hey, watch it with the insults, kid."

"She was, though. A slut."

"Just because she married two men doesn't make her promiscuous. Maybe she married the other guy for a good reason."

"Who knows?" Richie snapped. "Who cares?"

"You must care a little," I said. "She was your mom, after all."

If he teared up suddenly, he didn't want to show it. He turned his face away from me and got busy fluffing through the fabric on the table. He said, "We didn't get along. Never have. So it's no big that she's gone now, you know? Hell, maybe my life will get easier."

"That's pretty tough talk. You must be a strong person."

"I do all right," he said gruffly.

"So what's all this stuff?" I attempted to sound casual as I looked around the table. His piles of material turned out to be clothes, I finally discerned. A few finished dresses hung on a rack nearby. "Are you helping with a school play or something?"

"They're not costumes."

"What are they, then?"

"Couture," Richie said firmly. But a quick glance at him told me he wasn't quite so sure. His voice had a note of defiance, though. "They're clothing. Dresses, to be exact."

"Dresses, huh? Kinda weird looking."

"Cutting-edge," he corrected. "I'm working on developing my own vision."

"What? You trying to be a dress designer?" I couldn't mask my amazement.

"Why not?" he demanded. "It's like sketching and drawing. And designing dresses seems—I don't know—like an extension of that."

"Your parents okay with this hobby?"

"My father hates it. But my mom—my stepmom—she was kinda interested, I guess."

"Clarice thought it was okay for you to design clothes?"

"I made a few things for her, and she liked them, yes."

For the first time, I was hearing something good about Clarice's parenting skills. At least, she wasn't a total loss.

I nudged the kid with my elbow. "Got anything I can wear to a wedding on Saturday, kid?"

Firmly, he said, "I don't do special-occasion pieces. No red carpet, no prom or bridesmaids. Couture, that's what I do."

I flipped through a few of the hangers on the rack beside him. I had no clue what I was looking at. It was all ugly. Black and brown fabrics had been ripped and shredded, then somehow knitted back together in weird shapes. The occasional feather poked out. Some of the seams were held together with safety pins.

"What these dresses need is a little color," I said. "Maybe some buttons or a ruffle or something. It's all gloomy."

"Thanks," he said. "I'll keep that advice in mind."

I heard his scornful tone and grinned. "This seems like an unusual hobby for a kid like you."

"Like me?" he said carefully. "Are you insinuating I'm gay? Because I'm not."

"What I meant was, you're a young guy from Pittsburgh. We're a long way from Paris."

He sighed. "Don't I know it."

"Just seems like you could be spending all your free time watching reruns of old Super Bowl games like most of the guys in this city."

"I like football," he said. "Just so happens, I like making dresses, too."

I yanked out one of the so-called dresses. To me, it looked like a bunch of bandages wrapped sideways, dyed weird dark colors, and then frayed with cuticle scissors. I held it against myself.

The kid made an involuntary move—like he wanted to snatch the dress out of my hands. But he managed to say quite calmly, "That's really expensive fabric, you know. Maybe a thousand dollars' worth of silk."

"Holy shit." I almost dropped the hanger. Carefully, I put it back on the rack. "Where do you get that kind of money?"

He fell silent for a moment.

Then he said, "My stepmother gave me an allowance. She thought my creative outlet was good therapy after I got into some—well. Maybe it was good therapy. My father disagrees, of course. He thinks it's gay."

"He's wrong," I said. "Looks to me like you're actually interested in women's bodies. Which is normal for a kid. Actually, you're really gifted. Not that I know much about fashion, that is."

He looked me up and down. "That's painfully obvious."

I laughed.

To me, the kid seemed like he was trying to bluff his way past being very sad. The thought of him being left alone on his own the day after his stepmother was found murdered made me want to chase down his father and punch him in the face.

So I said, "Hey, I'm sorry about your mom. She might have had some faults, but I bet you miss her."

Kid shrugged. "I'll get over it."

I took a chance. "What's going to happen to Rhonda now?"

He sat up straighter, surprised by my question. "What?"

"Your grandfather was asking about Rhonda the other night. It seemed to me like he thought your mom was supposed to be looking after Rhonda."

Richie snorted and went back to concentrating on his weird fabric. "What's to look after? A bunch of bones, that's all."

"Where are they? At the Professor's house?"

"Who knows? Who cares? Not me. I don't care about any of that. What are you doing here, anyway? I think you should leave."

There was something in Richie Eckelstine that I liked. He was rebellious, judging by the criminal record, but he had standards. His dresses looked butt ugly, yet kinda sexy, but what did I know? It was probably a good thing that he was being creative. He was tough, too. I had a feeling he'd turn out okay.

But I made a mental note to check on him now and then.

In the meantime, I wanted to learn more about Mitch Mitchell.

❈ 15 ❈

Back in my truck, Rooney snored with his jaws clamped around his bone. It had begun to smell funky.

Cracking my window open for some fresh air, I pulled my phone out to call Bug to let him know I was on my way to meet him for lunch. I could hardly wait to tell him I'd figured out who Rhonda was. I'd have to leave out a few details, like breaking into the Eckelstine house, of course.

But my cell phone rang in my hand.

It was Flynn, and he sounded tense. "Hey."

"Hey, yourself. I haven't seen your friend the skater yet."

"That's not why I'm calling," he said shortly. "I need some help."

"You finally admit you want my body." I was feeling good again. I knew who Rhonda was!

The joke didn't amuse him. "Shut up and listen, will you? I'm in a jam."

I laughed. "What happened? The Health Department? They found out about Rooney in the kitchen yesterday?"

"It's a longer story than that. Where are you?"

I glanced around to decide what neighborhood I was passing through. "In Garfield. Why?"

"Pick me up behind St. Stan's, will you?"

"Sure. Let me drop off Rooney first. I'll be there in five minutes. That soon enough?"

He had already disconnected.

Intrigued, I dropped the dog off at the yard so he could sleep, and in a couple more minutes I pulled into the parking lot behind St. Stanislaus Kostka. St. Stan's was a Polish cathedral-style church in the Strip, famous for being one of Pope John Paul's tourist stops before he became everybody's favorite pope. Before that, back in 1936 when the nearby Banana Company blew up across the street, the church's congregation had to remove the ruined fancy bonnets on top of its steeples. But the church still looked like a special place, and the fact that it sat in the middle of the city's grimy warehouse district just made it more quirky and beloved.

Flynn came out of the shadow of the old church and crossed the asphalt in a few long strides. He wore a leather jacket with the collar turned up and a ballcap pulled low over his face. He looked like half the men in Pittsburgh, except he still had the best butt of any guy I've ever known.

Wistfully, I found myself remembering the old days when we used to push each other into backseats, dark corners, even his cousin's bed for hot sex. We fought a lot, but we laughed back then, too. Silly stuff would set us off, like the time we spent an afternoon on his dad's boat, rocking with the water, listening to some guys fishing from shore who talked about sneaking off while their wives went shopping.

We told each other we'd never be tied down the way those people were.

Well, we got our wish.

Flynn opened the passenger door and swung up into the truck.

"Jeez, what's all over this seat?"

"It won't kill you. Get in."

He slammed the door and said, "Let's go."

I spun the truck in a U-turn. It felt good to be on the run with him again. "What's going on? Who's on your tail?"

He shot me a sour glance, apparently not joining me in the flashback. "A writer from *Food* magazine."

"Uh, forgive me for asking a dumb question, but isn't that a good thing?"

"Under most circumstances, yes. Today, not so much."

"Tell, tell."

Flynn slumped in the passenger seat, staying low to avoid being seen. He took off his ball cap and ran his hand over his shaved head. "The dinner for Dooce last night? It went really well. He had this writer guy with him and a couple of musicians from his band—all of them serious about food. His assistant, that Jeremy guy, kept coming back, asking us for more. We gave them everything in the kitchen—the appetizers, the fish, the lamb, and some venison, too. Even the desserts were a hit. The bacon ice cream was, like, insanely good. But the soup—" Flynn stopped and shook his head.

"The soup was bad?"

I had never seen Flynn looking so flustered. With one hand, he toyed with his cap; the other rubbed the side of his face while he scanned the passing sidewalks. I wondered if he was thinking of roadside bombs in Afghanistan.

"No, no," he said. "The soup was fantastic. Calamari and mussels in a beef-marrow broth. Very light, but intense. The guys went nuts over it. Even I had to admit, it was pretty great. Maybe the best I've ever done. Soup is tricky, you know? It can be completely ordinary, but with a little nuance—"

"Cut to the chase," I said. "What happened?"

"The food writer wants my recipe. Jeremy brought him to the restaurant this morning. I told them I didn't give out recipes—I mean, most of the soups I make up on the spot—but Jeremy pulled a gun."

"A gun! Jesus! Did you shoot him?"

"Hell, no. To be honest, my gun was locked in my desk drawer. But jeez, he was serious. They wanted a whole symposium, practically. So I went over every ingredient. I mean, what's worth getting shot over? Then we got to the bones, you know?"

"The bones?"

"The soup bones. Did you see the box on the floor yesterday? I had a bunch of beef bones from a buddy I know. He raises Black Angus cattle, terrific sirloin and filet mignon. I use the bones for soup all the time. Yesterday afternoon, Julio cut up the bones with a hacksaw like always, and he threw a couple into a stock pot with some vegetables and a *garni* to simmer down the flavors. Standard procedure, nothing new. Except the bone was different. I should have noticed earlier, but I didn't until I fished it out before adding the calamari and mussels and serving the soup. I knew right away it wasn't one of the bones I got from my friend. It made all the difference, though. It definitely changed the whole composition, everything."

Faintly, I said, "One bone did all that?"

"Yeah, last night Dooce and his people went nuts over the soup. And I—I don't know how it happened, but the writer decided he had to do, like, the whole story on this damn bone."

"A story on a bone," I said, already thinking that if Flynn figured out even half the story, he was going to kill me.

"Yeah, so I went into the cooler to get a closer look at what was left. Rox, it's not anything I've ever seen before." Flynn pulled off his cap and ran one hand over the stubble on his head. "To tell the truth, it didn't look like anything people ought to be eating. It was really well aged. Julio was just doing what I told him to do, see? It's not his fault. It's my kitchen, my responsibility to serve only wholesome ingredients to the public. But the writer, he's insisting he wants to see this magic bone. And then a local restaurant critic got wind of the soup story, and she started calling me. Even the chef over at Mes Amies heard about it, and suddenly he shows up at the back door, asking questions, too."

"About the bone?"

"Right. A stupid bone." His energy suddenly evaporated like a kid's toy losing its windup. He rubbed his face. "I just need to get away for a few hours, you know? Normally, I'd go home and sleep, but Jeremy' got that damn gun—hell, I'm just beat."

"Because of a bone."

"Stupid, right? Look, I need a place to sleep before the evening service." He turned to me. "I thought maybe I could crash at your place for a couple of hours. Nobody would think to look for me there."

"Thanks."

"Sorry. What do you say? Can I use your bed?"

I had a lot to say, but Flynn wasn't going to like hearing it.

"Where's your gun now?"

"What? Back at the restaurant. Locked in my desk. Why?"

If he was unarmed, he couldn't kill me. "About the bone . . ." I began slowly.

"What about it?"

I was pretty sure his soup bone had been the one Rooney dug out of the Crabtree freezer. I hadn't noticed until long after we'd left the restaurant yesterday that Rooney's bone was considerably smaller than the one he'd started out with. At first, I thought he'd just gnawed it down to size, but now I realized he'd exchanged it for one of the bones in Flynn's kitchen.

Which meant the bone in Flynn's magic soup probably came from one of the extinct animals in Professor Crabtree's crazy collection.

"Flynn," I said, "how old do you think a bone has to be before it's considered inedible?"

"What?"

I didn't dare take my eyes off the road as I drove across the river and headed up to my house. "I mean, if it's frozen and then boiled, you probably cook out all the impurities, right?"

"What the hell are you talking about?"

"Nothing," I said hastily. "Forget it. What you need is a few hours of sleep before you go back to work."

"Mind if I use your bed?"

"Not in the slightest," I said. "I won't need it until tonight."

"By then," he said with a weary sigh, "maybe this whole soup thing will blow over."

I dropped him in front of my house and peeled the key off my ring. I handed it over. "Sweet dreams."

After he slid out of the truck and slammed the door closed, I intended to head back across the river. Maybe I could sneak into the restaurant and steal back the old bone before any of the employees came into the kitchen for the dinner shift.

But I saw Jane Doe sitting on the porch steps next door. She had her knees drawn up to her chin, and she was smoking a cigarette. She wore a pair of tan slacks with ballet flat shoes and a pink sweater—very Talbots. Her hair was pushed back with a pair of big black sunglasses. A Diet Coke sat beside her hip.

I eased the truck against the curb and rolled down my window.

"You hanging in there, Jane?"

She pasted on her brightest smile and waved. "Hi! Yes! I'm great!"

"Where are the kids?"

She tapped her forefinger on her lips, then pointed up. "Taking their naps upstairs. At least, they're supposed to be. I heard them singing a minute ago, though, so they haven't gone to sleep yet."

"Singing's good," I said. "Your boyfriend hasn't come around, has he?"

She shook her head quickly. "No, I haven't told him where we are."

"You've talked to him, though?"

"Well," she said, and stopped.

"Cell phone?" I guessed. "Did you call him, or did he call you?"

She got up from the steps, tossed her cigarette onto the sidewalk, and picked up her Diet Coke. She stepped on the cigarette and came over to the truck. Her hair was combed, her face scrubbed clean of makeup. But the bruises on her cheeks and around her eyes glared vivid blue and green—probably scary as hell for the kids to see.

She said, "He's sorry for what happened. He says it won't happen again."

I resisted the urge to scream at her.

Then I realized she had mixed some Jack Daniel's into her Diet Coke. I could smell it on her breath.

Instead of screaming, I said, "Where does a lady like you meet a fireman?"

Her expression brightened. "Oh, I love firemen! We met at a charity event. He was helping to sell one of the calendars—you know, the kind with pictures of guys without their shirts? He was Mr. April. I was asked to be the celebrity auctioneer. We met that night, and we've been together ever since. Well, until this happened."

"I don't think it just happened, hon. He did it to you all by himself."

The starry-eyed look left her face, and she backed away from the truck. She said, "I think I hear Emily calling."

I held back a sigh. "Okay. I'll check on you again later."

She nodded, mustering her usual perky enthusiasm. "Great!"

I put the truck into gear and pulled away. I wanted to wash her brain out with peroxide. In another day or so, if she had the chance, she'd move out and go back to the abusive fireman. I knew it. Before that happened, I needed to find a way to convince her otherwise.

And the drinking? Looked to me like she just needed a nip at noontime. I'd call Adasha to check on her later this afternoon, though. I didn't like the idea of the weather girl getting drunk when the kids were in her charge.

My cell phone rang.

I expected to hear Bug, wondering why I was late for lunch.

But Sister Bob said in my ear, "Roxana Marie, I'm going over to Shadyside Memory Support Center to visit Dutch Campisano. Want to come along?"

❈ 16 ❈

I picked up Sister Bob in front of Mary Frances O'Malley's house, where Bob had just attended a lunch party with some neighborhood ladies. Dressed in another colorful track suit, she carried some fancy Tupperware balanced on one upturned hand. A plastic bag from the CVS drugstore hung from her other elbow.

She clambered into the truck. "Boy, Tupperware sure has some wonderful inventions! See this? It's an egg carrier. Perfect for deviled eggs for a summer picnic."

"Do nuns eat deviled eggs?"

"Of course we do. And this? It's for an angel food cake! You put the cake inside, and the frosting doesn't get squished!"

"I'm sensing a theme. Angels and devils."

Sister Bob cackled. "You're a hoot, Roxana. Here, I saved you a tuna sandwich from the luncheon. Mary Frances made it herself. The tuna has pickles and grapes in it. Delicious!"

I already had a little indigestion just thinking about a big-time rock star and his entourage eating food containing bits of an animal that had been extinct for a couple thousand years.

So I said, "Not right now, thanks. Maybe later. What's in the plastic bag?"

She opened it and pulled out a box of drugstore chocolates and a cheap set of checkers. "Our key to the Alzheimer's center. I never knew a nurse who could resist a box of chocolates."

"And the checkers?"

"A gift. They're a very calming pastime. Dutch loved checkers." She tucked everything back into the plastic bag. "Between jobs for your uncle Carmine, Dutch used to be a photographer, did you know that? He took all the school pictures for years, and then he got into trouble for selling different pictures on the street corner. So he took up checkers to take his mind off things. I used to play checkers with him for hours."

"How well did you know Dutch?" I wondered nervously if he'd ever taken Sister Bob's photograph.

"We were classmates a long time ago. Before he started taking dirty pictures. He deserves our forgiveness, Roxana."

Dutch probably deserved a jail sentence, but I let it go.

A few minutes later, I pulled through a set of stone pillars and stopped at the security gate. I noticed the layout of the center involved high fences, locked gates, and plenty of security cameras. A guard leaned out of his booth with a clipboard in hand and gave the mess of the Monster Truck a dubious look. "Visiting?"

"Yes."

"Sign here."

I signed, and the guard directed me to a parking space where he could keep an eye on the truck. Maybe he thought the graffiti and the soap and the eggs were going to jump onto other cars.

Sister Bob and I got out in front of a life-size statue of the Virgin Mary, holding her robed arms wide and looking pensive. Behind her was an eight-foot fence topped with razor wire.

"Our Lady of Incarceration," I said drily.

"Families expect their loved ones to be completely protected—from themselves as much as anything dangerous. A couple of patients walk off the grounds, and they'd have lawsuits up the wazoo."

Sister Bob led the way up a set of wide stone steps, and we pushed through a revolving door to get into the lobby. There, a bulletproof glass door swung open automatically before us. About ten feet ahead, a stout woman sat behind the circular desk. Her fingers with their talonlike nails hovered over a set of buttons that looked as if they could lock down the whole facility faster than Leavenworth.

She smiled up at us from her chair as we approached. "Why, Sister Bob! I haven't seen you in ages. What can I do to help you today?"

"Waysilla, we're here for a visit. This is my niece, Roxy Abruzzo. And look, I brought your favorite. Mint meltaways."

Waysilla's broad face brightened at the sight of the box. "Aren't you the sweetest thing!"

While Sister Bob and her friend discussed candy, I took a look around.

The lobby of the Shadyside Memory Support Center was divided down the middle by a fence made to look like a pretty room divider. On one side of the fence, the men's lounge was so heavily paneled in mahogany that it looked like the inside of a humidor. A handful of male patients sat in leather chairs and stared at a flat-screen television tuned to a baseball game that might have been recorded a couple of decades ago. The film was in black and white. The players wore baggy uniforms.

On the other side of the fence, the ladies' lounge was decorated with chintz sofas and so many oversized paintings of flowers that an English tea party might bust out any minute. Except the ladies were mostly sleeping upright in their flowered chairs.

Waysilla typed our names into a computer, and a nearby printer kicked out two neon yellow strips of vinyl. Waysilla rolled the strips into ID bracelets and fastened them around our wrists. "Now, Sister Bob, what's this I hear about you leaving the convent?"

"It's true, Waysilla. I'm a free woman."

"Well, don't let any of the old men around here catch you. They're all looking for young single chicks."

"A young chick who'll wipe their chins and wash their clothes. I'm not trading one higher calling for another."

Waysilla cackled. "You go, girlfriend!"

With our ID bracelets on, Sister Bob led the way, and soon friendly staff buzzed us through a series of hallways. Some employees wore hospital scrubs, but most were dressed in neat street clothes. Maybe I expected guard uniforms, but it seemed everyone was trying hard not to make the place feel like a jail.

Sister Bob knew half the people we encountered, and they all chatted with her pleasantly while I refrained from tapping my foot with impatience.

We passed a door that was painted red and decorated with photographs and more drawings of hairy elephants. I stopped. The nameplate on the door said, Leeford Crabtree.

"I'll be damned."

Sister Bob turned. "What now?"

"Sister Bob, would you mind talking to Dutch yourself for a while? There's someone else I'd like to see."

"Sure. Here, give these checkers to your friend. Try playing with him. It might help keep him calm."

"Thanks, Bob."

She gave Dutch's door a brisk knock and let herself in.

Conscious of the security cameras watching my every move, I likewise knocked on Crabtree's door and went inside when I heard a gruff voice.

Professor Crabtree was shuffling back and forth across his room, moving from the bed to the sofa to the window and back again like a caged animal at the zoo. His tall figure was dressed in a pair of khaki pants hiked high on his torso and held in place with a pair of suspenders decorated with dinosaurs. Underneath, he wore a white dress shirt, thin with age. His white hair had been combed, and in general he looked more presentable than when I'd seen him last.

"Professor Crabtree?"

He straightened his shoulders and turned around. "Yes?"

"I'm Roxy Abruzzo. Do you remember me?"

"I have dementia! Of course I don't remember you," he said, then squinted closer. "You're an attractive specimen, though. Good bone structure, a healthy complexion. I suppose I should remember who you are."

"Not necessarily. We only met once. Do you mind if I sit down?"

He remained at the window, keeping his distance and looking cautious as I eased down on the sofa. "What do you want?"

"To talk a little. About your daughter, Clarice."

"Clarice?"

"Right, your daughter who works at the museum."

"What about her?"

I wondered if I should give him my condolences. Or might that upset him? I chickened out and said, "She's—well, when was the last time you saw her?"

He shook his head and began to pace. It didn't take much to agitate him. "Why is that important? It's not important! Clarice can take care of herself. It's Rhonda I'm worried about."

"Right, Rhonda. Do you think something's wrong with Rhonda?"

"Of course not. She's perfect. The most perfect example of her kind I ever found. I want to know she's safe, that's all." The professor knocked his fist on the windowsill for emphasis. "I want to be sure she's in good hands."

"Was Clarice taking care of her?"

He swung on me, and his face darkened. "Clarice was supposed to be looking after Rhonda. But for years she hasn't let me see her. Not even a visit! But I—I—"

He lost his train of thought.

"You wanted Clarice to keep Rhonda safe. But you were worried, weren't you?"

The professor gave me a steady examination, as if trying to figure out if I was someone to be trusted. "I thought she was safe. Should I be worried now? What has Clarice done to her?"

"What do you think Clarice might have done?"

"That's the whole point!" He stalked across the floor and flapped his arms peevishly. "How am I supposed to know about Rhonda when I'm locked up here all the time?"

"Did you go looking for her a couple of nights back? The night you went to your house? You were looking for Rhonda there?"

He frowned. "What are you talking about?"

"You left this place and went to see Clarice."

"Clarice," he announced suddenly, "can't be trusted."

"Why not?"

"She's sneaky. Always looking for money. Always more money! She has expenses, she says. Who could have that many expenses?"

A woman trying to finance two families could have a lot of expenses, I thought. Especially if one family included a skater who trained extensively and traveled all over the country. And who knew how much it cost to finance a budding fashion designer?

But I asked, "She tries to get money from you to pay her expenses?"

"I don't have any money!" The professor leaned so close that I could smell the harsh hospital soap on him. His attention wavered, and he lost the thread of conversation. "What's in the box?"

"Checkers. Want to play?"

"Now?" I had startled him. "Here? With you?"

"Why not?"

I opened the box and unfolded the board on the low table in front of the sofa. He grabbed the package of game pieces and organized them on the red and black squares. Watching him, I wondered how his brain worked these days. He obviously knew how to play the game, and he was eager to start. But more recent events confounded him.

We played a game, and he cleaned my clock.

In five minutes, he'd taken all my pieces and jumped the last one in the center of the board.

"Damn," I said. "You're good."

"You let me win. It's very insulting to be patronized."

"I did not let you win!"

"No? Let's play again."

This time, he whipped my ass in under three minutes.

"You're not even trying," he complained. "Where's your strategy?"

"Strategy? In checkers?"

"Young lady, you're a sad excuse for an intellect. Set up the board again. There now, see? You're going straight up the middle again. That's just asking to be decimated. Take the side route instead, where your piece is protected. Get it? Then move this piece, so. Your goal is to get as many pieces crowned as possible, so sacrifice this one—yes—to escape and there—! Well done. The escape tactic is a good one. It requires planning, sacrifice, a diversion, and voilà! Now, let's try a basic pursuit, and I'll show you how to trigger a trap."

The game absorbed me, and it wasn't until he'd guided me through a slightly less humiliating defeat that I realized how the game invigorated Crabtree. He seemed sharp and engaged. His eyes gleamed, and when he instructed me, his face took on more animation than before.

"I get it," I said. "There's skill involved."

"Not just skill, but planning and strategy. And a predatory attitude. My grandson, for example, is especially gifted at the game. He should be playing chess by now, but he likes the swiftness of checkers."

"Richie," I said. "I met him."

Professor Crabtree smiled. "He's a sharp one, isn't he?"

"What about Sugar? Sherelle?"

The old man's confidence wavered. "Who?"

"The ice-skater."

He bent his head over the board and began to gather up the pieces. "I don't know any ice-skaters. Richie had a skateboard for a while. I wish he was more interested in science."

I was sorry to see Professor Crabtree's confidence fade again. But it gave me an opening. I leaned forward. "What happened to your wife, Professor?"

His face froze. "I don't know what you're talking about."

"It's okay. I'm not trying to trick you. I'm just wondering about your wife's murder."

"I don't like to be tricked."

"Me neither. I hate it, in fact." I smiled at him and decided I couldn't ask if he'd had any part in her death. "Okay, here's an easy one for you. How did you get past all the locked doors and the staff, Professor?"

He slanted a grin up at me, his wits returned. "I pulled the fire alarm. It's still the surest way to get out of a building."

❧ 17 ❧

From Dutch, Sister Bob learned the name of his road-ragey son. Tony Campisano. "He's been on a cruise since Sunday."

"A cruise? Isn't he on probation?"

"I don't know. Dutch didn't mention that. He lost his train of thought. We had a cigarette after that," she said sadly. "He doesn't remember his own name, let alone any information that you might want."

"Wait a second. Nuns smoke?"

"Why not?"

"Do you know how much cigarette smoke I blew out of bathroom windows so the nuns wouldn't catch me?"

"And aren't you smarter for having figured out how to do that? We improved your education, Roxana."

"It's a damn sneaky way to educate," I grumbled.

After dropping off Sister Bob at Loretta's house and declining her invitation to come inside to watch *General Hospital,* I sat in the truck for a few minutes and thought about what to do next.

I figured Clarice had been making extra cash by selling off bits and pieces of Rhonda. And now that Clarice was dead, it looked as if Husband Numero Uno, Eckelstine, was doing the same thing. I was willing to bet he'd had a bone in his backpack early this morning.

I checked my cell phone and found Stony's number.

He picked up after three rings, sounding sleepy. The boss of Rusted Roses rarely got out of bed before midafternoon.

"Hey, Roxy," he said on a yawn. "Did you listen to the tapes I sent you? Know the harmonies yet?"

"Yeah, I'm almost finished," I said. "Stony, is this for real? I mean, are we really gonna work with Dooce?"

I heard the snap of a lighter, and Stony drew a long breath. Probably his first weed of the day. Impatiently, I waited while he held the smoke in his lungs.

Finally, he said, "Yeah, babe, it's a sure thing. He's an old buddy of mine. You in?"

Stony had always claimed to be pals with Dooce, but none of us ever believed him. "Sure. We going to get a chance to rehearse with him before the concert?"

Stony let out his smoke on a long, lingering sigh. "I doubt it. That's just not cool, you know? We might meet him at the sound check, but that's it. I don't have to worry about you asking him for autographs and pictures, do I?"

"Don't worry about me. Listen, Stony, do you know what kind of stuff Dooce might collect?"

"Huh?"

"Does he collect anything?"

"Like beer bottles or something? Hell, I don't know. He's an old friend, but c'mon, we're not, like, dating, you know?"

"Do you know his assistant? Jeremy? Could you ask him?"

"Jeremy's a surly SOB. He's Dooce's knee-breaker. Stay away from him, Roxy. He does anything Dooce tell him to do, and more. But he's not exactly housebroken, if you know what I mean."

"He hurts people?"

"If he thinks it's in Dooce's best interest, yeah."

"Okay, never mind. Where do I show up?"

"Come to Entrance B. I'll have a stage pass waiting for you."

"Thanks, Stony."

"Peace out, babe."

I hung up. I had wanted to know if the collecting Flynn had mentioned Dooce did might include woolly mammoth bones. Stony was no help. I'd have to wait until I met Dooce myself. That is, if I didn't get into trouble with the Jeremy dude. He sounded like a jerk to avoid.

I checked my watch. I could have called Bug to apologize for standing him up at lunch, I supposed, but he might have a few uncomfortable questions for me to answer.

Instead, I decided to drive out to the skating rink to talk to Flynn's friend, the figure skater.

Because of traffic, it took almost forty minutes to reach the Harmar Rink. I spent the drive singing harmony to Dooce's greatest hits. When I got to the parking lot, I found myself swept along on a tide of little hockey players—mostly preadolescent boys carrying big sticks over their shoulders and jabbering with excitement. Their mothers lugged heavy bags of gear through the double doors of the cavernous rink.

I found Jenny Osterman in the locker room, and she agreed to talk to me over a drink at the bar next door. We walked across the parking lot together. If all the hockey moms carried bags for their sons and shouted encouragement from the bleachers, it looked as if a fair number of the hockey dads came to the bar to watch sports on the big-screen televisions.

"I've had a long day," Jenny said when we'd ordered a draft apiece. She nibbled from the bowl of the pretzel mix the bartender put in front of us. "I start teaching lessons at five in the morning. Kids come in at crazy hours—before school, after school. By the end of the day when the hockey leagues start, I'm dizzy from spinning."

"I bet. How do you know Sugar Mitchell?"

I'd already asked her about Sugar, but it had been my connection to Flynn that intrigued her.

"You're Roxy?" She had looked at me with open curiosity when I'd introduced myself back at the rink. "You're not what I expected, I guess. Patrick has mentioned you once or twice."

"In flattering terms, I'm sure."

"Yes, actually. He's a great guy. How come you're not together? I mean, with a daughter and so much history, what's holding you back?"

"Do you know Flynn very well?"

She had smiled. "Not as well as I'd like."

"He comes with a few problems."

"Don't they all," Jenny had said on a sigh.

In the bar, after a delicate sip of beer, Jenny said, "Sugar Mitchell is a good skater. Maybe she'll be a great one. But she's hard to coach."

"What does that mean exactly?"

"I was her instructor when she was a beginner. But I wasn't advanced enough for her. At least, that's what her dad told me five years ago. Now Sugar trains with Nadia—a skater from Minnesota who flies here twice a week to coach a select few girls who are on the fast track to the Olympic team."

"Sugar is Olympic caliber?"

Jenny shrugged and sipped more beer. With her slim, athletic figure and pretty face, she could have been a beauty queen. No pretensions, though. She had the grammar and the manners of someone raised in the suburbs and educated in a nice school with good teachers. I pegged her for a hard worker who was trying to make a living at a sport she probably loved as a teenager. Living the dream. I respected that.

She said, "Sugar has the drive. Whether she has the talent and personality to grow beyond where she is now—that's the question. If she was more open to coaching, she could really make it. She has a big ego, and that's important. She needs to be mentally strong as well as physically capable. But—she's difficult."

"What do you mean, difficult?"

"Sugar's ego . . . well, she can be hard to handle. Which is good and bad. Her parents were very supportive, and that helps."

"Is it expensive to train as a skater?"

"Depends. You can do it on a shoestring, if you must. My mom volunteered in the snack bar. Dad swept the ice. You can take group lessons, not private sessions, to save money. I couldn't travel to competitions every weekend. But Sugar? She's going first-class all the way. And her dad is devoted. He's here all the time."

"And Sugar's mother?"

"Wow, shocking that she was murdered, right? I have to admit, I never saw her here. In all the years I've worked at the rink, I never met her. I'm kinda glad, actually. What kind of mother raises a kid who's so nasty to be around?"

"Sugar is nasty?"

"You won't repeat this, will you?" Jenny had clearly decided to trust me, because she finally confided, "Sugar's a bitch on wheels. Rude to everyone. Very demanding. She doesn't have many friends at the rink. Which isn't unusual. The girls compete against each other, and it's hard to learn to be a friend to someone who beats you out for a ribbon. But most girls learn to handle it. Sugar, though? No way."

I thought about the girl I'd seen at the Crabtree house the morning Eckelstine and Mitchell learned they'd shared a wife. She had seemed sweet to me. I wondered if Jenny had some kind of grudge against the kid.

Jenny said, "I mean, what girl comes to practice the day her mother's found dead? That's cold, isn't it?"

"Maybe she needed to be where she feels happiest. Everybody handles grief differently."

Jenny looked doubtful. "If something happened to my mom, I'd never get over it."

"Yeah," I said. "Unless she was a drunk who didn't pay the electric bill and threw dishes when she got mad."

Jenny blinked. "Sugar's mother was that bad?"

"No," I said hastily. "Not Sugar's mother."

"I heard her mom was going to make some changes, though."

"What kind of changes?"

"Nadia said Sugar was dropping out of private lessons. Apparently, Sugar's mother objected to the cost of coaching and everything."

"She was pulling the plug on Sugar's skating career?"

"That's what Nadia said. I saw Sugar bawling in the locker room a couple of weeks ago. I tried talking to her, but she had a tantrum, so I walked away. I never got the full story."

If Clarice wanted to end Sugar's skating, that suggested a whole new bunch of theories. I wonder if Bug knew about Clarice's decision to withhold the money. And what Mitch Mitchell might have to say about that.

I realized Jenny was watching my face with curiosity, so I tried to smooth away my frown. "Listen, I really appreciate you talking to me."

"No problem. If you don't mind, how come you're asking all these questions?"

"I knew Clarice, Sugar's mom. And I hate the thought of her kids growing up without a mother. Without answers."

She bobbed her head. "That's nice. Patrick says you're nice."

That surprised me. "Then he hasn't been paying close attention."

With a smile, she finished her beer and set it on the bar. "He says you're funny, too. That can be very sexy."

"Yeah, well, the sex was never the problem." I pulled some cash from my hip pocket and waved it at the bartender. "Thanks for talking with me."

"Sure. Tell Patrick I said hi."

Fat chance.

I climbed back into the truck and started the engine to warm up. The late-afternoon air smelled like snow, and I found a pair of gloves in the mess of junk behind the front seat.

I'd learned a lot from Jenny. More than I'd expected.

I tried phoning Bug Duffy, but he didn't answer his cell. I decided not to leave a message.

I needed more information—the kind the cops probably had already. For me, there was only one way to learn stuff from the police without actually asking an officer of the law.

I dialed Sage's cell phone.

"Mom!" She sounded guilty. "How are you?"

"Drop the innocent routine, kid. I'm not calling about where you've been all day."

"What do you mean? I've been at school."

"Save it. I need Zack Cleary's cell phone number."

"Zack," she said blankly. "What for?"

"I just need some information."

"Is everything . . . ? Are you . . . ?"

"You have his number or not?"

She rattled off Zack's cell phone number, and I scribbled it on my hand with the leaky ballpoint I kept under the sun visor.

Then Sage said, "Are you mad at me, Mom?"

Maybe my parenting skills weren't the best. But I knew sometimes it's better to let the guilt simmer.

I said, "I'll see you tonight. We'll talk."

And I hung up.

Half a minute later, I reached Zack Cleary on his cell phone. He was equally surprised to hear from me.

"Hey, Mrs. A. What's up?" Then, sharper, "Is it Sage? Is she okay? What's wrong?"

"Sage is fine. Jeez, kid, I didn't realize you panicked so easily."

"I just—aw, hell. With that Brian guy hanging around, I wasn't sure. What are you calling me for?"

"Information. Where are you?"

"I'm still at work. You wanna pick me up? My car's in the shop. You'll save me a bus ride."

I debated. Did I want this kid to start thinking he could call me every time he had an empty gas tank?

He said, "I'm off in half an hour. I could tell you what I heard about the Crabtree case."

"I'll pick you up," I said.

He laughed. "Okay, I'm at the gun range, Bullseye Target. Know where that is?"

Of course I did.

I didn't like the suburbs. Everything looked the same to me—and I liked them even less during rush hour. But I took the dreaded Route 28 along the Allegheny River and eventually drove onto the Fort Pitt Bridge and through the tunnels. The Parkway traffic moved pretty fast, and other drivers tended to get out of my way, so it wasn't long before I took an exit and popped up in a commercial area that featured a sprawling cemetery and a couple of hotels that filled up only when downtown overflowed or the airport hotels were jammed.

Bullseye was a squat cinder-block building that some genius had painted bright red with a gigantic cartoon bull on the side. A target had been painted around the bull's staring eye, and I parked right under it. A motion-detector light came on, casting a circle of illumination around my truck.

Unlike rural rod and gun clubs that truly facilitated hunting and fishing in more rural areas of western Pennsylvania, Bullseye attracted mostly suburban gun advocates—churchgoing middle-management types beset with work-related anger issues that needed an outlet.

Only a couple of cars sat in the otherwise empty parking lot. One was a Toyota sedan with bumper stickers advertising Ducks Unlimited, the Sierra Club, and a local high school basketball team. The other vehicle was a beat-up Ford Escape, painted green. It sported a Steeler flag on the antenna—a standard automotive accessory in Pittsburgh between September and January.

I jumped down from the truck and went inside, pushing through a door decorated with signs warning patrons to keep their weapons holstered until they were on the range.

The narrow lobby—little more than a hallway with a concrete floor and fluorescent lights—featured a trophy case displaying rifle team pictures and a couple of tarnished trophies dated twenty years ago. Somebody had also posted a photo of himself with the carcass of a twelve-point buck. The dead animal's tongue was hanging out, and the hunter was imitating him. The rest of the case showed empty boxes of ammunition—all the brands offered for sale.

"Can I help you?"

I turned around and strolled over to lean my hip on the sale counter. Behind the thick glass stood Irene Stossel. I had just seen her a couple of nights ago in Loretta's kitchen, delivering wedding cookies.

Tonight she was methodically checking the chambers of a rack of handguns. She took each one out, slammed the moving parts around, and peeked into chambers—all with the aplomb of a woman flipping burgers at a griddle.

"Irene." I took off my gloves. "I forgot you worked here."

"I sure do." She didn't break rhythm. Her voice echoed from behind the bulletproof protection. "What can I do you for, Roxy?"

She was dressed in jeans and a puffy down vest that made her shoulders seem broader than ever. A set of muffling earphones was slung around her neck. She'd pulled her brown hair back with a no-nonsense rubber band into a ponytail. In the holster at her hip, though, I could see the butt of a sidearm. I was willing to bet she didn't carry the weapon when she drove her mother to the church bingo hall.

"I talked to Zack a few minutes ago. He said he needed a ride home."

"He's with a client at the moment. He'll be done in ten minutes or so. I thought maybe you came to shoot some targets."

"Me? Nah, I don't carry."

"No kidding?" She plunked the last weapon into the rack and leaned her elbows on the counter. One odd tic was that Irene didn't blink much. "Why not?"

"It's just not something I think is necessary in my line of—okay, to tell the truth, guns make me nervous."

She grinned. "I never took you for the nervous type."

From her tone, I got the impression she was needling me, but I shrugged. "I get nervous all the time."

I didn't know Irene very well, but she'd always been around the edges of my life, I guess. Her family owned the neighborhood bakery where I stole the occasional cannoli, and her mom was one of the bossy ladies behind the scenes at St. Dom's.

She said, "That surprises me. I didn't think Abruzzos were scared of anything."

"Not much," I agreed. "You going to Shelby Martinelli's wedding this weekend?"

"I don't know yet." She stretched her arms overhead, and her puffy vest opened just enough to show she was wearing Kevlar protection underneath and a handgun on her belt. "Shelby's mother is my mom's cousin, so I should probably go. But I may have to work."

"This place is open on Saturday night?"

"One of our busiest nights. Where do you think all those single guys go who can't get dates?"

"Sounds dangerous for you."

She shrugged. "If I got worried every time some jagoff pointed a gun at me, I'd be in a mental hospital by now. Hell, last year, a guy almost took off my earlobe, see?"

She pulled back her hair and showed me her ear. Sure enough, part of the lobe was missing. I couldn't help noticing a couple of long scratches down her neck—the kind Rooney sometimes gave me when he got carried away.

I said, "You must save a bundle on earrings."

"I never thought of it that way." She laughed with a weird hiccough. "I stopped in to visit your uncle Carmine yesterday. I took him some of my mom's soup."

"Oh yeah?"

"He hasn't been feeling well."

"Yeah, Carmine puts out that bulletin when he needs a favor done. Brings everybody running."

From inside the shooting range, a series of muffled gunshots had been steadily kapowing while we talked, but finally the shooter was out of ammunition. A minute later, two guys pushed through the steel door—both of them pulling earplugs out of their ears. The first was Zack. The second was a burly man wearing a button-down shirt and khaki pants with a Windbreaker. Wedding ring, tassel loafers. He looked like your average suburban insurance agent except for the shoulder holster.

"Good job today, Mr. Glick." Zack twirled his ear protection. "Best score yet."

"Thanks, kid. Hey, Irene. See you next week."

Irene waved through the glass. The customer gave me a warm once-over before he went out into the parking lot.

Irene said to Zack, "Did that creep try to impress you with his new Python?"

Zack shrugged into his coat. "He's pretty excited about it."

Irene rolled her eyes. "Big man needs a big gun, I guess."

"Right. See you, Irene."

"You want some extra hours? I could use you Saturday."

"Sorry. Can't."

"Let me know if you change your mind."

I almost dragged Zack out of there by his ear. When we reached the parking lot, I said, "Man, she's a weird chick."

"Tell me about it."

"Why doesn't she ever blink?"

"She asked me about you when I got hired."

I missed a step. "Really? What did she want to know?"

"I forget. Just if you were still in business, I guess."

I found myself frowning. "Exactly why did you get this job?"

Zack zipped his coat against the cold. "Because she needed somebody who could handle firearms, I guess, and she heard I just finished the police academy."

"You and forty other guys, right? Out of all of them, why you?"

"Maybe she heard I was the best on the gun range."

I snorted.

"Well, it's true!"

We climbed in out of the wind, and I started the engine.

"How's Sage?" Zack asked.

"She's skipping school with that Brian kid."

"I knew it!" Zack kicked the dashboard. "I knew he was going to be trouble."

"Worse yet? He's taking her on a ski weekend this Friday."

"Like hell he is. I mean—" Zack turned to me. "You're not going to let her get away with that, are you, Mrs. A?"

"Why didn't you do something about this situation before it got started?"

"What was I supposed to do? Punch the guy in the nose?"

"Surely you could be more creative than that." I pulled out of the parking lot and headed back toward the Parkway and the city. "Get in the moment. Envision something."

Zack turned to me on the seat. "What kind of envisioning?"

"You hang around with cops, for cripesake. You can't pick up a few pointers from them?"

"You mean, something sneaky?"

"There are lots of ways of slowing down a guy like Brian."

Zack said, "Why don't you do it?"

"Because I'm Sage's mother. If I get caught, it's a world scandal. But if you get caught, it's no big deal. And besides, wouldn't it feel good?"

Zack mulled over whether or not he'd be happy to have Sage's new squeeze out of the picture. "I want to be a cop. I need a clean record."

"If you can't think like a criminal, what kind of cop can you make? Jeez. What do I have to do? Lead you around by the nose?"

"Okay, okay, I get it." He slumped in his seat, staring ahead without really seeing the road. His brain cells cooked for a while. "What should I do?"

I sighed. "Nothing dangerous. Drive him crazy a little. Every time he gets near Sage, put a banana in his tailpipe. Or siphon the gas out of his tank. Get some weed killer and use it to write a rude message on his old man's yard. Or—hey, you know what's a good trick? Go buy one of those birthday cards with the electronic song inside. Throw the card away, but stick the little music thing under the hood. It'll play for hours. Very annoying."

"Wow, really. You have a lot of ideas for pranks."

"Now that I've jogged your imagination, when do I get the return favor?"

"Huh?"

"I need information."

"Okay, sure."

"The Crabtree murder. What does your dad have to say at the breakfast table?"

Zack Cleary's father—a former colonel in the United States Army, a Gulf War veteran, and a local cop who climbed the ranks by virtue of an immaculate record and a rumored interest in becoming a political candidate eventually—was the city's newly appointed chief of police. He looked good on camera and supposedly ran a tight ship. So far, he hadn't presided over any police scandals, although it had been a near miss when two undercover cops arrested a high school honor student a few months back. The kid's family claimed he had been arrested for nothing more than Walking While Black, but later it came out that he'd been running drugs into a local high school and was the baby daddy of no fewer than six toddlers, so the scandal blew over before it turned into the kind of mess that took down chiefs of out-of-control undercover cops.

Zack said, "I heard him on the phone when he left the house this morning. They think one of her husbands killed that lady."

"What's their proof?"

"I didn't hear anything about proof. He said they were going to lean on both husbands today and see which one breaks first."

That would be a toss-up, I thought. Neither one of Clarice's husbands seemed particularly strong-willed to me. "What about an autopsy?"

"Uh—it was pretty obvious she died from two gunshots."

"Yeah, but what caliber?"

"This morning was too early for those results. They'll know by now, I suppose."

"Can you call your old man?"

Zack looked anxious. "Mrs. A, I really, really want to get a job on the force. I think the department will take a dim view of me blabbing about police business before I'm even sworn in."

"Okay, okay."

"There's one interesting thing I did overhear," Zack said.

"Oh, yeah?"

"The Mitchell guy. One of his friends heard him on his cell phone the afternoon before his wife died. He was having a hell of a fight with her."

"About?"

"Money. Maybe that's nothing new, since most married people seem to fight over money, but—"

"Was he mad because his wife didn't want to pay for any more skating lessons?"

"I don't know."

If Mitchell was as obsessed with his daughter's future in ice-skating as I thought he was, I wondered if he might be moved to murder to keep financing the kid's expensive lessons. But then, why kill the cash cow?

❀ 18 ❀

It was very dark by the time I dropped Zack a block from his home. A sharp wind had kicked up and blew a few snowflakes against the windshield—not enough that I needed to put on the wipers, but I could feel the temperature dropping fast. I stopped at the yard to pick up Nooch and take him home.

I checked on Rooney before I left. He was still green, but his paint job didn't seem to bother him. He was still focused on his bone. I left the dog to guard the yard and took Nooch home for his dinner.

I took Penn Avenue out through the Wilkinsburg and Churchill neighborhoods, then hopped on the Parkway East just long enough to hit the suburb of Monroeville. As I drove, I sang along with Dooce's recordings, listening to the way he built a song, changed key when the emotion shifted, hit the usual pop crescendo, but then sustained the song's musical motif long into the sound bleed. He made good use of his backup singers, too, unlike most rockers. The women's voices added another layer of sound, but also an emotional cadence—like a good gospel group. Sometimes the backup singers were the dominant vocals, carrying the melody while Dooce used his raw, shouting voice to embellish.

I could hear the part Deondra would want in most of the songs. A contralto, she had the biggest and most trained voice of the three of us who sang with Stony, and she was a local star in urban gospel churches. If it were up to me, I'd give her the lead backup. I was better at the screaming stuff. Kate had a lyrical soprano for the high notes. Deondra, though, she had the chops to lead.

The Monroeville traffic slowed me down considerably. I remembered the Miracle Mile being one of the first strip malls in the city, but now it was jammed with hellish traffic, no miracles. Fast-food joints, car dealers, and four lanes of bumper-to-bumper vehicles with traffic lights jamming up everybody in both directions was my idea of satanic city planning.

I stopped at a gigantic Sheetz convenience market to get some gas and asked a guy at the next pump where Kenyon Road was, and he gave me typical Pittsburgh directions—all landmarks.

"Make a right at Lowe's, go past the Outback Steakhouse, through the light at the Exxon station, then past the high school and hang a left. Go past the second church and the house with the tropical Christmas lights. Kenyon is on your right."

I followed those directions easily. The roads dipped and curved in the dark. Most of the houses were decorated for the holidays with lights and lawn ornaments. As I drove, I wondered whatever happened to icicle lights. Used to be, all these suburban houses had icicle lights dripping from their gutters, but not anymore. Too bad. Icicle lights are pretty.

I ended up parked in front of a modest two-story house with brown vinyl siding. In the front lawn was a blow-up Christmas decoration that looked like a giant snow globe. Inside, a mechanical figure skater twirled in jerky circles–as if she'd had a couple of wine coolers.

I shut off the Monster Truck's engine because it was loud, and this neighborhood was disconcertingly quiet. No traffic, no buses. I could see families moving around inside the houses and the blue gleam of television screens. Their cars were neatly parked in driveways. Their dogs were safely behind backyard fences. Taking it all in, I sat in the truck and thought about where we might have been if Flynn hadn't gotten into heroin and I hadn't come from where I did. Would Sage be attending some white-bread suburban high school, dating lots of kids like Mr. Squishy with the Escalade? Would we be taking her to skating practice? Coming home to a split-level house with curtains in the windows? Somehow, I couldn't make any of the three of us fit that picture.

Only one other car was parked on the street. It was a couple of houses down, facing me. I saw the interior lights flash on as the driver popped open his door and got out. Then he crunched up the street toward me, hands thrust into the deep pockets of his coat, his head bent against the wind. He opened the door and got into the passenger side of my truck.

"Hi, Bug. Sorry about missing lunch."

"No problem," he said. "I got tied up, too. What are you doing here?"

"Hoping to give Mitchell my condolences on the death of his wife. Unless he killed her himself. In that case, I'll withhold my sentiments. Is he here?"

"He arrived about half an hour ago. We questioned him most of the afternoon. Now he's alone."

"Where's his daughter?"

"After her skating lesson, he dropped her off at the mall. I've got an officer watching her at the Clinique counter. Mitchell's alone in the house."

We both looked. The curtains were pulled, blinds drawn, blocking any view of the inside. We could see only thin slivers of light beneath some of the blinds.

I said, "You think Mitchell's the one who killed Clarice?"

Bug got comfortable in the seat, stretching out his legs and leaning his head back against the headrest. "I don't know. He seemed genuinely upset about losing her when I interviewed him today. Unless he's a heck of an actor, I think he's sorry she's gone. But the night she died, he had dropped their daughter off at a skating lesson and disappeared for a couple of hours. Enough time to kill his wife and dump her body."

"Is he smart enough to get away with murder?"

"Well, nobody got away with it. The body floated up right in the middle of the three rivers. Even a moron would've known to tie a concrete block to the carpet, right?"

"So, by reason of his low IQ, you're putting Mitchell at the top of your list."

He sent me a wry smile. "Are you questioning my deductions, Watson?"

I smiled, too. "You know what I've been thinking about? The way the carpet was tied around Clarice. Nice and neat."

"Like a pork loin."

"Exactly. Maybe it's just because I haven't had a home-cooked meal in a while, but, yeah, I was thinking of the way Loretta ties up her rolled steak. Does one of the husbands cook?"

"Mitchell does. Eckelstine sends out for a lot of pizzas. I checked on the cord. It's an ordinary kind of rope you can buy at Home Depot and Lowe's. We're checking to see if anyone bought some recently, but it's something lots of people would just keep in the garage. Tell me about Eckelstine. I heard you were at his house today."

Damn that reporter. He'd seen me at the house and blabbed to the cops.

Bug said, "Did you talk to him? Or do something else?"

I turned sideways in the seat to get a better look at Bug. "Is that your Boy Scout way of asking if I had hot, satisfying sex with Eckelstine?"

Bug didn't meet my eye, but kept up his surveillance on the Mitchell house. Attempting to sound uninterested, he asked, "Did you?"

I had to make a conscious effort not to grit my teeth. "I gave that up."

He shot me a glance. "I know a lot of guys who say they're going to give up beer, but then a game comes on the TV and the refrigerator calls. It's tough changing an ingrained behavior."

"What the hell would you know about that?"

"Never mind," he said. "Forget I brought it up."

I had worked up some temper to argue with him and was surprised that he waved the white flag already. "Is this how you fight with Marie? Float your opinion and give up when she goes into attack mode?"

"I don't fight with Marie. She always wins. I'm a wuss."

I smiled at the thought of family strife in the Duffy household. Bug seemed happily married, with the sweetest kids who never got in trouble.

His thoughts must have strayed in the same direction, because he was quiet for a minute, then said, "How is it going with you and Flynn and your daughter? I mean, is she getting used to having a dad on the scene after all these years?"

"She's adapting. Already, she's trying to play us against each other."

Bug gave a soft laugh. "Yeah, I know how that works."

"Flynn's doing okay, though," I said. "He's trying to do things right—checking with me before he takes a position, you know?"

"Presenting a united front is key with teenagers, I hear. Gotta be a team."

I didn't want to talk about how Flynn and I ought to be a team.

Bug said, "I looked up Mr. Squishy, by the way. To check if he had any kind of—you know, criminal record. He's clean, except for some speeding tickets. His kids are okay, too."

"No stalking charges?"

"Stalking?" Bug turned his head, interested. "You think the boyfriend is stalking your daughter?"

"He's a pest, that's all. Calling her a lot."

"What do you mean by a lot? Every hour?"

"Yeah, maybe."

"Hm." Bug thought things over for a moment. "That kind of thing can escalate. You want me to have a talk with him?"

"I can talk with him myself."

"Yeah, but you don't have a badge." Bug smiled. "You'd be amazed at the power of waving a shield under a teenager's nose. Suddenly he starts thinking about what happens in prison showers."

I liked the mental picture of Bug intimidating Sage's boyfriend. "You'd do that for us?"

"For you," Bug said.

For a second, I wasn't sure how to take that.

Smoothly, Bug went on, "All parents need a little help now and then. And threatening the Squishy kid would give me the opportunity to blow off a little testosterone."

"You don't seem like the type. I mean, blowing off steam."

"You might be surprised. I didn't become a cop by accident."

An odd second ticked by, and I said, "Speaking of parenting, I wonder how Clarice Crabtree managed with two kids in separate households. I mean—two adopted teenagers, each with a different father. Plus her own dad losing his mind. She had a complicated family life going on. And that busy career she was so proud of. How'd she make it all work?"

"Yeah, usually it's a guy who's married more than one woman—a con man looking to cash in on their incomes."

"But in this case, Clarice is the big wage earner."

Bug said, "Sometimes people want everything like they're items on a résumé. Usually, it's a guy who thinks like that—wants a family with two point two children, nice car, and the important career, all the trimmings. It's unusual for a woman to think that way, but not impossible, I guess. She seemed to opt out on most of the real parenting. She let Mitchell take charge of the ice-skating lessons, for instance."

"And I get the impression Richie Eckelstine was pretty much left to fend for himself."

"About the boy. Do you think maybe he could have gone off the rails? Is he capable of killing his mother?"

I thought about Richie. He clearly felt abandoned and resentful, but he'd done something healthy about it by finding a skill to get good at. But had I let myself be influenced by the leave-me-alone-I'm-fine facade he put up? I was susceptible to that kind of kid—one who had a tough life but was determined to rise above it. I tried to think clearly about whether or not the kid had played me. Could he have killed Clarice? He wouldn't be the first teenager to shoot a domineering parent.

But suddenly we saw two flashes beneath the pulled blinds of an upstairs window in Mitchell's house. Two lightning flashes, I thought. Or maybe a camera?

And a single heartbeat thumped by before I truly realized what I'd seen.

Bug said. "Oh, hell. Was that muzzle flash?"

We bailed out of the truck together.

"Please," Bug said as we ran across the front lawn of Mitchell's house past the plastic ice-skater. I knew Bug wasn't talking to me. "Please don't let him be dead."

Bug had his sidearm out. With his other hand, he pounded on the front door. "Police," he shouted in a voice that boomed. "Open up!"

I cursed. Backing up, I tried to look up into the second-floor windows, but I couldn't see anything. I cursed some more.

Bug hauled out his cell phone and hit 911.

I was operating on instinct when I took off running around the house. In the dark, I jumped over a coiled garden hose, forgotten in the grass, and nearly lost my footing as the side yard fell away in a steep bank of grass coated in a skim of snow. I found myself in the backyard a moment later, under a wooden deck and some leafless trees that hissed in the wind. The driveway curled around the house on the other side, ending in a garage located in the basement. A motion-detecting light was already on, casting a yellow light across the grass toward a line of trees. I saw a thick woods there.

Then a freight train hit me, and I went flying. I hit the ground and rolled into the grass, and I felt more than saw the person who'd hit me run out of the yard and down into the woods.

I scrambled to my knees and heard someone crashing through the underbrush, heading away from the house. Maybe it was a deer, but I thought deer would be lighter on their feet. Whoever was running away sounded heavy-footed and already out of breath.

I got up and ran toward the trees. But I stopped at the edge of the woods. The ground slanted away from the house, looking treacherous in the dark. I took a few steps into the woods, but my boots immediately got tangled in a thick carpet of fallen leaves and the jagged roots of trees and bushes. I'd be flat on my face within a few yards. Plus, I'm a city girl. Those suburban woods might just as well be a jungle with poisonous snakes and little bloodthirsty guys with blowguns.

Besides, Mitchell was upstairs, maybe hurt. Maybe dead.

I ran back to the wooden deck and took the steps two at a time. I nearly fell over a patio table, but I caught my balance and reached the sliding door. Grabbing the handle, I threw my weight against it. Unlocked. The door slid open and I went inside. The first room was a den—TV set, sofa, clutter on the coffee table and floor. A light left on in the kitchen showed me the way to the carpeted stairs, and I leaped upward.

"Mitchell? Mitch?"

The upstairs hall was little more than a landing with three rooms radiating from it. I followed the light shining from the room on my right.

And found him on the bed.

One bullet had hit him in the shoulder. But blood also gushed from a head wound.

I wrestled the towel from around his hips and pressed it to the side of his head.

Bug must have run around the house too, because he came into the room a half a minute later, breathing hard.

"Oh, shit," he said.

The shooter had waited just outside the door, I guessed. Shot Mitchell twice as he came out of the bathroom. The momentum of the shots had propelled him onto the bed.

Mitchell's eyes fluttered. His breathing was shallow and uneven.

Bug still had his phone to his ear. He spoke curtly to the dispatcher, demanding an ambulance.

I kept steady pressure on the side of Mitchell's head, but the blood was already everywhere. I tried not to think about it and took an inventory of his room. It was tidy except for Mitchell's clothes and shoes on the floor. His wallet lay on the dresser. The walls were covered with photos of his daughter—skating, smiling in her sparkly costumes, proudly holding up her trophies.

Bug spun toward the closet and kicked the door wide, weapon ready. "The guy could still be here in the house, Rox."

"He's not here," I said. "I followed somebody down the backyard, into the woods."

Bug stowed his gun, turned on the overhead light, and came over to the bed. "Don't die on us, Mitch. Don't die."

I don't remember what Bug and I said to each other after that, and Mitch didn't do anything but gurgle. The ambulance showed up fast—that's the suburbs for you—and Bug went downstairs to let them in. When the paramedics took over, Bug grabbed my arm.

"Show me where the shooter went."

We ran down the stairs together and I led the way across the deck, down the outside steps, to the edge of the woods. Outside, the wind had kicked up. Or else I was cold from shock.

"There." I pointed into the trees. "Whoever it was took off down through that gulley. I could hear him, couldn't see exactly where he went."

"There must be another road down that way. Maybe a different neighborhood."

At that moment, a suburban squad car came down the driveway, bubble-gum light sending a whirl of red flashes against the trees and nearby houses. Bug turned from me and went up to meet it, pulling out his shield to show the patrol officer.

I stayed at the edge of the trees. The quiet neighborhood had already noticed the ambulance and the police car. Curious people were poking their heads out of the nearby houses. It was different here. In the city, neighbors would stay indoors until they knew it was safe. But in the burbs, people were more trusting.

Perhaps more observant, too. Maybe somebody had seen the shooter arrive. Had noticed him slip inside through the sliding door to try ending the life of a devoted father.

The patrol car backed up the driveway, going fast. The officer threw the car into gear and roared off up the street.

Bug returned to me. "Local cop says there's another housing development below this one. He's going down now to look for your shooter. But the street empties out onto a local road and goes straight up to the turnpike."

"So the shooter planned a quick escape."

"Looks that way. You all right?"

I didn't bother to answer.

He pulled a flashlight from inside his coat. He shone it up at the house, then down the yard, systematically casting the light from side to side, looking for footprints in the skiff of snow on the grass.

Simultaneously, we both saw a small black item on the ground. Together, we walked closer, and Bug crouched down for a closer look. He put the light directly onto it—a glove.

I recognized it at once.

I must have made a sound, because Bug looked up at me. "Recognize this?"

"Yes. It's mine."

He picked it up and started to hand it to me.

I took a step back. "No. I lost that glove. Yesterday or maybe sometime today, I can't remember when. Give me a second."

"Wait, so—?"

"So the shooter left it here."

"Left it? Or planted it? You mean—? The shooter knows you? Is trying to implicate you?"

I met Bug's gaze for a second, but sank down to sit in the snow. My hands were smeared with something dark and sticky, and I tried not to think about what it was. Upstairs, Mitchell was still alive, but barely. And whoever shot him had left my glove here to be found by the police.

Bug put his hand on my shoulder and squeezed.

❊ 19 ❊

Around one in the morning they reluctantly turned me loose, and I staggered over to my truck. I sat behind the wheel, breathing raggedly for several minutes before I could work up the guts to turn on the engine. I'd had a close call with someone who had shot Mitch Mitchell. I gotta admit, I was spooked.

And keyed up. I drove into the city, listening to Dooce sing about heartbreak. But this time I didn't sing along. What he didn't know about heartbreak could fill an ocean. My head was full of images I wished I could erase. Clarice dead in a carpet. Mitchell bleeding out on his bed.

I should have been crying for Sugar—a kid who might be an orphan by now. But I couldn't. Instead, I felt a boiling rage start bubbling inside. White heat so searing I couldn't think straight. I needed something to stop it. If Gino had showed up in my headlights just then, I'd probably have beaten him senseless.

On autopilot, I cruised past a couple of bars, thinking I might slip inside. Get a drink. Cool down a little. Make my brain stop whirling.

Wangdoodles on the South Side would be a good bet, I thought. Nobody knew me there. I parked on Carson Street and walked two blocks before turning up the alley, jingling my keys in one hand. I passed a couple of college hangouts on the way, but tonight I didn't feel like getting puked on.

Wangdoodles catered to firefighters and cops, I realized as I stepped inside. I remembered I'd been in the place before—a few years ago. It was a dark, sour-smelling honeycomb of rooms radiating from a central bar tended by a string of bored women who wore red T-shirts with the bar's suggestive logo printed on the front.

I recognized the faces of two guys at the first table. They were vaguely familiar to me, so I walked on by. I didn't want to talk to anybody I knew. I really didn't want to talk at all.

At the bar, three single men sat looking up at a TV screen playing football highlights, all nursing drinks. Two looked too drunk to function, but the third guy would do. Big shoulders, a day's worth of beard, clean jeans. He wasn't bad. I slid onto the stool next to him and signaled the girl behind the bar for a draft. Her nametag said EDIE.

"Hey," I said to the guy next to me. "Do I know you?"

Surprised, he turned and looked me over.

Before he could respond, though, the two guys from the first table strolled up, drinks in hand. One was tall and whippy, his pal shorter and built like a weightlifter.

The weightlifter said, "Hey, buddy, be careful. This broad can hurt you."

I spun on the stool. "What's the matter, fellas? Your feelings get wounded?"

They looked at each other and laughed. The taller one said, "No, we just were thinking you might want to party again."

Okay, I knew their faces, and I was pretty sure I'd had a brief booty call with both of them before. The tall one made me think of a time in a no-tell motel somewhere, but I wasn't sure. The weightlifter—he didn't ring any bells, but that didn't mean anything. In my bad-girl days, I could have done something with him without looking at his face much.

The weightlifter leaned close, beer on his breath. "What about both of us this time, baby?" he said. "My place is a couple of blocks from here, on the Slopes. I could really use a BJ, and Stevie here likes to watch. Gets him hot. Then you could do whatever you want with him. What do you say?"

The guy on the stool said, "I wouldn't mind watching first, either. But I got to get home to babysit my kid. My girlfriend goes to work in a couple of hours."

First of all, I don't do group events. You put multiple partners in the room, and it starts being all about performance and stops being about me getting my needs met.

But suddenly with all three of them looking at me like I was a strip steak, I heard Adasha's voice in my head.

"Understand why you're doing it," she said.

The weightlifter touched me, rubbing my arm up and down with his knuckles. "C'mon, baby. If not you, we're gonna have to go with Edie."

Edie came back with my draft. She set it on the bar and smiled widely. She was missing her front teeth.

All of a sudden, I had the shakes. I pulled a few bills from my hip pocket and tossed them on the bar for the beer.

"I'm not your baby," I said.

And I couldn't get out of Wangdoodles fast enough.

I got back into the truck and tried to find my way home. I made a wrong turn, though, and got lost. Down by the Monongahela River, I gave myself a mental head slap.

"C'mon, Roxy," I said aloud. "Man up."

I liked to be in charge. The one with the power. The whole idea of losing control messed with my head so much I felt dizzy. I needed to crash at my own place tonight, not Loretta's house. I needed to be alone. To think some things through.

I'd given my door key to Flynn—when? Yesterday? This morning? But fortunately, I kept a spare in the truck. I rummaged it out of the glove compartment and let myself into the silent house. I kicked off my boots inside the front door and headed for the kitchen.

In the fridge, there was beer, but also a quart of skim milk with a past-due date stamped on the carton. It didn't taste bad yet. I drank half of it and padded upstairs to get some sleep.

I flipped on the light and nearly hit the ceiling when Flynn rolled over in the bed.

"Jesus!"

He sat up slowly and squinted at me. "I thought maybe you were staying at Loretta's."

I sagged against the doorjamb and pressed my hand over my heart to keep it from jumping out of my chest. "What the hell cat dragged you in here?"

He rubbed his face. "I'm still dodging a bunch of people."

"You couldn't hide in your own home?"

"No." He stretched across the bed and grabbed my alarm clock. "What time is it?"

"Late. You can't stay here, Flynn. You hear me?"

"It's two in the morning." He set the clock down and flopped back against the pillows. "I'll be out of here at five to go to the market, I promise. I just need a little more sleep."

"Five o'clock isn't soon enough. I need to be alone."

I saw he'd dropped his jeans and pullover on the floor and kicked off his shoes. In the bed, he wore a T-shirt, and God only knew what else was under the sheets. He hadn't shaved in a while.

Flynn opened one eye and gave me a dour look. "Three hours. You can put up with me for three hours."

I stayed leaning against the door and tried to muster some gruffness. "Isn't Marla waiting for you?"

He shook his head. "She thinks I'm staying at my brother's place."

His brother had three little kids who all needed Ritalin, plus several hysterical little dogs and a wife who'd been in the army and did a lot of shouting. They lived in a big, crowded house in a tough neighborhood with the laughable name of Friendship. Anyone who knew anything about Flynn would bet big money he'd rather eat nails than stay at that house of madness.

If Marla thought he was there, she didn't know him as well as I'd assumed.

He gave a huge yawn. "You wouldn't believe the craziness about this damn soup. It's like I invented caviar or foie gras or something. And since Julio did all the prep work, they're hounding him now, too. He practically had a panic attack this afternoon."

"Who's hounding him?"

"*Food* magazine. Dooce's people. The restaurant writers. And Dooce's sidekick, that Jeremy guy, who actually made another threat. Julio could have cut him with a knife, but instead he took a powder to get away from it all. Never showed up for the evening service."

"All because your soup is so delicious?"

"Crazy, right? So I came over here, left my truck a few blocks away, and sneaked in for a few hours of sleep." He looked at me at last, and his attention sharpened. "What's wrong with you?"

"Nothing," I said automatically. Then, shakier, "Everything."

"Sage?" He sat up straight in the bed.

"No, no, she's fine. As far as I know, that is. No, it's—"

He swung his long legs over the side of the bed. He was still wearing his boxers, thank God. He reached for me. "Jesus, Roxy, sit down before you fall down."

I was shaking like a leaf in a tornado. In my own bedroom, I suddenly saw Mitch hanging on to life by a thread. That, and the guys in the bar who'd wanted me like I was a hooker.

Flynn took my hand and pulled me to sit on the edge of the bed. "What's going on?"

After a couple of false starts, I told him about Mitchell. About getting shot at myself. I skipped the part about the bar. He didn't need to know what I'd almost done.

He had a gentle arm around my shoulders by the time I finished the whole story.

Flynn swore softly. "You okay now? Not hurt, right? Just shaken up?"

"I'm okay," I said, surprised to hear my voice tremble.

He hugged me to him, side by side. "What are you doing, anyway, poking around in that murder?"

"I don't know. I hated Clarice back in the day. But—her kids." I wiped my nose on the sleeve of my sweatshirt. "I know it's nuts. For me to care about her kids."

"No, it isn't."

"They don't deserve what's happened."

"You're right."

"It's unfair they're going to have to pay the price."

"It is," Flynn agreed softly. "You know all about that, don't you?"

"This isn't about me."

"It isn't?"

I pulled away from him.

Flynn stayed quiet and let me get to my feet.

I was soon pacing the room. "Of course it isn't. They're innocent, caught in a mess they didn't make. I got over what happened to me a long time ago."

"If you say so." Flynn climbed back into the bed. He stuffed two pillows behind his head and leaned against them. "It was pretty bad for you, though. I remember you talked about it a few times."

"Hey, I'm over it. I'm not going through life wishing my mommy dearest was still alive."

"Is that the issue? I think it's more about what kind of a mother you are. Isn't that what bugs you?"

"I'm not like her."

"I know that."

"Her whole life was about my dad. She was madly in love with him, and he . . ."

"And he beat the shit out of her on a regular basis, right?"

"He never hit me, though."

Flynn narrowed his eyes. "What does that mean? He didn't hit you, so he's a hero?"

"No." I shook my head. "That's not what I— No."

"But you cared about him?"

"Except when they fought." I used to hide from them when the screaming started. I squeezed my eyes shut at the memory. It was like a storm, the two of them crashing from one room to another, throwing things, hitting each other.

"Rox," Flynn said.

"I don't want to talk about this. Not tonight."

"Okay, okay. Not tonight."

"Not ever."

"Come to bed," he said.

I opened my eyes and gave him a glare. "I'm not getting into bed with you," I said. "So forget it."

"I just want to sleep, that's all."

"I might believe you if you weren't staring at my tits."

Flynn smiled at last, his gaze warm. "I can't help myself. You've always had beautiful—"

"Get out of my bed," I said wearily. "Go home to your pretty girlfriend, Flynn."

"I won't touch you, I promise."

Looking at him there, propped up and relaxed in my bedroom, I realized something with a funny twist in my gut. "Know what? Since we were together, for me, it's been easier to have sex with strangers. Why is that?"

"I don't know. It's more than I can think about right now." He yawned again. "I gotta get up early, so let's just go to sleep, okay? No funny business, I promise."

He looked comfy there in the bed, and I felt myself weakening. "Why do you have to get up so early?"

"To go to the market. And," he added, "I take Marla to the clinic every morning at nine."

"For her methadone."

Flynn didn't answer, but I knew the truth. He was helping his girlfriend stay off heroin, making sure she got her methadone every day instead. It was his way of staying off drugs himself. Helping her seemed to keep him clean, too.

He said, "I don't want to fight with you about Marla."

"You're really into her, huh?"

He shrugged. "Sure."

"You love her?"

His gaze darkened. "Why the twenty questions?"

"I don't know. It's nothing."

Outside, the city made no sound. The room was very still, except for the pounding of my heart.

"Rox?"

"Adasha wants me to start going to therapy," I blurted out. "Group therapy."

"For what?"

"You know," I said.

He leaned forward, intent. "You gotta say it, Roxy. Admit it to yourself. Say it. Own it."

"What's that?" I laughed. "One of the twelve steps?"

"Why are you going to therapy?"

"I didn't say I was going!"

"But you're considering it. So say it. Why do you need therapy?"

I realized I'd been hugging myself, but I couldn't let go. Quietly, I said, "Maybe I need to get a handle on what I've been doing."

"Which is?"

I closed my eyes. "I like sex. Maybe in a way that's kinda twisted."

"So why do you do it?"

With a shake of my head, I said, "Once in a while, it's nice to—you know, be with somebody. Most of the time, I don't want to know his name. I don't want to know anything about him. I want to hold on to somebody, get it? I'm not hurting anybody, but . . ."

"But?"

Almost too soft for him to hear, I whispered, "I don't want Sage to find out."

After a moment, he nodded his head. "I like heroin. I like it a lot. But I know it's wrong, makes me stupid. I was doing hurtful things to get more of it, and I finally realized it wasn't just ruining my life, but a lot of lives. So I had to quit. To get to know myself without heroin."

"How's that going?" I asked.

"It's lousy sometimes." He grinned a little. "Other times, it's pretty good. I'm glad I can be with my daughter now. Without influencing her in a bad way."

"You think that's what I'm doing? Influencing her with my behavior?"

"She's a great kid, Rox. We did something really terrific when we made her. I don't want to screw that up now."

"I don't either."

"So," he said. "You going to get some therapy?"

I couldn't answer. I climbed into the bed with Flynn, wrapped my arms around his neck, and let his body heat soak into mine. He felt strong and familiar and delicious. Against his chest, I murmured, "How about enabling me a little first?"

"Roxy," he said.

"C'mon. For old time's sake?"

He disengaged my arms and rolled out of the other side of the bed. "That would be a very bad idea."

"You must be the only man on the planet who'd turn me down."

He was already grabbing his jeans from the floor and climbing into them. "It might surprise you to know that a lot of men would turn you down. You're not as irresistible as you think you are. In fact, you're kind of . . ." He stopped himself.

"What am I?"

"Mixed up," Flynn said finally.

I threw myself out of the bed. "Thanks a lot. Is that why you left, all those years ago?"

"You mean, when you got pregnant?"

"When *we* got pregnant, jerkwad. Only you couldn't handle it and took off."

"You're right, I couldn't handle it." He stood his ground, zipping his jeans. "To begin with, I was scared of where we were going, and then adding a baby—"

"Where were we going?"

"Face it, Rox, we were off the rails. Doing crazy stuff, stealing cars, getting into trouble. And then the sex started to get really wild. Remember? Eventually, one of us was going to get hurt."

"That's not true," I said, but I heard the doubt in my own voice.

"No?" he asked. "You weren't afraid I'd hurt you? Or you might lose your head completely? That we'd end up like your parents?"

Maybe I remembered things differently than he did. My memory was full of laughs and good times. Maybe things got out of hand now and then, sure, but I liked it that way—on the edge, heart pounding, brain going blank while the body took over.

"I don't know," I said slowly.

"One of us was going to get hurt bad," Flynn said. "And with a baby coming, I didn't know—I was scared of what might happen. And then— well, Loretta."

"Loretta?" I stopped pacing. "What about her?"

Flynn met my gaze. "You knew what she did, right? She told you, didn't she?"

"Tell me now," I commanded.

Flynn sat back down on the bed and searched my face with narrowed eyes, looking for clues to what I knew. Slowly, he said, "She came to see me at my dad's house. Told me that either we needed to get married, or I should get my act together some other way. Go into the military—that was her idea. She said I'd grow up, and boy, she knew what she was talking about. But—"

"She had no right to do that."

"You were in the hospital, remember? You were bleeding or something, and so you—"

"That was nothing. It went away. Sage was fine. I was fine."

"Yeah, but it scared Loretta. I don't know what she thought. Maybe that I'd done something to bring it on. So she had to protect you. She came to the house, sat me down with my parents, and we talked it out." He shrugged. "And I joined the marines."

"Because you thought we'd hurt each other."

"We had a lot pent-up frustration going on, Roxy. I started thinking it was all about your parents. We were acting it out, you and me. Their fighting, her death."

I started getting that room-spinning feeling again. Like everything I knew about myself was whirling around me.

"You okay?" he asked. "Rox?"

"Yeah, great." I snatched a blanket off the bed, in a sudden rush to be alone. I hated feeling this way—confused and uncertain. It made me think I was going to blunder into a big mistake. "You're right, this is a bad idea. I'm going downstairs and sleep in a chair."

He caught my arm. "Hey."

I shook him off. "Don't. Just leave me alone."

I had to think. I didn't want to talk anymore. He must have seen that in my face, because he released my arm as if I were suddenly too hot to handle.

"Okay," he said. "Good night."

I pushed past him. "I doubt it."

I stomped down the stairs and threw myself into a chair. Bundling up in the blanket, I tried to sleep. I thought I heard Flynn walking around upstairs, maybe pacing. I thought I heard him start down the stairs once. Or maybe not.

❊ 20 ❊

In the early hours of the morning, he stopped beside my chair long enough to ruffle my hair.

"Screw you," I muttered.

"You wish," he said, and kissed the top of my head.

The next thing that woke me was my cell phone.

In my ear, Adasha said, "I'm outside. Let me in."

I groaned. "I can't go running this morning."

"Me neither. It's pouring down rain. Let me inside, will you? And hurry up. There are two thugs out here, and they're looking for trouble."

I staggered out into the hallway and unlocked the front door.

In the act of snapping her phone shut, Adasha pushed her way inside, still wearing her scrubs under a rain slicker that sluiced water onto my floor. She had a brown paper bag clamped under one armpit and juggled a cardboard coffee carrier laden with two tall cups that smelled like heaven.

"God," she said. "I can't even walk in my own neighborhood without getting menaced. See those kids? Where are their parents?"

From behind the door, I pulled an aluminum baseball bat. I hefted it easily and went out onto the porch.

Sure enough, a couple of young gangbangers had followed Adasha from the coffeeshop, and they hung around under the shelter of the tree outside my place, clearly trying to stay dry while planning their next move. They hunched their shoulders against the cold sleet, but their baggy pants had soaked up so much water that they were both hanging on to the insides of their pockets. Their hoodies were pulled tightly over their faces. But I could see their eyes.

"Go home," I said to them, taking a batter's stance.

They shoved off without a word, heading toward the river.

I went back inside and kicked the door shut.

"I tried talking with them," Adasha said. "But you look especially scary this morning. What's wrong with your lip?"

"No big deal."

"Scary, though."

I felt scary, too. Sleeping in an armchair had given me stiff muscles where I didn't even know I had muscles. And my neck felt as though somebody had clobbered me. I rubbed it with one hand. "I slept in a chair."

"Why on earth?"

"Because—never mind."

"I saw Flynn." She handed over the paper bag. "So don't bother lying. He left just as I rolled in from the hospital. You gonna tell me what happened?"

"Nothing happened. He needed a place to stay, that's all."

"That's all?" Adasha kept her mouth serious.

I lightened her load by taking one of the cups of coffee, then led the way to the kitchen. Over my shoulder, I said, "I tried seducing him and failed. I'm losing my touch."

Adasha followed me, shrugging out of her rain slicker. "Or else he's a nice guy in a committed relationship."

"I don't care. He can have whatever relationships he wants as long as he doesn't screw things up with Sage."

"That's really how you feel?"

"Am I supposed to feel something else?"

I didn't want to talk about Flynn. Or my stupid feelings. I'd had enough of that last night and didn't care to revisit my past.

I flipped on the overhead light. Nooch and I had laid most of the hardwood kitchen floor a couple of weeks back, so at least the room was usable. I'd bought an old refrigerator that sounded like a lawn mower from time to time, and a used microwave, too. No stove, just an empty hole, but I wasn't doing any cooking. The sink functioned, but the countertops consisted of some old planks laid across the lower cabinets. For a kitchen table, I used a rusted patio set with only three chairs. The table was littered with empty takeout containers. I pushed them to one corner and opened Adasha's paper bag.

"What's in here?" I stuck my nose in the bag and inhaled deeply, hoping to catch the fragrance of freshly made doughnuts.

"Granola," Adasha said. "My own recipe. I'm using dried cherries and apricots with the nuts and oats. Lots of antioxidants, low on the glycemic index. It'll give you quick energy, plus the long-lasting effects of protein. Eat this for breakfast for a week, and you'll be running like a top."

"After a week eating this, I'd have a hole in my colon. What do you have against blueberry scones? Or maybe a bear claw?"

Adasha sat on one of the patio chairs and pried the lid off her coffee cup. If she'd had a difficult night saving citizens in the hospital emergency department, she didn't show it. She had taken the time to scrub off her makeup and tuck her hair into the checked Aunt Jemima kerchief she sometimes affected, but otherwise, she looked fresh and lively. "I won't dignify that with an answer. Tell me what happened last night."

"Like I said, Flynn only needed—"

"I'm not asking about Flynn. I heard on the news that Clarice Crabtree's husband got shot. One of her husbands, that is. You hear about that?"

"Is he still alive?"

"For the moment. I hear he's pretty bad off."

I let out a sigh of relief. "In fact, I was there when he was shot."

Adasha stared. "You gotta be kidding me."

"I wish I was."

"Are you okay?"

"I'll admit, I was shaky. But I'm okay now."

My friend sipped her coffee, and then she shook her head in wonder. "Crazy, huh? Old Clarice being married to two guys?"

"And one of them was kinda hot." I sipped coffee and let the heat slide down my throat. "Mitchell isn't the sort of guy either one of us would expect Clarice to end up with."

Adasha's face was worried. "So who shot him? The other husband?"

"That would be my first guess." I got a handful of Slim Jims out of a drawer and ate one while telling Adasha about my evening at Mitchell's house. She listened, aghast. Or maybe she was horrified watching me eat my usual breakfast.

"Holy shit," she said when I was finished talking. "You could have been killed."

"It wasn't that bad." I sat down at the table. "The worst part? I had just about decided Mitchell was the one who shot Clarice."

"Why would he have killed her?"

"He might have been upset that she was cutting off the money to finance their kid's Olympic dreams."

Adasha's brows rose. "The kid has Olympic dreams?"

"Ice-skating. Mitchell was really invested in the kid's skating. If Clarice decided to stop paying for it all, maybe he got upset and killed her. Sounds stupid when I say it out loud. But frankly, there was no other likely suspect. Until last night's shooting, I didn't think the other husband, Eckelstine, had the stones. And unless there's some nutcase working at the museum—somebody who hated Clarice or had a fight with her—I just don't see anybody else who could have killed her."

"Her father?"

"I guess he's a possibility. Bug Duffy is going to check on him today, make sure he hadn't busted out of his jail again."

Adasha said, "Alzheimer's patients can get violent, you know. But they're not good at planning anything. If Clarice had been simply killed, I might believe her father could do it. But wrap her up in a carpet? Drop her body in the river?"

"Then try to kill her husband to shut him up?"

"You think that's why Mitchell was shot?"

I shrugged. "Just guessing."

"What about the teenage son?"

I finished my Slim Jim and took a cautious peek into her bag of healthy granola. "Yeah, I've been thinking about him."

"And?"

"He got into some trouble a while back, kind of went adrift. Needs a parent. Maybe he hated Clarice for all the usual reasons a kid hates a stepmother. But . . . I doubt it. She encouraged him in the one thing he's good at—making clothes." I saw Adasha's surprise and said, "Yeah, he designs stuff. Looks ugly to me, but Clarice bought him fabric and wore the results. That's not the kind of stepmom who'd push a kid to violence."

"Lack of affection can be just as damaging as any other emotional abuse."

I sampled some granola. "Not bad for bird seed."

"I'm serious," Adasha said. "Father hunger is very real."

"Don't start," I said.

"Okay, I won't. But a parent who's distant, withholding, self-involved—that's just as cruel as the one who beats the child with a stick."

"You're saying the boy got sick of hearing Clarice talk about how wonderful she was and killed her?"

"I don't know him. You do."

I sipped coffee and thought about Richie for a while. Any kid might snap under the wrong circumstances. "Depends on transportation, I guess.

How does he travel? He can't drive a car. At least, I don't think so. It's a long way from the city out to Mitchell's house."

"How could he have gotten there last night by himself?"

"I'll find out." I shoveled up a handful of granola and began picking out the sweet dried cherries. Without looking Adasha in the face, it was easier to say what needed to be said. "There's something I probably should have mentioned."

I felt my friend giving me a steady stare. She said, "Do I want to hear what's coming?"

"Probably not. But here goes. Somebody tried to hire me to kidnap Clarice."

She sat back in her chair, eyes wide. "Who?"

"I don't know. Maybe Marvin Weiss knows, but he skipped town to avoid getting sucked into this mess."

"Did you—?"

"Take the job? No. I'll do favors for my uncle when it's petty stuff," I said. "But there are lines I won't cross, Dasha. Despite what everybody thinks about me."

"Nobody thinks—"

"I turned down the job. But I think it's possible that somebody did kidnap Clarice. And when things went bad, maybe the kidnapper decided to pop her instead."

"Pop her?" Adasha looked serious. "Does that kind of language make killing somehow more acceptable?"

"I'm not trying to make it acceptable," I said quickly. "I just—it's a way of talking. What it all means is this: I think I need to be looking for two people. The one who hired a kidnapper, and the kidnapper who killed Clarice. And maybe shot Mitchell, too."

Adasha sat back and folded her arms over her chest—the picture of disapproval. "There you go again. Taking responsibility. Let Bug do this, Rox."

"I can't tell him. Not about the kidnapping."

"Why not?"

"Because he's going to ask questions. I'll get in trouble. It'll all lead to

Marvin and Uncle Carmine, and pretty soon we'll all be in jail. And I don't want Sage coping with that."

Adasha looked deeply into my face. "I understand that part."

I didn't say it, but I was afraid of Sage's reaction.

I wondered whether, if she knew the real me, my daughter might choose Flynn to be her parent. Or worse, take up with one of her boyfriends and forget about her family. Either way, I was going to lose my daughter, which felt like the worst consequence in the world.

Adasha said, "So what are you going to do?"

"I think the kidnapper made two big mistakes. The first was killing Clarice. The second must have something to do with Mitchell. Why did he have to be shot? Because he saw something? Knew something? Or was he the target all along?"

"Maybe he witnessed the killer shooting Clarice."

"I've got to find out more."

"How?"

Good question. I said, "I think I need to learn more about Rhonda."

"Who?"

"Not who. What. She's a mastodon. Or a woolly mammoth. I don't know the difference."

Adasha gave a huge yawn and then blinked, dazed. She said, "Either you just said something that makes no sense, or I just hit the wall. And right now I don't have the brain power to figure out which it is. I need some sleep."

"Thanks for bringing breakfast," I said. "Thanks for coming over."

"You mean that?"

"Yeah, I do."

She dragged herself to her feet. "I haven't even mentioned the therapy thing yet."

I laughed shortly. "Quit while you're ahead. How's Jane Doe?"

"I checked on her last night. She's okay."

"Y'know, she's been talking to her shithead boyfriend by phone."

"Dammit! She didn't tell me that. I better go see her, I guess."

"Good luck."

"Same to you." She gave me a big hug, squeezing hard.

When Adasha was finished showing her affection, I said gruffly, "Get some sleep."

From my doorway, I made sure the gangbangers were gone and watched her run through the rain to the house next door where Jane Doe was staying. After Adasha knocked and was safely admitted inside, I went upstairs, stripped naked in the bathroom, and took a hot shower. My shampoo and soap were rearranged, so I knew Flynn had showered before he left. I found some clean clothes and dressed quickly, trying not to think about Flynn putting on his clothes in the same place earlier.

I pulled on my boots and went downstairs.

In the kitchen, I grabbed my keys and went out into the rain. That's when I discovered some jagoff had punctured one of the Monster Truck's tires with a screwdriver.

I cursed and kicked the flat tire a few times. Either the gangbangers had taken their revenge, or Gino hadn't gotten the message I'd stapled to his hand.

It took me about fifteen minutes to change the tire. I was soaked by then, but strangely invigorated. Directed rage has a tendency to perk me up. I drove across the bridge and up into Lawrenceville. Nooch was waiting on the corner. Fortunately, his face didn't look so bad. The swelling had gone down a little.

He climbed into the truck, wet through a couple of layers. "Where you been? You're late this morning."

"Some asshole stuck a screwdriver into one of my tires."

"Don't cuss," he said automatically. Then he looked surprised. "Was it Gino again?"

"I settled things with Gino yesterday. At least, I thought I did. Probably, the flat tire was some kids from the neighborhood."

"They should be in school," Nooch said. He gazed out the window at the passing scenery. "Sometimes I wish I was back in school. The cafeteria food, the gym. Football practice."

"The sleeping in class."

"Yeah, that was okay, too."

Thinking about high school gave me an idea, so I made a U-turn in the street and swung into the parking lot of a CVS drugstore. I dashed into the store and came out two minutes later with a plastic bag full of supplies. First, I gave Nooch a pack of powdered doughnuts, which kept his mouth full long enough for me to reach the back alley behind Gino Martinelli's house.

Nooch wiped sugar from his face. "What are we doing here?"

"You're staying in the truck," I told him. "And if anybody asks, I'm looking at some old windows in a house down the street. Got that?"

Nooch might keep the story straight if I didn't add too many details. I fished a tube of Ben-Gay out of the drugstore bag, and I bailed out of the truck. Silently, I hotfooted my way up the back steps to the kitchen door. I peeked inside and saw Gino's wife, Carlene, drinking coffee while Regis and Kelly blared on the television. Carlene wore a woolly bathrobe, and her hair—freshly dyed an unlikely black for the wedding, no doubt—was rolled up in pink curlers.

She appeared to be grooming a small animal, and then I realized she was combing out Gino's toupee.

I eased away from the door before she saw me, then scouted the back of the house for a way inside. As luck would have it, they'd left a basement door ajar, and I slipped inside. A cat box sat at my feet, stinking up the place, but explaining why the door was open. I found myself in the old coal cellar, although now it was full of yard equipment, including a greasy lawn mower old enough to be in the Smithsonian. I tipped an interior door open and walked into the Martinelli laundry room.

Perfect.

The dryer rumbled, almost at the end of its cycle. I opened the dryer door and found the drum full of Carlene's unmentionables. Carefully, I closed the dryer again, hoping Regis and Kelly were loud enough that Carlene couldn't hear me. On the floor I found two laundry baskets full of dirty clothes. Disgusting. On top of the washer sat another basket full of freshly laundered and folded items—including Gino's collection of extravagant boxers and briefs. Apparently, he liked underwear with funny sayings printed on them.

Lone Gunman, said one pair.

I said, "You'll be alone, all right, Gino. Just wait and see."

Opening the tube of Ben-Gay, I hummed while liberally applying the heat-inducing cream to the insides of Gino's clean underwear.

"The heat is on, Gino," I said as I tossed his clothing back into the basket.

Five minutes later, I tiptoed out of the basement. The family cat watched me throw the tube of Ben-Gay into an open trash can by the back steps. I slipped away and climbed into the Monster Truck.

Nooch woke with a grunt. "Huh?"

"Shh. Ready to go?"

"Why do you have that look on your face? That's not your positive look, it's your scary look. Like you did something that's going to blow up later."

"Go back to sleep," I told him, putting the truck into gear.

"I wasn't sleeping. I was visualizing!"

My cell phone rang as I drove out of the alley.

"Hey," Adasha said. "Did you have a problem with your truck this morning?"

"A flat tire. Why?"

"Just so you know," she said, "it wasn't those kids in the neighborhood who did it. Jane Doe tells me her fireman boyfriend came around last night. And he got the idea that you were keeping her away from him."

"Oops," I said. "I wish I'd known that five minutes ago. I thought it was Gino Martinelli."

"Sorry. The fireman threatened Jane, and he said he'd cause trouble for you, too."

"Bring it on, babycakes."

"Rox, don't taunt him. That will only make things worse for her and for the kids."

"Want me to talk to Jane? I've had some experience with situations like this."

"I don't know," Adasha said doubtfully.

"Hey, you brought her to me because the system doesn't always work. So let me take care of this in my way."

"I can't think straight. I'll get some sleep before I give you an answer."

"I'll take that as temporary permission to do whatever's best."

"Just don't let anybody get hurt."

We hung up. I wished I hadn't thrown away the Ben-Gay. There had been half a container of the stuff left, and I could have used it on the fireman.

We roared up to the gate of the salvage yard a little while later. The sight that greeted us surprised the hell out of me.

"Holy cow," Nooch said.

Two kids had parked a bicycle in front of the gate, and Rooney was licking their hands through the iron bars. They looked like a couple of orphans from Charles Dickens, except with clothes from the mall.

Richie Eckelstine and Sugar Mitchell.

Both of them were frozen and miserable. But Richie wore a fashion-forward checked scarf knotted around his neck, skinny jeans, pointy boots. A snug leather jacket with epaulet. And an expression of teenage mortification on his face. Beside him, Sugar was weeping.

As Nooch jumped down to open the gate, I leaned out of the truck's window and said, "What are you two doing here?"

Teeth clenched to keep them from chattering, Richie Eckelstine said, "We have to see you."

Nooch boosted Sugar into the truck, and Richie scrambled in behind her. I drove them across the yard, and then we bundled them into the barbershop. I turned on the space heater, and I started heating up some water to make instant hot chocolate. Rooney skidded to a stop on the floor beside me, ever hopeful for a handout. I gave him a pat for not biting the kids.

Richie struck a rigid model's pose and said, "I know this is awkward, us showing up like this. But I didn't know who else to go to."

I grabbed him by the elbow and steered him to the corner. "What's

Sugar doing here?" I asked in a mutter. "How do the two of you even know each other?"

"The police brought her to our house early this morning. Her dad's in the hospital. She doesn't have any other family, except us. It was either foster care or my dad. Dad couldn't say no."

I turned to the girl, who was elaborately drying her eyes. She looked bereft.

"She okay?" I asked Richie.

"She's the devil," he replied. "She'd be okay in the fires of hell."

I took a closer look at her. For her flight from foster care, Sugar wore a white fake fur jacket over a very short pink skirt and black leggings, with very high heels. She looked a little like . . . a junior hooker.

Richie rolled his eyes for my benefit. "I know, right? Who picks her clothes?"

Sugar had been hogging all the warmth that wafted up from the heater on the floor, but she must have seen my expression in the fragment of mirror left on the wall, because when she finally turned on us, she had a satanic fire in her eyes. "I don't know what the two of you are complaining about. You both look like homeless people. And this guy"—she hooked her thumb at Nooch—"should get arrested for smelling like rotten pepperoni."

She went on in a voice dripping with venom. "I'm not here by choice, that's for sure, but Bitchie seemed to think you were the person who could help."

"Bitchie?" Richie said. "That's what I get after pedaling you down here in the freezing cold?"

"We could have called a cab!"

"Neither one of us has any money!"

"You don't even have a debit card? What a dweeb!"

I cut across their bickering. "Wait. Hold on. How did you know where to find me?"

"Bada Bling Architecture Salvage." Richie pointed out the window at the logo emblazoned on the side of the Monster Truck. "I looked up your address. Look, things are totally out of control—"

"Things are horrible," Sugar corrected.

"My dad is no help at all," Richie said. "He locked himself in the bathroom this morning."

"The only decent bathroom in the whole house," Sugar added.

"Is he okay?" I wondered if the last parent standing might be on the verge of hurting himself.

"He's just overwhelmed," Richie said. "He'll pull out of it. He always does."

"Does he know where you are right now?"

"No."

"You should call him. This minute." I pulled out my cell phone.

Richie shook his head. "Right now, he's talking to the police again. He'll be busy with them for hours."

"Can we get down to business?" Sugar asked. "We want to know if we can become emancipated minors."

"What?" I remembered how Flynn's friend the skating coach had said Sugar was nasty. I hadn't quite believed her. But the obnoxiousness of this girl was finally starting to be real to me. "Emancipated minors?"

Patiently, Richie said, "It's a legal term that means—"

"I know what it means." I began to understand why Eckelstine was overwhelmed. "Why do you want to be emancipated? And why now? I mean, it's a little soon, isn't it? Your mother is barely—"

"That's the thing," Sugar broke in, businesslike. "We want to make sure we get our fair share of our mother's estate. Before Eckelstine gets awarded everything of value, not to mention the power to boss me around."

"Boss *us* around," Richie said.

"Whatever." Sugar had Clarice's bulldozing thing down pat. She pulled a fancy cell phone from her pocket and began to thumb the keys at lightning speed. "I've done all the research on emancipation. I'll show you. We certainly don't want to get trapped in any Youth Services hell. Now, I don't know you from a clerk at 7-Eleven, but Bitchie seems to think you have a brain and might be trusted. Although, anybody who'd wear such heinous boots as those should be shot." She pointed at my feet and shuddered.

"My name is *Richie*."

"Save your breath. You'll need it to blow up your next date. That's all you can handle, right? An inflatable girl?"

"Watch your mouth, crankypants," I said while Richie tried to figure out what the insult meant. "He's your brother now. And I'm the one you're asking for help, remember?"

Nooch spoke up. "Roxy's always helpful. Most of the time, she's a very positive person, except for some cussing. But she helps lots of people—especially people who can't go to the police."

"Right," Sugar said with sarcasm, still busy on her phone. "And we're supposed to trust your judgment? I don't think so, rhino man."

Shock might be to blame for Sugar's bizarre bad temper, but I was having a hard time not giving her a smackdown.

I turned to Richie. "I don't know what you think I can do," I said to him. "I'm supposed to temporarily adopt you or something? Is that even legal?"

"Do we have to explain every detail? Look." She thrust her phone at me. "All the information's right here on the screen. You can read, right?"

Before I could verify her Internet research, a big vehicle pulled up outside the office window. The driver tooted the horn cheerfully.

"Wait here," I told the kids, and I went outside.

Mostly, I needed fresh air to cool my temper. Two minutes in the presence of Sugar Mitchell, and I felt like spanking her.

Out in the parking lot, I did a double take. A big black Escalade had arrived, exactly like the one Sage's new boyfriend drove.

Except slipping out of the driver's side was none other than Zack Cleary. He walked around the back of the truck with a wide, if uncertain, grin on his face. "Morning, Mrs. A. How do you like my new wheels?"

I pointed at the SQUISHY license plate. "This is Mr. Squishy's Escalade. What did you do? Steal it?"

"Yep," Zack said proudly. "Isn't she a beaut?"

"I thought you were clear about the difference between an annoying prank and a real crime that might get you arrested, Zack, not to mention get you tossed off the police force before you even get hired."

"I know, but I was in the moment." His eyes were bright, and he was bouncing with energy. "Crazy, right? I saw this baby sitting outside your house, and I couldn't stop myself. I knew Brian was inside with Sage and—well, it was an irresistible urge. Besides, Brian left the keys in the ignition, and anybody that much of an idiot deserves to get his truck moved, right?"

"You didn't *move* his truck. You stole it."

"What's your point?"

"You stole it, and then you brought it here!"

At last, Zack's good cheer began to waver. "I thought you could help me plan my next move."

❧ 21 ❧

My day had shaped up into a full-blown shitstorm. I could see the faces of Nooch, Richie, and Sugar staring out through my office window. Sugar's mouth was moving a mile a minute. They disappeared when they saw my glare.

"Give me the keys, tiger." I put out my hand to Zack. "Then get inside before somebody arrests you."

When we entered the office, Sugar was sitting at my computer. She broke off a diatribe she had been addressing to Richie. "This machine is totally outdated," she said to me. "How am I supposed to function with a computer this old? I'm trying to find a lawyer, and this thing takes forever."

Then she took one look at Zack and immediately assumed an angelic expression with shades of seduction.

"Hi," she said, catching Zack off guard with some batting of eyelashes.

He stepped back as if she'd brandished a Taser.

"Okay, listen up," I said to the group assembled around my space heater. "Here's what's going to happen. I'm leaving for an hour." Over a chorus of objections, I raised my voice and continued. "All of you are going to stay here and behave yourselves while I take care of business. Zack, you can babysit."

"I do not need a babysitter!" Sugar said hotly.

"Neither do I," Richie said.

"I don't mind," Nooch said. "But what about lunch?"

Zack grabbed my sleeve as I headed for the door. "You're punishing me, aren't you? That's not fair!"

"I've got to get rid of Mr. Squishy's truck before the police figure out it's missing. So you're elected for child care, tiger."

"But—"

I got a handful of his shirt and dragged him out the door. Outside, I turned on him. "Listen, Zack, I'm not leaving you here to spoon-feed the applesauce and supervise the afternoon nap. Those kids have lost their mother, and that girl's father was almost murdered last night. Now, I haven't figured out why yet, but there's a fifty-fifty chance that one or both of them are in danger, too."

"Huh?"

"You've got some police skills, right?"

"Uh—"

"You just finished the damn academy, didn't you? So today your job is to protect those two kids until I get back. Nooch can help. Give him a direct order, and he'll do what you say. Just make sure those kids are safe."

"Okay." Zack gulped. "Okay, I can do that."

"If something happens to the little monsters, I'm going to blame you."

I took Rooney with me. He dragged his bone into the Escalade and left a greasy swath on the white leather upholstery.

As I pulled out of the yard, my cell phone rang again.

I groaned and checked the ID, expecting more bad news.

But the display read CARNEGIE LIBRARY.

I answered the call and heard Sister Bob's voice crying, "Roxy! Roxy! Come quick!"

I cursed and floored the Escalade.

We arrived in the parking lot of the library in a spray of gravel. I bailed out of the truck with Rooney hot on my heels. We ran through the employee entrance. Inside, I nearly stepped on the broken remains of a glass coffeepot and several cups.

In the stairwell, I ripped open the glass fire door and grabbed out the fire extinguisher. Rooney leaped up the steps ahead of me, his nose leading him straight for the trouble. Like a speeding bullet, he went through the double doors at the top of the stairs and disappeared.

I ran up the stairs behind him and reached the top in time to see through to the library's big lobby. The skylight sent a glare of sunlight down on a pudgy kid in a baggy sweatshirt stained with orange dye. He held a shaky handgun on three terrified librarians cowering behind the circulation desk.

Rooney charged the kid, who swung the gun on the dog, but not in time. The librarians screamed. Rooney leaped into the air, and the kid shrieked at the sight of a green dog headed straight for his throat. The gun went off. A chunk of the ceiling exploded overhead. Everybody started screaming—maybe even me. I saw the gun go flying.

Rooney's jaws closed around the kid's forearm, and his momentum whirled the kid around so that I could see his face at last. He looked ludicrously terrified.

I kicked the gun soccer-style, and it skidded under a table.

Another gunshot—this time higher pitched. The kid yelped and clutched his butt. I swung around to see Sister Bob flat on her belly, pointing a BB gun at the library robber.

By that time, Rooney was shaking the kid by his arm. I knew the dog was so far gone into attack mode that he could no longer hear me shouting at him. So I pulled the pin on the fire extinguisher.

The extinguisher had more kick than I expected. Before I got control of it, I had sprayed the circulation desk and everybody around it with soapy white foam. Then I grabbed the nozzle hard and trained the stream on Rooney and the kid.

Rooney released the boy's arm and backed off, his face full of foam.

"Get down on the floor," I ordered the kid.

But he was scared, plastered with orange dye and foam, plus he was bleeding and probably in pain. He grabbed his own arm and bolted for the stairs.

"Let him go!" someone cried, and I recognized Sister Bob's voice. She scrambled up from the floor.

The huddled group of librarians sorted themselves out into a cluster of middle-aged ladies who were frightened and outraged, but otherwise unharmed. One of them headed for the telephone and called 911.

"Tell the police to look for an orange kid," Sister Bob suggested.

"Who's all soapy-looking," added another librarian.

While the rest of the librarians advised the police, Sister Bob rushed over and hugged me. "Oh, Roxana, I can't thank you enough for coming! He's never brought a gun before. We were so frightened!"

"It's okay. Everybody's fine. Unless you shot someone with a BB."

"I think I hit that kid in the tushie."

"If it's only a BB gun, he'll just be walking funny for a while. It's his arm I'm more worried about. Good thing he was wearing that thick shirt, or Rooney might be chewing on a wrist bone."

Sister Bob hugged Rooney. "What a dear, sweet dog!"

"Uh, look, Sister Bob, I have to be going."

"But why? You should stay and talk to the police. You can identify the boy."

There was no way to explain that I didn't want the cops to see the vehicle I'd driven over. By now, surely they were looking for a stolen Escalade with a SQUISHY plate.

"You can identify him just as well as I can. Besides, nobody's going to miss seeing a kid who's orange and butt-shot. I don't want Rooney to get unfairly impounded. He's had all his shots, but—"

"I understand," said Sister Bob.

I edged for the stairs. "Sister Bob, did Sage go to school today?"

"Yes," said Bob. "Her boyfriend came to take her."

"Did you see her leave the house?"

"Well, no, but she said she was going. She promised to lock all the doors."

If I had any motherly instincts at all, they were telling me that Sage was home alone with her new boyfriend. "Okay, Sister Bob, I'll see you later, right?"

"Thank you, Roxana. Thank you, thank you."

All the librarians had to hug me after that, but I finally tore myself away.

Rooney and I pulled out of the parking lot just as two police cruisers showed up. One officer craned his neck around to see who was driving the Escalade, but I think I managed to escape before he saw my face. The license plate, though, was clear.

I drove up to Loretta's house to see if Sage was skipping school again. I parked the Escalade in the back alley and used my key to get into the house.

But nobody was home.

Next I drove over to Sage's school.

It had been my school, too, years ago, but now it was very different.

For one thing, the place had as many security systems in place as the airport. I had to pass through a metal detector manned by a mouth-breather who packed a Taser, a nightstick, and breath so bad he could have killed a terrorist with it.

Eventually, I made my way to the school's administrative office, where a former friend of mine was typing at warp speed on a computer. An open bag of M&M's sat beside her coffee cup. She saw me and waddled over to the counter to chat. Sometime during the last decade, she'd added about a hundred pounds to the body she'd so easily squeezed through a locker room window to steal Girl Scout cookies from a coach's desk drawer.

"Roxy Abruzzo," Megan Schnorr said with a smile, planting both dimpled elbows on the counter. "What brings you here? Back to finish your detention at last?"

"Very funny, Megan. Seems to me we spent a few hours in detention together. No, I'm just making sure my daughter made it to school today."

Megan made no effort to deny her own high school hijinks. "Sage? Just so happens I saw her in the hallway this morning. I noticed because she looked upset."

"How upset?"

"Not crying, which is all part of an ordinary day around here. But she had a group of girlfriends around her, and they were all chattering like a flock of birds. My radar told me something was up, but not big enough for me to interfere. Want me to check to see if she's in class like she's supposed to be?"

I hesitated.

Megan must have seen something in my face, because her smile broadened. "It's a stupid mother who trusts any teenager these days, Roxy. Why don't I rustle up Sage, and you can see for yourself?"

I caved in. "Okay, thanks."

"No problem. Wait here. School security rules."

I hung around, keeping an eye on the school principal's closed office door while Megan went looking for my daughter. I'd spent a lot of hours in that same office, sitting on the same wooden bench, waiting for the principal to come out and decree my latest punishment. In fact, I'd had time to carve my name into the bench. But somebody had sanded down the wood and refinished it. Either that, or so many girls had carved the bench that it had finally collapsed into a pile of toothpicks, and now a new one stood in its place.

At last, Sage showed up in her school uniform, carrying her backpack. She looked surprised to see me, but didn't exactly throw herself into my waiting arms. "Mom! What are you doing here?"

"C'mon." I pulled out the keys. "Let's got for a ride."

Sage held back. "I have class. An English quiz next period. It's Emily Dickinson."

"I bet you know enough about Emily Dickinson already. Let's go. Megan, we're going to go look at colleges this afternoon. That okay with you?"

231

Megan's phone was ringing, so she waved us off and went to answer it.

I put my arm around my daughter's shoulders and pulled her out to the parking lot.

Outside, Sage stopped dead on the sidewalk and gaped at the Escalade. In the passenger seat, Rooney sat looking green and smiley with his tongue hanging out. He spotted Sage and barked, happy to see her.

Sage saw the SQUISHY plate and cried, "That's Brian's truck! Where did you find it? He's going to be so—oh, God, Mom, you didn't steal it, did you?"

"No," I said. "But if I see you skipping school with him again, I might. Get in. We'll take a ride."

I shoved Rooney into the backseat and used a scrap of McDonald's napkin to swipe up the worst of the mess his bone left on the passenger seat.

Sage started talking even before she slammed the door. Her words tumbled out in a rush. "Brian came over this morning, Mom, but I didn't invite him. He just showed up. I swear we didn't do anything."

"Why the hell did he come over then? To check on you? What is he, your stalker?"

"We had a discussion about that," Sage said firmly. "I laid it on the line. He has to trust me, or we're done. We had a big fight, but he saw it my way, honest. He was going to drive me to school, but when we went outside, the truck was gone! He was so upset. He called the police and everything, but I had to go to school and— Where did you get this? Did you find it? Did the police bring it to the house?"

"None of the above." I turned the key in the ignition. "Fasten your seatbelt. What else do I need to know about Brian?"

"I should have introduced you. I know that, and I'm sorry. Loretta told me weeks ago I should make sure you met him. He's really nice and— Okay, okay, I was wrong not to make sure you got a look at him. But Mom, you're so— You're very scary sometimes. Especially to my friends who are guys. You intimidate them."

"Zack isn't intimidated."

"Zack." Sage sighed. She snapped her seatbelt into place and sank back against the seat as if the weight of the world suddenly landed on top of her.

"Yeah, Zack. What are you doing, stringing him along while you date Mr. Squishy, too?"

"I'm not dating Mr. Squi—Brian." She looked at me sideways to see if I bought that fib. "Not exactly. I'm not sleeping with him either, if that's what you're thinking."

I put the truck into gear and concentrated on driving. It was easier not to look at her when I asked the next question. "Are you sleeping with Zack?"

"Not anymore. Honest, I'm not. I don't want to get pregnant, Mom. I really don't. I learned from my mistake."

"Well, that's progress."

"Look, I know Brian's a little nuts with the calling. He says it's because he cares abut me, but it's—"

"It's a way of controlling you."

"He can't control me, Mom. I'm an Abruzzo, for crying out loud!"

"I can't help being worried."

"Do you think I haven't noticed all the abused women you bring around? I'm not dumb, Mom. I can see how they got into bad situations. I know how to say no, and I know how to kick Brian's butt if he keeps up the annoying phone calls. I'm your daughter!"

"Are you serious about him?"

"Serious?" she asked on another sigh. "I don't know. He's—he's not Zack."

"What's that supposed to mean?"

"He's not a yinzer, y'know?"

I knew, all right. A yinzer is a born and bred Pittsburgher with blue-collar values, maybe a few bad habits, and certainly a way of talking that sounds uneducated. A yinzer uses the word "yinz"—a word that might be "y'all" in the South—the plural of "you" with a Burgh accent. A yinzer drinks beer, rarely reads a newspaper, and throws his sofa into the back of his pickup once a year and drives it down to sit outside the hockey arena because he can't afford a ticket to the game. But he wants to be where the action is.

Yeah, Zack was a yinzer in the making.

I drove, not caring where we went. What mattered was inside the truck.

"I just can't see myself spending my life with Zack," Sage said. "Mom, the last book he read was a biography of some football player. And that was back in high school for a book report."

"Okay, so he's not exactly sophisticated. Brian is?"

"No," Sage said, sounding miserable. "He isn't. But at least he can buy me lunch. Take me to a movie. Zack just wants to stay home and watch TV while we . . ."

Her voice trailed off, so I said, "I know what he wants. Look, why are you bothering with these two losers, anyway? You've got your own life to live."

"Yes, but . . ."

"But what?"

"The Christmas dance is coming up. It's just nice to have a real date, you know?"

"So? Ask somebody else. Ask anyone. Nobody's going to turn you down. I'm thinking ahead, Sage. What about college?"

Miserably, she said, "I don't know."

"You haven't filled out your applications, have you?"

She stole another look at me. "Not exactly."

"Not at all. How come? And don't tell me you don't know."

"I don't— Okay, it's just too much right now."

"Right now is when they have to get done," I insisted. "You can't put them off any longer or you'll end up at the community college."

"What's wrong with that?"

"It's where Zack went, for one thing. You want to be a yinzer, too?"

"God, no," she said with a shudder.

"Then you need to get those applications done. You can't let Brian talk you out of going to college."

"Where'd you get that idea? Mom," she said, then stopped.

"What?" I demanded. "What's the problem? Brian?"

Sage took a deep breath. "The problem is you can't afford to send me to college."

I hit the brakes and pulled over to the curb. "What the hell are you talking about?"

"You can't pay for college. It's incredibly expensive, and you don't have the tuition money."

I turned sideways in the seat to face her. "Don't worry about where the dough comes from. That's my job—mine and Flynn's. He said he'd help. And Loretta. There's always Loretta."

Sage was teary. "You won't take money from Aunt Loretta. She says you never have, never will."

I hadn't. Borrowing anything from Loretta always felt like cheating. Like I couldn't manage on my own. And now I didn't know how I felt about Loretta at all. Turns out, she'd changed the course of my life by sending Flynn off to the Marine Corps. Life could have been a lot different for all of us if she had minded her own business back then.

But here was Sage, sounding both panicky and resigned to a dismal fate.

I said, "Maybe I've been stubborn about Loretta helping. But college is different, Sage. We're going to get you there, no matter what it takes. If that means borrowing from Loretta, that's what we'll do."

She didn't speak.

"I mean it," I insisted. "Let us worry about the money. All you have to do is the paperwork. Flynn and I will figure out the financial stuff."

She peeked at me. "You talk to him about this? About me?"

"Of course I do."

"You—I mean, the two of you really talked?"

"We talk a lot. What—you think all we do is yell at each other?"

"I don't know. You don't yell exactly. It's weird. Sometimes you act like total strangers, and then suddenly there's this look in your eyes, and I'm invisible."

"You're never invisible. Flynn and I go way back, that's all. There's history. Some good, some bad, but it's us, you know? Right now, your future is the most important thing to both of us."

"Do you love him?"

I grabbed the steering wheel and looked out the windshield.

"See?" Sage said. "That's weird, what you just did."

"It's not weird," I insisted.

"Then answer the question."

"I love you," I said. "That's what counts. Family is the important thing."

"Flynn is family. My family."

"Yes, he is," I said, trying to sound like an adult. "And he loves you like crazy. But me? And him? It's difficult. For one thing, he's with Marla now."

"Marla." Sage's singsong had some ridicule in it.

I looked at my kid. "What's wrong with Marla?"

"She's a yinzer," Sage said, and I laughed.

"So am I," I told her.

"No, you're not. Not exactly. But Marla pretends not to be. She wants to be a fashion model or something, and she's just—okay, she's dumb, I guess."

"She needs help, that's all. Or Flynn wouldn't be with her."

"Really?" Sage sounded curious. "He's like that? Like you?"

"What?"

"You're always helping people. If Sister Bob wasn't living in Loretta's house, you'd have some girl with a black eye staying in that room. Flynn does the same thing?"

"I don't know," I said, suddenly tired. And hungry. Disoriented, too. I couldn't figure out my relationship with Flynn right now. It was all too damn complicated. "Let's get some lunch, okay?"

"Thanks, Mom." Sage lunged across the seat and gave me a hug. "Most of the time I don't expect you to act like a real mother, but sometimes you remind me that you really are."

"I hope that's a compliment." I messed up her hair. "Where do you want to eat?"

At her request, we drove through a Wendy's and ate sandwiches in the truck in the parking lot.

Once, I saw a cop car cruise by, and I realized I needed to make a decision about Brian's Escalade. At the very least, I needed to find a new license plate.

At that moment, my phone rang, and I checked the ID.

"Who is it?" Sage popped a French fry.

Carmine. Sage didn't know much about Carmine. She probably saw him as the friendly old guy who waved at her in church and brought over Easter candy and Christmas mints.

I said, "Nobody important right now."

Sage's cell phone gave a chirp, and she checked its screen. "Text message," she reported. "From Brian. He's at the police station, reporting his stolen vehicle. Uh, what should I tell him, Mom?"

"Nothing yet. I have to decide some things first."

"Did you steal this car?" she asked, flat out. "Tell me the truth this time."

"No. But I'm in possession, and that's all the cops are going to care about. So don't answer, all right? Let me think about the best way to handle this."

"Who did steal it?"

"Sage—"

"Oh my God!" The realization hit her. "It was Zack, wasn't it?"

Rather than looking angry, Sage suddenly had pink spots on her cheeks and a glow in her eyes.

My phone rang again. It was Zack this time. I decided to pick up.

He said, "You need to get back here. These kids are driving me crazy."

"Remember that feeling next time you don't have a condom. Be there in ten minutes."

I closed the phone to find Sage's gaze on me again. Full of affection, she said, "Thanks, Mom."

"For what?"

"Being cool, I guess." She grinned. "I need to go to the bathroom. Then you better take me back to school, okay?"

"Okay."

She grabbed her backpack and bailed out of the Escalade. I sat there for a while feeling pleased with myself. Turns out, I could be a mom after all.

That feeling didn't last long. The next phone call was from Bug Duffy. He said, "Where are you?"

I told him, and he said, "Stay there. I'm coming."

I decided it would be smart not to be found sitting in a stolen car by a police officer, so I got out of the Escalade, left it unlocked, and carried my Coke over to a bench under a tree. A bus stop stood a few yards away, but it was obvious that a lot of public-transportation patrons had eaten their fast-food meals on the bench while waiting for their rides. Greasy bags and wrappers were mashed into the ground around the bench.

Two minutes later, Bug's battered cruiser took the corner too fast, bumped the curb, and careened into the parking lot. He parked carelessly, got out, and walked over to me.

I offered him my Coke. "Looks like you need to cool down, Detective."

He ripped off his sunglasses and glared. "Just what the hell have you been doing?"

"Sit down. Relax."

"I don't feel like sitting with you." His voice was icy. "Want to know who I interviewed this morning?"

"Can I buy a vowel?"

"Your uncle Carmine. And he had some interesting things to tell me. About you."

That didn't sound good.

✻ 22 ✻

He said, "You were hired to kidnap Clarice Crabtree."

"That's not true."

"The hell it isn't!"

"Now, Bug—"

"Your mobbed-up uncle told me himself. Said you were supposed to kidnap Clarice the night she was murdered."

"Nobody hired me. I turned down the job."

"But you knew it was going to happen."

"No." I got to my feet. "As far as I knew, they couldn't find anyone to do it, so—"

"Who's 'they'?"

"I don't know. All I saw was a photocopied letter."

"Who showed you the letter? Carmine?"

"Yes, Carmine." If the old crook could throw me under the bus, I could do the same to him. "Indirectly."

"What were the details?"

"There was a phone number."

"Who answered?"

"I didn't call."

"How much money was exchanged?"

"None that I know of."

"Why was Clarice the target?"

"I don't know any of these answers, Bug! Someone was supposed to make a phone call for instructions, but it wasn't me. I rejected the job at the very beginning."

"And just when were you going to mention all of this to me?" Bug demanded.

"Probably never," I shot back.

"And you don't see anything wrong with that? Why were you at Clarice's house the night she was snatched?"

"I went to see her because I knew somebody wanted to kidnap her."

"You went to watch?"

"To warn her! But I didn't have enough time. She had to rush to a meeting. And besides," I added, "she was a pain in the ass."

Bug stared. "You didn't warn her because of some high school grudge?"

"That's not what I—"

"Did you see who grabbed her?"

"Of course not. I'd have told you if I had."

"Oh, really? That's the point when your conscience kicks in?"

Bug turned away, muttering under his breath. At that moment, Sage came out of the restaurant. She slung her backpack over one shoulder and headed across the parking lot in the direction of the Escalade. Bug's gaze sharpened on her.

"Is that—?"

Then his attention traveled past Sage to the vehicle.

He spun around with fresh outrage. "For God's sake, on top of everything else you stole your daughter's boyfriend's car?"

"What car?"

Bug cursed and yanked out his cell phone. "I don't know why I bother trying with you. I ignored what everybody was saying at the station house. I thought you could clean up your act, be a normal human being. I thought you had a heart. But you're as screwed up as ever, aren't you? With a twisted sense of right and wrong. Just like your crooked uncle."

"Sometimes things happen," I said. "Sometimes going to the cops is the wrong thing to do."

"This time it was the right thing," he said. "I'm finished standing up for you, Roxy. You're a hustler on the edge of the law. Well, this time you can go to jail, for all I care."

He punched in a call and spoke tersely into his phone. Whoever was on the other end of the line heard exactly where a stolen Escalade with the SQUISHY plate could be found.

Sage spotted me and changed direction, happily heading my way.

I thought fast.

About then, a city bus pulled up, and a half a dozen passengers straggled off. Two university students headed in the direction of the campuses, but the others mingled on the sidewalk for a moment, aimless. Among them, I spotted a youngish guy who looked every inch a panhandler— shoes held together with duct tape, shapeless clothes that needed time in a Laundromat, bushy hair, and a face that hadn't seen a razor in weeks.

While Bug snapped orders on his cell phone, I pulled a ten-dollar bill from my pocket.

With the instinct of a pigeon catching sight of a shiny object, the panhandler spotted the ten and ambled toward me.

Sage reached my side about the same time.

"Sweetheart," I said to her, "got a piece of paper and a pencil?"

From her backpack, my daughter obediently produced both, and I scribbled a fast note.

I handed the ten and the note to the panhandler and pointed him in the direction of the restaurant. "Grab yourself a burger," I said to him. "And while you're at it, could you give this note to the nice lady at the cash register?"

He headed straight for the front door.

Bug snapped off his phone and swung on us. But Sage's arrival startled him, and he quickly smothered his anger at me. "Sage, right?"

My daughter smiled up at him, relaxed and confident that all was right with the world. "Hi, yes." She put out her hand to shake his.

He took it automatically, and I could see him struggling with the instinct to be nice to a pleasant teenager while wanting to strangle me with his bare hands.

I said, "This is Detective Duffy, Sage. He used to be a friend of mine."

"Oh," Sage said, "one of my girlfriends babysits for you sometimes. Bailey Jones."

"Right, yeah, Bailey. Nice kid."

"She loves your boys. Says they're a lot of fun."

"Thanks."

While they made small talk, I could see the anger drain out of Bug. He couldn't stay mad.

But I held my breath, hoping the scene would play out the way I hoped.

Another cop car arrived. And another and another. They were soon swarming the place, lights flashing. Officers jumped from their cruisers. But instead of surrounding the Escalade, they converged and made a dash for the front door of the restaurant.

"What in the world—?" Sage looked around. "What's going on?"

A mob of customers came running out of the restaurant, hands waving, lots of yelling. Bug noticed the growing chaos and turned.

Another police vehicle barreled into the parking lot, and Bug flagged him down. "What's happening?"

"Robbery in progress," the cop reported.

"Robbery!" Sage cried.

Bug forgot about us and headed for the restaurant.

"That's our cue," I said to Sage. "Let's get out of here before they block off the parking lot."

I bustled Sage over to the Escalade, and we climbed in. Half a minute later, I was steering the big vehicle through the maze of haphazardly abandoned cop cars, and we hit the street at last. I floored the accelerator and headed away from the restaurant.

Buckling her seatbelt, Sage said to me, "Mom, what was that note you gave the homeless guy?"

I decided not to tell Sage.

But I'd written, "This is a holdup."

Hey, it bought me enough time to escape being arrested for grand theft auto.

When we arrived back at the salvage yard, Rooney scrambled over Sage to get out of the truck. She climbed out more slowly, and by the time we reached the hood of the Escalade, Zack was outside, blinking in the sunlight.

"What are you doing here?" Sage asked him.

"Why aren't you in school?" he said in the same tone.

"What, you're suddenly my dad? I don't need to explain myself to you."

"That goes both ways."

I said, "Stop it, you two. I've had an extremely long day already."

"You haven't tried ordering pizza for picky eaters," Zack said. "What the hell is a vegan, exactly? That Japanese girl is nuts."

"She's not Japanese," I said.

"Huh?"

"Is everything okay? They're safe?"

"Yeah, sure. No problems."

"Okay, thanks. Round them up now," I told him. "This place isn't secure anymore."

"What's wrong?"

"We have to find somewhere else for everyone. At least for a few hours."

"Speaking of hours," Zack said. "I have to be at work by three. Stadium security for the Dooce concert."

"That's tonight already?"

I checked my watch. Stony wanted me backstage by five. But first priority was getting Clarice's kids stowed someplace where their mother's killer couldn't find them. I considered calling Bug for that. After all, the kids would be better protected by the police. But I had to ditch the Escalade first. I didn't want Zack taking the blame for stealing it.

Plus I needed to figure out something to wear to the concert.

"Let's take everybody over to my place. Zack, go get the kids. Tell Nooch I want him to drive the Monster Truck. I'll take the Escalade."

"Got it." Zack turned tail and strode back inside.

Sage had watched the whole exchange without a word. But she looked thoughtful as Zack disappeared purposefully into my office.

"I'm sorry," I said to her. "We've had a few problems this morning."

When Zack herded everyone out, I grabbed Richie Eckelstine. "How's your expertise with men's fashion?"

"What?"

"Nooch needs a suit for a wedding tomorrow. If I sent you with him to the Goodwill store, could you help him pick out something that won't look stupid?"

Richie gave Nooch a practiced glance. "It's a challenge."

"A big one, I know."

The kid lifted his chin, undaunted. "I'll give it a shot."

I produced my last few dollars and handed them over to Richie. "No bow ties. I don't want him looking like a dancing bear."

"I get it."

He turned away, but I grabbed him one more time.

"Another thing," I said.

He waited.

He waited a little more.

Finally, he prompted, "Another thing?"

Although I'd rather poke a fork in my eye than say so, I admitted, "I need something to wear tonight. To a concert."

"The symphony?" Richie inquired, one brow raised.

"Listen, smart-ass, I could turn you loose with your obnoxious little sister anytime."

"Okay, okay, but I need more to go on."

"I'm singing. I'm singing backup for Dooce at his concert tonight."

Richie's bland expression gave way to something akin to being impressed. "No kidding?"

"Normally, I wear jeans and a sweatshirt. But I was thinking–"

He began shaking his head before I got any further. "No, no, don't think. Leave it to me. I'll find something for you."

"I don't want to look like an idiot," I cautioned.

"No dancing-bear outfit, you mean?"

"I'm no twenty-year-old sweet tart, either."

"I get it," he said. "Can I have my shirt back?"

I released him at last.

We split up. Nooch and Richie took the Monster Truck and went off to the nearest thrift store. Zack and I got into the front of the Escalade, Sage and Sugar into the backseat. Sugar was busy using her phone again. Did she never stop?

My cell phone rang, and I checked the screen. Loretta.

Her name prompted a surge of resentment. The least she could have done was mention sending Flynn off to the marines so long ago. But she'd kept it a secret for a lot of years. I needed time to process what I'd learned.

I let her call go to voice mail, but the phone rang again almost immediately. Infuriated, I opened the phone and snapped, "What do you want?"

"Roxy? It's Tito calling. From the museum?"

"Sure. Hi, Tito. Sorry, I thought—never mind. What's up?"

"You sound a little touchy, darling."

"It's been an interesting day."

"For me, too, as a matter of fact. Do you have time to stop in? I have something to discuss."

"Well, actually, I've got a few too many irons in the fire at the moment. Can it wait?"

"Of course. It's just that I was really shocked by Clarice Crabtree's murder—especially since you and I were talking about her shortly before her death."

"I know, crazy coincidence, right?"

"I hope that's what it was." Tito cleared his throat. "Meanwhile, something interesting has happened I thought you'd like to hear about."

Suddenly I was all ears. "Let me guess. It's about dinosaur bones."

"In a way, yes. Richard Eckelstine tried to sneak into our facility yesterday."

"Say what?"

"Oddly enough, he was trying to return something."

I thought of Eckelstine's heavy backpack. "Tell me more."

"He tried to break in, but unfortunately, he tripped the backup security system. He was discovered with a large bone from our collection. So I did a little digging." Tito paused. "That's archaeology humor, Roxy."

"Hilarious."

"Yes, well, I looked into our inventory records. I discovered that Clarice Crabtree had signed out a number of items from the megafauna department. Over the last several years, Clarice systematically removed over two dozen valuable bones from the museum's collection."

"I bet she didn't keep them for herself."

"You seem to be a step ahead of me."

"She sold the bones?" I said.

"How did you guess?"

I guessed because if I had my hands on some valuable dinosaur bones, I'd probably find a lucrative way to get rid of them myself.

Tito went on. "I can't make specific accusations, of course. Not until her office gets a thorough going-over. But judging by her husband's eagerness to return a very large vertebra yesterday, I assume Clarice stole and sold a lot of items."

"Why would her husband return a vert—a verta—one of those things you said?"

"He's a scientist with a moral code. I think he discovered what his wife had done and was trying to do the right thing. He was returning something she stole."

"If he wanted to protect her reputation, he was a little late."

"There's more," Tito said in my ear. He dropped his voice as if someone might be eavesdropping. "After the Eckelstine incident, I looked through our really old records. Before the catalog was put on computer. We have old ledger books dating back to the days when the museum first opened for business. I found information dating back to the days when Professor Crabtree was associated with the institution."

My chest felt tingly inside—like the first time I figured out how to make an algebra problem work. "What did you find?"

"Don't quote me. But I think the Professor stole items, too. Mind you, most of it was things he gave us in the first place. But it's bad form to make donations and then take back the stuff. The interesting part is that I found at least one of the skeletons he checked out of the collection twenty-five years ago."

"What do you mean, you found it?"

"The skeleton is now owned by a movie star who collects all kinds of strange things—carousels, Native American pottery, Stickley furniture. And dinosaur skeletons. I think it's pretty clear the Professor sold his skeleton to her. For a lot of money."

"Wow. Twenty-five years ago?"

Twenty-five years ago, his wife had died in a supposedly random shooting.

Tito said, "You there, Roxy?"

"Yeah, sorry. My mind wandered. What's the next step?"

"We've started an internal investigation. It will take months to track down all the facts. And the police will be notified."

"You'll let me know what happens? And if you notice anything else?"

"Of course. Listen, Roxy. I don't want you to get into any trouble with the police, but . . ."

"Hey," I said sharply, "I didn't have anything to do with what happened to Clarice, Tito. So don't hold back when you talk to the cops."

Beside me in the passenger seat, Zack turned and got interested in the conversation.

Tito said, "That's a relief to hear. I'll be in touch."

I hung up, and thought about Richard Eckelstine trying to undo a small part of Clarice's low-down thievery. Maybe he wasn't such a dick-head after all.

Then I tried to remember what Clarice had said about her mother's death. How had it happened, exactly? And when? What did the Professor selling off an expensive dinosaur skeleton have to do with his wife's murder—if anything?

Meanwhile, Zack watched me think. And I found myself trying to figure out if Eckelstine was returning Clarice's bones to cover up her murder.

"Mom?" Sage said, yanking me back to the present.

"Yeah?"

"What's that?" Sage leaned forward and pointed out the windshield.

On autopilot, I had driven over to the North Side to my neighborhood.

The scene unfolding in the middle of my street was a typical domestic disturbance—nothing out of the ordinary in my corner of the world. A few of my neighbors, in fact, were hanging out their doors and windows to watch the action.

Jane Doe was shrieking while a Neanderthal dragged her by the hair toward a waiting car. Both of her children stood on the porch of the house, screaming.

To Zack, I said, "Push in the cigarette lighter, will you, tiger?"

"Huh?"

"I need to light a fire. So heat it up. Sage? See those kids on the porch? Go pick up the baby. I'll be there in a minute."

In the backseat, Sugar never looked up from her phone's screen. "This is so boring."

I bailed out of the Escalade and grabbed the only weapon I could find on short notice—a plastic ice scraper the vehicle's owner kept alongside the driver's seat. To Zack, I said, "See the garbage can over there? Go set it on fire."

"But—"

"Just do it," I said.

"Shouldn't we call 911?"

"No need."

I walked up the street and gave Jane Doe's boyfriend a solid shot upside his head with the ice scraper.

I gotta say, it doesn't pay to buy cheap automotive accessories at a gas station, because a flimsy ice scraper is going to break when you need it most. This one shattered on contact, but Jane Doe's boyfriend did not go down like I'd hoped he might. Instead, he turned on me like an enraged bull.

Like most firemen, he was big and strong, and he knew how to use that size and strength. He had a bulldog jaw and the insanity of rage glaring in his red eyes.

But he dropped Jane when I hit him, which was a good thing, and she had the presence of mind to stumble back toward the house, where Sage was just gathering up her children.

I figured my best move was to knee the fireman in the nuts. Not a fair fight, and I hated getting in close in case things didn't go my way, but it was a quick and easy solution.

Trouble was, he dodged my kick. And grabbed my hair. He swung me against a parked car, and I heard Sage cry out. I made a fist and jabbed the fireman squarely in one eye. He howled and tried to punch me back, but his blow went wide and he hit the car window instead. Another howl, and he clutched his injured hand.

Which gave me the opening to knee him squarely in the groin.

Except I didn't need to.

Jane Doe came back and hit him over the head with a porch chair.

It was like she suddenly had superhuman strength. She hoisted the chair over her head and brought it down on him with every ounce of muscle she had.

He went down on the pavement like a stone. He sprawled on the street, eyes spinning in his head. He was breathing, but he wasn't going to have a coherent thought for a while.

Meanwhile, from behind me, I heard a *whoosh* and a small explosion.

Then Zack cursed in surprise and came running toward me. "I don't know what was in that garbage, but it blew up!"

We looked down the street, where the trash can was already burning merrily. We could see the plastic melting fast, and an aerosol can suddenly popped up and disintegrated with a bang.

"Hairspray," I said. "The lady who lives in that house is a hairdresser."

The neighbors who had been watching the fight in the street suddenly turned their attention to the fire, and a few of them began shouting directions for putting out the flames.

"C'mon," I said to Zack. "Help me get everybody into the Escalade."

Sage carried the baby, and Jane Doe scooped up her little girl. They were all half crying, half laughing.

Jane was giddy. "Did you see what I did? I can't believe I did that!"

Sage said, "I was so scared! Mom, are you okay?"

"Sure, no problem."

Jane Doe burst into sobs. "Thank you. Thank you so much. He was—he came—I never thought I could—but you—and then I— Thank you, thank you."

"You did great." I put a calming hand on her shoulder.

She snuffled up her tears. "I didn't want my kids to see him treat me that way."

"That's progress."

As we left my neighborhood, we passed the first fire truck arriving on the scene. I figured Jane Doe's boyfriend would be happy to see his buddies.

❋ 23 ❋

Used to be, rock concerts played in the old Civic Arena—a round-domed municipal relic that had hosted everything from the Beatles to Pink Floyd to country shows like the Dixie Chicks, not to mention a lot of great hockey back when Mario Lemieux played and more recently when Sidney Crosby led the Penguins to the Stanley Cup. But that crumbling hulk had been retired, and beside the old site was now a shiny new multi-purpose arena that still had to prove itself to the locals, most of whom liked their Pittsburgh landmarks rough around the edges.

I parked the Escalade among the tractor-trailers that hauled Dooce's show around the country. At least a dozen uniformed city police officers hung around the trucks, but none of them seemed to be on the lookout for a stolen vehicle. We piled out of the Escalade. Zack took off for the security office. The rest of us made an odd parade going through the performer's entrance.

I gave my name to the guy double-checking security—a bearish, bearded guy who gave me a look in the eye that I recognized as an invitation. A heartbeat later, I read the name on the backstage credentials hanging around his neck: Jeremy Dranko. Dooce's right-hand man.

I returned the look and said, "You're Dooce's badass assistant."

"Personal manager," he said. "What's it to you?"

"I hear you're the man behind the man."

He had a crooked smile and gave me another slow once-over. "I do as I'm told."

"Sounds promising. Party after the show?"

"You bet, baby," he replied, then jutted his chin at the crowd behind me. "Who's this? Your entourage?"

"Family and friends. They'll behave, I promise."

"Too bad," he said. "What about you?"

"No promises there."

He laughed and distributed backstage credentials for everyone—even Jane Doe's baby. We slipped them around our necks, and I mentioned that I had two more people coming—Nooch and Richie Eckelstine.

"This isn't a backyard barbecue," he protested.

It seemed like a good idea to string him along. He'd been outside the Crabtree house the night Clarice disappeared. And the leather bomber jacket he wore inadequately covered the sidearm in his belt. I said, "But it could get hot later, right?"

He grinned again and relented. "I'll keep an eye out for them. As long as you make time for me, baby."

"Can't wait," I said.

I winked and we went through the metal detector.

We could hear the squeal of guitars tuning up in the arena, punctuated by the rattle of drums and someone counting into a microphone. We followed the sound along the wide concrete corridor to the first set of double doors. Another guard opened them for us. Inside, the work lights shone down on thousands of seats radiating from a big stage set up in the middle of what was usually the hockey ice.

Onstage, a dozen roadies and local guys from the stagehand union were finishing up threading cables, setting lights, and otherwise hauling junk around.

In the stadium, a group of observers sat in one cordoned-off section. To me, they looked like family and friends of the band or the roadies.

I put Sage in charge of the kids and told them to sit in the stadium seats with everyone else. Jane Doe still looked a little shell-shocked. She had ice cream on her blouse, but she was smiling.

Stony Zuzak called from the stage. "Roxy! That you?"

I jogged down the aisle and climbed the stage, where Stony and his bunch of local musicians stood getting their orders from the woman I took to be Dooce's music director. A tough blonde with a headset and a clip-board, she wasn't in the mood for nonsense. She talked their language, and they all nodded and scribbled notes while Dooce's lead guitarist made wisecracks with the drummer.

Off in the shadows by the electric piano were Deondra and Kate, my partners in crime in the backup department. I joined them.

Deondra wore a huge floral caftan. Her hair was freshly braided and swept to the top of her head. "Good to see you here, Rox." Her big voice was relaxed and vibrant. "Kate and me—we were worried we'd have to do this gig by ourselves."

Kate—very thin, very white, and very nervous—was sipping from a huge plastic water bottle. I knew from experience there was more than water in the container. She said, "Did you review the tapes Stony sent? You know your part?"

"Unless Dooce adds something fancy, I think I'm ready."

"Dooce won't do anything fancy," Deondra said. "He's performed this same concert so many times he could do it asleep. There won't be any surprises."

"Is he going to rehearse with us?"

"No, he doesn't get here until the show starts."

Kate said to me, "Is that what you're wearing?"

Kate favored short, skintight dresses and a hairdo that looked as if she'd cut it herself with hedge clippers—a look that worked for her. She glanced up and down my jeans and less-than-clean sweatshirt.

"Nah," I said, putting in a silent prayer for Richie to come through for me. "I'm going to change."

I saw Jeremy come down to the edge of the stage. He lounged there, keeping an eye on everything while talking into a cell phone.

The music director called us together, ran through the order of numbers without referring to her clipboard. She told us when Dooce would talk to the audience and give us time to get a drink, smoke, or run to the john. One intermission lasted twenty minutes, and we weren't to leave the building. She gave the musicians some specific cues, then turned and shouted at the guys in the light booth. They talked back to her using the arena's speaker system.

Then we checked every microphone on the stage to fine-tune the levels. I counted to three when it was my turn—that was it.

At last, they decided we should run through a number, and the music director chose one of Dooce's classics, a song called "Summer Drive." It was one of Dooce's American anthems—a song that glorified youthful indiscretions in the backseats of cars. Written by a man, there was no mention made of teenage pregnancies, but what else is new? The lead guitarist struck a major chord, nodded at the drummer to start the beat, and we were off. Stony played bass, and Dooce's keyboardist could really riff. The music director sang Dooce's part in a half voice—she wasn't bad—and the rest of us jumped in where we were supposed to.

Backing up a lead vocalist isn't like singing a solo in church or even harmonizing in a school choir. It's usually a lot of harmonizing with "ooohs" and "aaahs" and the occasional riff on the melody, but the art is in watching the way the lead singer breathes and creates his phrases. Deondra had a big voice with the kind of power that could drown the lead sometimes, but she was great at the technical stuff of backing up. She dropped the right consonants, let her voice fade so the lead could soar. Best of all, she blended. I had learned by following her, and after a few years I could confidently take my own part in the harmonies. Best of all, I liked getting noisy, raising the roof.

Okay, I wasn't usually a team player, and I liked being my own boss. But singing in clubs, working with Deondra and Kate and Stony's rotating band—it felt good to me. I liked the hard, driving music, but I also liked making myself part of a big sound.

The lyrics for "Summer Drive" were all Dooce's to sing, with the backup singers stuck with a long bunch of "c'mon, c'mons" and repeating the title phrase about two hundred times. Piece of cake. But fun.

Deondra and Kate and I were grinning at each other when the song came to close. We knew we'd nailed it.

But the music director came over and told us not to break in too early or Dooce would get mad. She made him sound like a jerk, which was a bit of a downer. Watch him for cues, she lectured. Don't sing too loud or the sound guys would cut our microphones. When she was finished, Deondra rolled her eyes at me and mouthed, "Anal."

"Okay!" The music director raised her voice to address everyone on the stage. "Show's in two hours. Please don't leave the venue between now and then. Stay in the designated backstage area. There's food set up, and lots of drinks, but go easy on the booze, okay?" She gave Stony's musicians significant looks. "We want a good show tonight."

At the edge of the stage, Jeremy Dranko snapped shut his cell phone and barked, "Backstage, everyone! House opens in half an hour."

While the guys stashed their instruments, the people who'd been watching from the stadium filtered down to the stage.

Sage bounded up to me, her face alight. "Mom, you were so cool!"

Sugar was right behind her, eyes glued to her phone. "This is so boring, I can't stand it."

Jane Doe had the baby in her arms and her daughter by the hand. They all looked beat. Any minute, the three of them were going to bust out bawling.

I said, "Let's go backstage and find a place to relax."

I'd never been behind the scenes for a big concert. In the greenroom,

I was prepared to see young groupies in skimpy clothes and a smorgasbord of recreational drugs. The clichés of the business. But everybody was disappointingly average—relaxed and hanging out in front of a couple of big-screen TVs watching ESPN and reruns of a sitcom. Mountain Dew and light beer seemed to be the beverages of choice. The roadies were all covered in tattoos, but they huddled together, straddling folding chairs and playing some kind of group computer game that sounded like machine-gun fire.

Jeremy disappeared down a hallway marked Dressing Rooms. I guessed only Dooce rated his own private place to chill.

What surprised the hell out of me was finding Flynn supervising a buffet. He slung a few hot trays and directed his assistant where to put the silverware. Wearing his black ninja chef outfit with the skullcap, he managed to look dangerous while peeling plastic wrap off a big bowl of salad greens. But just barely.

"Hey," he said when he saw me. "You sounded great out there."

"You could pick out my voice in all that noise?"

He grinned. "Not exactly. But the whole thing sounded good to me."

Sage rushed up and threw herself into Flynn's arms. "Dad! What are you doing here?"

He hugged her. "Hey, honey. Helping out, that's all. You should try the hot wings."

"Oooh, I'm starving!"

She launched herself toward the long tables of food. Still in her school uniform, she drew a few sidelong glances from the video gamers.

I threw flame their way. But to Flynn, I said, "Hot wings? That's not your usual menu."

"No," he admitted. "But a request. It's some kind of good-luck charm for the band, I guess. There's some better stuff. Lamb chops. A gumbo, too."

"Has Dooce asked to marry you yet?"

He allowed a wry grin. "In a way, yes."

I felt my own smile fade. "What does that mean? You're not going on the road with him, are you?"

"He asked. I haven't answered."

What about Sage? I almost blurted out the question.

He responded as if I had. "I don't want to leave Sage."

I tried to seem nonchalant about it. "Is there any of your famous soup here?" Because I didn't intend to eat any.

"Not tonight."

"I saw Jeremy, Dooce's assistant."

"Did he try to scare you?"

I smiled. "I haven't lost my touch completely."

"I get it. His mood must have improved. A while ago, he was screaming about losing his purse."

"His purse?"

"I dunno. Some kind of bag. He claims somebody stole it. He had a temper tantrum. I'm betting he dropped it somewhere."

"Was it, like, a messenger bag?"

"What's a messenger bag?"

I thought about the bag the bomb squad blew up. If it had been Jeremy's, that meant he'd been at the Crabtree house. He'd gotten out of the car, too. Maybe he'd snatched Clarice? If so, was it on Dooce's orders? And why?

Flynn said, "You okay?"

I pulled myself together. "Sure."

"Look, I don't want to be a jerk, but is this the right place for Sage to be?" He had also been watching the roadies ogling our daughter.

"I've seen bridge clubs more exciting than this scene."

"Things are cool for the moment. But that will change." With a jut of his chin, he pointed toward the unopened bottles of liquor standing alongside the soda pop and fruit drinks. "There's other stuff going on, too."

"Drugs?"

"Big-time in the men's room. This is not exactly a wholesome environment for kids."

"Sage probably passes six drug deals on her way to school every morning. She knows how to handle herself."

Flynn nodded at the rest of the brood that had followed me into the greenroom. "What are you doing playing Pied Piper with all these other kids?"

"Long story. Including a chapter that has the police looking for me in a stolen Escalade."

He turned on me. "Did you steal it?"

"Zack Cleary did. Which would reflect badly on a lot of people, including your daughter and his father, the chief of police, so I'm trying to figure a way to make it all go away."

"You couldn't just explain things to the police?"

"Without Zack getting arrested? And ruining his life? No. I'll figure something out. In the meantime, I'm keeping everybody out of sight. This seemed like a good hiding place, and the security guy at the gate saw things my way."

"So you're protecting Zack? Keeping him away from the cops? There must be a hundred of them working in this venue tonight."

"And he's one. So far, the security guys seem to be looking at pretty girls."

Flynn grunted in agreement. "Well, good luck. Who's the little girl with Sage? The Asian kid?"

"That's Clarice Crabtree's daughter."

"The one whose father was almost killed last night? Why isn't she sitting at his bedside?"

"That would be boring," I said.

We both looked at Sugar, who was pouting on a folding chair. For once, she wasn't staring intently at her cell phone. She ignored the action around her, which was an accomplishment in self-control, considering. How many kids got to see backstage at a rock-and-roll show? But she was acting as if someone had refused to buy her a candy bar.

I said. "Her reaction to her father's shooting is that she's decided she wants to be an emancipated minor."

"No tears?"

"She's in shock."

"Either that, or she's a psychopath." Flynn's gaze traveled past Sugar, and his eyes widened. "Wait—is that Nooch?"

I turned around to see my sidekick and Richie Eckelstine come through the door with backstage credentials around their necks. Richie carried a large, squished brown paper bag under his arm, but he managed to make it look like a fashion accessory.

Nooch had been transformed. Instead of his orange-stained sweatshirt, he wore a dark sport coat over a black turtleneck sweater with a checked scarf wrapped rakishly around his thick neck. Someone had brushed his crewcut hair into trendy spikes. He was . . . almost human.

My mouth must have been hanging open, because Richie said, "That's a good way to catch flies, you know."

"Nooch?" I said.

"Hey, Rox. The book says I need to dress like the person I as—asp—the person I want to be. Richie helped me pick out everything." He opened the sport coat. "What do you think? Do I look like I envisioned myself right?"

"You look like a bodyguard for Tom Cruise." Either that or a metrosexual professional wrestler. "Kid, how'd you manage to get him stuff that fits?"

"It wasn't easy." Richie reached out and tweaked Nooch's lapel. "And try hiring a tailor at this time on a Friday afternoon. We had to go back to my house to use the sewing machine."

"That's why we're a little late," Nooch added.

"Did you see your father?" I asked Richie.

"He's still with the police."

If Richie guessed his father might be the prime suspect in two murders, not to mention an accessory to a felony involving dinosaur bones, he didn't show it.

Sugar appeared beside her brother. To him, she said, "I need a cell phone."

Richie was starting to get distracted by all the greenroom action. "What?"

"My battery died. I need a new phone."

"Who are you trying to call?" I asked.

"I'm not calling," she snapped. "I'm on the Web."

"Hey," Nooch said. "Are those hot wings?"

"Get a napkin!" Flynn and I said to him in chorus.

Sugar flounced away. I saw her catch sight of Dooce's drummer, who was tapping the keys of a laptop computer. She headed his way.

While Nooch went over to wreak havoc on the buffet, I said to Richie, "You're a miracle worker. Nooch looks great."

"You haven't seen anything yet."

"What d'you mean?"

Richie took my hand. "Come with me."

Flynn said, "I'll keep an eye on the kids. And Nooch."

I let Richie lead me to the nearest women's bathroom. He stuck his head inside and called, "Anybody home?"

When he got no answer, he grabbed my elbow. "C'mon."

I know it's not normal for a woman to be completely uninterested in clothes. But in my line of work, it's just easier to stick with jeans. I have to admit, I had butterflies.

Richie upended his brown paper bag, and a heap of things fell out on the floor—wisps of fabric, stretchy remnants, a thick leather belt. Not to mention a selection of shoes, including a pair of leopard-print stilettos.

"Wait a minute." I backed against the nearest sink.

"Are you actually afraid?"

"No! But . . ."

"Don't worry." Richie pulled a pair of scissors and a spool of thread from his pockets. "We'll make it work."

He ordered me to take off most of my clothes, and then he slipped a sleeveless, boring gray dress over my head. Over that, he pulled a second dress that was printed to look like wallpaper. He took the scissors and began to slash both dresses so that they turned into one, with pieces cut out. I started to look as if I'd been attacked by lions.

It took almost an hour.

But when the kid finally let me out of the bathroom, heads turned and Nooch dropped a quart of gumbo on the floor.

"Mom?" Sage said.

"I feel like a fool."

Nooch said anxiously, "Rox, is that you?"

Flynn left Jane Doe and came over. "Holy shit. I think that dress is made out of cobwebs."

"That's it," I said to Richie. "I want my jeans back."

"No, no, no." Flynn grabbed my hand to stop me from disappearing into the bathroom.

"You look fantastic," Sage protested.

"And the concert's starting," Richie said.

We'd heard the crowd growing in the arena. For the last hour, their noise had steadily intensified to a dull roar. Jeremy had come into the greenroom every fifteen minutes to announce the time, and now he called the opening-act performers to the stage.

The rest of us followed, just to watch. The stage was dark, and the arena lights began to dim. The crowd cheered as darkness fell, then held their collective breath for the show to start.

Dooce's opening act was a has-been woman singer who'd had a string of hits in the eighties, when female artists dressed in aerobic dance outfits and sang in front of synthesized recordings for MTV videos. She'd been hiding in another dressing room, but she swept past us in the backstage darkness, propelled by two bodyguards and trailed by Dooce's music director. She wore a dress that looked like a torn nightgown and enough makeup to spackle a retaining wall. Her pointy-toed, thigh-high boots would have looked right on the Wicked Witch of the West if she worked part-time as a dominatrix.

"Tch-tch," Richie said as she went by. "Someone hire that woman a decent stylist."

Stony and his band took the stage behind the woman, along with Dooce's musicians. They started playing before the lights came up, and the crowd roared, recognizing the song. The noise from the arena felt like a tidal wave backstage—a huge roll of sound and energy.

Then the lights blazed. The woman singer grabbed the microphone and held the front of the stage like the captain of a ship in a hurricane. She still had her voice, and she belted her old hits with a confidence that won over the audience fast.

I pulled Sage close and hugged her in front of me so she could see the show, but not get buffeted away from me by the backstage crowd. She sang along and vibrated with excitement. Beside us, Richie looked completely absorbed by the spectacle. Beyond him, even Nooch seemed happily overwhelmed. On the other side of me stood Sugar. She had taken possession of the drummer's laptop and looked hypnotized by the screen.

The last song in the opening-act set was the singer's big romantic hit, a ballad with a driving beat called "Hot Kisses." The whole crowd knew the words and sang the chorus along with her—a familiar refrain known to anyone who'd listened to a radio in the last twenty-five years. It was a good song, one that was probably mixed up in anyone's memory of youth and the excitement of first love.

From behind, Flynn wrapped his arms around me, and the three of us swayed to the exuberant beat. Sage threw her head back and sang the words along with the crowd. Flynn laughed warmly in my ear, and I thought about hot kisses long ago.

The moment was over too fast. The song ended in a long, dying note, and the lights went down, then up again for the singer to take her bows.

The stage crew arrived and backed us all away from the wings of the stage, clearing an opening for the singer to exit through. She rushed past us, and this time her face gleamed with energy.

Richie must have forgiven her the bad clothes, because he shouted, "Great show!"

She blew him a kiss and disappeared.

Dooce's music director showed up out of nowhere and began to shout orders. Out in the arena, the audience stomped and chanted for Dooce.

Flynn said, "Have a good show," and grabbed Sage. They melted away, taking Richie and Sugar with them.

Then Deondra and Kate appeared, and the stage crew shoved us through the darkness and into our places. The sound assistant handed over our earpieces, and we jammed them into our ears. Someone plunked microphone stands in front of us, and we saw the keyboard player take his spot. He grinned at us and flashed a thumbs-up.

All the while, the roar of the audience grew and grew until I feared I'd never hear the music over their noise.

Dooce's lead guitarist stood slightly to the right of the stage, and a pinpoint of light struck him from above. He banged his opening chord, and the reverberation shook the building. The crowd shouted back like a monster. From behind us, the stage crew formed a wedge and rushed past. Dooce went with them, and he burst onto center stage just as the lights exploded around him. The crowd roared at the sight of him.

Then it was time to sing, and I forgot about watching the lights and listening to the massive noise of the audience. I focused on the music that came clearly through my earpiece. We ripped through Dooce's opening number—a fast, feel-good song that rocked the house. It took me half the song to figure how to blend my voice with the rest of the band, but I got it. The second number—also upbeat and fun—kept the audience on their feet. Dooce was easier to follow than I'd expected. He was a pro who knew how to cue the band without cheating the audience. We segued into one of his biggest hits. Deondra took the backup solo, while Kate and I harmonized a bunch of "oooohs" and "la-la-las."

After that, Dooce took time to shout at the audience. He introduced Stony as his longtime buddy, and the crowd went wild for the local guys. Deondra, Kate, and I used the interlude to grab our water bottles and guzzle. My heart pounded, but I was ready for the next songs.

We took a twenty-minute break halfway through, but Deondra sat down right on the stage to rest, sweating buckets, so I stayed with her.

"I could never do this every night," Deondra said. "I'm shaking like a leaf."

Kate scampered off to pee and probably refill her vodka supply. When she came back, she brought energy bars for us. Deondra wolfed hers and half of mine.

The rest of the concert blew by like a storm. Dooce was a performer who knew how to give the audience a show worth the price they'd paid. He really rocked. He was still good-looking in a wasted kind of way—tall and lean and muscled. He had to be—his concert was choreographed to show off his athleticism as well as his music. But I could see that he dyed his hair black, and he'd had at least one facelift done by an overeager surgeon.

He came back to us once during a song that featured the backup voices. He and Deondra dueled during the gospel segment, and he did some grind dancing between me and Kate that brought a roar from the crowd.

But after that, it was all an adrenaline blur for me.

Dooce performed two curtain-call numbers, and then it was all over.

Kate and I helped Deondra stagger back to the greenroom, where she collapsed on a sofa and asked for a beer and a plate of hot wings.

Dooce made the rounds in the greenroom, wearing a towel around his neck and follwed closely by a glowering Jeremy. Dooce thanked the local musicians for their help. Stony looked happier than I'd ever seen any man. Dooce gave Deondra a big kiss, grabbed Kate's ass and pretended to rub it for good luck.

Then Dooce put his hand between my thighs and groaned with pleasure for the crowd. I let it pass. No big deal. He was a rock star, after all, not Mr. Rogers.

"I love Pittsburgh!" he crowed to all of us. "I'll jam with you anytime."

"Let's go, Dooce," Jeremy urged. "The bus is waiting."

But he hung around. In a minute, I realized what kept him in the greenroom, and it wasn't Flynn's food.

It was Jane Doe. Dooce had zeroed in on her, and within minutes he slipped one arm around her waist and pulled her with him as he spoke to everyone else.

He even scooped up her daughter, carrying the little girl over to the buffet to find a treat for her. Whether it was all for show, or he really did dig Jane Doe, I don't know. But he acted like a courtly gentleman with her.

Jane Doe looked starry-eyed.

Jeremy headed my way—probably looking for his payoff for letting me into the building. I braced myself. When I got him alone, I intended to ask how he knew the Crabtrees.

But Flynn appeared. He took me by the wrist and pulled me away. In my ear, he said, "Police are here."

"Shit."

"Take the kids. Nooch has the keys to your truck. Use the exit through the kitchen."

❧ 24 ❧

Sage didn't ask questions. Neither did Richie as we dashed through the service kitchen and out the door into the night.

But Sugar complained the whole way about giving up the laptop she'd appropriated.

Nooch finally picked her up like a sack of potatoes and carried her through the maze of tractor-trailers parked outside. Already, Dooce's crew scurried around opening the trucks and rolling handcarts toward the arena, preparing to tear down the stage and haul it to their next concert venue.

We spotted two police officers standing guard beside the Escalade.

I skidded to a stop, holding the kids back. "Can't go that way," I muttered.

Richie said, "We left your truck in Section D."

"Let's go."

But our path was barred by two more officers who stood watching the rowdy crowd of concertgoers head for the parking lot. The last thing I wanted was to end the evening getting arrested for car theft. One of the officers turned our way.

I realized we were standing beside a bus. I reached for the door handle and found it open. I shooed the kids and Nooch inside.

We found ourselves in what must have been Dooce's travel bus. A driver sat behind the wheel in a big captain's chair. He was reading a paperback and smoking a smelly cigar. He wore a vintage Dooce T-shirt that didn't do his belly any favors.

"Hey." He took the stogie out of his mouth and glanced at the back-stage credentials around our necks. "Dooce send you?"

"Yes," I said without hesitation.

"Wow. He always goes for the girls with kids, but you take the cake. Three, huh? And all grown up."

"Yes."

"Who's the muscle?" He pointed at Nooch.

"Bodyguard."

The bus driver shrugged. In his world, bodyguards were normal. "Okay. Well, there's drinks in the fridge while you wait."

Sage and Richie looked at me with big eyes. I gave them a throat-cutting gesture to keep quiet, but Sugar wasn't taking any orders—silent or otherwise.

"Put me down," she said to Nooch. "Before I kick you in the teeth."

Nooch hastily obeyed.

"I want to get out of here," she said to the bus driver. "Take me to a hotel."

The driver grinned. "The Ritz or the Waldorf?"

"One with room service and a computer room."

"Oh, yeah? Your mom have anything to say about that?" The driver winked at me.

"My mother is dead," Sugar said.

That information startled the driver into dropping his cigar.

"Ha-ha," I said. "Very funny, Sugar. Now, come over here and get your-self a Pepsi."

"I don't poison my body with sweets."

The interior of the bus was set up like a standard recreational vehicle with a living room and kitchen combo behind the driver's seat. A laptop sat on the fold-out table. Sugar headed straight for it.

Toward the back, a doorway led, I presumed, to a bedroom and bath. What caught my attention in the front of the big vehicle, though, were the heavily framed shadow boxes on the walls. Dooce didn't display his gold records on the bus.

He displayed bones.

Big bones.

Big animal bones.

Leg bones, skulls, tusks, teeth. All kinds of bones.

"Wow," I said to the driver. "This is an interesting collection."

"Oh, yeah, Dooce loves this stuff." He retrieved his cigar and waved it at the framed boxes. "Picks up items all over the country. You should see his house. He's got a whole dinosaur in his basement."

"No kidding."

"And he's working on a whatayacallit—a woolly mammoth now."

I said, "That must be an expensive hobby."

"Oh, you know. These guys all make a fortune on tour. They gotta spend it somewhere."

"Does Dooce have any help? Doing his collecting?"

"What d'you mean?"

"You know—Jeremy. He seems to help out a lot. Does he have a hand in Dooce's collection?"

"Nah. Jeremy's just a glorified maid. He opens car doors, picks up the hamburgers. That's about it."

Richie had been staring at the bones on the walls. When he turned to me, I saw tears on his face.

I put my arm across his shoulders. "It's okay," I said.

"But my mom," he began.

"I know."

"Did she—?"

"Let's not jump to conclusions," I said.

"She was in contact with Dooce. I know she was. She talked to lots of celebrities, but she always said it was because they wanted to meet her. I heard her on the phone a lot. But I didn't think . . ."

Sage had been peering out the windshield of the bus. Over her shoulder, she called, "Boy, there sure are a lot of people out there."

I got the message.

"C'mon, kids." I grabbed Sugar's hand and dragged her away from the laptop. "It's time to go home."

"Hang on," the driver protested. "Dooce should be here any minute. You should wait."

"That's okay. I'm starting to get a bad feeling about this."

"Hey, Dooce ain't no creep. He just likes to show kids all the dinosaur stuff. Kids go crazy for dinosaurs." He winked. "Nothing too raunchy for the moms. He has a wife and kids at home."

"Right. Well, sorry, we've got to be going."

"Good thing your kids saw the bones, I guess, huh?"

"Wonderful," I said. "Good night."

We bailed out of the bus. I figured Jane Doe was on her own with Dooce. She'd probably be safe enough—especially if there were any chairs handy to hit him with.

The mob waiting for Dooce outside had quadrupled. Our backstage passes got us past a security guy who appeared outside the bus, and then we found ourselves plunging into the crowd that had gathered around. The people carried signs and waved T-shirts. Already, Dooce's guitarist was among them, mingling with the fans, signing autographs. Cameras flashed. Kids shouted. Somebody played a Dooce song on a tinny radio.

"Let's hit the road," I said to the kids.

We blended into the huge crowd and slipped past the police. In a few minutes, we found the Monster Truck and piled in. Stuck in the traffic exiting the arena lot, I pulled out my cell phone and checked the screen.

Six missed calls from Bug. Two from Loretta.

It was Loretta's attempts to contact me that puzzled me. Instead of calling her, I passed my phone to Richie. "Call your dad. See if he's home yet."

If Eckelstine had been arrested for murdering his wife or for breaking into a museum without authorization, I didn't know what I was going to do with the kids. But fortunately, Eckelstine picked up, and he told Richie to come home. Half an hour later, I dropped off Richie and Sugar.

I grabbed Richie's sleeve before he bailed out of the Monster Truck. "Thanks, kid. The clothes are great."

"No problem." He took a steadying breath and finally looked up at me. "Those bones in Dooce's trailer? Those came from my mom, didn't they?"

"Some of them, probably."

"She sold them to him?"

"Looks that way to me."

"That's how she paid for everything, right? Selling Rhonda."

That was the way I figured it. Clarice had been selling off her father's important paleontology discoveries to pay for Richie's dressmaking hobby and Sugar's astronomical ice-skating expenses. She'd kept it secret because selling to collectors was bad form among the scientific set.

But Richie looked shaken by the idea.

I said, "Parents do whatever they can to make their kids happy. Sometimes they make mistakes, but— Look, kid, your mother wasn't my favorite person in life, but she really loved you. She wanted to help you become whatever you want to be."

Richie struggled to hold back his feelings, but the dam broke. He hung his head and cried. I'd been there, at the moment when I knew my mother was gone—the woman who gave me life, but tortured me, too. The loss mixed with terror. The fear of being alone fought the relief of seeing the end of someone who frightened me in life.

I hugged Richie, and he let it all out, sobbing hard against my shoulder.

Finally, he sighed and sat up. He wiped his tears with both hands.

I gave him a gentle shake. "You'll be okay, kid. You're amazing. I meant what I said before. I'm grateful for all your help. If you can make me look good, you're obviously a genius. And Nooch? Hell, what you did for him was miraculous. You're going to be a star."

He smiled wanly. "Maybe."

"I'm sure of it. I just . . ."

"Yeah?"

"I need to know if I can wear this dress to a wedding tomorrow."

Richie regained his composure. "Is it Mick Jagger's wedding?"

"No."

"Then the answer is no." He shook off my hand and slid across the seat to exit the truck. But then his mood softened and he glanced back. "Okay, take off the belt," he coached. "It looks too S and M for a wedding. And add a slip. Do you own a slip?"

"Of course I do," I lied.

"A bra would help, too."

"Good suggestions," I said. "Thanks, kid. Keep in touch."

Sugar slid out of the truck and turned back long enough to say with a sneer, "I hope I never see any of you ever again."

I opened my mouth to make a wisecrack, but Sage elbowed me in the ribs.

"You're welcome," I said to Sugar after Sage closed the truck's door. I didn't know what to think of Sugar, but she sure as hell wasn't normal.

Sage said, "That chick is definitely screwed up. You should have heard what she said about her mother earlier."

"What did she say?"

Sage shrugged. "Rotten stuff. How she hated her. How she finally got her wish."

"Her wish?"

"That her mom's dead, I guess. She's a real creep."

I agreed. Sugar was one young lady destined to grow up alone, with her tech gadgets to keep her warm. And she seemed to prefer it that way.

We dropped Nooch off next. I noticed he had a new bounce in his step as he headed into his grandmothers' house.

"I guess clothes make the man after all," I said to Sage.

"He's cute," she replied with a yawn. "Everybody had a good time, Mom."

"That's good, because it felt like corruption of minors a couple of times," I said. "I'm going to drop you a block from Loretta's house."

"Why? Aren't you coming with me tonight?"

I saw the anxiety in her face and soothed: "You'll be perfectly safe. There are probably half a dozen cops watching Loretta's place."

"I'm not scared for myself. It's you I'm worried about."

"Hey, no worries. I've got some business to take care of, that's all."

"With Dad?" Her eyes twinkled.

No. But it seemed cruel to tell her otherwise.

I gave Sage a kiss and told her she was wonderful. And that she should set her alarm clock for seven and spend the weekend filling out college applications. The reminder about the applications put a cloud back on her face as she slid out of the truck. I waved good-bye, turned the truck around, and watched her walk away in my rearview mirror. When she turned the corner onto Loretta's street, I pulled away. But not before seeing a police car ease around the same corner. Sage would be safe.

I, on the other hand, put my leopard-print stiletto on the accelerator and floored it.

I cruised past my salvage yard, but the police presence there looked like somebody had set the national-security alert on neon red. I felt bad about Rooney not getting his supper, but maybe the cops were feeding him doughnuts. He'd be okay until morning.

I figured it was crazy to go across the river to my own house for the night. The streets were too narrow there, and I'd get trapped by the police for sure.

But I was tired. All the adrenaline I'd burned up that day was making my eyes itch and my brain feel fuzzy.

So I drove up into the dark and quiet neighborhood of Stanton Heights and parked in front of a nice little brick house that even had a picket fence out front. I pulled a packing quilt from the back of the truck. Wrapping up in its smelly folds, I stretched out on the front seat and went to sleep thinking about who most wanted Clarice Crabtree dead.

I woke in the morning when somebody tapped gently on my window.

I opened one eye and saw Bug Duffy holding two cups of coffee.

I groaned and fought my way out of the quilt to unlock the truck. He climbed in and closed the door. He was wearing a police department sweatshirt over a pair of flannel pajamas and the kind of slippers guys like him probably received on Father's Day.

He handed me one of the coffee cups. "You could have knocked on the door. Marie would have made up a bed for you."

"I didn't want to frighten your kids."

"Thanks." Bug eyed me cautiously. "What exactly are you wearing?"

I used one hand to open the quilt to flash him. In daylight, the dress Richie had made for me looked even more bizarre. Kind of like a shedding snakeskin. Tight except for the wispy bits. "I'm told it's couture."

"Wow. Looks scary." He sipped his coffee. "But a little sexy, too. By any chance, did you wear that getup to the Dooce concert last night?"

I took a tentative sip, too. Steaming hot and sweet. The caffeine went straight to my heart. Not the same kick as my usual morning Red Bull, but good enough. I figured I should dodge his question. "Marie makes a great cup of coffee."

"On the weekends, I make the coffee. I'm only asking because we found a stolen Escalade in the parking lot of the arena."

"I'm glad to hear you found it. The owner will be grateful. Maybe even drop the charges. Did you catch the thief?"

"Not yet," he said darkly.

"How's Mitch Mitchell?"

"Alive. Not talking yet. But he's going to make it."

We drank a little more coffee. A goofy-looking Labrador retriever waddled over to the gate of the picket fence, and stood there watching Bug and wagging its tail. The dog had a pink nose and carried an extra ten pounds.

"What's your dog's name?"

"Bonnie."

Bug let me wake up, and we sat in silence for a minute or two. I sipped a little more coffee and finally said, "I think I know who arranged to get Clarice kidnapped."

"I'm listening."

"It's a crazy idea, but I think I'm right."

"Eckelstine?"

"No. Sugar Mitchell."

"She's just a kid!"

"A kid who knows her own mind."

Bug shook his head. "You're right, Rox. That's a crazy idea."

"Hear me out. The thing she wants more than anything is to be a famous ice-skater. She took the most expensive lessons. Her father drove her everywhere and made her the center of the universe. He is more like a groupie than a parent. Her mother paid big bucks for everything, but finally shut off the monetary spigot. Sugar thought her ice-skating days were over."

"So she hired somebody to kill her mother? Rox, she's only—what? Twelve?"

"Fifteen and a computer genius. She could have found Uncle Carmine's name by doing a simple Google search for organized crime in Pittsburgh. The note I saw definitely looked like something a teenager would make. She knows all about cell phones and tech stuff, so she could have managed the logistics. Thing is, she has no feelings for other people—not even dear, devoted Daddy. I'm telling you, she could have done it."

"She hated her mother that much?"

"She loves herself a lot more."

Bug stared out the windshield, thinking. "Somebody from the museum called me yesterday. He had a story about Clarice maybe stealing museum property and selling it to collectors."

"To pay for Sugar's skating expenses."

"Why did she stop? Did she get worried she was going to be caught?"

"Maybe. Or she was running out of bones." I thought of the last bone left in her freezer—the one Rooney stole. "What matters is that Sugar's cash stream ended."

Bug looked unconvinced. "You really think the kid did it?"

"Either way, she needs a shrink," I said. "Last night, I watched her with her cell phone and computer. She was fixated. But most of all, she's completely self-obsessed. Put her alone in a room with a smart psychologist, and I'll bet she confesses. In fact, she's probably proud of herself. What have you got to lose?"

"But," Bug said slowly, "if Sugar hired the killer, who actually did the killing?"

"I'm guessing it's somebody in Carmine's organization."

"Who?"

"I don't know yet. Maybe one of the old guys thought he could pull off a kidnapping, but screwed up."

"And tried to kill Mitchell, too?"

"I don't know about Mitchell's shooting. Seems out of character that Sugar would want him out of the picture. I mean, he was her biggest fan. And he's useful to her. But maybe he'll be talking soon, and you can ask him yourself."

Bug had forgotten about his coffee. He sighed heavily. "If I round up all the usual suspects from Carmine's posse, it's going to look like geriatric week at the station house."

"Sorry. It's the best idea I've got."

He turned to me again. "How come you're giving up Carmine? What happened to honor among thieves?"

I shrugged. "I never cared much for Carmine. If he spends the rest of his rotten life in jail, that's okay by me."

"Does the rest of your family feel the same way?"

I doubted it. Loretta still cared about him. And Sister Bob did, too.

Bug said, "Forget I asked."

"Okay. Listen, I gotta pee, and I need a shower."

He sat up quickly, like a good host remembering his manners. "Sure, right. Come inside. Marie's making pancakes for the kids."

"No, thanks. I don't want any of them to think you're friends with a scary lady like me. I'll go home. That is, if you'll call off the cops waiting there to arrest me."

"Roxy—"

"Really, I'll be fine. I just need a shower."

"I am your friend," Bug said. "Even if you wear those shoes."

I waggled my foot. "You don't like?"

He bailed out of the truck, then leaned back inside to take my empty coffee cup. He said, "I'll call off the cops. Enjoy your shower. Just one thing."

"Yeah?"

"Burn that dress."

I flipped him a send-off and started the truck.

On the way out of Bug's neighborhood, I thought about how to convince Carmine to tell me who had kidnapped Clarice. I wondered how hard I'd need to lean on the old coot.

I stopped at the salvage yard to check on Rooney. He was happy to wolf down the kibble I gave him, but seemed just as pleased to get back to gnawing on his bone. I left him to it, and on the drive over the river to my place, I ejected Dooce's CD and listened to the radio instead. The concert felt like a long time ago.

At home, I stripped off my clothes and stepped into a hot shower. After a cold, uncomfortable night in my truck, the heat felt good. I washed the gunk that Richie had put in my hair, then lathered it up and washed it again. I tried not to think about Sugar and Clarice, but the whole mother-daughter dynamic floated up in my mind again and again. Had my own mother lived, might I have been moved to hurt her? I kept my head under the stream of hot water in an effort to wash the thought away.

When I finally shut off the water and opened the shower curtain, Flynn handed me a towel.

❧ 25 ❧

I squelched my surprise, took the towel from him, and stepped out onto the rug like it happened every day. "Did Jane Doe get away safely last night?"

He leaned easily against the doorjamb, playing it just as cool as I was. "Depends on what you call safe. For Dooce, it was love at first sight."

"I have a feeling that happens to him after every concert."

"She looked pretty happy, too. I talked to her during the concert—got the whole story. I don't think you need to worry about her."

"Do I need to worry about you?"

His mouth twisted wryly. "I lost my job."

"*What?*"

"The restaurant owner fired me."

"Jesus, over the soup?"

He shrugged. "I'll get another job."

"With Dooce," I guessed, and felt cold inside.

Flynn wasn't smiling either. His gaze was dark and intense. "I saw the way he felt you up after the show last night."

"That?" I started to towel off. "It was nothing."

"Not to me it wasn't." He reached out and stopped my hands.

I knew the look in his eyes. I hadn't seen it in a while, but I knew it, and it wasn't just about losing his job.

I boosted myself up onto the edge of the sink.

Flynn took the towel from me and wrapped it around my shoulders. Then, watching my face, he parted my knees with his hands, and I let him do it. In the next second he kissed me between my thighs, and I felt a shudder inside. He said my name against my skin. I closed my eyes and slipped my hands around the back of his head to hold him close.

It had been a long, confusing night. But now I felt as if I was home.

His tongue was hot and slow and sure, and I caught my breath as every sensible thought emptied out of my mind. I leaned back against the mirror and sucked in as much air as I could hold.

He still knew how to rock my world.

After, I took him into the bedroom and peeled off most of his clothes.

We didn't talk about Marla. Or his job or Dooce. Or anything else. Mostly, we told each other what to do. What we wanted. Where, how hard, and how fast. It was long and exhilarating, and we lost our heads, got high on each other just like long ago. Eventually we collapsed together, panting and laughing.

In a while our smiles faded. He said I was softer than he remembered. He was stronger, I told him. I found his shrapnel scars and he traced the burn on my thigh—an accident at work, I said, but it had been candle wax. Maybe he knew I was lying, because he didn't respond.

We dozed a little, wrapped around each other in a tangle. When he woke, we started all over again, but slower this time and with our eyes open.

Whispering.

In the afternoon, the sun came out and sent a blaze of golden light across the bedroom floor. It didn't feel as if we'd done something stupid yet. It felt like a climax that had been building for a long time. I didn't understand it, and maybe it was wrong, but I didn't want to think about that while the sunlight shone on the floor.

But finally, I said, "I need to get to a wedding."

"Me, too."

It was better not to talk anymore. Instead, we took a shower together. And then he got dressed, kissed me again, and went down the steps.

I zipped up my jeans and went out to the top of the staircase. With my heart hammering, I worked up the courage to ask, "Are you going with Dooce?"

Flynn turned on the landing, but didn't look up at me. "Maybe."

It sounded more like yes. "Is that smart? With all the drugs available?"

"Maybe not."

"And what about Sage?" What about me? I wanted to ask. But I didn't.

"It's not forever. Tour goes on hiatus in December for a couple months."

"And then?"

"Europe. Australia."

He might as well have punched me in the gut. "Jesus, Flynn. Can't you go farther away from us?"

He glanced up at last. "It's not forever."

"Right. It was only sixteen years the last time. Nice of you to drop by. Send a postcard now and then, will you? Sage could start a collection."

He said, "Can't you make things easier? Just this once?"

"You mean, because you brought me off a few times this afternoon?"

"Rox—"

"You want to know something?" I asked. "I switched the bones in your kitchen. It was me."

"What?"

"Rooney stole a bone out of the dinosaur lady's collection. That's what you cooked. That was your secret ingredient. Two thousand year-old woolly mammoth marrow, dug up from the permafrost in Siberia. I'm glad to hear it was delicious."

He stared up at me. "You did that? On purpose? Roxy, why?"

"Why not?" The words burst bitterly out of me. "You want to know how miserable you made my life?"

"So you sabotaged my job?"

"You sabotaged my whole existence!"

He came up the stairs fast and grabbed my shoulders. "How can you say that? You've had it good. You had Sage this whole time, all to yourself. What else do you want?" His hands bit into me, and he gave me a shake. "What else do you want?"

I couldn't answer. Couldn't say it.

He let me go. He cursed and turned away. I tried to reach for him, but I couldn't make myself do that, either.

He went down the stairs and out of the house.

I sleepwalked back to the bedroom and found a bra. Put it on. Then I stood for a while, looking at the dress on the floor with a storm in my head.

My phone rang, and I saw it was Loretta. My hands were shaking as I opened the phone.

"There you are," she said, sounding miraculously friendly. "I've been looking for you. Are you coming to the wedding with us? You haven't forgotten, have you? You're coming, right? Roxy? Are you there?"

In the mirror, my face didn't look like the face of a woman who ought to be in church unless it was for confession. My voice sounded hollow. "Not the ceremony, but I can make the reception. Pick me up?"

"We'd be delighted."

"Do you have a slip I could borrow?"

"I'll find one. You're at home, I hope? Not in jail? I hear you're an enemy of the whole fire department." When I didn't answer she said, "Five o'clock. Be ready."

We hung up, and I put my dress on. I went downstairs to find something to eat. I was famished. After a Red Bull and a Slim Jim, I was almost ready to face anything again.

Even Uncle Carmine.

I tried calling Adasha to talk to her about Jane Doe, but she didn't pick up. I left a message on her voice mail, though. I told her I thought Jane was going to be okay.

At five o'clock, I hear a horn honk outside, so I tucked a lipstick into my bra, grabbed a thick scarf that would have to be enough of a wrap for the night, and went out to see Loretta's big Cadillac waiting in front of the house.

Loretta's face and Sister Bob's face both goggled at me from inside the car. I opened the rear door and slid into the backseat.

"My God," Loretta said. "Put this on, and do it fast before somebody sees you."

She tossed the slip over the seat to me.

Sister Bob turned around as far as her seatbelt would allow. She wore a black suit left over from her days as a nun, but had jazzed it up with a string of green and purple Mardi Gras beads probably from a pre-Lent party. "Holy moly, that's some outfit you're wearing, Roxana. What happened? Somebody run over you with a lawn mower?"

"It's supposed to look this way. A famous designer made it. Well—he'll be famous soon." I kicked off my leopard shoes and wrestled the slip up over my hips. While Loretta drove, I scooched around until I had the slip on under my dress. "Where's Sage? Isn't she coming?"

"She has a date." Bob rummaged in her gigantic black nun purse and came up with a ChapStick.

"Oh yeah? Is she with Brian?" I wondered if he was back to driving his Escalade.

Bob slathered her lips and stowed the ChapStick back in her purse. "She wouldn't say."

"Didn't she show up at the church?"

"Hardly anybody goes to the church anymore. It's all about the reception."

I put my hand to my forehead and groaned. "I forgot! I didn't help deliver all the wedding cookies. Did you manage to move them up to the restaurant in time?"

"We rented a U-Haul," Loretta said. "Nooch came over to help this morning, and he was very useful."

"He hardly ate any," Bob added. "But he carried all the boxes for us. He said he was making himself into a magnet. Does that make any sense to you?"

"More and more." I slipped my shoes back on and sat up in the backseat. "How was the wedding ceremony at the church?"

"You should have seen Gino," Sister Bob said. "It's the first time I ever saw the father of the bride run up the aisle. Like he had ants in his pants. I've never seen a man's face so red. I think he had a fever."

Looking at me in the rearview mirrow, Loretta said to me, "Are you okay?"

"Gino was sweating like a horse," Bob went on. "Perspiration was gushing out from under that toupee of his. Something was definitely wrong with that man."

"Nothing he didn't deserve," I said mildly.

Loretta frowned into her mirror.

As dusk fell over the city and lights began to blink on around us, Loretta drove across the bridges and up the winding road to Mount Washington—so named because George Washington himself had surveyed the place where three rivers converged and made what looked to George like a great place to build a fort. Fort Pitt had long since disappeared under the railroads and steel mills, and now the department stores and skyscrapers made the downtown of Pittsburgh. I felt a tug of emotion for my hometown. It was a tough place that had survived a lot of hardship. I belonged here.

At the restaurant, Bob and I got out of the car while Loretta talked to the parking valet. From the ridge of Mount Washington, the city radiated from the Point, and we could see all three rivers glinting with the colors of the sunset. A tugboat pushed two empty coal barges down the Monongahela toward West Virginia. I saw the casino far below, and the spot where Clarice Crabtree's body had washed up on the bank.

Loretta accepted a ticket from the valet and tucked it into her tiny evening bag as she came over to the sidewalk to join us. Maybe she knew what I was thinking, because Loretta put her arm around me.

"Let's join the party," she said gently.

We went through the rococo front doors of the restaurant. Inside, the overblown decoration—the marble floor, crystal chandeliers, flecked mirrors in heavy frames—still looked ridiculous to me, but it was a grand place for an Italian wedding.

The Martinelli family had formed a receiving line inside the door of the restaurant—all except for the bride and groom, who were probably off getting pictures taken. Gino was missing, too. Probably changing his underwear someplace. The bride's sisters, Caprice and Malibu—so named, said neighborhood legend, because of where they'd been conceived—greeted Sister Bob and Loretta enthusiastically.

Me, they tolerated because they had good manners.

"Oh, hello, Roxy."

"Yeah, nice of you to come."

"Thanks, girls. You both look great."

Caprice and Malibu could have passed for twins in their big hair and poufy red bridesmaid dresses, wearing enough mascara to cause blindness.

Their mother, Carlene, was dabbing her eyes with a wadded-up tissue as she talked to Sister Bob. "I don't know what's wrong with Gino. He hasn't been himself since he got dressed this morning. I never expected him to get all emotional about the wedding, but— Oh, Roxy's here?"

"Hi, Carlene." I pumped her hand and hoped she hadn't seen me skulking out of her basement with my tube of Ben-Gay. "Thanks for inviting me. Beautiful wedding. Sorry Gino's not here."

She gave my dress a startled look, but Loretta nudged me down the line before we could exchange further pleasantries.

The groom's parents were perfectly nice people. But they both had highballs in their hands already. A good strategy for surviving a Pittsburgh wedding.

The tow truck business must have been good, because the Martinellis were throwing a big bash. A Frank Sinatra look-alike sang us through to the ballroom, where swan ice sculptures glittered beside towering flower arrangements.

The restaurant was a Pittsburgh landmark that cantilevered over the edge of the cliff overlooking the rivers. At the back of the ballroom, a wall of windows allowed a wide-angle view of the city below. Tonight, people mingled around the antipasto table and could see the nearby Incline—a funicular railway left over from the days when steel workers lived up on the hills and needed a quick route down to the mills along the rivers. Now it was a touristy thing for the most part—twin red cars that ran up and down the steep hillside.

The room filled up fast. The men peeled off their jackets and hustled over to join the line at the bar. The women preened in dresses cut so low that a dairy farmer wouldn't know where to start. Plenty of rhinestone jewelry. Torturous shoes. Half the crowd were busily moving place cards around so they didn't have to sit with their parents.

I knew most everybody. Irene Stossel's mother tottered past. I hadn't seen her since buying my last bag of doughnuts at the family bakery. Pepper Petrone, the owner of the gas station where I filled the Monster Truck, a woman usually dressed in overalls and axle grease, looked adorable in pink. Stony Zuzak's brother Archie, who spun pizzas at a joint in Lawrenceville, gave me a salute with his beer bottle.

Around a four-tiered wedding cake, a group of aunts gathered to discuss its towering design the way jealous artists probably argued about Picasso.

The cookie tables were already set up along one wall, but to keep eager fingers off the goodies until the dancing started, long yards of tulle had been laid over the cookies and weighted down with strings of white Christmas lights. Just to be on the safe side, Gino Martinelli's mother kept an eagle eye on the display. She was the size and shape of a storybook troll, and nobody crossed Mrs. Martintelli.

I saw Flynn come in with Marla Krantz. No surprise, she was the most beautiful woman in the room. Big eyes, high cheekbones. Heroin can do that, I thought. I noticed she clamped Flynn's hand in hers. They moved like a couple that had been together a long time—with easy body language and murmurs. If he saw me, he pretended otherwise. They headed for the bar.

Abruptly, I turned around and worked my way through the crowd, going the other direction.

A man I didn't know appeared in front of me and blocked my path. He had two glasses of champagne. "I hear your name is Roxy."

It's a proven fact that just about anybody can get laid after a wedding except total nerds or retirees who can only talk about their health. This guy wasn't going to have any problem in that department. Tall, good-looking, great shoulders. Suit and tie that hadn't come from a thrift store. Better yet: no ponytail, no stains on his tie, no stupid pickup lines.

He handed me one of the champagnes and said, "I'm Nolan McKillip."

"Yeah, I'm Roxy. Thanks."

He slid one hand into his trouser pocket and looked relaxed. "I feel like I know you already. My studio's right behind your office. I feed your dog at night sometimes."

"You're the blacksmith artist guy?" I blinked up at him in surprise. "The one who burns charcoal and pounds on steel at all hours?"

He grinned. "I guess that's as good a description as any. I have a forge. Does the noise bother you?"

"Not really, no." Hell, if I'd known he was such a hottie, I'd have visited him long ago. "My dog hasn't bitten you yet?"

"No, we're good buddies."

I looked into his face and tried to decide if he was on a mission to get laid later. But he had a nice smile and warm eyes.

He said, "Listen, I don't know anybody here. You mind if I hang out with you for a while?"

"How'd you get invited if you don't know anybody?"

"I know the bride's sister a little. She works at the deli where I get lunch. She invited me, but—well, to tell the truth, I'm a little afraid of her. All she talks about is weddings."

Caprice Martinelli, I guessed. She'd been engaged three times, and her obsession with the perfect wedding had chased away all the men who'd ever thought about slipping a ring on her finger.

I clinked my glass against his. "Sure, you can hang out with me. It'll be fun."

At that moment, Sister Bob rushed up to us and waved place cards in the air. "The Martinellis put me at a table with Father Mike! Can you believe it? So I'm moving seats around. Where do you want to sit, Roxana? And who's this nice young man?"

She peered up at Nolan McKillip with interest. "Would you like to sit with us?" she asked. "I can switch place cards."

"Why not?"

I gave him points for being nice to old ladies.

The Frank Sinatra look-alike stopped singing and called for everyone's attention. He announced the bride and groom, and that's when Shelby Martinelli and her new husband swept into the ballroom. Lots of applause, and then there was a rush to the bar to get more drinks before the dinner started.

Through the melee came Sage, looking adorable in a short blue dress and carrying a little bag shaped like a fish. She was much prettier than Marla Krantz. With her hair up and dangly earrings, she looked surprisingly grown-up. Behind her trailed Zack Cleary in a sport coat that was too big for him.

"Hey, tiger." I punched his arm. "Where's Brian?"

Zack shrugged, looking both sheepish and proud. "Who cares?"

Sage gave me a kiss, but she seemed subdued. "Hi, Mom. I hope you don't mind, but Zack and I are sitting at a different table with some friends of his."

"Sure. You okay?"

She glanced up, and I saw tears. In a heartbeat, I knew she'd talked to Flynn. The bastard had told her about leaving with Dooce. I grabbed her hand. "We'll be okay," I said.

She nodded but didn't look convinced. I almost ran across the room to deck Flynn in front of four hundred wedding guests. I wanted to smash his face into the wedding cake and drown him in frosting.

Zack stuck his hand out to Nolan McKillip. "Hi, I'm Zack."

"Sorry," I said, remembering my special-occasion manners. "Sage, Sister Bob, this is Nolan McKillip. This is my aunt Roberta. And my daughter, Sage. Her friend, Zack Cleary, too."

Nolan didn't run screaming when he learned I had a grown daughter. He shook everybody's hand and looked charmed.

As the crowd began to fill the tables, I saw Irene Stossel sitting with her mother. Irene was rooting around in her purse—a purse at least as big as Sister Bob's. Who the hell carries such a big bag to a wedding? Except maybe a nun?

A lightbulb went on in my head.

"Excuse me a minute," I said to Nolan McKillip. "I'll be right back."

I left him talking with Sister Bob and went over the talk to the Stossels.

"Irene?" I said.

She stopped digging in her purse and looked up at me, not exactly surprised. "Hey, Roxy."

I gestured at the otherwise empty table. "Are you sitting with my uncle Carmine?"

"He's not coming," she said. "He thought he might stop by for the dancing later, but not for dinner. His stomach's upset."

"You're getting to be a regular family member," I said.

"I don't mind looking in on him now and then."

Mrs. Stossel had been glaring at me, but her deafness prevented her from hearing our conversation. Finally she piped up: "That dress is disgusting, Roxana Marie. I can see your nipples."

"I can see your dentures," I said. "They're slipping."

Irene suddenly grew a backbone, because she said, "You can't talk to my mother that way."

"Irene, I've had a really bad week. If you want to try stopping me, be my guest."

Her eyes narrowed. "I could pop you right here."

"You have your gun in that ugly purse?"

"Of course I do."

"The same gun you used to kill Clarice Crabtree?"

The Frank Sinatra look-alike was urging all the wedding guests to find their seats, and people began to jostle past me. I could see Gino and Carlene heading to the microphone to make their welcome speeches. Gino's face was brick red. I imagined his dick was pretty hot, too. He was probably terrified that he'd caught a venereal disease overnight.

Irene stared at me.

I said, "You did a lousy job, Irene. Did you shoot Clarice by accident the night you kidnapped her? Or you just couldn't resist?"

"You—," she said, still not blinking.

"Just tell me this much," I said. "How come you tried to shoot Mitchell, too? Did the kid ask you to do that? Or were you freelancing?"

"I don't have to listen to this."

Irene got up from the table. She was wearing a shapeless dark dress with big buttons that ran from her chin to her knees. Which put her squarely in the nonlaid category for the evening.

She said to me, "If you were good to your uncle, he'd never need me. But you turned your back on him."

"Maybe because he deserved it."

"Bitch," she said through gritted teeth.

She put her hand on her weapon inside her bag and shoved it against my belly. I could feel the snout of the gun.

"You're not going to shoot me here," I said to her. "With all these witnesses? That would be colossally stupid. But then, that's your trademark, right? Stupidity."

"I don't have to listen to you."

She jammed her gun deeply into her purse and turned for the door. I followed, weaving my way through the tables of guests. People called my name, but I stuck on Irene's tail. We passed the waiters in the hall, all standing ready with the trays of wedding soup help aloft, ready to carry them into the ballroom.

Outside, she cut to the right on the sidewalk, heading for the Incline and walking fast.

Nooch was standing outside, a few feet from the parking valets. He had dressed himself in the clothes Richie Eckelstine put together for him, and he looked great. Clearly, however, he was debating with himself about whether or not he should go into the wedding reception. "Rox!" he cried, relieved to see me. "Where you been?"

"I can't talk, Nooch. I need you to call 911."

"No kidding? What for?"

A minivan pulled up, and the valets surrounded it. The passenger door opened, and Marie Duffy put a shoe on the pavement. From the driver's side of the minivan, Bug emerged, digging into the pocket of his suit trousers for a tip.

He saw me, and my expression must have registered immediately in his brain. He forgot about the valet and came straight for me. "What's up?"

"Irene Stossel," I said. "She killed Clarice."

"Who?"

I pointed. "That's her. She's armed."

Someone came out of the restaurant behind me. "Roxy?" Flynn's voice.

Bug cursed and turned toward his wife. A valet was helping her get out of the minivan, and I could see that Bug was going to use precious seconds explaining to Marie why he had to dump her to chase a killer.

So I took off after Irene myself. Nooch in hot pursuit. Flynn not far behind.

We ran up the dark sidewalk and skidded through the door of the Incline's ticket office. I could see Irene already making her way onto the car, so I vaulted the turnstile and clattered after her. Irene turned in the doorway, pulled the gun from her purse, and fired.

Instantly, Nooch said, "Hey!"

He clutched his arm. "Hey, that *hurt*!"

I could have stayed with him. Maybe I should have. But seeing him take a bullet made me nuts. I went down the ramp and shoved my shoulder through the door of the car just as it began to slide shut. The door slammed, pinning me against the side of the Incline car and forcing a cry from my throat.

"Hey!" Nooch shouted louder. He sounded panicked. "Hey, stop!"

Behind me, Flynn arrived. He jammed his shoulder against the sliding door. His impact was just enough to bounce it back so I could slither through.

"Rox," he said. "Wait—"

He thrust himself through the door, too, but his momentum sent him sprawling on the floor.

The door banged shut, leaving us alone in the car with Irene.

I caught my balance just as the car lurched and began to descend the cliffside. Flynn rolled clear, staying down. He'd seen the gun. Unsteady, Irene backed away from me and pulled the trigger again. The gun went off—incredibly loud in the small cable car—and a bullet slammed into the wooden door frame beside me.

I threw myself at her arm, and we grappled, stumbling over Flynn as he tried to get out from under us. The gun went off again. Glass shattered. Irene fired once more, and this time I felt the weapon recoil against me. I used my body weight to slam Irene against the hand railing. Together, we crashed onto the wooden bench seats, wrestling for control of the gun.

"Are you crazy?" she panted. "I've got a weapon!"

I elbowed her in the teeth. Flynn came up and seized her gun hand.

"Where's your gun when we need it?" I demanded of him.

He gasped for breath. "I didn't think I'd need it at a wedding!"

"Clearly, you haven't been to enough weddings!"

Irene was strong, and fought us hard. The three of us rolled sideways, fell off the bench, and dug at each other on the floor.

"I've had a *really* bad week," I grunted. "Let go before I hurt you, Irene."

It was a pretty good catfight, I was told later. With the lights turned on in the cable car, everybody at the wedding could see us kicking and scratching and otherwise showing our panties. One of Irene's bullets went through the window of the restaurant and hit an ice swan. It keeled over onto the cookie table and ruined twelve dozen lemon tarts, anisette-flavored butter cookies, and some peanut butter meltaways made by Grandma Martinelli, which was a tragic loss. I love peanut butter meltaways.

But somehow I ended up with the gun. Irene lay on her back on the floor, and Flynn was on top of her, facing me, too. He put his hands in the air, eyes wide on mine.

I stepped on his thigh, put the muzzle of the gun against his chest, and gripped the weapon with both hands. Irene froze and stared up at me from beneath his body. Her eyes were wide open, too.

Breathing hard, I said. "If I pull this trigger, the bullet will go through both of you, right?"

"Right," Flynn said.

"Then don't move, either one of you. All I need is one tiny reason to shoot you both."

When the car reached the bottom of the mountain, two police officers were waiting there, service weapons drawn.

The cops grabbed the gun from me and pounced on Flynn. It took only seconds to sort out who was who, and then they had Irene cuffed and it was all over.

"Damn," I said, glaring at Flynn. "I had my chance and blew it."

"Roxy?" one of the cops turned on me. "Is that you?"

I hoped he recognized my face. I pulled my skirt down.

At the hospital, while Nooch was bandaged up, I stole myself a set of scrubs with pants, and that made everybody happier, I think. It certainly made Nooch stop blushing, and Zack quit staring at me like I'd fallen from the planet Venus.

Later, eating cookies in Sage's bed, I apologized for making a scene that got my family kicked out of the Martinelli wedding.

"I heard there was going to be a band for dancing," said Sister Bob wistfully. She had changed into her fluffy bathrobe and sat in Sage's desk chair with her feet propped up on the bed. "I love to dance."

"Sorry," I said.

"Don't be sorry," Sage told me. She had admitted to hiding some wedding cookies at the back of the freezer and had fixed us a tray to nibble. "You were really brave, Mom. Even Zack said so."

"It was stupid," I said. "But I couldn't help myself."

Sister Bob chose a mini cream-filled cannoli. "You were really something, chasing that woman down. Who could have imagined? Irene Stossel a killer! Just goes to show, she should have kept that cashier's job at the bakery."

"Right," I said. "Without a college education, what other choices did she have?"

Sage groaned. She lay flat on her back, having changed into her basketball jersey and sweatpants. "All right, all right! I'll start filling out applications tomorrow, I promise. I just wish my boyfriend hadn't seen my mother's butt."

"Zack's back to being your boyfriend?"

Her dimple popped as she tried to smother a smile. "Maybe. Kind of. For the moment."

"He's okay," I said. "Not a bad kid."

We heard the doorbell downstairs, and Loretta's voice called up to me. I went down to see who'd come calling.

Bug Duffy stood inside the front door. When Loretta disappeared into the kitchen, he said, "My wife's not speaking to me. That wedding reception was supposed to be a big date for us. And because of you, I ended up working tonight."

He didn't look mad, though. Tired, maybe, but smiling.

"Tell you what, Bug, I'll babysit the boys for you next weekend, and you can take Marie out for dinner."

"Forget it. I'm not letting you near my children."

I thought he was going to say good night and leave, but he lingered. I said, "Coffee?"

"No, thanks. I just wanted to tell you that you were right about Sugar Mitchell. She did hire Irene Stossel to kidnap her mother."

Bug sat on Loretta's couch, and I perched on the arm of the recliner. I said, "So she didn't plan on her mother getting killed?"

"From what we pieced together, sounds like Sugar contacted Carmine to do a kidnapping only. She wanted her mom to be threatened into giving her more money. The kid has amazing Internet skills. That's how she found Carmine, made the arrangements. When you turned down the assignment, Carmine hired Irene. But Irene lost control of the situation and killed Clarice by mistake."

"Irene was no match for Clarice."

"Then Irene started worrying Mitchell knew about the plan, and she decided to kill him, too, to keep him quiet. She thought she'd pin that shooting on you, by leaving your glove at the scene."

"Kinda clumsy planning."

"Killers aren't usually brain surgeons."

"What's going to happen to Sugar?"

"I don't know yet. Here's the kicker. Know what she's telling us? That her mother hired Carmine to kill *her* mother, twenty-some years ago."

"Clarice had her own mother killed?"

"You don't sound surprised."

I shrugged. "Mothers and daughters, that's a complicated relationship sometimes."

"Looks that way." Bug eyed me for a while and finally stood up to leave. "We're trying to build a case on Carmine now. We're going to take our time, though. We want to get it right."

"Good luck."

"You're not worried? About your uncle?"

I got to my feet, too. "He gets what he deserves. And me? I haven't done anything I'm ashamed of."

Bug smiled. "Not even the public catfight?"

"You saw it, too?"

"Who could miss it? You were just lucky the television helicopters didn't show up in time."

"Get out of here," I said, giving his arm a punch. "Go home to your wife."

Without warning, Bug gave me a hug. It actually felt kinda nice. "Take care of yourself, Roxy."

I let him out the front door, and Loretta came in from the kitchen. She was drying her hands on a kitchen towel, still dressed in her wedding finery, but with an apron.

I leaned against the front door. I was too tired to explain everything Bug had told me. But I said, "Flynn told me today. About you sending him off to the marines."

Loretta's hands went still. "I didn't send anyone anywhere. I suggested, that's all."

"You interfered."

She folded the towel carefully, not looking at me. "What did you do for Sage this week? With Brian and Zack?"

"I . . ."

"You protected her," Loretta said. "Because you love her."

I wrestled with my emotions for a while, struggling with the words. But there, in Loretta's warm house, I finally said, "I love you, Loretta."

I heard her voice catch. She tried to speak, but couldn't.

I went across the room to her and wrapped her in my arms. I said, "You've been wonderful to me. You still are. You're the mother I should have had."

"Light years away from Agatha Christie's Miss Marple... grittier and more sexual than Laura Lippman's Tess Monaghan."
—*Pittsburgh Tribune Review*

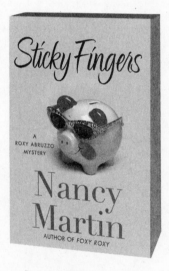

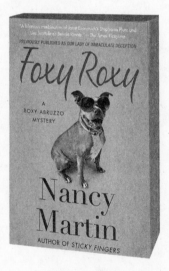

Roxy tries to stay one step ahead of trouble while working for her Mob boss uncle, but trouble finds her anyway when a kidnapping victim turns up dead.

When Roxy steals an ancient Greek statue, she gets caught up in the sordid events surrounding the murder of its original owner.